Also by Seán Cullen

Hamish X and the Cheese Pirates

Hamish X and the Hollow Mountain

Hamish X

Goes to Providence, Rhode Island

SEÁN CULLEN

PUFFIN
CANADA

PUFFIN CANADA

Published by the Penguin Group

Penguin Group (Canada), 90 Eglinton Avenue East, Suite 700, Toronto, Ontario, Canada
M4P 2Y3 (a division of Pearson Canada Inc.)

Penguin Group (USA) Inc., 375 Hudson Street, New York, New York 10014, U.S.A.

Penguin Books Ltd, 80 Strand, London WC2R 0RL, England

Penguin Ireland, 25 St Stephen's Green, Dublin 2, Ireland (a division of Penguin Books Ltd)

Penguin Group (Australia), 250 Camberwell Road, Camberwell, Victoria 3124, Australia
(a division of Pearson Australia Group Pty Ltd)

Penguin Books India Pvt Ltd, 11 Community Centre, Panchsheel Park,
New Delhi – 110 017, India

Penguin Group (NZ), 67 Apollo Drive, Rosedale, North Shore 0745, Auckland, New Zealand
(a division of Pearson New Zealand Ltd)

Penguin Books (South Africa) (Pty) Ltd, 24 Sturdee Avenue, Rosebank, Johannesburg 2196,
South Africa

Penguin Books Ltd, Registered Offices: 80 Strand, London WC2R 0RL, England

First published 2008

1 2 3 4 5 6 7 8 9 10 (RRD)

Copyright © Seán Cullen, 2008
Illustrations copyright © Johann Wessels, 2008

*Publisher's note: This book is a work of fiction. Names, characters, places and incidents either are the
product of the author's imagination or are used fictitiously, and any resemblance to actual persons
living or dead, events, or locales is entirely coincidental.*

Manufactured in the U.S.A.

ISBN: 978-0-670-06854-8

Library and Archives Canada Cataloguing in Publication data
available upon request to the publisher.

Visit the Penguin Group (Canada) website at www.penguin.ca

Special and corporate bulk purchase rates available; please see
www.penguin.ca/corporatesales or call 1-800-810-3104, ext. 477 or 474

Hamish X

Goes to Providence, Rhode Island

A Note from the Narrator

At last! The final book in the trilogy of Hamish X. We've fought Cheese Pirates. We've battled Grey Agents and their evil machines. We've met kings and raccoons, friends and foes. Now, we arrive at Book III. It's time for the chickens to come home to roost.[1]

I hope you've been paying attention to the developments in the books. I've taken great pains to lay everything out as simply and clearly as I can. Not too simply and clearly, of course. I wouldn't want to insult your intelligence by assuming you were incapable of understanding more complex plot points and challenging words. If you are still reading by this, the third book, I assume you appreciate my efforts and I haven't lost you. If I have lost you, why are you still reading? Are you trapped in an airport or on a bus or in some other equally dull place and forced to read things you don't really understand just to pass the time? If so, put this book down and find another diversion: thumb-wrestling,

---

[1] There are no actual chickens. It's just an expression that means all the loose ends will be tied up . . . which is another expression that means . . . oh, it just means that the story will end! All right? All right.

nose-picking, nail-chewing, or some other less taxing way to occupy your tiny, bewildered mind.

We're coming to the most important part of the story now: the end! When I first entered the ANCC,[2] we were told that the end is the most important part of any story. Really, it's quite obvious. Why even bother telling a story if you aren't going to end it? What's the point? If stories ended in the middle and never seemed to have any real conclusion, they would be very unsatisfying. Why, they'd be just like our daily lives that go on and on without any really well-defined stops. That's one of the reasons people like reading stories: they get to see the beginning, middle, and end. Nice and neat. I try to do that with my own life. I get up in the morning and right before I eat breakfast I say, "Once upon a time, the narrator ate his breakfast." When I go to sleep I say, "The End!" Very loudly. My neighbours think I am slightly mad, but I find it gives me a certain amount of personal satisfaction and closure.

My editors wanted me to recap the action from the first two books so that readers are up to speed with the story. I really can't be bothered. I find it tedious to repeat myself, so I won't. If you can't remember the first two books, read them again right now. I'll wait . . .

Done? Fine. And for those of you who are just picking up this third book without bothering to read the first two, I must say I think you are extremely lazy, cutting to the end

---

[2] Advanced Narrators' Certification College in Helsinki. See Book I.

like that. You don't deserve to have a summary of the first two books at your disposal. All the other readers took the time to read those books and so should you. Shame on you! Shame! Big disgusting buckets of steaming, sticky shame.

Oh, my. I'm becoming a little cranky and short-tempered. Please forgive me. The strain of telling this very complex story is starting to wear me down. Who knew this tale would have so many amazing escapes, daring adventures, and powerful smells?[3] Have no fear, dear readers! I will tough it out to the end. There is nothing that will keep me from reaching the final chapter. Narrators have a sacred duty to complete their stories. I take that duty seriously. Not finishing a story once started can carry stiff penalties enforced by the Universal Narrators' Guild.[4]

Without further nonsense, let's get to our story. Turn the page and join me as we begin the first chapter of the last book in the tale of Hamish X and his friends, Mimi and Parveen.

---

[3] Originally, the books were to be accompanied by a scratch-and-sniff card highlighting some of the more thrilling odours featured in the story. Sadly, budget constraints have forced me to cancel the cards. If only you were able to smell the sea captain's rust-stained trousers for yourself! Alas, it was not to be.

[4] One instance of these terrible punishments occurred in 1768 in Portsmouth, England. A narrator was telling the story of the Tortoise and the Hare to a group of children when he stood up too quickly, bumped his head on a low beam, and knocked himself unconscious. As a result of the blow to the head, he couldn't recall the end of the story and therefore couldn't finish it. The Guild was swift to enact their punishment. The narrator was forced to marry a fish. The Guild was not without sympathy for the poor man. As it had been an accidental lapse, they made sure the fish was very pretty indeed.

Part 1

ON WATER,
BELOW WATER,
AND
UNDERGROUND

Chapter 1

MIMI

Mimi stood on the edge of the stone platform. All the children were silent, awed by the sight they beheld: a subterranean vault with black water stretching out beyond the reach of their battery-powered torches. The soft slap of the underground lake was the only sound ... besides the sniffling and crying of a few of the youngest refugees from the destruction of the Hollow Mountain. Even these snufflings were subdued by normal standards.[5]

Cara stood at Mimi's side, her eyes desolate and red from crying. Mimi was glad the girl had finally gotten a hold of herself. Cara had wept incessantly and inconsolably for the entire long fall in the escape pod. She had no idea what had happened to her brother, Aidan. She knew only that he had stayed behind when the escape hatch closed to face the invading army of Grey Agents with King Liam. Mimi had understood the pain Cara was experiencing. Parveen was nowhere among the escapees.

---

[5] The sound of a crying toddler is the most piercing noise in nature. There is no sound more capable of destroying the mind of an adult human being. In ancient Parthia, the armies of the King commonly sent in front of their invading forces a corps of soldiers wearing wax plugs in their ears and crying infants strapped to their chests. These Babytroopers completely demoralized the enemy, driving them mad, making conquest much simpler. Of course, in ancient times, babies were much angrier and therefore more deadly.

Mimi was tempted to have a good cry of her own, but she had to hold it together for the sake of the frightened children around her. She had to lead by example: Hamish X had taught her that.

Mimi thought back to how they had arrived on the shore of this dark sea.

Aidan had slammed the hatch shut, automatically launching the pod on its journey down the escape shaft. What followed was a hair-raising fall accompanied by the screams of the occupants as the contents of their stomachs threatened to paint the inside of the pod. The blackness made the fall worse. Mimi couldn't orient herself. Her terrified mind tried to focus on something to make the fear go away, but there was only darkness.

After what seemed like an age, the pod took a sloping turn, pressing the inhabitants against the restraint straps. The pod picked up speed and began a slaloming[6] series of S turns, throwing the passengers back and forth.

"Oh," squeaked Mrs. Francis. "Why can't they flick on the lights?"

As if in response to her question, a light went on overhead, shining a yellow glow down on the pale faces of the passengers. Mrs. Francis and Mr. Kipling were holding hands. Cara's cheeks were slick with tears. Two other

---

[6] Slaloming, the act of skiing back and forth as one descends a mountain slope, is named for its inventor, Gustav Slalom. He discovered the manoeuvre accidentally while trying to avoid bears that he believed were leaping out at him as he skied down a mountain in Austria in 1772. The bears were a hallucination, induced when Slalom drank a keg of tainted corn syrup. Observers were delighted by the manoeuvre and began to imitate Slalom's style. (No one ever learned why Gustav had drunk an entire keg of corn syrup.)

young children Mimi didn't know looked decidedly green about the gills.[7]

"Maybe it was better in the dark." Mrs. Francis grimaced as the pod jerked side to side. Mimi focused on a rivet above Mr. Kipling's head in an effort to keep her stomach settled.

The escape pod had finally come to rest after a long, tumbling descent. The pod had some kind of gyroscopic system that generally kept the passengers right side up during the descent, but the twisting and turning was hard on the stomach nonetheless. Mimi was relieved when the pod finally rolled to a stop, the hatch facing upward. She unfastened her harness and spun the wheel that unsealed the hatch. With a hiss of air, the heavy steel hatch swung open. Mimi popped her head out into a dark, cold space. She pulled her electric torch from her belt and switched it on, piercing the darkness with the beam and discovering they had come to rest at the end of a long stone corridor. Confident that there was no immediate threat, Mimi turned back to the hatch and said, "I guess we're here ... wherever here is."

Mr. Kipling and Mrs. Francis immediately began to unfasten their harnesses. Cara sat with her head buried in

---

[7]   *Green about the gills* is an expression meaning sickly or on the verge of vomiting. The expression comes from the Mediterranean Sea where one fish in particular, the Regurgitrix, is known to throw up when cornered, much as an octopus releases ink. The warning sign is when the Regurgitrix's gills turn a brilliant green. Fishermen know to throw the fish back when the gills turn green or receive a faceful of the fish's last meal. The Regurgatrix feeds exclusively on rotting vegetation and fish poop, so one really doesn't want to experience a shower of said material if one knows what is good for one.

her hands, her hair hanging like a curtain around her face, making no move to get out of the pod.

Mimi grabbed Cara's shoulder and shook her. Cara looked up, her eyes red and puffy, her face smeared with a paste of soot and tears.

Mimi made her voice as firm as possible. "Cara. We need ya to snap out of it."

Cara wiped her tear-streaked face with her sleeve, blinking. "But he's gone. I was supposed to take care of him."

"We cain't think about that now. We gotta keep movin'. It ain't like I know where we are. Yer a Swiss Guard. You gotta start actin' like one."

Cara covered her face with her hands and sobbed anew. Mimi didn't know what to do. She caught Mrs. Francis's eye. Mrs. Francis nodded and slid next to Cara. The former housekeeper looked quite bizarre in her white wedding gown, now soiled and torn from the battle and their flight from the Hollow Mountain.

"There, there, dear. It will be all right. I'm sure he'll be fine," soothed Mrs. Francis. Cara turned her face into Mrs. Francis's shoulder and wept. "If anyone could survive, it would be young Aidan," the former housekeeper assured her.

Mimi then caught Mr. Kipling's eye and jerked her head towards the lightless corridor. "Mr. Kipling," Mimi said, "let's have a look-see."

Mr. Kipling nodded and smiled. "Shall we?"

Mimi gripped the rim of the escape hatch and pulled herself up. She swung herself around and slid down the side of the smooth pod until her feet hit solid ground. Standing still, she listened.

There was silence, save for a soft humming. She couldn't place it in an exact location. It seemed to come from all around her. Pale yellow light shone up from the escape pod, a cone of illumination piercing the gloom and bathing the ceiling in a circle of gold. The ceiling was made of solid rock smoothed and sculpted by hands or tools, Mimi couldn't be sure.

She sniffed the air. It was cool and moist but smelled fresh. There was a slight tang of salt.

"I smell the ocean," said Mr. Kipling. He dropped down beside Mimi, steadying himself with a hand on her shoulder. "We must have travelled a great distance underground."

"Yeah, but where to?" Mimi reached out and brushed her fingertips on the smooth stone surface. "This place ain't natural. Somebody dug this tunnel."

"I agree. They had very sophisticated tools at their disposal as well." There was a scratching sound, and suddenly a match flared in the darkness, casting Mr. Kipling's long bony face in a stark reddish glow. He smiled and lit his pipe. He puffed softly until the bowl of the pipe burnt like a coal in the dimness. "Shall we take a look down this tunnel, then?"

Mimi nodded in agreement and pointed her torch down the corridor. They were at one end of a stone tunnel now blocked at their end by the escape pod resting in a depression on the floor, stoppering the corridor like a cork in a bottle. The tunnel stretched away for several metres in the other direction and seemed to widen out into a larger chamber.

Mimi reached out and took the older man's hand in her own. "I think we wanna go that way."

"Where are you going?" Mrs. Francis had popped her head out the pod. Her face was visible in the pod's interior light as she looked down at Mimi and Mr. Kipling. Her brow was knotted with worry.

"You stay in there with Cara and the others, Isobel," Mr. Kipling said. "We're just going to reconnoitre the tunnel."

"Just don't reconnoitre yourself into any trouble!" Mrs. Francis said sharply. "You're my husband now and I expect you to look after me!"

Mr. Kipling answered sheepishly, "Yes, dear."

"And you shouldn't be smoking," Mrs. Francis said. "It will make you ill. And it's a poor example for the children."

"Yes, dear."

"And it makes you smell."

"Please sit back down and wait for us to return, my dear," Mr. Kipling pleaded with mild exasperation. Mrs. Francis frowned and ducked back into the pod. Mr. Kipling shook his head. "She's such a worrywart." He smiled, put out the pipe, and tossed it away. It struck stone and rattled in the darkness. "Still, it's nice to have someone to worry about you. Come now, Mimi. Let's find out where this tunnel leads, eh?"

"I'm gonna switch off the torch and save the battery. We'll have ta wait a second ta let our eyes adjust."

"Good thinking, sweetheart."

Mimi clicked off the torch. The only light came from the hatch of the escape pod. After a few moments, Mimi was able to discern the walls around her in the dimness. "Let's go."

Mimi shuffled right and reached with her right hand while Mr. Kipling did the opposite with his left. Just before they were extended as far as they could while still holding hands between them, they each touched the respective sides of the tunnel.

Carefully, they shuffle-stepped their way forward for a few minutes until they reached the end of the tunnel.

They stopped, sensing a vast empty space opening up in front of them. The salty sea smell was stronger here.

"Listen," Mimi whispered, and though her voice was quiet, it sent echoes scurrying and chasing one another all about them. When the echo died down, Mr. Kipling heard the sound, too: waves lapping against stone.

"Hello?"

Mimi and Mr. Kipling started at the sound of the human voice. It was a boy's voice and it came from a good distance away, echoing throughout the chamber. "Is somebody there?"

Before Mimi could answer, another voice piped up, "Here. Over here," this time from a different side.

"Hey," Mimi cried, throwing caution to the wind. "Hey! Who the heck are y'all? I'm Mimi Catastrophe Jones."

Mimi's declaration seemed to break a verbal dam. Children's voices were calling from all over.

"I'm Tiny! We were in pod seventeen!"

"Jarko and Semina! Pod thirty-two."

"Ursula! Pod twelve!"

"Hold it! Hold it!" Mimi raised her voice, shouting until she had silence. "We've escaped from the Hollow Mountain. But does anyone know where we are?"

Cara's voice sounded close by Mimi's ear. She had been utterly silent in her approach and startled Mimi with her flat tone.

"We are in the Staging Area. According to the King's escape plan, all the pods were designed to converge at a central chamber. I can only assume that this is the Staging Area. We were told about it in security briefings, but I don't think any of us have ever been here."

"Great. That sounds peachy. What are we supposed ta do now we've all converged?"

"We will be met." Cara's voice was hoarse, the memory of weeping still rasping at its edges.

"Who will meet us, Cara?" Mr. Kipling said softly.

"We were never told who would meet us. The King said it was important for security. A 'need-to-know' situation."

"Well, now we need ta know!"

"Like I said, I just don't know. Security."

"Security? Whose security?"

"Ours ... theirs ...," Cara guessed. She squatted down and cupped her hand, scooping some of the water up and tasting it. She spat. "Salt water."

"Well," Mimi said to the refugees now gathered around her. "Now what?"

No one had a ready answer. And so they stood at the shore of a dark sea with no idea what was coming next.[8]

What happened next was a sound. Well, not a sound, exactly. Remember the hum mentioned awhile back when Mimi emerged from the hatch of the pod? Well, it had continued, but as is the way with humming noises, the human ear tends to register them at first, but as time goes on and the hum continues, the brain dismisses the hum as part of the background clutter of noises that exist in the world. Oh, silly brain, so easily deceived! So lazy! Sadly, it is the only thinking organ we have, so we'll have to muddle through.[9]

---

[8] As is usually the case in such junctures in a story, something did happen. Otherwise, there would have been many pages spent describing the shore of the lake, the rocks, the saltiness of the water, the darkness, Mr. Kipling's pants, etc. That would be very, very boring. How lucky for you, dear readers, that you will be spared such a boring passage by what happened next.

[9] There is a tribe in the Central Andes who believe they can also think with their elbows, but there has been no clinical investigation of their claim. It is interesting to note that the funny bone is located in the elbow, which seems to indicate that the joint in question has its own quirky sense of humour.

Back to the point! The hum! The hum began to swell. Mimi's brain registered the change as the hum grew louder and became more like a pulse, rumble, or vibration.

It was like being on the sidewalk when a subway train passes deep below the pavement. Not that Mimi had ever been to a city big enough to have subway trains, but her father had told her about a trip to New York when he was playing baseball and the great throb of the trains below the streets. The tone grew in strength, becoming more insistent. The children fell silent, waiting for whatever was coming.

Mimi was suddenly aware of a light growing all around her. As the illumination brightened, she saw that they were standing in a domed chamber hollowed out of the rock. There were numerous doorways cut into the chamber and in each one stood a cluster of children, refugees from the Hollow Mountain, staring with wonder and trepidation as the light intensified. When the groups saw one another they quickly moved into one clump, herding together for protection. The light was coming from the water, shining from beneath the surface and steadily waxing.[10] The ceiling had begun to glow as well, as if in response to whatever was in the water. The water began to froth and churn as an object rose from the depths.

The waters parted over a glowing dome of crystal that shimmered wetly with a light so powerful that it hurt the children's eyes. It was as if a small sun was rising. Mimi took a step forward and shielded her eyes with her hand over her brow, peering at the object through slitted lids.

---

[10] *Waxing* in this context means "growing." It has nothing to do with wax. When someone says, "The waxing moon shone above," they do not mean there will be wax raining down from the sky, nor is the moon made of wax. The moon is made of cheese. Everyone knows that.

The dome stopped rising, a hemisphere of crystal radiating softly with its own inner illumination. A crack opened on the side nearest Mimi, widening steadily until an aperture that looked like a slice of pie spilled illumination onto the water's surface. From the opening, a tongue of the crystalline material emerged, a gentle hum accompanying the movement until with a grinding *chunk* the extension stopped a few centimetres short of the pool's edge.

Mimi took another step towards the bridge, for so it was, before Mr. Kipling laid a hand on her shoulder to stop her.

"Wait." Mr. Kipling drew his sabre and stood at the ready.

There was movement in the opening of the crystal hemisphere. Forms, backlit by the light from within, shuffled out onto the bridge. The children gasped as the creatures emerged from the radiant dome.

The creatures were dressed in tattered rags pulled over glittering but tarnished armour that seemed to be cobbled together from many different sources. They were short in stature and they were pale, with eyes the colour of polar ice. Their hair was almost colourless, and twisted into their tresses[11] were bits of shells and odd scraps of shiny metal. They were obviously adults, but Mimi towered over them. In their knobby, powerful hands they carried a variety of strange weapons manufactured of a dull black material. The weapons ranged from staves[12] and crossbows to swords and axes.

---

[11] *Tress* is another word for a lock of hair. The word *mattress* is derived from the word *tress*, as people used to sleep on bags full of hair. Not a lot of people ... but still.

[12] *Staves* is the plural form of *staff*. This is an exception to the rule for most "aff" words. For example, one doesn't call a group of giraffes "giraves." That would be wrong. I don't know why ... but it would be.

One of them stepped forward and levelled his crossbow at Mimi. His hair hung in greasy ropes about his face. Tangled in his straggly beard were scraps of fish bone, seashell, and tin. He looked Mimi up and down, his gaze haughty and imperious.

Finally, he stood up to his full height (still inches below Mimi's chin), drew back his shoulders, and barked in a sharp, raspy voice:

"You're trespassing! Leave ... or *die!*"

Having made that dire announcement, he took a step forward and fell face first into the water.

Chapter 2

The man struggled to his feet and pulled himself out of the water. Pointing at the bridge and the gap between its end and the shore, he spoke an odd gurgling language to his fellows. It appeared that he was complaining about something. Finally, he turned back to Mimi. He summoned his rumpled, drenched dignity and said again:

"You're trespassing! Leave or *die*!"

The declaration reverberated off the surrounding walls, bouncing back and forth ominously along the stone. The children were obviously quite impressed and frightened by the odd party of newcomers levelling their weapons at Mimi and Mr. Kipling. Mimi merely stared at the man. He stared back. After a long moment, his brow furrowed and he frowned. Lowering his crossbow, he said, in a wounded tone, "What? Did I say it wrong?"

One of the other strange people, a woman, jabbed him in the ribs with a gnarled staff. "Xnasos, you ninny. Of course you said it wrong. They don't understand you. What a dumdum!"

"I didn't say it wrong, Xnasha. And don't call me a dumdum."

"Sorry, brother. You're right. You're not a dumdum. You're a nitwit."

"I am not a nitwit."

"You're right. A nit has more wit than you could ever dream of having. You're a sub-nitwit."

"I said it right!"

"Why is she looking at you then? She obviously doesn't understand what you're saying."

"I'm telling you, I said it right ... and anyway, I'm the spokesman. We all voted."

Xnasos and Xnasha started shoving each other and would have come to blows if Mimi hadn't interjected. "Hold on! Hold on! Settle down, y'all." She stepped between the two combatants, placing a hand on each of their foreheads and holding them at arm's length from each other. "I understood ya fine, little fella, but here's the thing: I don't take kindly ta people pokin' a bow and arrow in my face."

The man called Xnasos looked at the bow in his hands and smiled sheepishly. "I'm sorry about that. We can't be too careful. One can't be too sure these days." He suddenly frowned fiercely. "Who are you calling little? I'm the tallest person around."

"I'm just as tall as you are," the one called Xnasha said. "Almost all of us are taller than you."

"You're wearing shoes with very thick soles," Xnasos scoffed, waving a gnarled hand dismissively. "In sandals, it's no contest."

"I still think she's taller ...," someone in the back pointed out.

Xnasos gritted his teeth and ignored the comment. Turning to Mimi, he announced once again: "You're trespassing! Leave at once or else." The whole group shook their weapons in what they thought was a menacing way, but it ended up looking rather silly. Eventually, the strangers realized that they weren't impressing Mimi and so they stopped, shuffling their feet restlessly.

"Now what?" Xnasha asked sarcastically.

Xnasos cut her off with a slash of his hand. "Enough!" The little man turned to Mimi and pointed up into her face. "You *are* trespassing!"

Swift as an enraged donkey,[13] Mimi grabbed the finger. "It's rude ta point," she snarled, gently twisting the finger backwards.

"Ow!" yelped Xnasos. "Ow! Ow! Ow!"

"You don't seem ta git it, so I'll say it slow," Mimi growled. "We ain't trespassin'. We came here 'cause we ..." Mimi shrugged and let go of the finger. "'Cause we ain't got nowhere else ta go."

The strangers stared at Mimi as if she were crazy. They stepped back out of reach of the wild-haired girl.

Mimi decided to state the refugees' case. "Well, uh ... Xnasos, my name is Mimi. And this here's Mr. Kipling and we ... that is, all of us ... just escaped from the destruction of the Hollow Mountain. And well, we ended up here ..."

Mimi's declaration brought a hush to the group of small folk. As if for the first time, they looked past her to take in the crowd of children standing in the shadows behind Mr. Kipling and Mrs. Francis.

"Look!" the one called Xnasha said in an awed whisper. "They're children." Hushed debate erupted among the party. They spoke in a hissing, gulping language that Mimi couldn't understand. She watched with growing impatience

---

[13] This may seem like a ridiculous and inaccurate simile to the ignorant and uninitiated. However, few people have experienced the speed and agility of a truly irate donkey. When enraged, donkeys move with blinding speed. In Mexico, they are called Los Cheetahs del Sol (the Sun Cheetahs). One donkey, poked with a sharp stick, was recorded at a land speed of 155 kilometres per hour as it chased down the possessor of the stick and bit him on the ear. I won't be poking a donkey with a stick again any time soon.

as the one claiming to be the spokesman argued with his sister and several other of his followers. Finally, he turned back to Mimi. Xnasos stared at the tall girl, his eyes cold and calculating.

"You're still trespassing. Get lost."

The crowd of strangers jeered their agreement. They shook their weapons and banged their staves on the stone floor.

Mimi suddenly felt annoyed with these bizarre people who were being so disrespectful. She had already had a long day.

"You look here, pipsqueaks!" Mimi's sharp voice silenced the strangers. They blinked their huge pale eyes at her. "I ain't got time fer all these shenanigans. I've had a bad day." She stepped closer to the spokesman and towered over the group. "I've been shot at, scorched, shocked, and beaten. I've been chased outta the only home I ever had. I lost one best friend to a pack o' Grey Agents and the other to I don't know what!" At the mention of Grey Agents, Mimi thought she saw a flicker of fear in their eyes. "I fell down a hole and ended up here, and I ain't got the patience left ta deal with any guff from you bunch o' shrimps. Are you gonna help us or are we gonna have to make ya sorry ya didn't? I started this day at a wedding. Don't make me end it at a funeral."

She planted her fists on her hips and stuck out her chin, waiting for a response.

The little people looked at one another, then at the hawkish face of the girl glowering at them. They looked at the crowd of children who stared back with determined faces. Mr. Kipling's hand fell to the hilt of his sabre.

"Surely, there's no need for threats." Xnasos smiled unctuously,[14] showing yellow, unhealthy-looking teeth. "We just have to be cautious. Our realm is a secret that has been kept for centuries—"

"Millennia," one of the others offered. She was a short, bandy-legged female who wore a skirt of what looked like fish skins.

"I'm talking! It's me who's the talking one. My turn. We agreed."

"Well, just be accurate," the woman said evenly. "It's more like millennia."

"Fine. Millennia."

"Fine."

"Fine."

"Hey," Mimi interrupted the witty repartee. "Are ya gonna help us or not?"

The one called Xnasos rubbed his chin thoughtfully. "Grey Agents, you say?" He shot a worried glance at his sister, who frowned. "Most dangerous, they are. We certainly don't want to attract their attention. Another good reason for us to send you packing."

"But we did swear a pact with the King of the Hollow Mountain," Xnasha insisted. "And, brother, they are children!"

The little people murmured their agreement. Xnasos looked vexed. He glared at Mimi and her companions.

"Xnasos," Xnasha repeated softly. "We swore an oath."

---

[14] *Unctuous* is an old word meaning unpleasantly suave, smug, or smooth or resembling or containing oil, fat, or grease. It comes from the common word *uncle*, and it's derived from the practice of taking uncles who were dishonest and packing them in greasy barrels until they learned to be more trustworthy.

"I heard you the first time!" Xnasos barked, furious. He glared his sister into silence.

"Well?" Mimi prompted.

Xnasos stepped forward, and after one more disdainful look at Mimi, he sneered. "We refuse your appeal for shelter."

Cara's voice was sharp. "You can't do that. You had a deal with the King of Switzerland. We were to come here for help."

The strangers scuffed their sandals against the stone floor, looking uncomfortable. Xnasha seemed embarrassed. Xnasos shook his head and raised a pedantic[15] finger. "We had a deal with *a* King of Switzerland. Not necessarily *the* King of Switzerland who is *your* King of Switzerland!" The pale eyes flickered back and forth. "And I don't see a King of Switzerland anywhere. So ... the deal's off."

Mimi reached over her shoulder and pulled her fighting stick from its sheath on her back. She swung the stick once around her head and settled into a combat stance, her left foot forward, the stick held menacingly in front of her. "All right. I ain't gonna take no fer an answer. I've had a bad day. The worst. We ain't gonna leave."

Cara took up position next to Mimi. Mr. Kipling drew his sabre, the slice of steel on leather echoing off the stone walls. The little people shrank back, raising their various weapons and retreating towards their weird shining dome.

"Stop this foolishness at once!" Mrs. Francis's voice froze everybody in his or her tracks. She pushed her way through the ring of children to arrive in front of the

---

[15] *Pedantic* is a word that means too concerned with rules. I had a pedantic finger once. It was so bossy I had to wear gloves so it wouldn't tell me what to do all the time.

fierce-looking pack of stunted creatures. Mimi was alarmed to see Mrs. Francis place herself within striking distance of the weapons in their gnarled hands. The former housekeeper showed no sign of fear, however. She puffed herself up as large as she could and stamped her soiled satin-encased foot. "How dare you refuse shelter to these children? They are hungry and frightened and in need of your help."

"I wasn't really—," Xnasos began, only to be cut off by Mrs. Francis.

"No, you weren't really! Really!" Mrs. Francis's face flushed with fury as she stamped her small foot again. "I demand that you live up to your promise to provide aid and assistance to the King. Why ... it's the right thing to do, seeing that the Hollow Mountain is destroyed and the King probably ... probably ..." She burst into tears, burying her face in Mr. Kipling's shoulder.

Xnasos and his fellows lowered their weapons and hung their heads, suddenly finding the stone floor fascinating in the extreme. Finally, Xnasos said sheepishly, "Madam, there's no need for tears. We were just being cautious. We can't be too careful any more. The Grey Agents are formidable enemies. We can't risk war with the ODA. There are not so many of us as there once were." He looked up and his big blue eyes were full of sadness. "The Hollow Mountain destroyed?" He shook his head. "The pact we made was one of mutual protection and safe haven. I never thought we'd see the day when the King of Switzerland needed our help. But this is a grave decision, affecting us all. We must debate." He bowed and his fellows followed suit. "We have to be certain that you are deserving to enter the great and hallowed undersea realm of Atlantis!"

Chapter 3

PARVEEN

A sudden, jarring thud woke Parveen from a fitful sleep. He groaned, stretching his stiff, cramped muscles. The compartment he shared with his unconscious sister was barely spacious enough to accommodate one person, and that was under the assumption that the person in question was drugged, stunned, or otherwise incapacitated. Parveen had spent the entire trip from the Hollow Mountain jammed to one side of the cubbyhole, fighting a growing claustrophobic panic.[16]

Parveen had no idea how long the journey had taken between the Hollow Mountain and their destination. Initially filled with terror, anxious that the Grey Agents might discover him as a stowaway, he had done his best to stay alert. Eventually, however, the lulling sound of the engines and the featureless dark of the compartment had conspired to drag him down into sleep.

---

[16] Claustrophobia is the fear of enclosed spaces, not, as is often assumed, the fear of Santa Claus. Although I would hate to be enclosed in a cramped space with Santa Claus, as he is quite obese and would take up that much more room, making any cramped space even more cramped. Granted, he is a charming person with many wonderful personality traits, but he does take up a lot of real estate. Not his fault that he is overweight. I hear it's a glandular disorder. Also, he would bore you to death with stories about reindeer veterinary issues. Or so I've been told.

Now, it appeared, they had arrived at their destination. The low throbbing of engines, whose deep vibration had pervaded the entire craft, suddenly cut out. Parveen felt its absence pulsating in his bones.

"Now what?" he whispered to himself. He had taken to talking to himself, just to keep from losing his grip. The fear and panic were so close to the surface. He had always thought he didn't need any company, preferring to immerse himself in lonely study and solitary pursuits, but something had changed. Being part of the community of the Hollow Mountain, finding his sister again, and the adventures he'd experienced with Mimi and Hamish X had changed him. Now, in this dark coffin, he wished he could speak to anyone, see a familiar face.

"I guess we're on our own," he said to the inert form of Noor, asleep or unconscious beside him. He couldn't tell. Her breathing was regular and steady, but she didn't stir as a normal sleeping person might. Parveen dug in his knapsack and fished out a small but powerful flashlight. He twisted it on and looked at his sister's sleeping face.

Her normally dark skin was pale and sickly. Her smooth black hair was gathered in a ponytail, coiled behind her head like a pillow.

"I wish you'd wake up," Parveen whispered. "I could use your help."

He shone the thin flashlight beam around the enclosed compartment. Just after he had crept into the cubbyhole with his sister, a hatch had slammed down, sealing them in. He had tried everything he could to open the hatch, but there was no catch on the inside. Even if there had been an inner access panel for the electronic lock, he didn't have the tools to deal with it. He had explored every inch of the compartment and found only a small drain at one end, down by his sister's feet, presumably to sluice away any unfortunate accidents the unconscious prisoners might have. Luckily, he had brought a couple of bottles of water and a number of protein bars. The bottles had come in handy when he found he couldn't hold his bladder any longer. He'd had to use only one, so he reasoned that the trip hadn't been too long, probably a day or two.

Now, the trip appeared to be over. Parveen heard a clank and the rattle of chains on the hull of the compartment. With a hiss of escaping air, the hatch opened. Parveen cringed back, trying to make himself invisible at his sister's feet, as far from the hatch as possible. Cold air flooded the compartment, carrying with it a faint whiff of plastic, oil, and some sort of disinfectant. The little boy blinked in the sudden blue-white glare of lights. His eyes, tuned to the almost total darkness of the compartment, watered behind his thick glasses. His hand dove into his knapsack, the fingers closing around one of his hamster bombs, waiting to toss it into the face of any Grey Agent who might thrust his or her way through the hatch.

He sat, his muscles taut, adrenalin pumping, for more than a minute. Nothing happened. No face appeared. He relaxed his grip on the bomb and crept to the opening. Screwing up his courage, he peeked out.

Down the length of the cargo pod, all of the hatches stood open. He watched as the last row of compartments unlocked with a sigh and their hatches folded neatly into the wall, disappearing through slits in the dull metal. A pale blue light washed in through the large open cargo door at the far end. The light was blindingly bright after the hours of darkness Parveen had endured. After a moment of adjustment, he was able to discern objects moving into the long corridor that ran the length of the cargo ship.

Boxy shapes and trailing hoses and wires drifted into the cargo pod, hovering a few centimetres above the deck by some means Parveen couldn't guess. "Robots equipped with magnetic repulsion units?" he mumbled. "Air cushions, perhaps." Even in these moments of extreme danger, he couldn't switch off the part of his mind that was fascinated with technology in all its forms. Several of the items floated in, dispersing along the length of the cargo pod. They appeared to be completely automated. There was no sign of a Grey Agent operating them. One by one, they stopped at a pre-ordained cubbyhole, moved in close, and with a click connected to the pallet under each unconscious child. The device then drifted back, lifting the entire pallet out, and trundled off out the cargo door to be replaced by another robot. They began to work their way down towards the cubbyhole that housed Noor.

Parveen felt a worm of panic uncoil in his belly. What would he do when the robot came to take Noor away? If he tried to disable the machine, an alert message would no doubt be transmitted back to whomever was controlling the robot. An agent would be sent to investigate. Parveen would be discovered and taken prisoner, helpless like all the other children captured in the attack. No, he had to remain at large and find a way to escape and a way to take at least Noor and as many of the others with him as possible.

He had to keep his presence a secret. He had to bide his time. He would learn as much as he could about the Grey Agents, try to find a weakness that might help destroy them. He had to be ready when Hamish X and Mimi came to rescue him. He was sure they would. It was just a matter of time.

Hiding would be very difficult, but he had an advantage. He dug in his knapsack and pulled out a compact bundle of cloth. Shaking out the grey fabric, he struggled into a tight-fitting jumpsuit, an operation made much more difficult by the confined space. In a desperate minute, he succeeded in donning the suit and zipped it up the front, pulling a hood over his head that left only his face visible.

A robot lifted the child out of the cubbyhole next door. Noor's would be next. Parveen donned a pair of goggles that covered the last of his bare skin. He made sure he had packed everything up, leaving no evidence of his presence. Satisfied, he leaned over his sister's sleeping face and whispered in her ear: "Don't be afraid, Noor. I'm with you. I won't let anything happen to you." Parveen brushed a stray hair from her forehead and pressed himself against the side of the cubbyhole, trying to make himself as small as he could, which was very small indeed.

Chapter 4

The robot arrived at Noor's cubbyhole. A small camera fixed to its black plastic front whirred, the lens extending and contracting as the robot scanned the inside of the compartment. Satisfied, the robot extended its two mechanical arms to grasp the pallet on which Noor lay and slowly pull it out into the cargo pod.

Why didn't it see Parveen, you ask? Ah, well. One would have to blame the jumpsuit. Parveen had adapted it from the "sneaky sheet" of the airship *Orphan Queen*. Remember the camouflaging skin of the Chameleon whale?[17] While staying at the Hollow Mountain, Parveen had been inspired to develop a synthetic version that could be manufactured and sewn into garments. The suit he wore was the prototype. The testing process had yielded excellent results. He had been in the midst of completing the final tests before making suits for all the Royal Swiss Guards. The invasion had cut short the work. He now wore the only working "sneaky suit," and he thanked his lucky stars that he had stuffed it into his backpack (sewn from the same material) before he had set out on this mad rescue attempt.

As a result, when the robot surveyed the inside of the compartment, Parveen, pressed against the wall, had appeared to be just another innocent piece of the interior. A handy trick. Anyone searching the compartment would have

---

[17] See Book II of Hamish X's adventures: *Hamish X and the Hollow Mountain*.

to step directly on the hidden boy to discover him. He had also insulated the suit from heat and infrared because he had a suspicion that the Grey Agents' goggles allowed them to see in spectra that normal humans couldn't.

Lifting the pallet, the robot backed out and turned to make its way down the pod to the doors. Parveen had always been a very small and slight boy, making the extra weight as he clung to the underside of the pallet that held his sleeping sister negligible. He positioned himself so that he hung head forward, back to the floor, his fingers wrapped around the plastic struts of the pallet and his toes jammed under the short lip that ran around the edge. He lowered his head so that it skimmed the floor of the pod as they approached the doors and headed down the loading ramp.

He found himself in a giant open space brightly lit from above by banks of blue-white lights burning with nauseating intensity. The cargo pod he had arrived in was one of perhaps a hundred arranged in a semicircle around a central metal loading dock. Its surface was rubberized and textured to reduce slippage. All around the loading dock, robots were transferring their cargo of immobilized children on pallets into large racks. The racks, stacked with trays of humanity, reminded Parveen of the tray racks at the back of the cafeteria in Windcity Orphanage. Intent on sliding Noor into one of the vacant slots, the robot trundled across the loading dock towards an empty rack. Parveen quickly scanned the area to make sure no one was watching. He was just about to drop from his perch and roll to his feet when he heard a voice say ...

"Stop!"

The robot carrying Noor and Parveen jerked to a halt. Footsteps approached until Parveen saw two pairs of polished grey shoes standing to one side of the pallet. He gripped the pallet tighter and prayed that the suit would hide him from close scrutiny.

"A good haul, Mr. Sweet."

"Yes, Mr. Candy. Most will be utilized to provide conductivity for the final phase. Some may be eligible for promotion. This one here looks like she might be a fine candidate. A little young perhaps, but definitely a potential candidate."

"The surgeons will have to decide, Mr. Sweet."

Parveen clenched his teeth. *Surgeons?* He couldn't understand what they were talking about, but it didn't sound good. He wanted to leap out then and there, attack the agents, and attempt an escape. He held himself back with great difficulty. Best not to be hasty. He knew that if he were to make his presence known now, he could never fight his way free with Noor in her present state. His fingers and toes ached from clinging to his precarious perch under the pallet, but he gritted his teeth and hung on.

"Yes," Mr. Candy said after a short pause. "She looks to be just about right. Unfortunately, most of the children we've netted are too young to be useful. I guess they can be hooked into the matrix and used for auxiliary power sources. Mother is always hungry for more power. But soon we won't require these headquarters any more. The whole world will be ours. Still, for a while longer we need all the energy we can muster."

"Indeed, Mr. Candy. Waste not, want not."

"Indeed, Mr. Sweet. Indeed."

At last, when Parveen's fingers felt they would snap off, the grey shoes moved away from the pallet. The soft fall of the Grey Agents' feet retreated across the loading dock. A hiss of hydraulics heralded the opening of a door and then a muted thud indicated that the agents had left the area.

"Headquarters?" Parveen's mind reeled. He was in the *ODA HQ?*

Parveen dropped from the pallet, falling the scant inches to the cold metal floor. His fingers screamed in agony as he flexed them to force the blood through once again. The pallet moved silently away, leaving him exposed in the middle of the loading dock. He rolled onto his hands and knees and looked around.

The loading bay was a rubberized metal square with walls of brushed steel pierced only by one large white sliding door. The room was roughly the size of a football field. Banks of halogen spotlights burned from above, eradicating any trace of shadow, Parveen noted with some relief. The sneaky suit would meld with the grey surface of the floor, but he would still cast a shadow if the light hit him at the right angle, giving away his location to anyone who might be watching. Everywhere robots were lifting pallets, sorting the human cargo from the pods, shuttling inert children according to some predetermined system. Parveen stood for a moment, trying to puzzle out a pattern to the activity. With a start, he realized that the pallet carrying Noor was heading for the large white door on the far side of the loading dock. He had to hurry if he was going to keep it in sight.

Padding as softly as he could, he dodged robots and machines, following a winding path in pursuit of his sleeping sister. A steady stream of robots carried the children through the door and out of sight. Parveen desperately wanted to know where they were being taken, but he had to stay with Noor. All the prisoners were heading in the same direction, so he assumed that if he followed his sister he would learn the fate of all the others on the way.

He caught up with Noor's pallet as it approached the large white door. The robot got into line behind a row of other robots steadily inching forward through the door. One by one, they passed through the portal.

Parveen found himself in a long, plain corridor lit from above by fluorescent tubes. Once again he was reminded of the cafeteria and dormitory at Windcity. Windcity Orphanage and Cheese Factory seemed like a pleasure palace compared with the dismal sterility of ODA Headquarters. The robot headed off in procession behind its fellows as Parveen trotted alongside his sister's sleeping form. Every few metres a fiercely bright light shone down from recessed holes in the stone ceiling, casting a harsh white beam over the pallets as they passed along. Parveen tried to stay against the wall to avoid making an obvious shadow. He couldn't see any surveillance cameras, but he didn't want to take any chances: they might have been hidden or too small to be seen by the naked eye. He had a suspicion that the ODA wasn't terribly concerned about security inside their Headquarters. He doubted any child would have been crazy enough to want to stow away in a Grey Agent cargo pod before he had done it.

Parveen still wondered at his sanity. What could he possibly hope to accomplish? He looked down at his sister's pale, sleeping face and felt a sliver of helplessness slide into his heart. He was completely alone. Hamish X wasn't going to save him. Mimi was lost to him, too. What could he hope to achieve here in the belly of the beast that was the home of the Grey Agents? He would have been better off if Hamish X had never come along. At least when he was back in the Windcity Cheese Factory, slaving under the loathsome Viggo Schmatz, life had been simpler. All he had to worry about was getting up, doing his work, eating porridge, and going to sleep.

With a supreme effort, he pushed the rising despair out of his mind. No. Back in Windcity, he had lived from day to day, without hope, without a dream. He hadn't really been alive then. Now he had Noor and his friends, and he had to do what he could for them.

"We are a family," he whispered softly, reaching out to touch his sister's cold hand as she glided along beside him. "I'm not alone any more."

The corridor turned sharply and ended in a glass doorway that whisked aside as each robot and pallet approached, admitting them one at a time. Bright, antiseptic light flooded through the opening, blinding Parveen momentarily. He adjusted his goggles, filtering out the strongest glare, but he couldn't see what waited on the other side of the doorway. Parveen kept in step with Noor's pallet until it was next in line. The door whisked open and the robot trundled forward. Parveen moved after it.

He found himself in a glass chamber in the shape of a cube. The glass was fogged and impossible to see through. Parveen soon found out why. As soon as the glass door hissed shut behind them, the chamber filled with jets of cool steam, surrounding the pallet, Noor, and the robot. Parveen felt a shiver of panic but kept calm. It seemed to be some sort of disinfectant bath. Noor showed no signs of ill effects. After a few seconds, the other side of the cube slid back. The robot edged forward and Parveen went with it.

He stepped out of the steam cloud and almost blundered straight into a Grey Agent. He caught himself centimetres from collision and stepped to one side, his heart pounding so loudly he was sure the agent would hear it. The agent was oblivious to his presence, however, standing still as the steam bathed his grey-clothed body. Holding his breath, Parveen carefully sidled out of the chamber through another set of sliding glass doors and found himself on a metal catwalk, where he almost bumped into another Grey Agent waiting for his fellow to finish in the steam room. *Sterilization chamber?* Parveen guessed. The agent was dressed in a long grey lab coat and wore a filter mask over his mouth. As the first Grey Agent stepped out of the steam room onto the catwalk, Parveen managed to avoid contact by a hair's breadth, sidestepping quick as a cat. He turned and looked out into the vast space beyond the chamber.

The room was enormous, the size of several football fields. Harsh blue light shone down from banks of halogen spotlights, adding to the overall impression that the chamber was a sports arena. The ODA didn't seem to be playing any games here, though. Everywhere Parveen looked, automated machines swarmed about, performing strange tasks, moving hither and thither[18] carrying pieces of equipment, machinery, and crates. There were Grey Agents supervising the activity, scurrying like drab ants through a bizarre picnic of metal and plastic.

What caught Parveen's eye immediately was a vast pale grey hoop suspended over the far end of the chamber. The thing was immense, dwarfing all the other objects around it. The hoop hung above the activity below by a web of shining cables, pulsing eerily with a greenish-yellow light that made Parveen vaguely nauseated if he looked at it for too long. The cables ran down to the chamber floor and connected to a small mountain

---

[18] *Thither* is quite a fun word, as is its companion, *hither*. It's quite fun to say. More fun, certainly, than saying here and there. Probably twice as much fun as saying hither and yon, although *yon* is quite a sweet little word. But I have spent too much time distracting your attention hither. Perhaps you should return to the main text, thither. (So much fun!)

of black plastic, encrusted with clumps of crystal that pulsed with the same malevolent light.

Parveen stood with his mouth open, awestruck and sickened by the spectacle and scale of the ODA's evil handiwork. He wondered what function the hoop might serve. And the thing below: was it a power source, a computer? He couldn't figure it out without a closer examination. The scale of the operation threatened to overwhelm his fragile confidence. When faced with the scope of the ODA's powerful technology, his heart almost failed him.

I'm just one boy, he thought to himself. *And a small boy, also. What can I hope to do against the might of these creatures?* He gripped the railing of the catwalk and mustered[19] his courage. *I have no choice. I have to be brave for Noor. There's no one else who can help her.*[20]

Parveen was so rapt in contemplation of the evil spectacle that he failed to notice when the robot carrying Noor set off along the catwalk, the two Grey Agents on either side of it now. He started out in pursuit as quickly and stealthily as he could.

The catwalk where Parveen stood was suspended a hundred metres above the floor below and ran the entire length of the chamber. Parveen caught up with his sister and her escort as they passed through another set

---

[19] *Mustered*, not *mustard*. One is a verb meaning gathered or assembled. The other is delicious on a sandwich. If people are gathering on your sandwich, don't eat it.

[20] Do you know what's wonderful, my dear readers? Small people like Parveen find it in themselves to be brave every single day, every place in the world. They carry on in the face of failure, loss, and hopelessness and so make the world a little better. Try it yourself sometime. But I digress.

of sliding glass doors. He nipped in just as the doors hissed shut.

Once inside, he stopped dead in his tracks. Looking up into the room he had to bite back an involuntary cry of horror.

The room was big, not as vast as the one he'd just left but very large. He stood at one end of a long stone causeway. On either side of the causeway was a yawning empty space. Well, not exactly empty. The space was filled with children.

Children were suspended in rows above and below him. Like fruit from a vine of wires and cables they hung, motionless and inert. They wore pale grey body stockings that clung like a sickly second skin and made them seem even more deathly pale, their faces wan and slack, eyes closed, comatose. Wires stretched from harnesses affixed to their shaven scalps. A tube ran from each of their mouths through which a sluggish green fluid oozed slowly. Parveen felt a horrible revulsion. As he watched, several metallic creatures with multiple silvery legs scurried up and down the wires and tubes like spiders, servicing the sleeping orchard of children. *What is this place?* he asked himself. He was so horrified that he had to shake his head to clear it of the vile setting. Keeping his attention on the path ahead, he set off after his sister.

The stone causeway stretched out across the chamber, passing through the terrible orchard of children. Parveen concentrated on the back of the robot as it carried his sister's pallet flanked by the two Grey Agents in their surgical clothes. He felt terror uncoiling in his stomach like some tentacled creature at the bottom of the ocean that rarely felt the warmth of the sun. Was his sister doomed to become one of these children, hooked up to a bizarre network for who knew what purpose? He staggered along behind the party as they approached another black metal hatchway.

As the party approached the hatchway, it slid open with a soft, asthmatic hiss to reveal a dim room beyond. Parveen scooted in after them as the hatchway slid shut. After the relative brightness of the child orchard, this new place was quite dark. Parveen's goggles took a moment to adjust to the ambient light. When they did, he almost fell to his knees. He stifled another cry of horror. He thought that nothing could be more terrifying than the child orchard. He was wrong. Horribly wrong.

"Noor," he whispered softly. "Oh, Noor, no."

Chapter 5

HAMISH X

Hamish X lay very still. He lay perfectly still because the knife at his throat was very sharp and the young girl holding said knife seemed very serious indeed. Lying still is always the best option when someone serious is pressing a knife to one's throat.[21, 22]

The boy named Thomas looked at Hamish X with cold blue eyes.

"I think we should kill him now," he whispered. "We don't need his help and we can't trust him."

---

[21] In fact, the Surgeon General of the United States released a report citing sudden movement as the number-one cause of serious injury and death in those having sharp objects held against their throats.

[22] Why is there a young girl holding a knife to Hamish X's throat, you ask? Didn't you read the last book? I mean, really! It was the bit right at the end! The last thing you read! Oh, I suppose I should refresh your memory or else I'm never to hear the end of it. In a nutshell, Hamish X had left the Hollow Mountain to pursue his destiny, find Professor Magnus Ballantyne-Stewart, and learn the truth about himself. He stowed away on a rusty old freighter bound for Africa, where the Professor in question was last known to be located. Having stowed away onboard the ship, he settled down for a snooze in the cargo hold only to wake up and find a girl named Maggie holding a knife to his throat and announcing that she and her associates were going to take over the ship. So, that's the end of the refresher course. May I continue now? Fine.

"I want to hear his story. How did he end up on this tub?"

"Who cares, Maggie? Just kill him and let's get on with taking over the ship."

"What are you talking about? Kill him? You wouldn't hurt a fly."

"I would, too."

"Well, I'm in charge, because I have the knife."

"Right, sister Maggie, dear."

"And I'm older," Maggie said pointedly. Thomas made a rude noise and fell silent. Maggie turned her full attention back to Hamish X. As she pondered his immediate future, he had time to examine his captors.

Maggie was a girl of roughly eleven years of age. Her hair was dark and, at the moment, a greasy mess. She had the same luminous blue eyes as her brother, but while his face was round, hers was long and sharp. She wore a striped orange-and-blue bathing suit that looked a little the worse for wear and a matching sarong wrapped around her waist. Thomas, the bloodthirsty brother, wore jeans with holes in both knees and a T-shirt that announced *My Grandma went to Aruba and all I got was this crappy T-shirt* in blue neon letters. He held a length of metal pipe in his hand. As Hamish X looked at him, Thomas slapped the pipe into his hand in a menacing fashion.

Gathered around them was a crowd of grimy, bedraggled children, eyes wide and white in their filthy faces. They warily eyed their captive and waited for instructions from the girl Maggie.

"So, spill the beans," Maggie demanded. "Who are you? What are you doing here? Are you spy or what?"

"A spy? What's there to spy on?"

Thomas thrust his face into Hamish X's. "Us. The Captain coulda sent you down here to see what we're up to. To rat us out!"[23]

"I'm not a spy," Hamish X said, his skin crawling under the edge of the knife. "I don't know anything about the Captain. Listen, I just stowed away on this boat to steal a ride."

"A ride? On a child-slaver? Are you kidding me?" Maggie shook her head.

"A child-slaver?" Hamish X asked. "This is a child-slaver?"

Upon hearing this news, Hamish X felt a flicker of anger ignite in his belly.

Maggie nodded. "They cruise around and snatch children, then sell 'em. At least that's what we've overheard from the crew."

Hamish X clenched his fists and felt a surge of power flow into his boots. "Sell them to whom?"

Maggie looked into Hamish X's golden eyes, and what she saw there made the knife waver in her hand. "The Grey Agents," she said softly. "The ODA."

"That's enough talking." Thomas spat and shook his head in disgust. "I'd kill 'im. It's simpler."

Hamish X glared at the boy. "But not very nice," he observed coldly. Something in the glare of his golden eyes made Thomas take a step back.

"Still." Thomas shrugged.

---

[23] Rats certainly have a bad reputation for being untrustworthy, a reputation that I for one doubt they really deserve. Have you ever been lied to by a rat? Have you ever been betrayed to your enemies by a rat? I sincerely doubt it. So let's try to refrain from bad-mouthing the rat population, shall we? Now mice, on the other hand, you can't trust as far as you can throw them, those dirty, lying mice!

A little girl, one of the many children in the dark cargo hold, stepped closer. Her face was smeared with dirt. She wore a ragged dress and carried a teddy bear under her arm. The bear was missing one eye and its left arm. She leaned closer and peered at Hamish X. "Hey," she said softly. "You ..." Her eyes went wide. "You're Hamish X."

In the darkness of the ship's hold, Hamish X felt a hush descend. Thomas's eyes were suddenly wide, all suspicion gone, replaced by awe. "Hamish X," he breathed. "*The* Hamish X?"

"I suppose so." Hamish X shrugged. Suddenly, children were crowding in, grasping at him as if to assure themselves he was real. Grimy hands reached out and brushed his clothing, touching the black surface of his boots as if they were some kind of hallowed objects. Hamish X looked into their faces and saw that, where only moments ago there had been despair, now there was a glimmer of hope.

Maggie lowered the knife but maintained a belligerent attitude, her lip curled. "Hamish X, eh? What are you doing here on this dirty, filthy tub?"

Hamish X stood up and stretched. "An accident. A total fluke. I just needed to hitch a ride and this is the first ship I tried. How lucky for you that this is a child-slaver ship in the employ of the Grey Agents."

"Lucky? Are you off your nut, buddy?" Thomas laughed humourlessly. "The *Christmas Is Cancelled* is the last ship you wanna get stuck on and the ODA are the last people you want to tangle with."

Hamish X thought about that for a second. "All right, that came out wrong. Being trapped on a child-slaver ship isn't the luckiest thing in the world that could happen to you. The Grey Agents are terrible people to be mixed up with. What

I meant to say was having me stow away on the child-slaver ship you happen to be trapped aboard is lucky in the extreme, especially since the Grey Agents are my sworn enemies! ... Wait a minute ... *Christmas Is Cancelled?*" asked Hamish X. "That's the name of the ship?"[24]

"Cute, isn't it. It's the Captain's idea of a joke," Maggie explained. "The *Christmas Is Cancelled* runs up and down the European coastline snatching kids. We were on a summer holiday in Turkey with our parents." She jabbed a dirty thumb at Thomas. "My brother and me. We were just wandering along the beach looking for shells when we got kidnapped."

"Our parents told us not to go out of sight," Thomas said bitterly. "But we didn't listen."[25]

---

[24] A strange name for a ship, certainly, but typical of the names chosen by child-slavers throughout history. Child-slaver ship captains usually name their craft after something that will depress and demoralize children. Some examples of ships that have struck fear into the hearts of unwary children through the ages are *The Bath-Time*, *The Brussels Sprout*, *The Wedgie*, *The Bee Sting*, *The Haircut*, *The Moustached-Auntie-Who-Pinches-Your-Cheek-And-Has-A-Big-Hairy-Mole-And-Bad-Breath*, *The Big Brother's Fart*, and *The Wet Willie*. So, *Christmas Is Cancelled* might be considered mild by comparison.

[25] An interesting phenomenon: children's hearing seems to fail when parents are telling them what to do. Studies have shown that when parents are dictating instructions concerning behaviour, comportment, manners, or safety regulations, the ability of the juvenile ear to discern sound and comprehend these instructions drops by an astonishing fifty-eight percent. New studies indicate that if parents wish their children to absorb and follow instructions, they should insert subliminal messages into their conversations. Dropping instructions into especially pleasing conversations is highly effective. For example: "Children, don't talk to strangers," is seventy-two percent less likely to be absorbed than "Children, don't talk to *who would like a chocolate ice cream sandwich* strangers."

"They were waiting for us behind a big rock outcrop," Maggie explained. Her eyes glistened in the feeble light of the cargo hold. "They grabbed us, gagged us, and stuck smelly sacks on our heads. They had a boat waiting and then brought us out to the ship." She shook her head suddenly, a quick snap that sent her greasy curls bouncing. "That was a few weeks ago. They've been picking up kids all around the Mediterranean. There's more than a hundred of us now."

"Where are they taking you?" Hamish X asked. His heart went out to these poor kids. He had a quest to complete, but he knew he'd have to postpone his own journey until he could deal with this situation. Then he would be back on his way.

"We've been trying to figure that out. The Captain and his crew have been careful not to talk too much. From what we've managed to overhear, we're going to a place called Morocco."

Hamish X pondered for a moment. "Morocco. There's a slave market there in a city called Marrakesh. I've been there before.[26] I suppose that's where they'll meet their bosses and hand you over. Any idea when we're to arrive?"

"We arrive at dawn. I overheard Captain Ironbuttocks talking to the guards," Maggie said.

"Captain Ironbuttocks?" Hamish X scoffed. "What kind of ridiculous name is that?"

"He isn't ridiculous," Maggie shot back. "He's mean and he's dangerous."

---

[26] Hamish X's reference to the slave market in Marrakesh is interesting. I have no solid information as to what he might have done there, but his adventures are too numerous for me to know about all of them. I can only do so much, you know! Perhaps he is referring to the mysterious Marrakesh Fire that consumed a cluster of warehouses and brought shipping to a standstill. The cause of the conflagration is still unknown.

"Ironbuttocks." Hamish X shook his head and laughed. "What is with these sea captains and their inane nicknames? Why can't they just be Captain Jones or Captain Wilson? Honestly!"[27]

"He isn't someone you should laugh at," Maggie warned. "He's a pretty nasty customer."

Hamish X stood quite still. Those closest to him took a shuffling step backwards when they saw the look on his face. A wolfish, sneering smile exposed his left incisor, giving his features a predatory cast. His fingers curled into tight fists, opening and closing slowly. A ghostly, bluish flicker skated over the surface of his boots like an echo of his growing hatred for his mortal enemies. The faces of the children in the dark, dank cargo hold reflected the faint flare of power.

"So am I," Hamish X growled softly. He grabbed his backpack and slung it over his shoulder.

"I bet you are." Maggie nodded.

I should be getting on my way, Hamish X thought. *I have to find the Professor.* He shifted his shoulders, feeling the weight of the book in his backpack settle between his shoulder blades. The *Great Plumbers and Their Exploits* book was the reason he was on this journey. *I have to find*

---

[27] Of course, Hamish X is referring to Captain Cheesebeard and Captain Soybeard (see Book I of Hamish X's adventures: *Hamish X and the Cheese Pirates*). It is true, sea captains, especially evil sea captains, tend to have quite ridiculous names, often associated with some distinguishing physical attribute; for example, Captain Hook, Blackbeard, Cheesebeard, etc. The interesting thing is that evil sea captains are required to register their nicknames with the Evil Sea Captains' Guild to avoid doubling up. There is nothing more confusing than having two Captain One-Eyes, but, that said, one wonders why the two Captain One-Eyes couldn't join forces and have two eyes in total. Sadly, evil sea captains are very argumentative and rarely manage to coordinate their efforts.

the Professor, but this is a chance to strike directly at the ODA, who did this to me. For the first time since I got some of my memories back, I'm able to do some good. I can't pass up this chance. Aloud, he said, "What's the plan?"

Maggie and Thomas exchanged a look. Maggie held up her knife. "I have a knife."

Thomas shrugged. "And I found a piece of pipe."

Hamish X frowned. "I was expecting more, but I suppose that's a start."

"We haven't got a lot of options," Maggie said defensively. "I managed to steal this from the kitchen while I was working there. Some of the other kids have done the same. Some have clubs, but mostly we're counting on numbers."

"There are only twenty or so crew members," Thomas added, then frowned. "Plus the captain."

"Ha!" Hamish X couldn't help but laugh. "Ironbuttocks! I still think that's a ridiculous name. I mean, Ironbuttocks. Really!"

"Sure," Thomas grumbled. "It sounds ridiculous! But he's no pushover. You'll see."

"Don't worry! Leave old Rustypants to me!" Hamish X puffed out his chest. "I've handled worse."

"Anyway," Maggie interjected, "we're getting ahead of ourselves. First we have to get out of the hold. The hatch is battened down every night." She pointed up into the gloom overhead. Hamish X looked up and could vaguely make out the outline of the hatch he'd climbed into hours before. It had been open then, but now a heavy wooden cover had been pulled over the opening, reinforced with steel bars.

Hamish X nodded grimly, taking in the fortified hatch with thoughtful eyes. Then he turned to the children huddled in the darkness of the cargo hold. He tried to look into each and every dirty, desperate face as he spoke.

"I don't know any of you, but you know me. I have faced some of the most dangerous people in the world and I've managed to come out in one piece. We have strength in numbers. We can escape this place if we are brave and strong and work together. Are you ready to do that?"

"Yeah!" The children shouted as one, filling the gloomy cargo hold with their defiance.

"Good! Thomas?"

"What?" the boy asked.

"You will take a third of our force and head for the engine room. If we control the engines, we control the ship."

Thomas nodded, his blue eyes blazing, as he immediately began counting off his squad.

"Mimi," Hamish X began, turning to Maggie. Seeing her confusion, he caught himself. "I meant Maggie, sorry. Mimi's a friend of mine from ... Never mind. Maggie, the rest of you will rush the bridge and subdue any crew member we run into on the way."

"That's a great plan, but aren't you forgetting something?" Maggie asked.

"What would that be?"

"We are locked in the cargo hold," she said. "Duh!"

"It's nice to see you aren't in awe of me any more." Hamish X laughed.

"Well, what about the hatch?"

Hamish X smiled his fierce smile. "Leave it to me." He turned and addressed the gathered children. "Are we all ready?"

Thomas nodded. Maggie nodded.

"Who wants to be free?" Hamish X shouted.

"Yaaaaaaaaaay!" was the thunderous reply.

Chapter 6

"There's that cheering again," Monkey-Knees observed.

Up on the deck of the *Christmas Is Cancelled*, the night watch was underway. Long, dark, and lonely, the night watch was the most onerous of all duties, and none of the crew was very eager to do it. Slavers are nasty, mean, and cruel, but what few people know is that the majority of nasty, mean, cruel people are the way they are because they are afraid of the dark.[28]

The night watch fell to Rodney and Monkey-Knees,[29] two sailors who were particularly fearful of the dark and so had hung a lantern from a pole. The lantern swung gently back and forth in sympathy with the motion of the sea. The men sat in the bright yellow glow of the lamp. Monkey-Knees had pulled up his trouser legs and was manipulating his knee muscles for the entertainment of Rodney, whiling away the final hour before dawn.

---

[28] It may seem surprising to you that people as evil, nasty, and cruel as slavers might be afraid of the dark, but the truth is many villains are the victims of phobias and fears. According to a poll taken by the University of California, Los Angeles Medical Center, thirty-five percent of evil people are afraid of the dark. A further twenty-seven percent of villains fear spiders, snakes, or crawling insects. Forty-two percent of nasties are chronic bedwetters, and a whopping seventy-two percent of evil villains think birds control the weather.

[29] His real name was Curtis, but his crewmates called him Monkey-Knees because his knees, when clenched, resemble the faces of monkeys.

"They're probably playing tag or something," Rodney said dismissively. "Kids are always playing stupid games."

"We're supposed to be guarding them, though," Monkey-Knees pointed out in a worried tone.

"Forget them! They can't get out! That hatch is solid oak reinforced with steel. They couldn't get out if they tried. Now," Rodney said, giggling, "do another one."

"Okay!" Monkey-Knees twitched his left kneecap.

"Oh, that's a cheeky one," Rodney chortled, pointing a stubby, filthy finger at Monkey-Knees's left knee. "Does he want a banana?"

"Ook! Ook! Eeek!" Monkey-Knees tensed his left kneecap as though said monkey was responding to the question. Monkey-Knees had become a fair ventriloquist as well as a knee puppeteer. "Ook!"

Rodney guffawed and slapped his own knee.[30]

"Quiet out there!" a voice roared above the two sailors. Monkey-Knees leapt to his feet and banged his forehead on the lantern, sending it swinging in wild arcs and splashing light around the oily wooden deck. Rodney simply fell backwards off the oil drum he had been sitting on.

---

[30] It must be pointed out that one of the side effects of being an evil henchman or lesser baddie is that one has a limited ability to grasp what is truly funny and what is completely inane. After years in the company of villains, one's sense of humour becomes stunted, mainly as a result of being required to laugh at whatever one's evil master says, even if it isn't particularly funny. One tends to lose perspective. Hence, knee puppetry and ventriloquism become extremely and disproportionately amusing.

"You two stupids don't give me a minute of peace!" Down the steps from the nearby superstructure[31] the slaver Captain approached. *Clang! Clang! Clang!* Each step he took was accompanied by the clash of his metal buttocks that gave him his name, or, rather, his nickname. (The Captain's real name was Georgiou Stroumboulopoulous. Even he had trouble spelling it, so he went by the simpler nickname.) The metal buttocks crashed together when he walked, making it almost impossible for him to sneak up on anyone. As a result, Captain Ironbuttocks was never invited to any surprise birthday parties, which contributed to his evil temperament: he loved birthday cake but rarely had the chance to eat any. The metal buttocks were also a safety hazard. When they crashed together, they tended to throw off showers of sparks that threatened to ignite flammable liquids, a real danger aboard ship. To avoid unfortunate conflagrations, Ironbuttocks's pants were lined with flame-retardant fabric (which was itchy in the extreme), further contributing to the Captain's ill temper. The ill

---

[31] The superstructure of a ship is the section that rises above the decks. The bridge is located here as well as most of the areas vital to the functioning of the ship: the radio room, radar room, map room, and the ping-pong table. What? You don't think ping-pong is vital on a ship? Things can get pretty boring when one is out at sea. Sometimes ping-pong is a captain's last line of defence, the last option before discipline fails, mutiny reigns, and madness follows. The only thing that kept the crew on Magellan's circumnavigation voyage from going mad was the intense ping-pong tournament they kept going en route. Magellan was killed when he went over the side in the Philippines to retrieve the ball after a particularly hard smash.

temper in question was now focused on the two sailors keeping watch over the cargo hatch.[32]

The Captain stalked down the metal steps from the superstructure. He was short, but he was solid. He wore a soiled undershirt that was stretched tight over a round paunchy belly, but his bare arms bulged with ropy sinew. On his head he wore a Greek fisherman's cap, stiff with grease. Down the length of his arms, tattoos writhed in concert with the movement of the muscles beneath the skin.

The tattoos were many and varied. There was a black panther clawing its way out of the Captain's right shoulder. Two snakes coiled down his arms. There was a Greek flag on his right forearm and an anchor on his left. On his right wrist he had a tattoo of an expensive watch. (Being a sailor, it didn't make sense to have a real watch because the salt water would ruin it. As a result, it was always ten past two in the Captain's world.) Last, and strangest of all, was the tattoo on his left shoulder: a little cat with big, sad eyes. Anyone who mentioned the cat was summarily executed.

"I try to get the sleeping and you are laughing! You two dumb-stupids keep me with eyes open!" The Captain stalked up to Rodney, who towered over him. "You!" he barked, poking Rodney in the stomach. "Bend over!" Rodney did as he was told. The Captain slapped him very hard across the face. "Stop laughing so much!"

---

[32] Readers might wonder how Captain Ironbuttocks came to sport his iron buttocks. A fair question. There are many stories that claim to tell the tale. One says he lost the appendages when he was waterskiing in shark-infested waters near Curaçao. Another source insists they were shot off in a gunfight. Yet another declares that his ex-wife sold them while he was asleep. Colourful options all, but I have learned the truth. He fell asleep on a waffle iron and singed them off. Weird but true.

"Ow," said Rodney.

The Captain slapped him again. "Don't say 'ow' to me." Rodney bit his lip and said nothing, tears standing in his eyes. The Captain's hands were very rough and they smelled bad, too. "I don't want no trouble. I want you to keep eyes open! I deliver these children to Marrakesh and *then* you play the knee puppet games! Until then, you pay attention and don't make noises." Rodney and Monkey-Knees nodded sheepishly and looked at the deck in front of them. Satisfied, the Captain nodded. With a hollow clanging, he set off up the steps and returned to his cabin.

When Monkey-Knees was sure the Captain was gone, he twitched his left knee and said, "Ook."

Rodney punched him in the arm, stifling a laugh. "You're so bad." He giggled as Monkey-Knees twitched his kneecap again. "Eek! Eek!"

Rodney collapsed into helpless, strangled giggles. They both started laughing softly, leaning on each other and trying desperately to bite the inside of their cheeks to avoid laughing out loud. They were so preoccupied with their own hilarious hijinks that they almost failed to notice the weird blue glow licking around the hatch-cover beneath their feet.

"Ha-ha-hey," Rodney said, wiping his eyes. "Do you see that?"

"Wha-wah-what?" Monkey-Knees gasped.

"That!" Rodney's giggles were gone now. The entire hatch, a square of wood and metal held in place by four heavy latches, was leaking a strange luminescence.

Monkey-Knees was suddenly serious. "That's weird. Is it a fire?"

"I don't know, but it's getting brighter."

Rodney was correct. The light was growing in intensity now, as though a train were approaching the hatch from below, its headlamp shining.

"Do we have a train in the cargo hold?" Monkey-Knees asked. Kind of a silly question, but what do you expect from a man who enjoys knee puppetry? Rodney was about to point out the unlikelihood of having a train in a boat, but he had only just opened his mouth when Hamish X smashed out of the hatch from below, his boots blazing.

Rodney and Monkey-Knees were flung aside in the impact, cartwheeling through the air and crashing heavily into the sea. Shards of the ruined hatch rocketed upwards as shrapnel from the explosion rattled off the metal bulkheads of the superstructure. The broad windows of the bridge shattered as the concussion wave struck them, raining bits of glass over the night watch inside.

Hamish X rose like a comet out of the cargo hold, a smear of blue power trailing after him into the black night. He arced through the air, suddenly and belatedly realizing that his trajectory would send him plunging into the sea. Thinking quickly, he grabbed hold of the communications mast on the top of the ship. The mast bent under his weight and then snapped back. Hamish X held on tightly, clinging to the metal pole like a fly. The mast thrummed like a plucked string but held. From his perch, he watched as Maggie and Thomas led a swarm of children up through the ruined hatch, boiling out onto the deck. There, the children searched about for weapons, picking up whatever they could find: sticks, weights, anchor chains, ropes, and gaffs.[33]

---

[33] Not, strangely, gaves.

"Let's get to the engine room," Thomas shouted, waving a wooden club. The swarm split in two, with a third of the shouting children setting off in the direction of the gangway to the lower decks. Maggie led the rest towards the bridge.

Clang! Clang! Clang! "What going on here?" Captain Ironbuttocks stomped out onto the upper deck, casting his furious gaze down. As he swept his eyes across the deck of his vessel, he took in the crowd of mutinous children. "Well, well, well!" He glared, stopping the children in their tracks. "What is this we have here?"

"We're taking over the ship," Maggie shouted, brandishing her stolen knife. "You might as well give up! We don't wanna hurt you, but we will if we have to!"

"Ooo! Is that right? You're taking over my ship! Well, whoop-e-dy, wheep-e-dy woo!" The Captain did an odd little prancing dance, waving his hands in the air before suddenly becoming deadly serious, his unshaven face set in a fierce scowl. "Well, I hate to be the disagreeing person, girlie, but I am disagreeing with you." He spat a contemptuous loogie[34] onto the deck. "Nah. I don't think so. This

---

[34] The origin of the term *loogie* is shrouded in mystery. As we all know, a loogie is a particularly nasty, snot-laden lump of spit. Some say it originated in the eighth century when Lord Loog of Snowdon held the first ever distance-spitting competition. Other scholars insist that the term is a descriptive one, likening the gob of spit and goo to the luge, a small, one-person sled. According to my sources, I believe *loogie* comes from a bizarre custom in medieval Scotland. On New Year's Day, the King would customarily spit out the window on his gathered courtiers. Whomever the spitty projectile happened to land on was appointed prime minister for the ensuing year. Therefore, it was considered a very lucky thing indeed to be spat on. *Lucky*, in medieval Scots dialect, was pronounced *looky* and over time became transmuted into the current form: *loogie*.

is ending now. No one gets hurt if you go back to the cargo hold and behave yourselves!"

Maggie stopped at the foot of the steps and glared up at the Captain. "You like the cargo hold? I'm sure we can arrange for you and your crew to stay in there as long as you like. As for us, we aren't going back there. C'mon!" She signalled for the mob of children to follow her up the steps. She stopped dead when she saw the large black revolver that the Captain drew from his waistband. The gun was heavy and dark, full of menace, the long snout of its barrel trained on Maggie as she stood frozen, one foot poised on the lowest step. The knife in her hand wavered. One must remember, Maggie was really just a little girl, and although committed to taking over the ship, she was only a few weeks removed from building sandcastles on a beach in a Turkish holiday resort. Now she found herself in a bit of a dangerous spot, having mistakenly brought a knife to a gunfight.

The Captain laughed. "Not so sure of yourself now, eh? Captain Ironbuttocks, he seems to be the cat who got your tongue!"[35]

Maggie hesitated for a moment, but, feeling the crowd of children behind her waver, she dug deep and found a hidden well of courage in her heart. She waved her arm to the crowd behind her. "He can't shoot all of us." She was

---

[35] The expression *Cat's got your tongue* originated in Portugal in the late sixteenth century. An ingenious burglar employed a group of very clever cats that would steal into people's homes and, using their tiny teeth, latch on to sleeping victims' tongues, preventing an alarm from being raised. The burglar would then rob the house at his leisure.

about to lead the charge forward up the steps when she heard the voice from above.

"That's hardly fair," Hamish X said. The Captain looked up to see Hamish X sitting on the communications mast, dangling his big boots and smiling broadly.

"What you do up there?" the Captain roared. "You get down here." He aimed the gun at Hamish X, who merely continued smiling.

"I'll come down when I'm good and ready, Captain," Hamish X said. "Please, don't make this any harder than it has to be. Drop the gun and surrender quietly."

"Or what?"

"Or I'll have to come down there and dent your bottom for you."

"You dare to threaten my magnificent behind? You will pay for that!" The Captain raised his pistol and took aim at Hamish X. "I don't have time for your games." He pulled the trigger and, with a ringing crack, fired at Hamish X.

Bullets move at extremely high speed. May you never find yourself in the path of a bullet because, truth be told, it is almost impossible for a human to duck out of the way of an oncoming projectile moving at such high velocity. The best policy is to avoid contact with human beings who employ firearms. If contact is unavoidable, the wise course of action is not to provoke the person with the firearm to discharge it in your direction. Don't say things like "Why don't you try to shoot me with that gun?" or "Hey, I bet you couldn't hit me with a bullet!" or "Yo, dumdum! Shoot me, why don't you?"

As I was saying, bullets move very swiftly and almost everyone in the world is slower than a bullet. Fortunately, Hamish X was blessed with reflexes that allowed him the luxury of being rude to people with guns. The bullet ploughed into the mast exactly where he had been sitting only a fraction of a second before. The mast splintered and a sizable shard of it fell, forcing the Captain to dance aside to avoid being skewered. Hamish X launched himself into a somersault[36, 37] that took him spinning out of harm's way to land easily on the deck behind the Captain. Within an instant of landing, Hamish X lashed out his left boot and connected with the Captain's right buttock with a resounding clang. The Captain staggered from the impact and crashed hard into the railing.

"Ow! Hey!" The Captain reached back and explored the buttock in question with his free hand. "You little stinker. You dented my beautiful bum!"

---

[36] *Somersault* is a fun word. *Somer* comes from the Latin word *supra*, which means above, and *sault* comes from the Latin word *saltus*, which means jump. This is the accepted origin, but many believe it comes from the name of a man who lived in sixteenth-century London and stood on the wharves at Greenwich and jumped over large sacks of salt in a very entertaining way. His name was Harry Somers and his salt-leaping was a tourist attraction until he was killed by a rabid anchovy.

[37] The anchovy is a family (Engraulidae) of small but common salty fish. They are found in scattered areas throughout the world's oceans. I think they are delicious, but that's really neither here nor there. Rarely do they get rabies, which is a disease that affects only mammals, but there's a first time for everything. Since anchovies travel in vast schools, an anchovy with rabies would quickly infest all of his fellows, leading to huge schools of rabid anchovies, terrorizing the seas. I shudder just thinking about it. Being bitten by a fish is bad, but being bitten by such a salty fish would really sting a lot. It would be literally rubbing salt in the wound, some might say.

The children on the deck below cheered. Hamish X laughed and shrugged. "You were warned. Now throw down your weapon and I'll accept your surrender."

Captain Ironbuttocks glowered. He was not used to being laughed at, especially by children. On top of that, his bottom was quite sore, which did nothing to improve his mood. He stood up and sneered. "You can't possibly be defeating me and my entire crew. It's you who should be surrendering before I call my men up here to deal with your little mob of ankle-biters, hey? I will take these rug monkeys, these carpet gnomes, these thumb-sucking, diaper-wearing . . ."

Before Ironbuttocks could think of another way of insulting the children, the ship rocked as an explosion from below decks sent Hamish X, the Captain, and the children crashing to the deck. Thomas was obviously up to some mischief in the bowels of the ship. Before Hamish X could stop Ironbuttocks, the Captain vaulted to his feet, leapt over Hamish X through the door to the bridge, and slammed the metal hatch behind him.

Hamish X stood up and grabbed the handle to find that it was locked from the inside. He braced his boots against the hatch and strained with all his might, but to no avail.

"Ha!" The thick steel of the hatch muffled Ironbuttocks's voice. "Not so smarty-mouthed now, eh Boot-Boy?"

Hamish X reared back and kicked the hatch, scoring the surface but denting it only slightly. "Open this hatch! There's nowhere to hide!" Hamish X shouted.

"No chance!"

Sometimes one becomes so focused on the task in front of one that one misses the obvious. Have you noticed? Hamish X was trying so hard to get in the locked hatchway that he failed to notice all the windows on the front of the bridge were gaping open, shattered when the explosion tore the cargo hatch off. Flummoxed by this hatch, he stood back, breathing heavily, and finally noticed his error. Unfortunately, so had Captain Ironbuttocks.

"Aha!" shouted Hamish X. He tensed to jump through the opening. Inside the bridge, the Captain staggered across the floor and slammed his hand down on a large metal lever. Metal shutters screeched down, sealing the windows from the inside. The Captain breathed a sigh of relief. He had bought himself some time.

"Tee hee!" Captain Ironbuttocks cackled, "Tee hee! I have stuck a fly in your ointment, hey, Mr. Boots? Tee hee!"[38] He looked around the bridge, hoping to find some way out of his predicament. All of the ship's controls, radar, communications equipment, and steering were controlled from the bridge. If he could wait the rebellious children out, he might still win the day.

Hamish X stood outside the bridge, frustrated by the metal shutters. Maggie, having recovered from the explosion, ran up the steps and stood by Hamish X's side.

"We gotta get in there," Maggie said. "Without the bridge, everything else is pointless."

"Yes," Hamish X agreed, running his hand over the scratched metal of the hatch. "This door is strong, but I don't doubt that with a little work," he tapped it with the toe of one massive boot, "I can get through. In the meantime, we should look for alternatives."

"Like what?"

Hamish X thought for a moment. "Leave this to me!" he said grimly. "You go and help Thomas. Get to the engine rooms and shut down the turbines. If the ship's dead in the water, there's nothing Ironbuttocks can do. He'll have to come out or we'll have all the time in the world to get in."

Maggie nodded and sped off in search of her brother.

Hamish X turned his attention back to the task at hand. He concentrated on his boots. In all his adventures they

---

[38] I know it seems strange that a grown man, and especially a grown evil man, would laugh in such a childish way, saying, "Tee hee" all the time instead of a more manly "Ho ho" or "Ha ha," but I assure you that I am merely being accurate. According to witnesses I have interviewed and former crew members (including Monkey-Knees and Rodney, who were thrown clear of the explosion into the sea and picked up by a fisherman after drifting for several days), Captain Ironbuttocks laughed in an odd and unlikely way. Don't doubt me. Ever.

had aided him in overcoming whatever obstacle he faced. Angry Yetii,[39] vicious pirates, fields of fire, oceans of ice: all these opponents had been vanquished by his boots. But since King Liam had freed him of the ODA's hold, removing their restraints and tracking devices, Hamish X had been forced to relearn how to access the power of his magnificent footwear.

He took a deep breath and focused his mind on his boots. Before, whenever he was in distress, the boots would respond immediately, coming to his aid. Now he had to make a conscious effort, but as he practised, the effort became easier, second nature.

"Like riding a bicycle," he muttered ... Where had he ever ridden a bicycle?

He had a sudden vivid memory of being up on the seat of a bicycle, wobbling ferociously as someone shouted to him: "You're doing it, Hamish! You're doing it!" A beautiful, woman's voice. He knew her. The voice was so familiar. "You're riding a bicycle, Hamish! I knew you could do it." Suddenly he was tipping over. He was falling, his hands thrust out in front of him ... Falling!

He opened his eyes to find himself on his hands and knees on the deck. What had happened to him? Was he remembering his life before he had become Hamish X? Were those memories still there, hidden in his mind? Was there hope that he might someday find his real mother?

---

[39] Yes, the plural of Yeti is Yetii. I'm sure you've never seen the plural of Yeti before as they rarely congregate in one place. Trust me. I am quite sure about this. If there is one thing I know, it is plural forms. One deer, two deer. One moose, two moose. One pie, pie squared. Ha ha ha! A little math joke for you. It may not be funny now but wait until you study trigonometry! You'll suddenly laugh out loud and be asked to leave the classroom.

Tears started in his eyes. "Ha! It's possible. Ha ha!" He started to laugh out loud.

"Hey!" Captain Ironbuttocks shouted through the hatchway. "What's so funny? Are you going crazy because you can't get me? That's it, isn't it? I'm driving you mad with the frustration, eh?"

Hamish X pushed himself up to a standing position outside the hatch. "No such luck, Rustypants," he called cheerfully. "I'm just laughing because getting you out of there is going to be so easy!"

Hamish X once again took a deep breath and focused on the boots. When he was a slave to the ODA, he had been forced to listen to that voice, Mother. Not his real mother but a presence guiding his actions for the evil intent of the Grey Agents. He was free of that presence now, and the hope that one day he might find his true mother and listen to her voice filled him with joy. He tapped into the swell of his emotion, reaching easily down into the boots and calling up a massive surge of glorious power.

"Are you ready, Captain Ironbuttocks? I'm coming for you!"

To his boots he cooed, "You've never let me down before, friends," and felt the power begin to swell. "Let's open this tin can and get ourselves a greasy little sardine!"

Chapter 7

Captain Ironbuttocks sat in his captain's chair and puffed on a cigar.[40] He was feeling pretty pleased with himself. He had thwarted the crazy boy with the boots and now he could dictate terms. The shutters and the hatch were made of the highest quality tempered steel. Nothing short of an industrial laser could cut through his defences. Back when he had purchased the ship, he'd made sure the bridge was reinforced as a final bastion. As a Slaver Captain and a member of the Pirates Union, Ironbuttocks knew that captains often had to face the danger of a mutinous crew or a rebellious cargo, so he'd made sure he had a fortified place to ride out any uprising. For once he was glad he'd been so paranoid and paid the extra money.

"I'm a pretty smart guy, me!" The Captain chuckled. "Super smart."

He was fairly certain that he had driven the nasty boy with the boots mad with frustration when he heard Hamish X laughing for no apparent reason. The Captain's aura of superiority evaporated when the boy shouted, "Are you ready, Captain Ironbuttocks? I'm coming for you!" Something in the tone of Hamish X's voice cut right through the Captain's wall of contentment.

---

[40] I hate to mention smoking in this story, but I have to be accurate. Ironbuttocks did, in fact, smoke a cigar. Don't you do the same! It is a very bad habit that will take years off your life. So does being evil, so Ironbuttocks was bound to have a very short life indeed.

The final vestige of Ironbuttocks's smug self-confidence was dissipated by a loud clang as Hamish X kicked the hatch with all the pent-up power his boots could muster. The impact knocked the Captain out of his chair and onto his metal bottom. The hatch held, but an alarming dent appeared in the centre. The dent was roughly the same shape as one of the mad boy's boots.

"Uh-oh," the Captain said softly. Another ringing clang saw the hatch dent grow even larger. The hatch wouldn't hold much longer. Captain Ironbuttocks felt a cold, burning hatred deep in his soul.

"I hate you, boy! I hate you and your silly, stupid boots!" he railed. He loathed the thought of losing his ship to these ragged kids. If he lost his ship, his employers would not be pleased. He doubted he would survive the displeasure of the ODA. "I won't give up my ship! I won't give up my ship! I ... I ..." He looked around the bridge and his eyes caught the radar screen. What he saw there made him smile. He leapt to the wheel and slammed the engines full ahead. The ship lurched forward.

"Hey, Mr. Big Feet! You think you have a lot of smart thinks in your mind? Well, phooey! If I can't have this beautiful ship, nobody will! Tee hee! *Christmas Is Cancelled* is cancelled!"

Though the threat was difficult to decipher, Hamish X still felt a trill of dread when he heard it. Outside the hatch, he was just rearing back for another powerful kick when he felt the ship change direction. Puzzled, he shouted to the Captain. "What's going on, Ironbutt? What are you up to?" He turned to look out over the bow of the ship, scanning the darkness. At first, he saw only blackness and the reflection of the ship's running lights off the wine-dark sea, but after his eyes adjusted, he saw a winking red light in the distance. Concentrating on it, he felt his vision shift. His pupils widened like telescopic lenses. The red light leapt into stark relief. The dawn was coming. Outlined in the growing daybreak, a series of jagged rocks rose out of the sea. On the largest of them a red beacon winked on and off to warn sailors of the danger. Hamish X's face turned ashen as he realized what the Captain was going to do. He turned and hammered on the dented hatch.

"What do you think you're doing? You'll wreck us on the rocks!"

"You won't get my ship, you booted freak-boy," came the muffled, manic reply. "You won't get my ship! Tee hee! Tee hee!"

Hamish X feverishly began to hammer the hatch with his boots. He had to stop the Captain from wrecking the ship on the rocks. "Hurry, Maggie," he muttered to himself.

Down below, Maggie hurried. She pelted through the corridors of the ship. Everywhere she looked, there were signs of a titanic struggle. She ran through the mess hall and found the tables overturned, chairs broken, dishes shattered. She ran down a corridor past the crew cabins. The doors hung open or dangled from shattered hinges. In a heap, four crewmen lay tied together with electrical tape and nylon rope, a child standing guard over them. She was about to ask the boy where her brother was when she heard shouting and the sound of metal clashing against metal. She followed the din and came to a steep metal ladder. The sounds were coming from below. She gripped the handrails and slid down the ladder, landing lightly on the metal floor.

She found herself on the lowest deck of the ship. The remnants of a heavy battle were strewn along the corridor. Two sailors lay unconscious. A little girl sat with her back to the wall, holding a rag doll against a cut on her forehead.

"Where's Thomas?" Maggie demanded. The girl pointed down the corridor and Maggie sped off. She came to the end and turned the corner, almost running into a knot of children gathered in front of a large metal door. Lined up against the wall, bound and gagged, was a group of vanquished crewmen.

The door was scratched and dented but seemed solid. Thomas swung a massive wrench. It bounced off the door with a sound like a metal gong, shivering the wrench from his grasp. The tool fell to the metal deck with a clatter. Thomas danced out of the way, avoiding a crushed toe, then examined the hatch. The wrench had barely scratched the surface.

"Ow!" Thomas winced and twisted his wrists experimentally. "This is hopeless! We can't get in!" He shook his head.

"What's going on?"

"The last of the crew is holed up in the engine room, Maggie. They've locked the hatch and we can't get through. We'll have to starve them out."

"Hamish X says we have to shut down the engines," Maggie insisted.

"Well, unless he has a blowtorch," Thomas snapped, "or a bazooka, we are not getting into the engine room."

Maggie shook her head. "Hamish X is trying to get into the bridge, but the place is like a fortress. Keep trying." She turned on her heel and ran back the way she came.

Thomas watched her go and shrugged. "Let's find a bigger wrench."

HAMISH X WAS DRENCHED WITH SWEAT. He had kicked the hatch with all his might for the last minute and, though it was severely dented, the portal would not yield. He staggered back and looked at the rocks. They loomed ever closer. Even without the enhanced vision afforded him by whatever alterations the ODA had made to his eyesight, he could make out the deadly obstacle in the growing dawn light. He calculated that, at their current speed, the ship would crash into it in a minute, maybe less.

Maggie burst out of the lower deck hatch and ran towards Hamish X. "The engine room door isn't going to break down any time soon. We can't shut down the engines."

Hamish X felt panic well up inside him. Fear wrapped itself around his heart and squeezed.

Maggie stood looking up at him, her blue eyes huge in her grimy face. She needed him to do something.

Before, when he remembered nothing about the past, he never felt this fear. When he was alone in the world on his adventures, he had never known fear because there was nothing and no one to lose. Now he missed Mimi and Parveen. They could have helped him, but he'd left them behind. He had found these new friends in need of his help, and now he was going to fail them.

Inside the bridge, the Captain had gone quite mad. He thumbed the switch on the Tannoy[41] system. The laughter of Captain Ironbuttocks rang out on the loudspeaker

---

[41] *Tannoy* is the name for the public address system on a ship. It comes from the name of the British manufacturer of public address systems, the Tannoy Company. Not very funny, not very interesting, but nevertheless true.

system. "Tee hee! Tee hee! We're all going to die! If I can't have my ship, no one can." He gripped the wheel of the ship with insane intensity, his eyes glaring and foam spraying from the corners of his mouth.

Hamish X snarled, "No. I won't let this happen." Suddenly, he had an idea. He ran down the steps to the main deck. As he passed Maggie, he pointed at the hatchway to the bridge. "Don't let him out!" He didn't wait to see if she obeyed but set off towards the bow, running as fast as his amazing boots could carry him.

Reaching the absolute front tip of the ship, he skidded to a halt, his boot soles sending up a shower of sparks. The rocks were looming ever closer. He had no time to lose. A spare anchor chain lay coiled on the deck. He grabbed the end, wrapped his fists around it, and dove out in front of the speeding ship, disappearing into the furiously boiling bow wave.

He plunged into a maelstrom of churning water, immediately losing track of which way was up and which way was down. He held on tenaciously to the anchor chain as if it were the only thing in his world. Wrapping the end of the chain around his forearm, he tried to orient himself. The barnacle-encrusted hull of the freighter rushed by overhead, the current threatening to bash him against the razor-sharp coating of shells.[42] Spinning in the fierce current, he got his boots up just in time to push the deadly surface away before his skin was scoured off.

---

[42] *Barnacles* are small shells that cluster on underwater surfaces. In a recent poll among sailors, "barnacle" was voted the third funniest name for a shell creature. Number one was "winkle," and coming in slightly behind it at number two was "whelk."

Holding his breath, though he was desperate for air, he began to bounce along the bottom of the ship as it rushed by, like a rock climber rappelling down a mountain face horizontally instead of vertically. His boots surged with power. He felt the bubble of joy expanding in his chest that always came when he used the power of the boots. If he hadn't been underwater, he would have laughed aloud.[43]

The hull began to curve upwards towards the bow where the propellers thrashed the water to foam, driving the ship forward. Hamish X felt the powerful suction created by the massive props' blades. Timing was critical. The keel loomed out of the darkness, a sharp fin of steel carving the water in two directly in front of him. Hamish X pushed off with his right foot, kicking with all his might. Swinging in a wide arc, he felt the pull of the propellers as he sailed past them and loosened his grip on the chain until he barely hung on. In seconds, the chain straightened out and, with a jerk, was pulled painfully out of his fingers, taking some skin as the propeller blades caught it.

The chain wound around the propeller like thread on a spool. The torque of the crankshaft was so powerful that the anchor chain was yanked from its housing on the foredeck and reeled in at high speed. In a matter of seconds the thick steel links were completely entangled in the propeller blades, freezing the crankshaft and stripping all the gears inside the engine room. The engine spouted black smoke as the tortured inner workings tore themselves

---

[43] Laughing under water is one of the leading causes of death among scuba divers. As a result, the World Scuba Organization has banned all waterproof joke books and passed a strict prohibition against undersea tickling.

apart. The sailors holding out in the engine room gagged on the poisonous fumes. They were forced to open the hatch to escape the toxic smoke. They ran into the waiting arms of Thomas and his cohorts, coughing and wheezing as they sucked in the sweeter air.

Hamish X kicked to the surface, finally heeding the cry of his aching lungs. He broke through the choppy seas, instantly swallowing a mouthful of brine as a wave swamped him. Choking and spitting, he scanned the waves to see the rear end of the ship sporting the name *Christmas Is Cancelled* in peeling black paint. Oily smoke billowed from the stern as the ship coasted gently, slowing as it lost momentum. Hamish X grinned. He had done it. He'd stopped the ship. He pounded the warm water of the sea with his fists, crowing with delight. "Ha! It worked! It worked! I did it ... I ..."

His delight suddenly ebbed when he saw how close the rocks loomed. In the gathering dawn light they glistened in the pounding spray. A rainbow hung over the black stone teeth, but Hamish X couldn't take time to appreciate its beauty. The ship, deprived of power, was drifting on the current. The inexorable pull of the sea would grind the ship to pieces.

His work wasn't over yet.

"Boy," he spat out another mouthful of sea, "you solve one problem and create another. Life can be very annoying." He smiled ruefully and began to swim after the wayward vessel.

Mr. Candy and Mr. Sweet

Mr. Candy and Mr. Sweet strode along the causeway through the forest of harnessed children hanging in the air. In a state of suspended animation, the children were oblivious to everything around them. They didn't notice the two Grey Agents passing below.

"Mr. Candy, we seem to be no further ahead than we were before."

"We've managed to destroy the King of Switzerland and root out his rat's nest of resistance. That's certainly a plus." Mr. Candy waved a gloved hand distractedly at the children hanging overhead. "And we reaped a good haul of battery power for the portal generator."

"Indeed," Mr. Sweet nodded, ducking his head in the odd, birdlike manner common to the Grey Agents to indicate his agreement. "The Hall of Batteries is completely full. Some of the units are rather immature . . ." He poked a little girl hanging at shoulder height, setting her swinging gently. "But that can't be helped. We'll need every possible source of energy to open the portal."

They walked through the sterilized airlock and onto the catwalk, looking out over the vast chamber that held the massive circlet, cables snaking away into the many machines at its base. Grey Agents climbed like ants on the giant structure as it pulsed faintly, casting a sickly glow over the faces of Mr. Candy and Mr. Sweet as they stood at the rail admiring the horrible apparatus.

"So beautiful," Mr. Candy breathed with an emotion and reverence rarely expressed in his cold, antiseptic voice. "Soon the worlds will align and the portal will be ready."

"Yes," Mr. Sweet agreed. Their rapt faces stared up at their horrible machine. Its flashes of energy were reflected in their insectile goggles as they admired the portal.

"But we still lack the final, crucial component, Mr. Candy."

"Indeed, Mr. Sweet. Indeed. We must retrieve Hamish X at whatever cost. The time is growing short."

They turned from the rail and headed down the catwalk to an elevator with dull metallic doors. When they were a few metres short of the elevator, Mr. Sweet stopped suddenly. He spun around and faced back the way they had come, cocking his head and scanning the catwalk.

"What is it, Mr. Sweet?" Mr. Candy stepped up beside him.

"Mr. Candy, I don't know. I thought I saw something out of the corner of my eye."

"What kind of something?"

"I'm not sure," Mr. Sweet said, annoyed. He hated not being sure. For an instant, he'd thought he'd seen a human shape just at the edge of his vision. He scanned the catwalk intently for a moment, but he couldn't see anything out of the ordinary. There was only stone and metal decking and nothing more. "I thought I saw someone. An intruder."

"Surely you are mistaken," Mr. Candy said. "Who could intrude on our Headquarters? Who could possibly penetrate our defences?"[44]

Mr. Sweet scanned the catwalk a final time and shrugged. "Indeed, Mr. Candy. I'm sure you are correct." Mr. Sweet turned and strode swiftly with Mr. Candy to the elevator.

As they approached, the doors whisked open to reveal an elevator car. The Grey Agents stepped inside as the doors whisked shut behind them.

"How can we find Hamish X? It would seem the King managed to neutralize the tracking devices we implanted in him."

"Quite clever." Mr. Sweet sighed as the elevator zoomed upward.

"Indeed," Mr. Candy agreed. "The King was clever. But what did his cleverness gain him? He's still dead."

The elevator stopped and the doors slid open to reveal ... a kitchen. The floor was tiled in black and white squares of

---

[44] I'm sure you are sitting there, saying to yourself, "Well, of course someone could penetrate your defences, and without much difficulty." Mr. Sweet probably saw Parveen out of the corner of his eye. But Parveen came into the Headquarters of the ODA in a most unusual manner as part of their own cargo. The Grey Agents are like almost every villainous organization in history in that they have an overweening arrogance in assuming that their defences are impenetrable. Thank goodness for that! If villains weren't so ridiculously overconfident, they would never be defeated. If only the evil people of the world would just sit back and consider the possibility that they might be wrong once in a while, they might succeed more often ... What am I saying? Let's hope evil people continue to cut their noses off to spite their faces until the end of time!

linoleum. There was a dinette set with four black vinyl chairs. The stove and kitchen were sparkling if a bit old-fashioned, and a shiny radio with a chrome speaker like the grille of an antique car sat on top of the shiny white fridge.

"Hamish X is the priority," Mr. Candy said, opening a cupboard and taking down a glass canister filled with little square tea bags. "He has to be found."

"Let me do that, dear."

Mr. Candy turned to see an old woman standing in the kitchen doorway. She wore a shawl around her shoulders and a flower print dress. Her hair was white as snow and pulled back into a tight bun. She smiled and her blue eyes twinkled, wreathed in wrinkles.

"Thank you, Mrs. Guardian." The woman took the canister and plucked out three tea bags, dropping them into the top of a white china teapot resting on the counter. She filled the chrome kettle and set it on the stove to boil.

"Any activity to report, Mrs. Guardian?" Mr. Sweet asked.

"Quiet as usual, dear," she answered. "Perimeter is secure."

The Grey Agents left her to make the tea and moved to the kitchen table.

"He could be anywhere," Mr. Sweet said, pulling out a chair and sitting down. "How will we find him? Biscuit?" He opened a tin on the table and offered an unappetizing grey wafer to Mr. Candy, who nimbly took it in his long, thin fingers.

"We must be watchful," Mr. Candy said. He reached up and turned a big black knob on the radio. "Mother?"

"I'm listening." The smooth feminine voice oozed from the radio speaker, filling the kitchen with its cold perfection.

"Monitor transmissions from our sources worldwide. If anything even slightly suspicious comes up, bring it to our attention immediately."

"Yes, Mr. Candy."

The kettle began to whistle. Mrs. Guardian took it from the stove and poured the boiling water into the teapot. "Three bags. One for each of you and one for the pot!"

"Hamish X will make himself known to us," Mr. Candy continued. "He is an arrogant little fellow who can't seem to keep his nose out of other people's business. He will stir up some trouble and then ...?"

"We will swoop down and snare him."

The two Grey Agents sat at the table, waiting for the tea to steep. Mr. Sweet cocked his head. "Why does he do it?"

"Do what, Mr. Sweet?"

"Why does he help people? I mean to say, it was never part of his programming, but he seems to do it ... naturally."

"Indeed." Mr. Candy reached for the pot. "It is a most puzzling development."

"Sugar or honey?" Mrs. Guardian asked sweetly.

"Both," the Grey Agents answered in unison.

The old woman smiled and her blue eyes glittered. "Of course."

Chapter 8

MIMI

Mimi sat with her back against the wall of the stone chamber. Even her threats of physical violence had yielded no results. Maybe the strange folk knew she was just bluffing. So the wait continued. After many hours of deliberation, the strange people who claimed to be Atlanteans still hadn't come to a conclusion as to whether they would help the Hollow Mountain refugees or turn them away. They stood in a small huddle debating in their weird burbling language, occasionally shouting at one another and gesticulating at the intruders.

There seemed to be two schools of thought about what the Atlanteans should do with the refugees. The factions appeared to be led by Xnasos and his sister, Xnasha. The siblings stood toe to toe in heated debate. Mimi could only hope they would allow the children to at least rest and recuperate before sending them on their way. The Atlanteans had provided jugs of water and sacks of dry, salty fish jerky as a meagre meal for the refugees while they continued their intense debate.

The refugees in question were spread out throughout the stone chamber, some sitting on blankets, others trying to get some sleep. Mrs. Francis moved here and there, her once-white wedding dress glowing in the dim light as she patted heads, pinched cheeks, and squeezed little hands in need of comfort. She paused to push a lock of hair out of her eyes and saw Mimi watching her. The woman smiled and winked at Mimi, who smiled weakly back.

Looking out across the chamber, Mimi saw the remnants of the Royal Swiss Guards reduced now to a knot of about twenty or so ragged members cleaning their weapons while keeping a wary eye on the Atlanteans. Cara squatted in their midst, speaking earnestly with the remainder of her command. The normally coiffed and groomed Guard was a grimy shadow of her former self. Her uniform was torn at the shoulder and the knee, her face smeared with soot and her hair a mess. Her eyes were as fierce as ever, however, and she had certainly pulled herself together after losing her brother. Mimi admired Cara's fortitude and wished she could be as strong.

She found herself thinking of Parveen. The little boy with the thick glasses would have been in his element.

"He'd have a field day with this place," she murmured and felt a sharp pang stab her heart. Where was Parveen now? She had no idea. The last time she saw him he was running for the workshops during the siege of the Hollow Mountain. They'd been separated during the exodus. Hoping he had gotten aboard one of the escape pods, she had carefully searched the entire complement of refugees, moving through the crowd with Mrs. Francis as they listed all the survivors, but he had not been among them. Mrs. Francis had comforted her, even though the chubby housekeeper had been on the verge of tears herself.

"Don't worry, Mimi," Mrs. Francis had said, stroking her hair as the girl wept. "He's a very clever little boy. I'm sure he's somewhere safe, worrying about you right now."

Now Mimi found tears prickling in the back of her eyes once again. She wiped her eyes on the filthy sleeve of her

Swiss Guards uniform. It wouldn't do to let the others see her in a moment of weakness. She had to be strong.

She turned her head and looked at Mr. Kipling, his dress uniform a mess, his long legs stretched out in front of him as he dozed with his back to the wall. His naturally gaunt face looked even more drawn. He'd suffered minor burns and bruises in the attack. Snoring softly, he rested his hand on the hilt of the sabre that lay unsheathed at his side, vigilant even in slumber. Mimi longed to curl up next to the old man who had become like a father to them all and just forget about the troubles they faced. Let an adult take care of things! That's what adults were supposed to do, wasn't it?

But that had never been her experience of the world. Ever since she lost her father and mother she'd had to fend for herself, counting on no help from adults and trusting her own strength and instincts to survive.

"But I'm so tired," she muttered to herself. She could barely keep her eyes open. "So tired."

She wished Hamish X were here. He'd know what to do. But he wasn't. The King had told her he was gone and now she had to lead. That's what Hamish X would expect of her. She still missed him though.

"And where are ya now, Hamish X?" she wondered aloud.

"Nobody knows," a voice answered her. Mimi turned to see Cara standing nearby. The other girl made a comb of her fingers and ran them through the tangled mess that was her hair. After a few tugs, Cara gave up. She had a bruise on her cheek, a remnant of the battle with the Grey Agents. "I've spoken to the other Guards, and no one saw him during the battle. In fact, the last place anyone can remember seeing him was at the wedding ceremony. It's like he just disappeared."

"The King said he was goin' ta Africa, of all places," Mimi said. "He musta had a good reason."

"We could sure use him now," Cara said. Gone was her habitual arrogance, lost when her brother chose to stay behind. She was serious and subdued now, with none of her usual sarcasm. She jerked her head at the group of Atlanteans. "How much longer can they argue?"

"It ends now." Mimi frowned and pushed herself to her feet. "It's time we put a stop ta this, one way'r t'other. Let's go."

Mr. Kipling stirred from his slumber and gripped his sabre. "What's happening?" he asked, instantly alert.

"Either they help us or we gotta move on. We cain't wait no longer." Mimi strode off towards the strangers, Cara and Mr. Kipling falling into step behind her. Mrs. Francis saw the determined set of Mimi's chin and joined the little party, slipping her hand into Mr. Kipling's. He smiled at her, squeezing her pudgy fingers in his own bony ones.

The Atlanteans saw their approach and fell silent. They gripped their staves tighter and fell back slightly when they saw the tall girl's face. Mimi stopped a couple of paces away and pointed a finger at the one called Xnasos.

"Enough jawin'. Are ya gonna help us or not?"

"You have no right to be rude to us, surface-dweller. I am the rightful headman of the great race of Atlantis," Xnasos said in an outraged tone.

"I don't care if you're the President of the Universe! We got kids here who need shelter and we got friends who need our help. Tell us if yer gonna help us or show us how ta get the heck outta this hole in the ground. We've waited long enough!"

Xnasos scowled. He cracked his staff against the ground. "We have endured for centuries ... *millennia*, even ... through caution and wisdom. We are not as powerful as we once were. Our numbers dwindle. At one time we ruled a vast kingdom beneath the oceans of the world, but now we are reduced to this one small refuge. Secrecy is our only defence. When we made the pact with the King of Switzerland hundreds of years ago, we were a much stronger people. Now ..." He hung his head. When he continued, his voice was less angry, more weary, and tinged with defeat. "Now we can barely hold our own in the world. Pollution from above destroys our means of growing food. There are no children among us now and our race fails." The others nodded. "You have powerful enemies. The Grey Ones ... They are not to be trifled with!"

"It was us who unleashed them on the world," Xnasha interjected, drawing an angry glare from Xnasos.

"What do ya mean by that?" Mimi asked.

"Nothing! She means nothing!" he snapped. "They are powerful enemies who could destroy us if they knew we helped you. Circumstances have changed since we swore the oath to your King."

Mimi felt her righteous anger fade. She looked at the Atlanteans and saw their ragged clothes and their fear, and she recognized in them a kindred desperation. They were refugees of a sort as well. She suddenly felt ashamed of herself for demanding something that would perhaps be difficult for them to give.

"We understand," Mimi said. "Sorry. I guess I was a little pushy, but I hope you see that we ain't got nowhere else to go. We don't wanna bring the ODA down on y'all. We know how bad that can be." She looked at Cara. "If you can just tell us how we can git outta here, we'll be on our way."

80

Xnasha's eyes went wide. She blurted, "Oh, no! *You* don't understand. What my brother is trying to say is that we will honour the agreement we made with King Gertomund. You are welcome in Atlantis for as long as you wish to stay!"

Xnasos stamped his foot. "Xnasha, really! I wanted to tell them. I'm the spokesman! Why can't you ever let me have any of the fun?"

"Sorry," Xnasha said sheepishly, sending a sneaky wink Mimi's way. "After all, it's only right we should hide you from the ODA. It's our fault they entered this world in the first place."

"Xnasha! Silence!" Xnasos barked. Xnasha immediately obeyed her brother.

"What did she mean by that? You're the reason the Grey Agents are here?" Mimi demanded.

"My sister cannot control her tongue." Xnasos aimed another pointed glare at Xnasha, who reddened and remained silent. "We will explain everything to you later. Right now, we offer our official welcome to the city of Atlantis. You are welcome to stay as long as you need to."

Mimi wondered what Xnasha had meant by her strange comment. She was about to demand an explanation, but Cara cut her off.

"Mimi," Cara said meaningfully, "we need a place to rest and regroup. Let's just get ourselves settled, and then we can ask our questions later."

Mimi glowered at Cara, about to shoot back an angry response, but she looked around at the state of their little company of refugees, the exhausted faces of the Guards, Mrs. Francis, and Mr. Kipling. The tall old sailor was practically asleep on his feet. Seeing that they were in desperate need of a safe haven to lick their wounds and make plans, she conceded.

"All right," Mimi nodded. "We accept yer invitation. But I wants some answers ... soon!" She turned to the waiting throng of Hollow Mountain refugees and shouted, "Hey, everybody! We got a place to stay!"

The children sent up a deafening cheer of joy that echoed around the stone chamber. Xnasos's face fell. "Oh, dear," he said softly. "I hope we haven't made a terrible mistake."

"Doing the right thing is never a mistake." Xnasha smiled and clapped him on the back. "Let's get underway."

Chapter 9

After the children had gathered up their meagre posses-
sions, Mrs. Francis herded them into rows, with each older
child holding hands with a younger one. The Guards took
up positions along the line, forming a protective escort
with Mimi, Cara, and Mr. Kipling in the lead. When the
chaotic mass of children was finally in a rough semblance
of order, Mimi signalled to Xnasos and Xnasha that they
were ready. The babble of excited conversation died down
to an expectant hush as the Hollow Mountain refugees
turned their attention to their hosts.

The Atlanteans faced the glowing dome, its surface
smooth and glassy. It was closed and had been since just
after the Atlanteans had departed from it. Now Xnasos
approached the dome, moving across the metal gangplank until he stood directly in front of the weird object.
He reached out, laid a hand on its surface, and uttered
a series of words in his own language. The dome
responded. The light pulsed brighter and the dome shuddered. A deep thrumming vibration filled the chamber so
strongly that Mimi could feel it resonating in her chest.
The children sighed in wonder as a section of the dome
slid back with a smooth hiss until there was a slice out of
the sphere. Golden light spilled over the faces of the
spectators. Mimi had to admit it was pretty impressive—
until the slice ground to a halt when the opening was
only a metre wide.

"How embarrassing!" Xnasos groaned, kicking the dome
in frustration. "It's stuck! Oh, what a piece of rubbish!"

"I'm surprised it opened at all," Xnasha said, exasperated. "We haven't any idea how any of our technology really works. Everything was built centuries ago and we've lost the manuals. Even if we had them, we probably wouldn't be able to read the ancient language, so it's hard to do routine maintenance. We'll have to squeeze!" Xnasha shook her head and squeezed through the opening. Once through, she stuck her head back into the gap. "Come on. It's a tight fit, but you'll manage." With that, she disappeared into the luminous dome.

Mimi shared a nervous glance with Cara, who shrugged and said, "Scared?"

Mimi scowled and stepped through the gap.

She found herself at the top of a wide stairway made of the weird glowing material. The stairway was long, leading down farther than Mimi could see. The walls and ceiling joined overhead in a smooth arch of the same stuff. The light was bright but not painful to look at. Xnasha stood on the steps below, beckoning and smiling. Mimi started down after her.

Mimi walked carefully down the stairs and found herself in a wide corridor. The floor was paved with huge pink flagstones covered with carvings of tiny shelled sea creatures, sea horses, and fish. On closer examination, the creatures weren't carved into the rock but actually embedded in it, fossils of ancient living things entombed forever in the stone.

"So beautiful," Mimi whispered. She'd seen fossils before, but never so many in one place. She looked to either side and saw that the walls were made of the same material. Mimi traced the curling tail of a crablike creature, her mouth hanging open in wonder.

"You're easily impressed," Xnasha laughed. "Wait until you see the city!" The Atlantean reached out her gnarled hand and grasped Mimi's elbow. "Come! It isn't far!"

Mimi looked behind her up the stair to make sure the others were following. Mrs. Francis was having difficulty negotiating the narrow opening. One Atlantean gently tugged her arm while another pushed firmly from the other side.

"Really," Mrs. Francis fumed.

Mimi couldn't help but laugh despite the housekeeper's obvious discomfort. Leaving Mrs. Francis in the care of the Atlanteans, Mimi let Xnasha pull her along.

The passage led on for the better part of a kilometre, slanting ever so slightly downward. The air was surprisingly fresh with a salty tang, more wholesome than she had expected any underground passage to be. Xnasha pointed at fossils as they went along, keeping up a running commentary. "Those are trilobites. They've been stuck in the rock for millions of years ... there's a sardine. Oh, and that one just became extinct a couple of decades ago. What a shame!" Mimi took the time to examine her companion more closely.

Xnasha was female, although her short, stocky frame was anything but feminine. Her nose was thick and bony, but it gave strength to her face. Her mouth was wide and thin, and her eyes were a very pale blue with flecks of green. Her pale hair, more white than blonde, was worn long, and wound in its tresses were fragments of coral, shark teeth, and shells.

"This is the Hall of Entry," Xnasha said, running her hand along the cool pink surface of the stone as they followed the corridor. "Down this hall, kings of the surface would come to ask our advice, beg for our help, ask us for trade." Xnasha smiled sadly and let her hand drop. "A long time ago. Now I doubt that anyone knows we exist or thinks we're anything more than a legend." Her eyes brightened. "Ah, we're here."

The corridor ended in a metal door. It might have originally been shiny, but years had coated it with a thick layer of black tarnish. The carvings on the surface were still clear: tangled fronds of seaweed intertwined in complicated relief covering the entire surface and two dolphins leaping over a giant shell in the centre. The door was vast, more than ten metres high.

"The mighty Dolphin Gate!" Xnasos and the others caught up with Mimi and Xnasha, gathering beside them. He sighed sadly while running his hand over the ornate metal. "Cast in a single slab of silver. Beautiful, isn't it? We really knew how to build in those days. We really ought to give it a good clean one day ..."

"Why bother?" Xnasha said irritably. "No one ever sees it. We never leave this place and no one ever visits." Mimi sensed frustration in the little woman, as if the isolation of Atlantis was a bone of contention often picked over between brother and sister. Xnasos stared daggers at his sister. Sensing his displeasure, Xnasha shrugged. "Frankly, I don't think there's enough silver polish in all of Atlantis to make it shine as it once did."

"Doesn't mean we shouldn't try," Xnasos said under his breath. Shaking his head, he reached up with his staff and tapped the centre of the shell. "Fendictus Blort!" The door split down a previously invisible seam, its two halves swinging silently inward. The children gasped.

"Oh, that's nothing," Xnasos chuckled. "Don't just stand there with your mouths open like a bunch of groupers![45] Come in! Come in!"

---

[45] A grouper is a species of fish that is renowned for having a wide, gaping mouth.

He strode forward through the mighty gate. After a moment's hesitation, Mimi and Cara followed him, leading the rest of the Hollow Mountain refugees.

Mimi stepped through the gate, blinking in the sudden glow of sunlight overhead. She stopped short and let her eyes adjust, but when they had, she almost refused to believe them.

Considering all the amazing adventures Mimi had enjoyed up to this point in our story, you might not credit that she could still be amazed. Sadly, you would be underestimating the human capacity for wonder. She had never seen anything so beautiful in her short life. Granted, her early experiences had been severely limited: she grew up in a tiny Texas town and then travel led straight to the remote and miserable wasteland that was Windcity. Still, she had trekked across the Arctic ice and witnessed the glory of the northern lights. She had soared via airship across the North Atlantic and watched the sun rise over the grey ocean waves. She had lived within the Hollow Mountain, the product of centuries of brilliant human engineers.

None of those sights could have prepared her for the majesty of Atlantis. She found herself standing in a huge paved square. The flagstones were fashioned from the same stone as the corridor, irregular in shape and fitted together with painstaking precision like a giant jigsaw puzzle. The musical rush of water drew Mimi's eye to the centre of the square, where a fountain towered above her. Crystal-clear water gushed up towards the sky in a single, graceful column to then fall in glittering drops into a circular pool below. A mist of cool droplets moistened Mimi's upturned face, gently caressing her skin. At the base of the fountain, a stone cluster of dolphins, octopi, shellfish, and mermaids sheltered under the broad arms of a man with a giant fork in his hand pointing high at the ceiling. The statue's face was grim and bearded, a layer of grime darkening the recesses of his features, making him seem dour and serious.

"Hettakarus," Xnasha said. "You know him as Neptune, god of the sea!"

"My great-great-great-great-great-great-great-grandfather," Xnasos said, puffing out his chest. "He was a mighty king in his day. Built most of what you see around you." He spread his arms wide to indicate the towering structures crowding in around the square. "The city of Atlantis."

Mimi stood dumbfounded, taking in the impossible city. Proud marble towers and colonnades lined the square. She looked to Cara and found her companion similarly impressed. Vast porches of stone carved to look like fronds of seaweed braced broad marble balconies. The towers stood at odd angles and were of varying sizes, lending the whole city a strangely natural feel, as if it had grown out of the seabed rather than having been built by humans. Thousands of windows faced onto the square. Some of them held beautiful panes of stained glass, but an equal number were gaping and empty, their panes shattered.

On closer inspection Mimi saw that many of the towers were cracked and leaning precariously. Some had already fallen into neighbouring structures, leaving stumps like rotting teeth in the otherwise beautiful skyline.

The more Mimi looked, the more she saw signs of decrepitude and rot. The magnificent buildings were in desperate need of maintenance, as if this whole civilization had seen better days.

Arranged around the square, a crowd of Atlanteans stood watching them. Their pale eyes and drawn faces did not look friendly. Mimi smiled at them and waved. They merely stared back, eyes filled with suspicion.

Mimi was so mesmerized by the vista before her that she hadn't noticed the arrival of Mrs. Francis until the housekeeper spoke.

"Oh my word!" Mrs. Francis cried. "Look at the sky!"

Mimi followed the housekeeper's gaze and couldn't help but gasp in wonder. She hadn't registered the sky as anything unusual because, as a surface-dweller, she always assumed there was a sky overhead. The sky above Atlantis wasn't a sky at all but a crystal dome that covered the entire city. The crystal was completely transparent, tinted a soft blue by the sea above it. Schools of colourful fish lazed by like clouds of stars illuminated by a soft glow that emanated from the crystal barrier. The schools scattered as the cold, pale body of a shark waded through their formation, its bullet head thrashing side to side in an attempt to snap up slowpokes in its razor-sharp jaws.

"Ain't that a sight to make ya sit down hard and stand up quick?"

"You have a strange way of speaking." Xnasha laughed.

"Yeah." Mimi smiled. "I've been told that b'fore."

The other children from the Hollow Mountain arrived at the gate and began to file in. They looked about at the bizarre undersea city. From the legendary home inside the Hollow Mountain, they had fled to find themselves in another hidden, mythical land. Their faces registered the confusion and awe at their new surroundings.

The children's reaction was predictable. What Mimi didn't expect was the Atlanteans' reaction to the children. They stared as the refugees flooded into the square. From their open-mouthed, wide-eyed reaction Mimi guessed they'd never seen so many surface-dwellers before. The Atlanteans began to whisper among themselves in their own language. Mimi tugged at Xnasha's sleeve.

"What's with them?"

Xnasha smiled. "It has been a long time since they have seen any children. We don't know why, but we can't seem to have any of our own. I was the last child born and that was more than three hundred of your years ago."

Now it was Mimi's turn to gape in astonishment. Being a child herself, she found it hard to judge how old adults were relative to herself.[46] She had guessed that Xnasha was an adult, maybe as old as her mother when her mother had died. Her mother had just celebrated her thirtieth birthday when the tapir[47] had plummeted from the sky and taken her life. So far, all the Atlanteans had pale white hair and their stunted stature made them appear older, but never would she have imagined she was off by several centuries. "That ain't possible! How can ya possibly be so old? It ain't natural."

"It's natural for us. We age differently from you. It has something to do with the environment we live in and our diet, too. And, of course, the Crystal Fountain in the temple."

She pointed towards a large, imposing building directly across the square. The temple was held up by ancient

---

[46] A common difficulty when it comes to children. Every adult is considered ancient.

[47] See Book I.

stone columns carved in the shape of human figures. The figures were inlaid with coloured gemstones that almost made them seem alive. An archway pierced the front of the building, flanked by armed Atlantean guards wearing heavy plate armour and holding long spears. The archway glowed with a soft pearly light that spilled down the steps, bathing the paving stones with luminescence.

"Temple? Crystal Fountain?"

"Enough!" Xnasos snapped, cutting off any further explanation. Xnasha waited for her brother to turn away before winking and smiling secretively at Mimi. "Later," she whispered. "I'll show you after you've rested."

Mimi returned her attention to the group. Now the Atlanteans were moving timidly forward, approaching the children with caution as if afraid these tiny beings might be figments of their imagination, prone to dissolving into air at the slightest touch.

The Hollow Mountain refugees, for their part, were wary of these odd creatures. Cara and the remaining Royal Swiss Guards took up defensive postures, watching the strangers approach. Mrs. Francis tried to look menacing but failed spectacularly. Mr. Kipling stood with his arm around his new wife's shoulders and his free hand resting on the hilt of his sabre. The children didn't know what to do. After the long day they'd had, many were practically dead on their feet. The younger ones hid behind the legs of the older children and peered at the Atlanteans with trepidation.

Mimi caught Cara's eye and gave a quick shake of her head. Cara lowered her fighting stick and the other Guards followed her lead.

One Atlantean, a woman with bright silver wire woven through her hair, approached a small girl about four years old. The woman knelt so that she seemed less frightening and smiled.

"My name is Axandra," she said in a soothing, friendly tone. "Who are you?"

The little girl stared for a moment in silence. Screwing up her courage, she said, "My name is Nicolette."

"Nicolette," Axandra said, savouring the word. "A strange and lovely name. Hello, Nicolette."

"Hello," said Nicolette. Then, shaking off her trepidation, she announced in a very loud voice, "I'm hungry."

The spell was broken. Everyone laughed, Atlanteans and Hollow Mountainers alike. All suspicion and wariness were dispelled. Xnasos raised his staff and called for silence.

"Of course you are hungry," Xnasos said. "You have had a long journey and a terrible heartbreak. But have no fear, you are welcome here in the realm of Atlantis. We will honour the pact made with the King of Switzerland. No enemy can reach you here. Tonight we will feast and celebrate the meeting of our two peoples. Our realm has missed the sound of children's laughter for too long."

He addressed his own people: "Make room in your homes for our guests. Bring food and drink and set tables for a feast."

To the Hollow Mountainers, he said, "Eat and rest for a while. You are welcome among us. When you are refreshed, we will discuss our course of action in the council chamber of the Temple of the Crystal Fountain. Tonight, let no worry cloud your minds. You are safe here. As in the days of old, when Atlantis ruled the world, my forefathers swore that—"

Xnasha interrupted him. "Enough of your speechifying, brother. They need food, not words."

Xnasos raised his hands and tugged at his white hair in frustration. "Why can't I make one little speech? How often do I get to make a speech?"

"Once is too often," Xnasha retorted.

Xnasos grumbled to himself and waved his staff. "Prepare the feast."

The Atlanteans hurried to their tasks as the Hollow Mountain children chattered excitedly, discussing their newfound refuge.

HOURS LATER, Mimi finally lay back in a comfortable bed in the house of Xnasos and Xnasha after a long night of merriment and feasting under the great dome of the sea. At first it had been quite disconcerting to sit at the long trestle tables laden with fish, prawns,[48] shellfish, and seaweed salads heavily laced with salt and strange spices while the weight of the ocean loomed above, but she soon grew comfortable in the company of the Atlanteans. The odd folk were quite taken with the children, chatting and singing to them as they ate, telling them wondrous tales of the distant past, of great machines and beautiful ships that sailed above and below the sea. They played music on harps, pipes fashioned from the shells of sea creatures, and bizarre stringed instruments with bows of ivory and twine wound from sea plants. Everywhere Mimi looked,

---

[48] *Prawn* is another word for shrimp. I prefer using the word *prawn* as it avoids the embarrassing ridiculousness that occurs when eating jumbo shrimp. I mean, really, jumbo shrimp?! It's silly! It's like saying, "Look at the huge dwarf!" or "Look at the honest politician!" or "Wow, this was tasty soil!" (That last one was a stretch, although if you've ever tasted soil, I'm sure you'd find it quite bland ... unless you are an earthworm, which leads me to wonder how you learned to read ... or even hold this book.)

children ate and laughed happily as their hosts looked after their every need.

The music of the Atlanteans fell weirdly on her ear, reminiscent of waves and the cries of sea animals, sad and slow and complex. Mimi studied the Atlanteans, watching their clever little faces and hands as they played, and sensed an underlying sadness, a loneliness born of isolation in their underwater home. Xnasha, courteous and friendly, sat at Mimi's side, asking many, many questions about the surface world.

Xnasha asked very funny questions: she wanted to know what the sun looked like, what the wind felt like. What did a tree smell like? Had Mimi ever seen grass? Was it true that there were millions of people on the surface and that they rode on the backs of animals and in machines over the land and even in the air? Xnasos frowned at Xnasha's open curiosity from his place at Mimi's other elbow. Mimi answered every question as best she could. She realized that the Atlanteans' knowledge of the upper world was quite detailed, considering they hadn't ventured there in what seemed like centuries or even thousands of years. Xnasha deflected Mimi's own questions, saying, "Tomorrow. You will hear everything tomorrow. Don't worry, there's plenty of time for us to bore you tomorrow."

Finally, having eaten her fill of the delicious food, drunk all the clear, cold, slightly bitter watered wine[49] she felt she could hold, and even sampled the ice cream made from whale milk, Mimi began to yawn uncontrollably. The feast

---

[49] The Atlanteans must be forgiven for allowing children to drink wine. They really didn't know any better. Also, the Atlantean wine, fermented from kelp, has incredible healing powers even if it does smell slightly of fish.

broke up and the children were taken to the homes of the people who would shelter them for the night.

Mimi followed Xnasos and Xnasha to a stone house just off the square. The furnishings were beautifully carved from ivory and dark wood. Xnasha took her to a bedroom on the upper floor. They walked along a hallway, passing other rooms that looked as though they hadn't been used in years, dust thick on the floor. Xnasha took her into a room with a balcony that looked out over the square where the people of Atlantis were busy cleaning up after the celebration. A bed was set out for her on the balcony, and a small table held a basin of hot water for washing. Xnasha bid Mimi good night.

Mimi splashed her face with water but had no energy for a more thorough bath. She stripped off her filthy Guards uniform and let it fall to the floor, putting on a fluffy robe Xnasha had set out for her. She fell into bed and pulled the soft blanket (woven from seaweed) up to her chin.

The air was warm and a light breeze wafted over her as she gazed up into the ocean overhead. Her eyes were heavy. She was glad of the safety and the food and the new friends. Tomorrow, she would make plans. They had to find Parveen and Aidan. They had to rescue the other children. She wondered where Hamish X was right now.

"He can take care of himself, wherever he is," she mumbled. "I just hope Parveen is okay."

And with a last thought of her little friend, she fell into a deep and dreamless sleep.

Chapter 10

HAMISH X

The stern of the ship loomed large above Hamish X as he fluttered his powerful boots. The pull of the current was strong and aided him in his pursuit of the vessel. Five minutes of dedicated fluttering allowed him to reach the rusty hull of the *Christmas Is Cancelled*, but having arrived there, he realized he had no way of reboarding the wayward ship. The hull was slick with algae and slime. The Captain rarely took the time to clean the hull, and as a result, Hamish X was forced to cling to the housing of the keel and rack his brain for options. He was at a loss until a length of rope fell from above, striking him firmly on the top of the skull.

"Ow," he said, rubbing his scalp. He craned his neck and looked up to see Maggie peering down at him, hanging over the ship's rail.

"I thought you might need a hand," the girl called.

"Thanks," Hamish X answered. Gripping the rope, he began to haul himself up hand over hand until, with much effort, he finally pulled himself over the metal railing and lay puffing on the deck.

"Good work," Maggie congratulated him, extending a hand and pulling him to his feet.

"We aren't out of the woods yet." Hamish X pointed forward to the looming reef. "The engines are ruined. We have no way of avoiding a crash."

Thomas ran up to them, his face flushed with excitement. "I don't know what you did, but it worked! The ship is ours."

"We may not hold it for long." Hamish X explained the danger they faced. Thomas took in the new situation and thought for a moment. Suddenly, he snapped his fingers.

"What about the anchor?" Thomas asked.

"I used the chain to foul the propeller."

"The lifeboats! There are lifeboats on the forward deck," he said. "We'll load everyone aboard and abandon ship. If Ironbuttocks wants to keep this ship, he can have it."

"Good thinking." Hamish X slapped Thomas on the back. "Let's get the boats in the water. Stand guard outside the bridge hatchway to make sure the Captain doesn't escape. Maggie and I will organize the kids!"

The three children dashed off to perform their tasks. Minutes later, they were faced with another dilemma. Maggie and Hamish X surveyed the condition of the lifeboats and soon came to the awful realization that the craft, like the rest of the systems on the ship, had rarely experienced any form of maintenance. All four lifeboats were completely devoid of supplies, and three of them were so full of holes as to be totally unseaworthy. One lifeboat would not be enough to carry all the children to safety.

"What'll we do?" Maggie asked Hamish X. "We can't leave anyone behind. There's no way we can get all the kids into one boat. One big wave and we'll capsize."

"Not to mention the crew and the Captain," Hamish X pointed out.

Maggie's mouth hung open in astonishment. "Are you kidding me? We leave 'em here! What do we care if the crew or the stinking, rusty-bummed Captain survive? They made our lives a misery! They stole us from our parents!

They were gonna sell us as slaves! If the tables were turned, they'd leave us here to die without a second thought!"

Hamish X smiled and nodded. "You've hit upon it there, Maggie. If we left them to die, we'd be just as bad as they are. That's the danger of dealing with bad people: after a while you start to act like they do." He shook his head. "No. We'll have to think of something else."

He turned and headed along the deck to the bridge with Maggie in tow. They found Thomas and four children prying at the bridge hatchway with a long metal bar. As they approached, the bar slipped and rattled to the deck. Thomas kicked the door in frustration.

"Darn it! The door is so bent in its frame it's wedged shut. We won't be able to get it open without some explosives. We'll never get in now."

"That's the least of our worries," Maggie said. "There's only one lifeboat. The rest are junk. There's no way we'll get all of us off the boat before we crash into those rocks. Captain Ironbuttocks can rot in there for all I care."

Hamish X ran a hand thoughtfully over the dented surface of the hatch. "No. I think not. The Captain can still be of some use."

"How?" Thomas and Maggie asked.

"First," Hamish X tapped the hatch with the toe of one shiny boot, "we have to get in there." Thomas held the pry bar out to Hamish X. The boy looked at it and raised a hand in polite refusal. "Thank you, no. I'll do this my way. See if you can rig an anchor, Maggie." Maggie nodded and dashed off. Hamish X turned to the hatch. He closed his eyes, took a deep breath, and concentrated on his boots.

INSIDE THE BRIDGE, Captain Ironbuttocks had begun to think they had forgotten about him. He'd felt the jarring shudder that announced the destruction of the ship's engines. He had cursed Hamish X roundly, pounding his fists on the ship's wheel in frustration.

Finally, he sat down hard in his Captain's chair and assessed the situation.

"They have escaped from the cargo hold," he said to no one in particular. He felt better speaking out loud and listing his woes. "They have trapped me in the bridge. They have broken my beautiful engines. All is lost." Tears streamed down his puffy face, leaving tracks down his dirty cheeks. His cheeks weren't dirty as a result of the battle with his prisoners. He rarely bathed and so was coated with a thin layer of filth at all times.

"What can a man do when faced with such a defeat?" he said. "What can a man do when all hope is gone?" He pondered the magnitude of his defeat for a long moment. "Ah, of course. A man can eat a very spicy sausage." And having so decided, he put his words into action. Reaching into his trouser pocket, he retrieved a lint-covered, greasy pepperoni, dusted it off with clumsy delicacy, and bit the end from it, chewing thoughtfully. "Yes ... the world seems better with a spicy, stinky sausage in my mouth. Things seem ... clearer somehow." He cast his gaze around the bridge and instantly saw that an option still lay open to him. He dreaded the option. He loathed the option. He feared the option. "But I have no other option."

Transferring his sausage to his left hand, he leaned over the radio console. He thumbed the power on and the transmitter hummed gently to life. He hesitated. Calling his employers was a last resort. They would not be happy with him. He had heard tales of ships and captains who were never seen again when they failed the ODA. The Grey Agents were never pleased with failure.

"Choices." The Captain shook his head. "Choices? I ain't got no choices." He pushed the send button and spoke into the microphone. "Mayday! Mayday! This is Captain Ironbuttocks aboard the *Christmas Is Cancelled*. Mayday! Mayday! I repeat. Mayday.[50] Ship requires assistance. Do you read me, Miss Cake?"

At that precise instant, the hatch exploded inward, driven by the right boot of Hamish X. He had gathered all his focus and concentrated all his will into a single strike, and that strike tore the hatch from its hinges. The metal door crashed into the far wall of the bridge, shattering a large glass map that the crew used to track weather formations. The Captain was showered with tiny bits of glass as he fell backwards over his chair. His buttocks struck the floor with a ringing clang and his sausage spun from his hand, splatting against the wall and slowly sliding down to the floor with a wet plop.

Hamish X gathered himself up from the floor where he had landed in a crouch and unfolded himself to his full height. He walked slowly over to the prone Captain, who scrambled backwards until his back was against the wall. Ironbuttocks's eyes were wide with fear, the white visible all around the irises.

"Don't kill me, you crazy boot-boy! Don't kill me!"

Hamish X chuckled softly. "Kill you? No, I won't kill you." He raised one boot and pressed it into Ironbuttocks's chest, pinning him to the wall. "You don't deserve to live,

---

[50] Mayday is the international verbal signal of distress for operators of ships and planes. It is derived from the French phrase *Venez m'aidez!*, which, translated into English, is literally *Come help me!* It replaces the older and more cumbersome *Bougez votre derrière! Je vais mourir, ici, idiot!* (Move your butt! I'm dying here, idiot!)

you miserable, metal-bottomed parasite, but I won't kill you. I ..."

Static hissed loudly from the radio. Hamish X jerked his head and saw that the transmitter was working. He reached for the switch to kill the machine when a flat female voice came through the tinny speakers. "*Christmas Is Cancelled*, this is ODA cargo helicopter 7A. I am reading you, Captain. However, I am not certain I heard you correctly. You need assistance? What are your coordinates? Please transmit them and we shall rendezvous with you immediately. Respond, over!"

The static returned. Hamish X pressed his boot harder on the Captain's chest.

"You called for help?" Hamish X hissed. "You little worm!"

"Hey! Who you calling worm? I am no invertebrate.[51] I have a bony, bony spinal column."

"I was speaking metaphorically, you crusty, rusty, greasy, slave-running, cowardly scum!" Hamish X growled then stopped, puzzled. "How do you even know what an invertebrate is, anyway?"

"I was going to be a marine biologist but—"

"But what?"

"But ... my little bum, she make me sink!"

Hamish X snarled and ground his boot harder into the Captain's chest.

"We have no lifeboats because your idea of shipboard safety is exactly like your personal hygiene: nonexistent!"

The Captain frowned, wounded by the remark. "Hey. I comb my hair!"

---

[51] Invertebrates are animals that have no spines. They include earthworms, molluscs, and bread.

"*Christmas Is Cancelled* ... Do you read me? Over." The voice of the Grey Agent named Miss Cake filled the ruined bridge. "Do you require assistance? Over."

The Captain wheezed as the pressure on his chest restricted his breathing further. "I have to answer them ... They'll be suspicious ..."

"Suspicious ...," Hamish X said thoughtfully, then he grinned his wolfish grin. "Yes ... Yes! You have to talk to them. And you will say exactly what I tell you or I'll kick your buttocks till they're as flat as a pancake and throw you over the side."

"Okay," the Captain agreed fearfully.

"So ...," Hamish X smiled. "Here is what you say ..."

Chapter 11

Miss Cake eased back on the throttle of the heavy cargo helicopter and peered through the clear plastic windscreen of the cockpit. The *Christmas Is Cancelled* floated below, precariously close to a spine of jagged rocks. The only thing restraining the ship from drifting to its destruction was a taut cable running from the bow down into the water, presumably to an anchor lodged in the seabed. No one was visible on deck. The ship appeared to be deserted.

Miss Cake frowned and pressed a finger to the side of her skull just below the brim of her fedora. A cable ran from the base of her skull into the control console in front of her, connecting her to the communications net and her partner riding in the hold aft. "No movement at all, Mr. Cookie. Where is Captain Ironbuttocks? The coordinates are correct, but he and his crew are nowhere in sight."

"Strange." Mr. Cookie's voice crackled inside Miss Cake's head. "Perhaps they were forced to abandon ship?"

"Negative, Mr. Cookie. I did a full surface radar scan of the sea out to a radius of ten kilometres. There are no lifeboats."

"What do you suggest we do, Miss Cake?"

Miss Cake tilted her head to the side and thought for a moment. Her dealings with Captain Ironbuttocks had always been smooth and simple. He was a greedy man who took the money he was offered and handed over his cargo without any questions or difficulties.

Miss Cake was the Grey Agent in charge of the ODA's interests in the Mediterranean, North Africa, and the

Black Sea. She had been ordered by Headquarters in Providence to wrap up operations. The gate would be opened soon. The ODA no longer required her to gather children for their purposes. She had been travelling around, closing down all her operatives one at a time. The call from the *Christmas Is Cancelled* had forced her to break the logical sequence of her travels, but now or later mattered little. She would take the final shipment of children and close down the project as per her instructions.

Implicit in these instructions was the eradication of any loose ends. The Captain and crew of the *Christmas Is Cancelled* definitely constituted a loose end. After picking up the cargo of children, Miss Cake had planned to send the ship to the bottom with all hands. Mounted under the belly of the helicopter were six high-explosive, armour-piercing missiles brought along for just such an occasion. Miss Cake caressed the launch button with her gloved thumb in anticipation.

"Miss Cake? Your orders?"

"We'll take her down and land on the deck. Arm yourself, just in case, Mr. Cookie."

"Indeed."

Tugging on the control stick, Miss Cake swung the huge helicopter around and set a course for the derelict ship. The helicopter was enormous, fitted as a personnel carrier capable of airlifting one hundred and fifty Grey Agents and depositing them anywhere within a thousand kilometres of their base of operations. Miss Cake and Mr. Cookie had only just taken off from an ODA operations base on the coast of Libya and were heading for a rendezvous point with the slaver ship just outside Moroccan national waters when the distress call had come in. 7A was converted to carry the human cargo aboard the *Christmas Is Cancelled* with room to spare.

Miss Cake deftly manoeuvred the aircraft over the gently rising and falling deck, easing off on the throttle and allowing the wheels to touch down with hardly a jolt. She turned off the engine. As the rotors spun down, she punched the clasp on her chest, releasing the safety harness. Climbing out of the seat, she reached up and pulled a stun rifle from the rack on the wall behind her pilot's seat. She ducked through the small door at the back of the cockpit and entered the cargo area. On both sides of the helicopter, small square cages lined the bulkheads, making the dark, utilitarian space reminiscent of a dog kennel or an animal experimentation lab. These cages were meant for the children aboard Captain Ironbuttocks's ship. Miss Cake walked briskly down the hallway formed by the lines of cages and joined Mr. Cookie, who nodded and checked his stun rifle. Satisfied, he reached out with one gloved hand and tapped a green button. The door to the helicopter slid open.

Miss Cake and Mr. Cookie leapt down and took up combat stances, scanning the empty deck for any possible threat. A ragged flag fluttered from the broken mast atop the superstructure. Otherwise, nothing stirred. The deck was strewn with the wreckage of the hatch cover.

"Let's check the bridge, Mr. Cookie," Miss Cake said crisply.

They moved across the deck, one behind the other, Miss Cake holding her rifle ready for any threat from the front while Mr. Cookie walked backwards, keeping his rifle trained on the rear.

"There's been a battle here," Miss Cake said, kicking debris out of her way.

"Indeed," Mr. Cookie confirmed. "Whatever became of the Captain and his crew might be our fate too if we are not vigilant."

They made their way through a maze of overturned crates to the steps that led to the bridge. Climbing up the steps, they found the hatch to the bridge lying next to the gaping door. After a quick scan of the deck to make sure they were still alone, the two Grey Agents leapt through the open hatch.

Inside the bridge they found chaos. All the instruments were destroyed. The radio was smashed, the navigation system pulverized. The radar screens were dark and silent. Moving to the radio, Miss Cake picked up the handset only to find that its cord to the radio was torn out. Mr. Cookie joined his comrade where she stood perusing the damage in confusion. Looking around at the destruction, he shook his head. Water sloshed around their grey-booted feet.

"Strange," Miss Cake said, indicating the water. "Why is there water on the floor?"

"It's bizarre," said Mr. Cookie. "What happened here?" he asked Miss Cake.

"Captain Ironbuttocks said there was a natural disaster and our help was required immediately."

"What natural disaster?" Mr. Cookie asked.

"That would be me."

They whirled around to find Hamish X leaning in the doorway, looking completely at ease. He smiled sweetly at them and gave a friendly wave. "I'm Hamish X."

The Grey Agents levelled their rifles at the boy. "We know who you are," Miss Cake said. "Don't move or we will be forced to shoot you."

"That's not very friendly of you." Hamish X frowned. "All I want is to borrow your helicopter."

"What?" Miss Cake's face was a picture of confusion. "Put up your hands and surrender at once or we will be forced to shoot you."

"Ah." Hamish X laughed softly. "How fast do you think you can pull those triggers?"

"Very fast," Mr. Cookie said honestly.

"Faster than it takes electricity to travel through water?" Hamish X raised his other hand to reveal a black power cable spitting sparks.

The Grey Agents barely had time to open their mouths in surprise before Hamish X dropped the cable into the water on the floor of the bridge. Instantly, thousands of volts of electrical current coursed through the water. Grey Agents are different from us in many ways, but in one respect they are the same: they make excellent conductors. Before they could react, they were dancing a jig to the tune of an invisible, silent band.

Hamish X, standing on the deck outside the bridge, waited a full ten seconds before kicking the cable out of the water and allowing the Grey Agents to fall to the floor with a splash, lifeless as marionettes whose strings have been cut. They lay still, their weapons half-submerged in the water that the children had laboriously hauled in buckets to set their trap.

Maggie and Thomas rushed up from their hiding place in the hold where the other children waited. Looking into the bridge, they laughed and gave each other a high-five.

"Awesome!" Thomas crowed. "We did it."

"Oh yeah!" Maggie laughed and slapped Hamish X on the back. "Nothing can stop us now."

Hamish X let them enjoy their victory for a full four seconds before barking out orders. "Okay. Load the children into the helicopter. We have to be long gone before

108

the ODA sends anyone to find out what happened here. With any luck, we'll be sleeping on the beach under African stars tonight."

"You're sure you know how to fly that thing?" Thomas asked as they set off down the steps.

Hamish X winked. "I think I can manage."

Chapter 12

PARVEEN

Parveen's sleeping arrangements were far less comfortable than Mimi's or Hamish X's. An African beach or an Atlantean bedchamber would have seemed like heaven to him. He woke from his fitful slumber and looked up at the aluminum sheeting gleaming dully overhead. The shadow of the giant exhaust fan swung across the ceiling of his little bolt-hole in the junction of a ventilation shaft deep in the bowels of the fortress that was ODA Headquarters. He had discovered the ventilation system quite by accident yesterday after reeling away from the horrible sight he had witnessed in the room where Noor had been taken. He had wanted only to hide himself away from the world. Staggering back along the corridors, he had happened on a loose vent cover and pulled it aside, crawling in as far as he could go.

After he had recovered from his shock, he realized what a boon the vents were. The shafts were warm and allowed him access to almost every corner of the facility. From his central location he explored the complex, looking for a way to help his sister and the others.

Parveen had very nearly been caught by Mr. Sweet while trailing the two Grey Agents along the catwalk. When Mr. Sweet had stopped and turned towards him, the agent's goggled eyes had been staring straight at where

Parveen pressed himself against the catwalk wall. Fortunately, the sneaky suit had concealed him, but he resolved that in future he would be more careful to avoid coming so close to any Grey Agent.

At first, food was a problem. He'd had a few protein bars in his knapsack, but they were hardly enough. The Grey Agents didn't seem to need food in the traditional sense: there was no central food storage to pilfer. In the end, Parveen found a source of nourishment that was slightly gruesome but efficient. He would go to the room the Grey Agents called the Hall of Batteries. When no one was looking, he went to the nearest child, pulled the tube that provided the comatose sleeper with nutrients, and sucked on the tube until he had his fill. The nutrient syrup was bland and tasteless, but it provided all the essentials he needed to survive.

Parveen was hungry, but he continued to lie on his back wrapped in the thermal blanket from his knapsack. He knew he should eat to keep up his strength, but he still postponed the effort. Going to the Hall of Batteries was a depressing affair. Looking up at all the captured children, their energy sapped to power the infernal machines of the ODA, was very sad and also frustrating. Here he was, at large in the enemy's home base, and he couldn't find a way to free all these children from their horrible fate, just like Aidan, Noor, and all the other children from the Hollow Mountain. He felt helpless.

He had always enjoyed spending time on his own without anyone to bother him. He had resigned himself to never having a family and friends. Then came Mimi and Hamish X and now Noor, his only surviving sister. He felt terribly alone and would gladly give up all the solitude he was enjoying now to see Hamish X or Mimi again.

His mind returned to the horrible sight yesterday that had sent him scrabbling into the ventilation shafts, his sanity fraying. A whisper of panic swept through his mind. He trembled and forced himself to think.

In the glass chamber beyond the Hall of Batteries, the Grey Agents performed their most fiendish work. The chamber was a surgical laboratory where the ODA perpetrated the most horrible corruption imaginable on the children they felt were eligible.

Parveen had almost shrieked out loud when he saw at least a hundred steel operating tables surrounded by clusters of Grey Agents in surgical gowns and masks and glistening medical instruments poised to invade the bodies of the unconscious children. He watched, powerless, as Noor was taken to a table. Her inert body was laid under a bright white light. Hanging above the table, a clutch of robotic instruments, a curl of metal claws like a sleeping spider, twitched to life. A red dot of light crawled across Noor's calm face, tracing the future path of horrible, cold steel instruments.

Parveen's heart hammered. He had to do something! He had to stop them. His sister. He reached into the pouch at his hip, his fingers grasping the furry lump of a hamster bomb, readying himself to attack the Grey Agents as they gathered like scavengers around the helpless children.

Parveen was distracted by Grey Agent activity at a nearby table. He stepped closer to investigate, letting Noor out of his sight for the moment.

What were they doing? Parveen's horrified mind shrieked. As if in answer to his silent question, the Grey Agents stepped back from the table, pulling rubber gloves from their pallid hands. On the table lay Aidan, his skin now a sickly grey, his eyes closed. His head was shaved, making him appear even more vulnerable with his bald skull pressed against the cold metal of the table. At the top of his head, where his blond hair had been, a nest of multi-coloured cables sprouted, snaking up into a thicker cable that ran into the ceiling out of sight. The wires pulsed with a nauseating bluish glow.

"He is ready for the download," one Grey Agent said, the flat voice muffled by a surgical mask fitted over the lower part of her face.

"Open the micro gate," another agent commanded.

"Opening," the first agent intoned, turning a dial on a sleek black box. There was a flash of sickening lightning that sped down the cable into Aidan's skull. The boy writhed in agony, but his limbs were secured to the table with straps. Aidan's eyes flew open, staring wide in terror. As Parveen watched, the irises flickered and changed from pale brown to a weird metallic golden hue. Parveen almost cried out. He'd seen that colour before. Hamish X had eyes like that.

The female agent turned the dial down and the light diminished. The other Grey Agents moved closer to the table. They deftly removed the restraints, and Aidan sat up and gazed curiously around him.

Aidan raised a hand to his face. The colour of his eyes wasn't the only physical change he exhibited. His fingers were longer and thinner: he'd grown another knuckle.

"Interesting sensation," Aidan said, but his voice no longer had any life; rather, he sounded as flat and emotion-less as all the Grey Agents. He held out a pale hand and turned it over, looking at the appendage as if he'd never seen anything like it before. "These bodies are quite loath-some. Moist and stinking."

"Indeed. Very inefficient, too. It is a trial," the female agent agreed. "One gets used to it."

The other agent handed Aidan a grey bundle of clothing with a grey fedora placed neatly on top. "It's only temporary. When the great portal opens, things will be much more amenable to us in this world. You shall be called Mr. Crisp."

"Mr. Crisp," Aidan repeated. All trace of the Aidan that Parveen knew was gone. An alien intelligence inhabited his friend's body now.

Parveen bit back a choking sob. He tried to understand what he had just witnessed. *This is what happens to the older ones*, Parveen thought. *They make them into Grey Agents! What had the agent called the device? A micro gate! A gate to where?* Parveen's thoughts flew back to the weird device he had seen hanging in the huge chamber with the banks of machines. Was that a larger version of the machine he'd just seen in operation? It must be. He vowed to take a closer look at the horrid device as soon as possible.

Noor! Frantically, he searched the room for his sister. Parveen moved as quickly as he could without being detected, weaving in and out of Grey Agents, robots, and banks of equipment, checking every table.

At last he found her. She lay cold and inert under a stark blue light. An agent held an electric razor poised above her skull. Another gazed at a small screen.

He wasn't too late! Parveen clenched his fists. He had never felt such rage before. He had never understood Mimi and her blazing temper, her fits of fury, and her lack of control. Finally, he knew what it felt like to want to tear something apart.

He was about to throw himself at the unsuspecting Grey Agents and sell his life dearly when the agent tapped the screen and said, "No. This one's cerebellum is not developed enough to accept a host yet."

"Oh." The agent lowered the shears. "What shall we do with her then? Destroy her, I suppose."

Parveen tensed, ready to spring to his sister's aid.

"Wasteful." The second agent shook its head. "Send her to the Hall of Batteries."

"Fine."

The relief that flooded through Parveen was enough to bathe his body with sweat. Noor had been spared the horrible psychic invasion that Aidan had experienced. At least in the Hall of Batteries, Parveen could keep an eye on her while he made his plans. He felt an urge just to grab her now and try to make a run for it, but Parveen was intelligent. He always weighed the positive and negative results of his actions. Even though attacking the Grey Agents now and attempting to free his sister would feel good, he knew that, ultimately, it was a foolish thing to do. He couldn't hope to overpower so many enemies and get away with Noor. For one thing, he didn't know how to get out of the complex.

No. He shrank against the wall, careful not to brush up against any of the Grey Agents as he backed away, heading for the entrance. *I have to make a plan. I have to use my brain.* He had limited resources, very few remaining weapons, and no allies. The one thing he did have in his favour was that the ODA didn't know he was there. He had to remain hidden until he could make his move. He would find a place to hide, learn the layout of the complex, and find out everything he could about the ODA's operations. Armed with that knowledge, he might be able to strike a blow that would free all the children.

And who knew? Maybe Hamish X and Mimi were on their way here right now. He hadn't told anyone where he was going when he stowed away in the cargo carrier, but

Mimi would have noticed he was missing. She would try to find him. Of course, she might not have made it out herself ...

No. Parveen shut out that possibility. *She will come. Hamish X will come. They won't abandon me. I have to be ready. I have to have everything in place to help them when they arrive.*

He watched and waited while Noor was transferred from the surgical table back onto her pallet. He trailed after the robot that carried her into the Hall of Batteries. He stood in the shadows as Noor was hooked up to a feeding tube and the strange harness. He waited until she was left alone, one of many inert children dangling in space. She hung on the lowest tier, at the height of Parveen's shoulder.

After the robot had trundled away, Parveen crept to his sister's side. He laid a hand on her cool forehead and said, "I'm watching over you. Rest now. I'll come and get you soon." He smoothed a strand of dark hair away from her face and padded away.

An hour later, after dodging many Grey Agents and searching several corridors, he had discovered the loose grille. Using the multitool from his pack, he quickly tugged on the grille until one side swung out from the wall. Ducking inside, he discovered a warren of tunnels carrying warm air throughout the complex. The shafts were a perfect height for him to walk upright and gave him access to everywhere he might need to explore. Settling on one central junction as a headquarters, he hunkered down and, wrapping himself in a thermal blanket, fell deeply asleep.

That had been yesterday. He sat up and looked at his watch. It read 6:00 a.m. He had slept for twelve hours. He didn't know what time zone he was currently in, but it didn't matter: he always kept his watch set to Greenwich Mean Time,[52] or Zulu Time as the military called it.[53] No doubt he had needed sleep. He stretched his arms and legs, wincing as his muscles protested the hard metal floor.

"Time to explore." He packed his knapsack, pulled his hood up, and trotted off down the tunnel in search of a shaft that would lead him to the ODA's evil gateway.

---

[52] Greenwich Mean Time is so called because it is the time at the prime meridian, or zero degrees longitude. Zero longitude is the imaginary line that runs north to south from pole to pole. Some English astronomer or other decided that the town of Greenwich was the centre of the universe, and so time is computed from there. A little egotistical, but there you go. I always like to think that I am the centre of the universe and so, wherever I happen to be, it is always noon. This is a confusing way to live, but I enjoy it.

[53] The military requires very precise timekeeping, as many of their operations are dependent on punctuality, and, of course, it is common knowledge that Zulus are the most punctual people on Earth.

Chapter 13

After many false turnings and dead ends, Parveen finally found his way to a shaft that ended a few metres short of the gateway. He huddled behind a broad-bladed exhaust fan, its metal arms swinging lazily as they siphoned away heat from the infernal machine.

Sitting so close to the gateway was difficult. First of all, the ring of metal emitted a sickly glow that was difficult to look at. Parveen raised a gloved hand to his goggles and flipped through a sequence of filters that blocked different kinds of light: infrared, ultraviolet, X-rays, and gamma rays. Nothing seemed to ease the nausea he felt as the weird light cast its glow over him. He hypothesized that perhaps the light was from a spectrum not of this Earth.

He observed the Grey Agents below as they scuttled here and there servicing the banks of computers that regulated the machine. They wore no special protective gear to shield them from the energy radiating out of the device. Either they were used to it or ...

"Maybe it's natural for them," Parveen whispered to himself. "Maybe it isn't dangerous to them because it comes from their home environment." He gasped as a realization struck him. "It's a gateway to their home world."

Parveen's ruminations were interrupted by a mechanical hum coming from the ventilation shaft behind him. Someone was coming! Had they found him? Had he tripped some alarm?

He was at the end of the shaft. There was no escape route. The only way out was back towards the approaching sound or out through the fan and into the gateway chamber below. That way would lead to certain discovery. He had only the camouflage of the sneaky suit to protect him. Pressing himself against the shaft wall, he checked his hands and his hood to make sure every centimetre of his skin was covered. Satisfied, he held his breath and waited.

The mechanical hum grew louder. After what seemed an eternity, a robot rounded the final corner. The machine was basic: a tracked vehicle with mechanical arms ending in articulated claws attached to a vague torso, making the robot vaguely anthropomorphic.[54] Parveen sucked in his breath, trying to make himself as small as possible as the machine passed by him and went straight to the fan housing.

A maintenance robot. Parveen breathed out softly. *Perhaps he hadn't been detected. The robot was doing routine upkeep on the ventilation system.*

The robot's arms extended, telescoping out until the articulated claws could reach the housing of the fan motor. A tiny nozzle emerged from the tip of one claw. With a hiss, oily liquid sprayed out of the nozzle into a hole in the housing. Having finished its lubrication procedure, the nozzle retracted, followed by the arms. The robot's inner workings whirred and clicked, its torso spun, and it headed back the way it came.

As it passed Parveen, it stopped. Parveen held his breath again. The torso spun in his direction. A tiny camera irised out from the centre of the torso. For a few seconds it tried to focus on Parveen's chest. After a number of whirs and clicks,

---

[54] *Anthropomorphic* is an old Greek word for humanlike. Why not just say humanlike? Because I like the word *anthropomorphic*. And I am telling the story, so there!

it gave up. The camera retracted, the torso spun, and the robot trundled off up the ventilation shaft without a backwards glance.

Parveen's heart slowed and he breathed deeply. He would have to be careful. The suit had succeeded in hiding him again, but he would have to be very cautious from now on. With a final look out at the terrible gate, he turned and headed off after the robot to continue his investigation of the ventilation shafts. He felt better and better every step he took away from the gateway. He didn't know how harmful the energy of the other world was to him, but he knew he didn't want to spend more time than necessary in close proximity to the horrible apparatus.

Already very difficult to detect in his sneaky suit, Parveen was certain he could become a veritable ghost now that he had the ventilation shafts as his own personal thoroughfare. He doubted that the Grey Agents ever entered the shafts. But he would have to be careful to avoid the little maintenance robots. He made his way by memory back to the place he had designated as his sleeping quarters. Ensconced in his hideaway, Parveen sat with his back to the wall. He reached into the hood of his suit to pluck the stub of pencil from behind his ear. Rummaging in his backpack, he found a crumpled sheet of paper. He smoothed out the paper on his knee and made a list.

"Number One: I'm alone," he said softly as he wrote. "Number Two: Noor is safe for the time being. Number Three: I know the Grey Agents use the older children as hosts. Hypothesis: The big apparatus in the main chamber is a huge version of the machines they use to possess their human hosts."[55] He shuddered at the thought of being possessed by one of the entities calling themselves Grey Agents. Who knew what their true nature was? Their human forms were gruesome enough. "Lucky that Noor didn't qualify," Parveen murmured to himself. He had no idea what the long-term effects of being used as a battery were, but they had to be better than becoming a Grey Agent. He wondered if the process of becoming an agent was reversible. Did the person

---

[55] A *hypothesis* is a proposed truth that needs to be proven through further investigation and experimentation, whereas a *theory* is proven beyond a shadow of a doubt. They are very different. One is proven and the other is not. I know this does not seem important right now, but I had this drilled into my mind by my extremely kooky high school physics teacher and I thought you ought to suffer as I had to. Thank you, Mr. Cowan.

possessed still exist somewhere within the unlucky body? He hoped so, for Aidan's sake. And for Hamish X's. The golden hue of the Grey Agents' eyes was so like Parveen's friend's eyes. What did that mean? Was Hamish X doomed to be like the Grey Agents? Was he one of them deep down in his soul? Did he have the potential for their wickedness and evil? Parveen could only hope that the colour of his eyes was the only trait Hamish X shared with these entities who were bent on enslaving the Earth.

A thought struck him: if the agents were really people who had been possessed by entities from another world, when they were killed was the human host killed as well? It was a terrible thought. He had cast a female agent from the *Orphan Queen* during the assault on the Hollow Mountain. Had he killed some poor human being as well as the agent? He felt a stab of guilt but ruthlessly crushed it a second later. They were at war with the ODA. The Grey Agents had to be defeated. When the war was over, there would be plenty of time for guilt and soul-searching.

Parveen looked at his list. What he knew was very scant indeed. He had to learn more and try to find a weakness to exploit.

"First things first," he whispered, turning over the sheet of paper. He began to draw the beginnings of a map of the ventilation system. The very act of making a blueprint calmed him. He was not exactly happy, but he was making a plan and that was something, at least. He always felt better when he had a plan.

Chapter 14

MIMI

Mimi looked up at the great dome of Atlantis. Above her, millions of tons of water and salt were restrained only by the frail crystal barrier that arched over the city where she stood.

She was in the Great Square. She was alone. Where was everyone? Had they gone and left her here?

A sharp rending sound drew her attention back to the dome above. With a boom like a gunshot, a crack appeared in the dome directly above her head. As she watched, terrified, the crack began to spread, radiating outwards like the web of a crazed spider. She wanted to scream but couldn't open her mouth. She wanted to run but her feet were fused to the stone.

Wide-eyed with terror, she watched as the first drops of water fell from above. The drip quickly became a torrent. Salty water pounded onto her upturned face. No matter how hard she tried, she couldn't turn away. Her nostrils and mouth filled with brine. She was choking! She couldn't breathe!

She awoke in the darkness, bathed in sweat, and her dream had come true. She couldn't breathe! Something was covering her mouth and nose. She was suffocating!

"Mimi," Cara hissed at her ear. "Mimi! It's me, Cara!"

Mimi relaxed. Cara stood over her in the gloom, the pale light of the dome washing in through the balcony doors. Cara's right hand was pressed over Mimi's mouth. When she saw Mimi relax, Cara took her hand away and raised a finger to her lips. "Quiet."

Mimi sat up, pulling the twisted sheets away from her limbs. "What's the big idea?"

"Shhh!" Cara said with a hushed urgency. "Xnasha woke me moments ago. She says she wants to talk." Mimi looked over to find the Atlantean woman standing in the doorway of the bedchamber. Xnasha smiled and beckoned the girls with a wave of her hand. In her other hand she held a glowing lamp in the shape of a seashell.

Mimi swung her legs out of bed and stood, pulling her Guards jacket on as she joined Cara. The floor was smooth and warm, but she stepped into her boots anyway. One never knew what might need a good kicking in the middle of the night. When she was ready, she nodded. Xnasha stepped back into the hallway, and when the two girls joined her, she led them through the silent house.

Silence, of course, is relative. Xnasos's snoring was a rumbling drone that swelled as they passed quietly by his bedchamber. Xnasha rolled her eyes and led them down the stairs and out into the square.

The public space was empty. All the refugees had been taken into the homes of the Atlanteans. Obviously, the sea folk didn't see the newcomers as any kind of threat because there were no guards on patrol. Most of the windows in the buildings around the square were dark. Here and there, a lamp glowed. The dome above was dim, blocking out the ocean. After the dream she'd just had, Mimi was thankful for that. The weight above seemed less oppressive when she couldn't actually see the swarming fish and pale blue water.

The Temple of the Crystal Fountain shone its weird blue glow and its guards stood stiff and straight. They took no notice of the little party as they passed below the great broad steps. Mimi assumed they were concerned only with what the temple held. As long as the group made no effort to approach, the guards would take no particular interest in them. Xnasha led the girls down the shadowed edge of the square, the glowing shell lamp guiding them along the stone walls until they reached an alleyway. Xnasha turned up the alleyway and increased her pace. Though she was short and stocky, the white-haired woman could certainly move at a surprising speed, which Mimi and Cara found themselves hard-pressed to match.

This part of the city was more decrepit than the area around the square. Moss grew on the damp stone walls and the air was scented with mildew and decay. Xnasha led them through a bewildering maze of narrow passages between buildings whose roofs were lost in darkness. The scuff of their feet was the only sound.

At last, Xnasha stopped at an archway with a black metal door. She fished in a pouch that hung from a belt at her waist and pulled out a slender, delicate key. Holding the shell lamp in front of her, the Atlantean found the keyhole, inserted the key, and turned it. With a soft whoosh of trapped air, the door swung inward. Xnasha stepped back and indicated that the girls should go ahead of her through the door. After a moment of hesitation, Mimi shrugged and stepped through, followed by Cara and Xnasha, who pulled the door shut behind them.

The lamplight illuminated only a small circle a few metres across, but Mimi felt that the room was vast, stretching out into the surrounding darkness.

"Where are we?" Cara asked, her voice throwing echoes off the hidden walls.

Xnasha pressed a button beside the door and soft light flooded the chamber. Mimi and Cara gasped in unison as they saw what the room held.

The room was divided in half. Where they stood, a solid stone platform housed a number of giant cranes and smaller vehicles resting on rails that allowed them to move from side to side and up and down. The cranes were meant to service the strange vehicles berthed in the piers that made up the other half of the vast chamber.

The piers were carved of the native stone of Atlantis, jutting like fingers into inky water. The wavelets lapped against the sides of some of the most alien and beautiful vessels Mimi had ever seen. Long and sleek, they had the shape of dolphins lying at rest alongside the piers. They were made of a silvery-grey metal that shone softly under the diffused light. Mimi counted twelve of the crafts bobbing slightly in the water. Eight of them were truly huge, measuring more than two hundred metres in length, but the other four were much smaller. One vehicle was only about twenty metres long.

"Amazing, aren't they?" Xnasha said reverently. She walked towards the smallest vessel. "We used to rule the waves with these ships. The ancients, fearful of what their primitive minds couldn't comprehend, called them sea monsters. We mapped the oceans of the world. We travelled the seas and dove beneath the ice of the polar caps ..." She stopped speaking and gazed over the piers, sadness plain on her pale features. "Those were great days ... but now they are gone." She shook off her sadness and beckoned the girls. "Come."

Mimi and Cara followed the Atlantean along the ancient stone pier. Mimi couldn't help but be awed by the amazing technology. "Submarines," she said in a reverent whisper. "Awesome!"

Xnasha looked pleased that Mimi was so impressed. "Yes, they are. So beautiful. They represent the most advanced technology our ancestors ever achieved. Sadly, none of us really knows how to operate these craft any more. The knowledge has been lost over time."

"What a waste," Cara said.

"Indeed, yes," Xnasha agreed. "Thousands of years ago, we travelled the world's oceans and explored her continents, discovering the mysteries of science and technology. We were curious, intelligent, and eager to explore. Now, however, we have turned our attention inward. We hide from the world. Our technology keeps us alive, powers the dome that protects us, increases our lifespan, but we have turned away from the world."

"Why?" Mimi demanded. "You have so much to offer."

Xnasha shook her head. "In a moment." They had arrived at a gangplank that ran from the pier to the foredeck of the smallest submarine. A modest console stood on a pedestal at the head of the gangplank. Xnasha reached out and tapped a triangular crystal on the console. On the deck of the submarine, a circular hatch slowly opened. "First, let's go aboard. We have much to talk about before you face the assembly tomorrow. We can be comfortable inside."

She started across the gangplank. Mimi and Cara looked at each other.

"I cain't think of nothin' better to do," Mimi said.

"After you." Cara bowed sarcastically. Mimi snorted derisively and set off up the gangplank. Cara was only a step and a half behind her.

Climbing into the hatch, they found the inside of the submarine even more amazing than the outside. Xnasha

led them down a passage into a control centre. Elaborate banks of crystals covered the walls and the ceilings. In the centre of the space were four comfortable-looking swivel chairs. Xnasha plunked herself down in one and the two girls did likewise.

"Amazing, isn't it?" Xnasha mused, looking about her at the shining instruments. "My people built this craft thousands of years ago. I cleaned and restored this one as best I could. I've even managed to puzzle out the basic power systems and the propulsion unit." She held her hands out towards a bank of crystals and they began to glow. A soft hum filled the cramped cabin. She lowered her hands and the hum ceased, the glow faded. "I think I could launch her if I had a reason to."

"Why don't you?" asked Cara, flipping a stray lock of brown hair behind her ear. Somewhere she had found a comb, and it looked like she'd even had a bath. Mimi hadn't bothered washing and had fallen straight into bed. Stuck in the tight quarters of the submarine control cabin, she sniffed her armpit and began to regret not having had a quick scrub.

"You mean launch her on my own?" Xnasha shook her head, rattling the many shells twined in her hair. "It'll never happen. I'm the only one who comes down here any more, and I'm not supposed to. We're forbidden to fiddle with the ancient technology." Her face clouded. "The rest of us have almost forgotten these things exist."

"So, yer sayin' you built this thing, but ya don't know how it works?" Mimi threw up her hands. "That's crazy."

"*Tragic* would be a better word." Xnasha sighed. "My brother wouldn't be happy if he knew I brought you here, but I thought I should show you what the people of Atlantis were once capable of. Our ancestors built this great city and now we scurry through it like mice."

"Why?" Cara demanded. "Surely if you all applied yourselves, you could reclaim these machines. Atlantis could rise again. Think of the gifts you could bring to the world."

Xnasha hung her head. "No. We can never reveal ourselves. It would be folly. They would find us and destroy us."

"Who? Who would find y'all?" Mimi asked.

Xnasha raised her eyes, and they were full of fear. "The ODA. The Grey Agents. They tried to destroy us once and very nearly succeeded."

"You told us you've been down here for thousands of years," Cara said. "The ODA arrived in our world only about a century ago—"

"No," Xnasha cut her off. "They *returned* to this world a century ago. The first time they tried to cross over into this world, we inadvertently invited them in."

"I don't get it," Cara said, confusion written clearly on her face. "What are you saying? Atlantis brought the Grey Agents here?"

"Yes." Xnasha nodded. "And we paid dearly for our mistake." She held up a hand for silence as both Mimi and Cara opened their mouths. "I will give you a history lesson. I hope it will explain everything." Cara and Mimi nodded and leaned forward in their chairs, listening eagerly as Xnasha told them the history of Atlantis.

Chapter 15

XNASHA'S TALE

"Thousands of years ago, when the Egyptians had yet to build the pyramids, contenting themselves by constructing very large stone cubes instead,[56] mammoths still roamed in the northern wastes—"

"One still does," Mimi interjected.

"Shoosh!" Cara hissed.

"I'm just sayin'," Mimi grumbled but fell silent again.[57]

"... and the world was greener and the sea bluer, before all the great civilizations of China, India, and Greece had risen above the Stone Age, Atlantis was already a noble and powerful nation. From our island capital in the centre of what you now call the Mediterranean Sea, we travelled the world in our ships above and below the waves, mapping the world and bringing enlightenment to our benighted

---

[56] None of these mighty cubes has survived. As soon as the Atlanteans taught the Egyptians how to build pyramids, the Pharaohs had all the Great Cubes dismantled because they thought they were extremely boring. Pyramids are way more fun because one can take a slippery metal sled and slide down the side of them into the soft sand. Pyramid Tobogganing has been banned in modern Egypt because the toboggans tend to scratch the stone and leave unsightly marks on the monuments. Still, illegal tobogganing expeditions are a bane to the local police.

[57] Mimi is referring to Amanda, the mammoth from Book I: *Hamish X and the Cheese Pirates*.

human relatives across the face of the globe. We taught farming and building techniques, studied medicine and science, mathematics and astronomy. There was no problem that we couldn't bring our superb intellect and culture to bear upon. We were proud. We were confident ... too confident, as it turned out. We sowed the seeds of our own destruction.

"Our scientists began to dream of reaching other worlds, other planes of existence just beyond the surface of our own. They began to experiment with potent and dangerous technologies that might open a gateway to these other planes and perhaps contact creatures that might live there. In our defence, we believed that any intelligent creatures in these other planes would be benevolent like ourselves. Such foolishness is its own punishment.

"High atop the highest peak on the Island of Atlantis, the Atlantean scientists constructed a vast machine. Drawing on the power of the molten core of the Earth, we opened a gateway, a rip in the fabric of space, and punched a hole into another plane of existence."

"You found the Grey Agents' world," Cara breathed.

"Yes." Xnasha nodded, her eyes reflecting the soft glow of the crystal instruments in the cabin. "And it was a bleak and hungry place populated by voracious, evil beings. Their world lacked life and energy. They had drained it of all its vitality. By opening a gateway to their world, we invited them into ours, and they must have thought their prayers were answered. They poured out of the gate and immediately began to possess our citizens, turning them into the kind of creatures you know as the Grey Agents.

"The destruction they wrought upon the Earth was appalling. We Atlanteans were not a warlike people.

We were not prepared for the attack. Quickly, we turned all our energies into creating weapons to combat the threat. We fought a war with the Grey Agents, and there was devastation on a scale that is impossible to imagine. Tidal waves shattered whole cities. Earthquakes altered the geography of the world. Fire rained from the skies. The moon, once a vital, living planet, was turned into a lifeless ball of dust.

"At last, we were victorious. We forced the remaining evil invaders back into their own plane and destroyed the gate forever. Yes, we were victorious, but at a terrible cost. Our civilization was in ruins. Most of our people were dead.

"With our remaining resources, we built this refuge in the sunken ruins of our capital. The dome was built and the shields went up. We went into hiding. Our great achievements were forgotten by the surface world, and the name *Atlantis* faded into myth and legend."

Xnasha heaved a great sigh and fell silent. Mimi and Cara sat lost in their own thoughts. Mimi tried to imagine the beautiful world as it had once been—the glorious city shining and alive, filled with magnificent wonders instead of the faded shell that now remained—but it was hard to grasp the magnitude of what Xnasha's people had lost in that long-ago war.

"So the Grey Agents have been here before," Cara said, finally breaking the silence. "How did they manage to come back if you destroyed the gateway?"

"I don't know. I can only guess that once they got a taste of the life and energy in this world, they have striven ever since to return. As I said, the gateway was a massive undertaking requiring all the resources of our great and powerful civilization. Perhaps it has taken them this long to find a way to return—and even then, managing only a small breach allowing just a few to come through—but I'm sure it is just a prelude to a much larger invasion. My belief is that they are trying to build a permanent gateway somewhere in our world, and then they will come in strength."

Cara turned to Mimi and nodded. "It has to be in Providence."

"Providence?" Xnasha asked.

"Thur Headquarters in Rhode Island," Mimi explained. "It's a state in America."

Xnasha clapped her hands in delight. "I've heard of it. They make chickens there!"

Mimi laughed. "I guess they do, kinda."[58]

Cara folded her arms over her chest and leaned back in her chair. "That's something I find curious."

"What?" asked Xnasha. "That Rhode Island has a chicken named after it?"

"No ... although that *is* weird. But what's weirder is that you know anything about Rhode Island and chickens and that you speak almost perfect English."

"Oh that! That is easily explained. Come with me."

A few minutes later, after being led back up to the city square, they found themselves in one of the strangest places they had ever seen. Considering how many strange places they'd been in before, that was quite an accomplishment.

---

[58] Xnasha is referring to the Rhode Island Red, a breed of chicken that takes its name from the tiny state on the eastern seaboard of the United States. Only one other U.S. state developed its own variety of chicken: the New York Taxi Driving Chicken. These chickens were capable of driving taxicabs and laying eggs at the same time. The variety has become extinct because hungry passengers caught in traffic jams tended to devour the chickens. It was not uncommon in the 1950s to see a passenger frying his driver on the hot block of an overheated taxi.

"So that's how y'all know how to speak American," Mimi cried in amazement.

"English." Cara rolled her eyes. "The language is English."

"Whatever." Mimi scowled. "Just answers a few questions, is all."

They were standing in a vast stone building beside the temple. Stacked haphazardly around the space were piles of artifacts from the surface world. There were cars, tires, wagons, and chariots. There were suits of armour from every era of history: plate mail from Europe, coats of metal rings, rusted and rotting, swords, shields, and helmets. There were licence plates and kitchen appliances. There were farm tractors and furniture. In short, almost every aspect of surface life was represented in some way. Most of it was the worse for wear from soaking for a long time in the salty depths before the Atlanteans scooped it up for their weird museum. All the junk was stacked willy-nilly in tottering piles, but one piece had been lovingly restored, cleaned, and polished. Standing in the most prominent place in the centre of the hall on a marble pedestal,[59] its shiny chrome gleaming in the torchlight, was a radio.

A soft glow shone from the dial. The radio looked as though it had been ripped out of a larger housing. Perhaps it had once been in a boat or car dashboard. A bent, twisted aerial sprouted from the top. Currently, it was picking up a gardening program.

---

[59] A pedestal is a short pillar upon which one might display a piece of sculpture or statuary. It looks like a stubby little pillar, but it is not, technically, a pillar at all. To call a pedestal a pillar would be utter madness. A pedestal is also definitely not a plinth, which is the stone block that supports the bottom of a pillar or pedestal. I would like to thank the Plinth, Pedestal, and Pillar Enthusiasts Society for its help in creating this footnote.

"I'd give those rhododendrons a good watering in the morning once a week, Doris. Anything more and you'll have root rot on your hands," a cultured voice advised from the speaker.

"Thanks, Reg, for taking my call," a lady answered.

"Thanks, Reg, for taking my call," Xnasha mimicked the voice perfectly. She reached over and turned down the radio by twisting a black knob. "I listen all the time. I love it. I would love to garden, wouldn't you?" Her pale eyes danced with excitement. She danced in a circle, her arms swept wide to encompass all the strange relics of the surface world. "All these treasures, so mysterious and amazing. Rhododendrons and root rot. It's just so exciting!"

Cara and Mimi exchanged a look. "You got some weird ideas about what's amazing and what ain't! You live in this amazin' place surrounded by amazin' things and yer listenin' to the radio?"

"What's the matter? Don't you like rho-do-den-drons?" She turned the tuning knob with her knobby fingers, filling the air with static as she searched for another channel.

"It ain't the subject matter," Mimi began, but she stopped when the confident voice of a female newsreader came in loud and clear.

"Leading off the international news this morning, geologists are still puzzled by the freak eruption in the Swiss Alps two days ago. Mount Nutterhorn, until recently thought to be completely stable, has now spewed molten rock over hundreds of square kilometres, raining ash and debris as far away as Brussels. Relief agencies are heading into the area, which is sparsely inhabited by humans. The region is home to many dairy farmers and local fauna such as the Alpine Puking Rabbit, an endangered species. More

136

on this story as it develops. Now to Bill in New York, who has a fascinating story about a cat who can type his own name! Bill?"

Mimi reached over and turned the radio off. "They wrecked it. They wrecked the Hollow Mountain."

Cara's face was ashen. "George, the King ... everything is gone."

Mimi's face reddened with fury. She slammed her hand down on the pedestal. The impact knocked the aerial askew. "We gotta make 'em pay."

"Careful of the radio," Xnasha yelped, leaping to adjust the wire.

Mimi grabbed the woman's shoulder and spun her around, glaring into her pale blue eyes. "That was our home. We gotta get outta here and get back at the Grey Agents."

Xnasha shook her head. "You can't do anything. They're too powerful! They crushed our whole civilization ..." She pointed at the radio. "They destroy whole mountains, remember."

"We gotta try! We need your people to help us."

"No." The Atlantean shook her head, rattling the shells in her hair. "We can't help you."

Mimi clenched her teeth to stop herself from shouting. She took a breath and said, "This place is amazing. You people of Atlantis are powerful, too. Why are you sittin' around here listenin' to the radio?"

Xnasha looked confused. "But ... but ... the radio *is* amazing! There's a whole world that I will never know. All I have is this radio. We can't go to the surface, so I listen to the radio and learn what I can."

"Can't go," Cara said. "Why can't you go? Is the light of the sun deadly to you? Is the air poisonous?"

Xnasha shook her head, suddenly quiet.

"No," Mimi said sarcastically. "The only thing keepin' them out o' the fight is fear. They're afraid. It's a good thing you heard about the Rhode Island Red 'cause yer a chicken yerself!"

Xnasha looked at Mimi with a puzzled expression. "I'm a chicken? I don't understand. You have the strangest manner of expressing yourself."

"I mean, you ain't got no guts!"

Again, Xnasha was confused. "I believe I have guts inside my abdomen."[60]

"Aw, ferget it. I cain't even insult ya proper." Mimi turned on her heel and stamped out of the museum and into the night.

Xnasha turned to Cara and asked, "She was insulting me?"

"She was basically calling you a coward," Cara said gently. "But don't listen to her. She's a little upset right now. I think you have good reason to be afraid of the Grey Agents. You know better than anyone what they're capable of." Cara yawned. "I'm so tired. Let's go and find Mimi before she gets lost. I need to sleep."

Cara began walking to the door, but Xnasha stood still, looking at the floor. Cara went back and touched the woman's arm. Xnasha raised her face and there were tears shining in her eyes.

"What's the matter, Xnasha?"

"I ... I am *not* a coward. I want to help you. I want to see the surface but ... my people are few. How can we hope to make a difference?"

---

[60] The *abdomen* is the region of the human body directly below the ribs and above the thighs. Lots of interesting organs are stuffed in the abdomen, including the stomach, the intestines, and the pancreas. I love the word *pancreas*. I'm not sure I know what the pancreas does ... but I love it anyway.

Cara looked her in the eye, pursed her lips, and shrugged. "I don't know. We all do what we can. I know that if my people were driven underground by a gang of evil creeps and forced to live in hiding for thousands of years, I'd want a little payback."

Cara turned and went out the door, leaving the Atlantean woman alone in the museum. For a long moment, Xnasha thought about what Cara had said. She looked around at all the piles of objects and saw them for what they were: stacks and stacks of junk, evidence of the lives of others. What about her life? Xnasha realized then that she could no longer sit idly by as a spectator. She could no longer hide while the world above moved on. She took one last look at the place she used to find so fascinating and decided it was a dead end. She wanted to see the living world instead. She set off to catch up with the girls.

Chapter 16

HAMISH X

Night came quickly in the Sahara Desert. Hamish X barely had time to appreciate the reds, oranges, and purples of the western sky spilling down to colour the pale brown sand when the sun ducked beneath the horizon. The moon would not rise for many hours. Though only a few metres below, the sandy ground was invisible to his regular vision. Sitting in the pilot's chair of the helicopter, Hamish X willed his vision to sharpen. His pupils widened to suck in all the available light. Now the ground was visible, as if there were a full moon.

He didn't really need to physically see the ground, but it was comforting for him. He gripped the control stick between his knees and checked the heads-up display on the instrument panel. The helicopter gave him a full three-dimensional projection of the landscape, and a cursor showed where he was on a map along with his exact map coordinates. There was no chance he could get lost. He wanted to get as far as he could with the stolen ODA aircraft before ditching it and continuing to his destination on foot.

Since leaving the children from the *Christmas Is Cancelled*, along with the vanquished crew and a furious Captain Ironbuttocks, safely on a beach just outside Casablanca, Hamish X had taken off again on his own to find Professor Magnus Ballantyne-Stewart.

Thomas and Maggie had protested loudly when he told them he was going alone.

"You have parents waiting for you," Hamish X pointed out. "They're probably worried sick."

"They can worry a little longer," Thomas said. "We wanna come and help you. The desert is no place to go alone."

"Really." Hamish X laughed. "Have *you* ever been in a desert?"

"I saw one on the science channel."

"I see. Well, I respect your expert opinion, but I have to go across this desert and I can't bring anyone with me. It's too dangerous. In the place I'm going to there is a war going on. I can't guarantee you'll be safe."

Maggie poked a stiff finger into Hamish X's chest. "You can't make us stay here. We're free people. We can go where we choose."

Hamish X winced as the finger drove into his skin and jabbed his ribs. "You really do remind me of a friend of mine. You have to meet her someday. Maybe after I find out who I am and the ODA are all gone. But until then, I need you both to stay here. These kids need someone to help them get in touch with the authorities in town, and after that ... call your parents and go home." Hamish X smiled sadly. "It's what I would do if I had parents or a home."

After a lot more argument, the brother and sister had finally, reluctantly agreed. As Hamish X rushed along over the darkened desert, he hoped they were with their parents right now. He imagined the joy on the faces of their mother and father when they were reunited with the children they thought were gone forever. He wished he could have seen that happy sight, but he had to find Professor Ballantyne-Stewart.

The helicopter was a huge bonus. Using the purloined aircraft, he had managed to cover a great deal of ground in a fraction of the time it would have taken on foot or in a vehicle. He checked the fuel gauge: the needle was just above half. Based on how long the previous tank had lasted, he would be able to fly for another thousand kilometres before having to abandon the helicopter and proceed on foot. According to the maps King Liam had left for him in the luggage locker in the train station in Athens, he would be only a hundred kilometres or perhaps less from his goal.

Two hours later the moon had risen, silvering the dunes. The sky sparkled with more stars than Hamish X had ever seen. As he neared his destination, he felt a sense of unease growing inside him. What would he learn from the man who had made him at the behest of the ODA? Sometimes he wondered if he really wanted to find out everything there was to know about himself. Couldn't he just be happy? He had these amazing boots. He could do amazing things! He was the unconquerable Hamish X! Why shouldn't he just turn around and forget this quest for knowledge, find Parveen and Mimi, and go and live out his life somewhere where the Grey Agents might never find him?

Even as he had those thoughts, he realized it was just a fantasy. He would always wonder. The Grey Agents would never let him go. They would find him wherever he chose to hide, no matter how far he ran. No. It was imperative that he find the Professor and learn the truth. Better to face the unknown head-on.

Glancing at the instrument panel an hour later, he saw that the fuel gauge hovered just above empty. He had to find a safe place to land the helicopter and proceed on foot.

Hamish X checked the maps and saw that an oasis lay a few kilometres ahead. Oases were tiny clusters of vegetation that grew around sources of water in the otherwise barren sands of the desert. According to Hamish X's charts, there was a well at the oasis where he could land the helicopter, fill his canteen, and begin the final leg of the journey on foot across the desert to the Professor's last known whereabouts. The file said that the Professor had been seen in the village of Al-Haleed only a month before. If Ballantyne-Stewart had moved on, Hamish X would track him down.

Easing up on the throttle, he cut his speed in half, searching ahead in the moonlight for any sign of the oasis. In a moment, he saw it: a ragged line of vegetation against the normally smooth profile of the dunes. He flew past the site, looking out over it. There were date palms and some scrub grass. A crude stone well marked the watering hole. He brought the aircraft around and was about to land gently amid a swirling tornado of sand when a rocket lanced up from the ground and smashed into the tail rotor of the helicopter.

The vehicle began to spiral out of control. Hamish X fought to hold the stick steady, but it bucked in his hands like a live thing. Hamish X braced himself for the inevitable impact as the whole world tilted to one side and the helicopter slammed into the sand. He was thrown against the restraining straps of the safety harness and banged his head on the side of the seat. Stars erupted in his head. For a second, his sight went dim.

He woke to find himself hanging sideways in the harness. The window below him was pressed against the sandy desert, the windscreen starred and cracked but still holding the weight of the helicopter.

Bracing his feet against the instrument panel, Hamish X punched the button in the centre of the safety harness. Grabbing hold of the door handle above, he swung himself around and stood on the side of the seat. He propelled himself off the seat and pushed the door open. The wind tore the door from his hands, slamming it back against the cabin. Carefully, he stuck his head out the door and scanned the surrounding desert. There was no sign of anyone in the dunes. Nothing moved but the skirling clouds of sand. Whoever had attacked the helicopter was nowhere to be seen. He waited a minute longer, threw his backpack out, then flung himself out the door and dropped easily into the soft sand, hiding in the shadow cast by the fuselage of the aircraft.

The wind was sharp and cold. Hamish X stood for a moment, listening. The hiss of sand and the ticking of the engines were the only sounds in the vast desert night apart from the rattle of the broad leaves of the date palms in the breeze. He studied the desert for any sign of human activity. There seemed to be nothing but sand, scrub grass, and dates littered around the base of the trees.

Who had fired upon the helicopter? Surely they mustn't be far away. Was he imagining the attack? Had it merely been a malfunction and explosion in the engine? Perhaps, but he didn't really think so. All the systems had been running fine up until the time of the crash. He had to be careful. He was in a war zone. He had to assume that whoever had attacked the helicopter would be here soon to inspect their handiwork.

First things first: he needed water if he was going to survive a hike through the desert. He made one more scan of the surrounding dunes but saw no movement at all.

Satisfied that he was alone in the oasis, Hamish X trotted across the soft sand to the well. The well was a pile of roughly hewn stones stacked on top of one another in a circle surrounding a deep black hole in the ground. Arranged over the opening was a tripod made of blackened iron. At the peak of the tripod hung a pulley and rope. Attached to the rope was a plastic bucket. Hamish X wondered who had hung the tripod and how long it had been there. Oases were immensely important to the nomadic people of the desert, being the only source of water in the rolling wasteland of sand. The oases were like islands in a dry ocean. The nomads travelled from one oasis to another like ships passing through a hostile sea. Someone had constructed this well, and now it was used by whomever might need it.

Hamish X reached up, grabbed the handle of the winch, and began to lower the bucket in the well.

"Where are we?"

Hamish X whirled around to confront the speaker and found Maggie and Thomas standing in the sand. Thomas had a cut over his right eye, sending a slow trickle of blood down the side of his face.

"What are you doing here?" Hamish X demanded. He let go of the handle and the bucket dropped with a hollow splash.

"You can't get rid of us so easily." Maggie laughed.

"We stowed away in the cargo bay," Thomas explained, smiling. "You didn't even bother to check."

"You should be more careful," Maggie teased. "And maybe you should learn how to land one of these things." She stabbed a thumb at the smoking ruin that had been the helicopter. "That was a little bumpy."

Hamish X was furious. "I told you to go home. Find your parents! This is no place for you. I have to do this on my own."

"Yeah, whatever." Thomas waved Hamish X off with a dismissive wave of the hand.

"Talk to the elbow," Maggie quipped, extending the bend of her left arm at Hamish X, "'cause the hand is too bored to listen."

"I'm serious," Hamish X said. "You shouldn't have come."

"Is that water?" Thomas asked, licking his lips. "I'm parched."

Thomas moved to grab the handle of the winch but stopped and stood staring past Hamish X into the darkness. Hamish X followed his gaze and saw a human shape outlined in the dim moonlight beyond the well.

"Stay where you are," a deep voice ordered. Hamish X tensed to spring at the figure but heard the click of a rifle safety being released behind him. Suddenly the oasis was full of robed figures, their faces hidden behind scarves that wound around their throats, covering their faces save for their eyes, then continued on to become a headdress. The figures seemed to coalesce[61] out of the sand and darkness into actual human beings. In their hands they held heavy

---

[61] *Coalesce* is a combination form of the words *coal* and *fluoresce*. Coal miners in Pennsylvania in the 1930s would become so blackened with coal dust that they were invisible to one another. Many dangerous accidental collisions led the miners to smear themselves with fluorescent or glowing paint so that they would be visible in the darkness. People would shout, "Hey, look! The coal miners are fluorescing!" That was shortened to "Look! They're coalescing." Now *coalesce* is synonymous with something seeming to solidify out of thin air. What does *synonymous* mean? Go look it up!

automatic rifles. The rifles looked lethal,[62] and all of them were trained on the three children.

"We mean no harm!" Hamish X said clearly, raising his hands so that the strangers could see he held no weapon. Taking his lead, Maggie and Thomas did the same. One of the robed men came forward, walking across the sand until he stood directly in front of the children.

---

[62] You may say, "Of course they look lethal. All rifles are lethal." How wrong you are. There are some rifles that fire tranquilizers and some fire rubber pellets that stun rather than kill. There are also rifles that fire tiny cream pies and are used exclusively by the Clown Armies of Central Nepal.

"Good evening," he said in English. "Would you mind telling me who you are and what you are doing at the oasis of Khar-el-Salaam? Please be quick about it as I do not know how long I can restrain my brethren from shooting you." His English was perfect, although accented. His eyes were pale blue, but the skin of his hands and face was dark from exposure to the desert sun. "Speak or you will be food for the vultures!"

Hamish X and his companions had no doubt that the stranger meant what he said.

Chapter 17

"We are merely passing through and so we stopped at the oasis for water," Hamish X explained. "Or at least that was my plan before you so rudely shot my helicopter out of the sky." In his mind he was calculating the chances of fighting his way free. He believed he could make it, but he doubted Maggie and Thomas would be so lucky. He decided to bide his time. "Surely the laws of courtesy haven't changed in the desert: the oasis is here for anyone to use."

The man's eyes narrowed. "You know the customs of the desert? There is a saying among my people: 'Beware the stranger who speaks the words of a friend.' It hardly seems possible that one so young as you could have been here before. I ask you again: who are you?"

"None of your beeswax, chump," Thomas said loudly. "Now back off or you'll be sorry."

The strangers laughed out loud at Thomas's bravado. The leader raised a hand for silence. "Ha! The tiniest hawk often has the sharpest claws. Ah, I hate to disagree with you, young fellow, but it is my *beeswax*, as you call it. I am responsible for the safety of everyone in my tribe. This oasis lies within our territory. You arrive in an ODA helicopter and that is most suspicious. The Grey Agents are our sworn enemies. If you arrive in one of their vehicles, chances are you will be allies of theirs. As the saying goes, 'He who rides the camel of my enemy is not my friend.' Therefore, I cannot allow you to leave here until you tell me what you are doing and where you are going. Indeed, I cannot allow you to continue to breathe the desert air, for you may pollute it with your falsehoods."[63]

Maggie was about to say something that Hamish X was almost certain would be an insult to the masked man, so he jumped in before she could let loose. "We mean no harm. Our purpose here is peaceful. If you must know, we stole the helicopter from the ODA."

The man's blue eyes went wide. "Is that so?" He shouted over his shoulder in a language the children didn't understand, and his fellows laughed. The man shook his head. "I'm afraid we find that a little hard to credit. Three children stole an ODA helicopter? How is that possible?"

Hamish X smiled. "As it is said among your people: 'The tiniest hawk often has the sharpest claws.' Nothing is impossible ..."

Maggie blurted, "Especially when one of those three children is Hamish X." Hamish X laid a hand on her arm, but it was too late.

---

[63] *Falsehood* is an interesting word. It comes from the Middle Ages when monks, if they were found guilty of lying, were forced to wear a bright red hood or "falsehood" so that everyone in the community would be aware of their guilt. Other transgressions had particular articles of clothing associated as punishments. Thieves were forced to wear bright green gloves. Chronic bedwetters wore bright yellow pants. Nose-pickers wore orange socks ... on their noses. This kind of punishment was very effective until monks started to gain some fashion sense in the early Renaissance and took to committing all the transgressions so they could flounce around in colourful outfits.

The robed men fell silent. Their leader reached up and lowered the scarf from his face, revealing a pointy black beard laced with strands of white. He went down on his knees and reverently touched Hamish X's boots. "Ah," he said, "I thought I recognized those boots. Now I can see how the ODA might come up one helicopter short. Please, forgive us for attacking you. How could we know we were firing on the magnificent Booted Sheik? Welcome, Hamish X, to our oasis. Welcome Companions of Hamish X. I am Sheik Harik Faraad and these gentlemen are members of my tribe." The others moved in closer now. All of them vied with one another for space closer to Hamish X. "We welcome you in fulfillment of the prophecy!"

"Prophecy?" Hamish X was confused and uncomfortable with this formidable desert leader bowing before him. "What prophecy are you talking about?"

"All in good time, Booted Sheik. All in good time." Harik turned to Maggie and Thomas. "Who are these that we might honour them with our friendship?"

"Booted Sheik?" Thomas laughed out loud. "That's funny. Maybe you should shake your booty, Booted Sheik!" Thomas slapped Hamish X on the back. His laughter died when all the desert men snarled and glared at him, their teeth gleaming in the moonlight.

"It does not please them when you mock the Booted One," Harik said softly.

Thomas gulped. Hamish X jumped in.

"I don't mind. They're friends. This is Maggie and her brother, Thomas ...," Hamish X faltered and laughed. "You know, I don't even know your last name."

"Schwinkel," Maggie said.

"Schwinkel?" Hamish X asked, incredulous. Maggie shrugged. "Thomas and Maggie Schwinkel. Until recently, we were all prisoners aboard a slaver ship operated by the ODA."

"A ship?" Harik's brows shot up in surprise. "There are not many ships in the desert, my friend.[64] You must sit with us, break bread, and share this tale, and I will tell you of the prophecy."

Harik called for his men to start a fire and prepare a meal. They set up camp in the lee of the crashed helicopter, using the wrecked vehicle as a shelter from the wind.

Instead of using wood to make a campfire, the men brought heaps of dry crumbly matter that burned steadily but smelled powerfully.

"Camel dung," Harik explained. "There are not so many trees out here in the desert. Burning camel dung is an old Bedouin tradition."

"Charming," said Thomas, waving the fragrant smoke out of his face.

"What's a Bedouin?" Maggie asked.

---

[64] There are truly no ships in the desert. There wouldn't be much point, would there? However, camels are known as the "ships of the desert" because of their capacity to carry heavy loads over long distances while requiring very little in the way of food or water. Animals are often characterized as vehicles in many cultures. The Belgians call ponies the "taxicabs of the pasture" and the people of India are known to call cows the "milk trucks of the jungle." I myself call squirrels the "roller skates of the forest," but I am completely alone in that.

"We are." Harik laughed. "We Bedouins[65] are the last of the nomadic bands of tribesmen who have criss-crossed the deserts for a thousand years and more. We are one with the desert. And we have many uses for camel dung." The man smiled mischievously. "Sometimes, we even eat it." Thomas choked on a brown cake he had been chewing. Harik pounded him on the back. "Dear friend, Thomas. Do not worry. There are only honey, dates, and flour in that cake!" Thomas looked with suspicion at the remainder of the cake in his hand, but in the end he kept on eating. Harik clapped his hands in delight.

"Harik," Hamish X interrupted. "What is this prophecy you spoke about?"

Harik became serious. "In good time, Booted Sheik. In good time. First, tell us how you came to have such a lovely helicopter."

Hamish X was less than pleased, but he realized he was at the mercy of these strange warriors and had little choice.

---

[65] Bedouins are a nation of nomadic peoples who roam the deserts from Saudi Arabia to the Western Sahara. They have a number of different linguistic groups and tribal divisions, but they constitute one single ethnic entity. The name *Bedouin* is shrouded in mystery, although some have said it comes from an ancient practice that saw tribal leaders, or "sheiks" as they are called, betting against one another on horse races. Sometimes these sheiks were compulsive gamblers, betting all their wealth on the outcome of a single race. When they had lost every-thing, they would be left only with the carpets they slept on, and some would even bet these, saying, for example, "I'll bet my bed on the black horse to win." Which was often shortened to "Bed to win!" And shortened still more to "Bedouin." But this may just be a long, amusing story that has no basis in historical fact.

And so, under the stars of the Sahara, Hamish X related the whole tale of the *Christmas Is Cancelled* and the success of the children's uprising. As Hamish X spoke, Harik translated his words into Arabic. The tribesmen listened with intense interest to the story, laughing when Hamish X described the flattening of Ironbuttocks's iron buttocks. Maggie took over whenever Hamish X tried to downplay one of his amazing feats of dexterity or courage.

They sat around in the mellow glow of the flickering firelight, sharing the food of the desert nomads. There were dates, dried beef, camel cheese, and pieces of flatbread smeared with yogourt and butter. They told their whole story up to the point where they landed in the oasis and found the Bedouins waiting for them.

When the story was finished, Harik sat lost in thought for a long time. Finally, he raised his blue eyes from the fire and looked deep into Hamish X's golden ones.

"A tremendous tale, my friends. You are very brave indeed."

"Thank you, Sheik Harik." Hamish X pressed his hands together and touched his fingertips to his forehead in the manner he'd seen the Bedouins use. "And thank you for your hospitality. Other than the fact that you shot us out of the sky, we cannot fault your hospitality. Now ... we have waited long enough. What is this prophecy you spoke of?"

Harik looked at Hamish X, his dark features unreadable. After a long moment, he raised his hands to the sky. "The Prophecy of the Booted One! Praise be!" All the Bedouin raised their hands and shouted aloud in their own language. Harik lowered his hands and smiled. "All of our tribe knows the prophecy of the Booted Sheik. It is an ancient tale handed down from generation to generation. According to the tradition of our people, a time will come when we are sorely oppressed and our livelihood threatened. There will come an enemy too strong for us to battle. Like locusts they will come to devastate our lands and take away all that we need to survive. When our need is most dire, a saviour will come to help us. He will come from the sky and under his boots our enemy will suffer a great defeat. We will be restored to our rightful place. He shall come and he shall wear great boots and he shall trample on the evil ones!" Harik reached up and pulled open his robe, baring his chest. There, over his heart, was a tattoo of a black boot. "We all bear this mark to show our devotion to the prophecy."

"That's a pretty slim prophecy, if you don't mind me saying," Hamish X interjected. "I mean, it could mean anyone with boots on. That's a lot of people. And tattoos?" Hamish X shook his head. "Those are quite permanent. You may regret having a boot on your chest one day."[66]

Harik's eyes flashed and he shook his head. "No, you are wrong. Everything in the prophecy has come to pass. Our people are oppressed by evil folk! We stand to lose everything! Just when the end seems inevitable and the only future for us is annihilation, you come to us! And you fall from the sky just as the prophecy foretold!" Harik reached out and laid a hand on Hamish X's forearm. "I know what

---

[66] Hamish X is right: tattoos are forever. I have never been tattooed because I have very beautiful, soft, pale skin that is completely without blemish. I wouldn't mar such perfection with an anchor or a flaming snake or a raging otter or what have you. I knew a man in Turkey who got a tattoo of a moustache on his upper lip. Utterly foolish. He grew a moustache on top of his moustache tattoo and was arrested because the intensity of his double moustache drove ducks insane. The Turks have some strange ideas, but they are very loyal to their duck population.

you are thinking: this is just a foolish superstition. These backward desert folk believe in old tales. I would have agreed only hours ago. You see, I have only just returned from Oxford where I was studying to become a doctor of medicine. I had left my people and thought their ways foolish and out of touch with the modern world. Then came foreign invaders who took the people's lands and drove them away from their traditional migration routes. They took the oases for themselves. I came home to help in the fight, though I thought the cause an impossible one. I didn't truly believe in ancient prophecies until I saw you climb out of that helicopter, but now I believe. More importantly, my people believe. They have hope again. If you would lead us, I know that despite the odds we can prevail. It is fate! It is destiny!"

Hamish X read the desperation in Harik's eyes. He cast his gaze among the other Bedouin sitting still as stones, cross-legged in the sand or on woven mats, their dark eyes shining in the firelight. Once again, he was expected to be the saviour. Once again, he was to fight a battle for people he hardly knew. What about what he wanted and needed? He had to find the Professor and know who and what he was! He looked down at the boots that had yet again brought him so much responsibility and silently cursed them.

"I don't know what to say," Hamish X admitted finally. "I came here for my own reasons and they have nothing to do with any prophecy. I just need to ... Well, I have my own reasons for being here, that's all. I don't believe in prophecies and I don't believe in fate! And these two ..." He indicated Thomas and Maggie with a dismissive wave of his hand. "These two aren't even supposed to be here! They should be at home with their mother and father!"

"Whatever," Thomas said, grabbing a piece of flatbread and taking a big bite.

"You need backup," Maggie said firmly. "That's why we're here."

Hamish X rolled his eyes and fell silent.

Harik turned to the brother and sister. "You were very brave."

"We did what we had to do," Thomas said, taking a moment to wipe his greasy chin with his sleeve.

"Yes, I see that," Harik said, continuing to look at Hamish X. "I just have one question."

"What's that?" Hamish X asked.

"If you don't believe in the prophecy and you don't believe in fate, then tell me ... Why are you here? At this time and in the desert, what are you doing? Where are you going? I realize we have a rather lovely oasis here. I would hazard to say that it is worth taking over a ship and stealing a helicopter to get here. But something tells me you must have a different destination in mind. So, I ask you again, where exactly are you going?"

"Why should I be going anywhere in particular? Maybe I'm just out for a little sightseeing."

"Ah, my friend. We have another saying among my people: 'If it walks like a camel and smells like a camel and groans like a camel ... burn its dung.' I know we have only just met, but I want you to trust me. Whatever your goal is, we will help you. My people are a people of honour. I promise you, we will not harm or hinder you, but rather we will help if it is within our power. I believe that by helping you, we help ourselves. Thus the prophecy will be fulfilled."

Hamish X didn't answer right away. Thomas and Maggie were watching him intently, along with Harik and all the Bedouin sitting around the fire. He took a deep breath.

"I'm looking for someone," he admitted. "I have reason to believe he is nearby."

"I see." Harik brought a hand to his chin and stroked his wiry beard. "This someone, does he have a name?"

"He's a doctor. I was told he was in this area, providing medical help to poor villagers. His name is Professor Magnus Ballantyne-Stewart."

Harik frowned. He turned to his tribe and spoke. Hamish X heard the Professor's name spoken. The others shook their heads. Harik shrugged. "There have been many doctors coming through here. There is a war raging and many people are driven from their homes. Our opponents try to discourage the doctors and aid workers from coming, but they are brave people. He may be among the doctors in the area, but I have not heard this name."

Hamish X reached for his backpack and dug out the green leather *Great Plumbers* book. He pulled the heavy file King Liam had given him after their basketball game from the centre of the book where he had stuffed it for safekeeping. Setting aside the book, he opened the folder and pulled out the photo of the Professor that had been taken at the unknown airstrip. He held it out to Harik, who took it in one brown hand, tilting it so that the fire-light illuminated the picture.

Harik's eyes widened. "You say there is no fate and no destiny? Ha! I have seen this man. He is one of the international doctors treating the sick and injured in the area. The last I heard, he was at the village of El Arak."

Hamish X's heart leapt. "That's fantastic. Is it far?" He jumped to his feet, eager to leave that very instant.

"It is not far from here, a night's ride through the desert. We know the place well, Hamish X, because as fate would have it, El Arak is our ancestral home. The evil ones occupy it as we speak, holding all those within, our women and children alike, hostage."

Hamish X retrieved the picture, the file, and his book, repacking them in his backpack. Satisfied, he heaved his belongings over his shoulder and smiled at Harik. "Call it prophecy, fate, or just dumb luck," he said. "It seems we have a common goal. Let's go!"

Harik raised a hand. "Hold, my friend. We have a saying: 'He who jumps into a dark hole is instantly blind and may break a leg.'" Harik thought for a moment. "That's a bit of a lame proverb, but it makes good sense. El Arak has been the scene of much fighting recently. It is an ancient stronghold, built into a cliff. The latest reports say that mercenaries[67] in the employ of the ODA have taken over the village and hold hostages. Your doctor is among them, I fear."

"Mercenaries? Hired by the ODA? What possible interest could they have in this barren wasteland?" Thomas asked.

"It might seem barren to some, but beneath the desert sands are minerals that the ODA require for some important project. They hired the mercenaries to secure the area

---

[67] Mercenaries are soldiers who are paid to fight. Soldiers who fight for a country's army usually do it for political reasons, to further the cause of their nation or defend it in times of war. Mercenaries are professional soldiers who sell their services to the highest bidder. Some mercenaries have been known to fight for food coupons, but they are very unsuccessful mercenaries for the most part. I once heard of a mercenary who fought for a sandwich, but he was very, very hungry at the time.

for their mining operations. They have turned El Arak, already a formidable fortress, into an armed camp."

Hamish X groaned and sank back down beside the fire. "I don't believe it. Can this whole journey become any more difficult? I just want to ask him some questions." Hamish X stamped the sand as a sign of his annoyance, his boots flaring in the blue flame. "I've already had to fight a gang of slavers, steal a helicopter, and fly across the desert, and now I have to get into a stronghold guarded by evil mercenaries?"

"Life is unfair," Harik said softly. "But all is not hopeless. We have an old saying: 'If all you have is a bucket full of sand, be thankful at least you have something to carry the sand in.' Why bother going after this doctor? Is it really that important?"

Hamish X looked down at his boots and then up at the star-encrusted black velvet of the night sky. He sighed. "Yes. Yes, it really is that important. I must speak with him if I am ever going to be free." He dusted the sand off his trousers and picked up his pack. "Do me a favour. Take care of these two?" He swept his hand towards Thomas and Maggie. They immediately began to protest.

"No way! We aren't leaving!" Maggie snapped.

"Yeah." Thomas crossed his arms. "We've come this far. We want to see how it ends."

Hamish X was about to argue with them when Harik stood. "Before anyone decides anything, we will show you El Arak. That may make your decision for you." Harik rose to his feet and shouted something to his comrades. Camels, harnesses, and saddles were brought from behind the large dunes. Minutes later, Hamish X, Maggie, and Thomas were trotting through the sand under the moonlight in the company of Harik and his warrior tribe.

Chapter 18

PARVEEN

Parveen scuttled like a mouse through the walls of ODA Headquarters. Using the ventilation shafts as his personal transportation system, he moved silently under the very noses of the ODA. Grey Agents went about their business without the slightest notion that they were being observed, their movements recorded, and their actions catalogued and correlated.

Parveen's plan of action was in fact a plan of no action. He had decided that he must observe his opponents and find a way to exploit their weaknesses. In the days that he had huddled behind access grates watching his quarry, he had come to realize one thing: the disturbing apparatus in the main chamber was the centre of all their operations. To strike a crippling blow against the gate would in turn cripple the ODA.

There were a number of problems facing Parveen as he sat in his little lair, cataloguing his notes and observations. How could he destroy the gate? Explosives would do the trick. He believed he knew where to obtain them in the storerooms of the ODA compound. The armoury was located on the lowest level. Unfortunately, electronic and robotic warders as well as a number of Grey Agents guarded it: a problem, but not an insurmountable one. He had some ideas in that direction.

Destroying the gate might be possible through tampering with the main computers. He had yet to get close enough to observe the mainframe, but given some luck and a little courage, that was also possible.

The only real worry was escaping with his sister and as many of the other prisoners as he could. Would the destruction of the gate bring about the immediate destruction of the whole ODA Headquarters? If he destroyed the gate, did it follow that the Grey Agents would cease to function, or would they remain as dangerous as ever? He didn't know the answers to these questions. He needed more information.

He reviewed his notes and decided it was time to make a move. He had a limited number of hamster bombs in his backpack. They were saved as a last resort. If he used one on a Grey Agent inside the compound, he was certain there would be a general alert. He had to make a choice: the gate and its computer or the armoury. He ruminated on the choices while eating a last protein bar he had found in the bottom of his bag. The bar was a welcome change from the nutrient syrup. Swallowing the final morsel, he made his decision: he would go for the armoury first. Without raw materials, he would not be able to take the computer offline.

He felt better now that he had a distinct goal. Pulling on the hood of his sneaky suit and donning his goggles, he checked his tools and his backpack one last time, taking out a single hamster bomb and tucking it into his pocket. Thus prepared, he ventured off down the main shaft.

He padded softly along the shaft, stopping twice to allow maintenance robots to trundle by, pressing himself against the wall to avoid detection. The robots never registered his presence, leading him to believe that they were not monitored directly by the Grey Agents. The ODA probably never imagined anyone would ever infiltrate their inner sanctum, so they were not specifically looking for intruders. *Their arrogance and overly developed sense of invulnerability could be used against them,* Parveen mused. He watched the second robot trundle away down the shaft and a thought struck him: the Grey Agents paid absolutely no attention to the army of service robots that wandered around the facility. The automatons were practically invisible. That may come in handy. He mentally jotted a note to that effect before heading off to the grate that led out into the main catwalk.

Waiting until the catwalk was relatively clear of traffic, he pushed the grate outward and slipped through, crouching and looking around. He'd had a close call when Mr. Sweet had almost seen him that one time. He had learned to stay as still as possible until he could move without anyone looking directly in his vicinity. The sneaky suit had trouble blending in with the background when that background shifted swiftly. Parveen pressed himself up against the grey wall and stood still for a moment.

He took a look out across the vast chamber at the gate that pulsed softly with its nauseating radiance. Even at this distance, the sight still made him feel ill. The chamber floor was busy as ever. The Grey Agents didn't seem to need extended periods of sleep. At least, they didn't follow any pattern of night and day as human beings tended to do. They worked around the clock without rest.

Parveen took a few deep breaths and tried to remain calm. He hated being out in the open, sneaky suit or not. He was certain that his luck would soon run out. Someone would see him or trip over him and he would be caught.

He pushed his fears aside and waited for someone to pass by on the way to the elevators.

After what seemed like hours, a Grey Agent in a combat jumpsuit strolled by on his way to the plain metal elevator doors. Parveen allowed him to get a few metres ahead before trotting off after him. The Grey Agent strode purposely to the elevator and stopped in front of the doors. He punched a small keypad beside the door, his overlong fingers dancing quickly over the keys as Parveen crept up to within a metre of his back.

The elevator was the only way to get down to the lowest level of the facility. All the ventilation shafts were fitted with proximity alarms and stout steel grating. Parveen believed that, with time, he could have circumvented the alarms, but he would have needed an acetylene torch to burn through the metal grating. Therefore, the elevator was the only option. He would have preferred to crack the code on the keypad lock that protected the elevator and ride down himself, but he decided against it in the end. Even if the sneaky suit had withstood security scrutiny, he imagined that the arrival of a seemingly empty elevator on the lowest level would have sparked undue curiosity. Parveen watched the Grey Agent manipulate the keypad. He wished he could just watch and steal the code, but each Grey Agent seemed to have a different one and the writing on the keypad was not in any alphabet that Parveen had ever seen. There were strange characters on the keys, and he theorized that the Grey Agents had colour codes that registered only in spectra peculiar to their otherworldly eyes. In the end, Parveen had chosen the more dangerous but sure method of sneaking onto the elevator with another rider.

The Grey Agent finished punching the keys and stood back as the elevator door whooshed open. He stepped into the elevator car. As he did so, he heard a rattle and a clink in the rear corner of the cabin. He turned and bent over, finding a small metal screw lying on the floor. He plucked it from the ground and held it up between the thumb and forefinger of one grey-gloved hand. He tilted his head from side to side, puzzling over the tiny screw. He turned his goggled eyes to the ceiling of the car, trying to see if there was an obvious place the screw might have fallen from. Finding no clue as to the screw's origin, he pressed a finger to the side of his head.

"This is Mr. Pastille. Log a request for a maintenance check on the main elevator."

"Acknowledged," came the reply in his ear.

He nodded and tucked the screw into his pocket, watching the doors slide closed.

For the thousandth time Parveen silently thanked heaven that he'd thought to bring along the sneaky suit. Without it he would have been sunk long ago. He had taken a screw from the ventilation shaft cover, and the little object had provided him with the distraction he needed to board the elevator car behind Mr. Pastille. Now he stood pressed against the back wall praying that the Grey Agent would not turn around.

His prayers were answered. Mr. Pastille stared resolutely forward as the car lurched and dropped down the shaft, slowing and stopping seconds later at the armoury level. The doors whooshed open to reveal a long corridor stretching out away from the elevator. Mr. Pastille stepped out of the elevator unaware that Parveen was right on his heels.

Parveen stayed as close to the Grey Agent as he dared, trotting silently in the creature's shadow as Mr. Pastille made his way along the corridor. Every two metres a bright light shone down from overhead. Parveen tried to stay out of the harsh pools of light, keeping close to the metal wall of the corridor. Still, he felt horribly exposed. If he made even the slightest sound or Mr. Pastille decided to turn and look carefully along the corridor behind him, the game could be up.

After a hundred metres, the corridor came to an end in a heavy steel door. In the centre of the door was a winking red light. Mr. Pastille stopped in front of the door.

"Identify," said a feminine voice. Parveen had grown used to the voice of the computer called Mother. She was the central nervous system of the whole Headquarters.

"Pastille," Mr. Pastille announced in a clear, lifeless voice.

There was a second's pause before the computer said, "Identification affirmative. Enter."

The winking red light turned a solid green. The door swung silently inward. Mr. Pastille stepped through the door. Parveen waited until the door began to swing shut before slipping through. He immediately stepped to one side and crouched down.

The armoury was packed to the rafters with weaponry. Rack after rack of rifles and pistols hung suspended from the ceiling. The grey combat armour favoured by the ODA hung on rails along one wall, looking like the hollowed-out husks of vile, human-sized insects. Hanging from the ceiling in the centre of the room was a huge crystal sphere filled with the multicoloured butterflies that the Grey Agents had unleashed upon the inhabitants of the Hollow Mountain during the assault. The beautiful, deadly things were lifeless now. Dormant, awaiting the dark command of their masters, they clustered on the transparent walls of their container.

Arrayed on the wall opposite the combat armour was a series of metal cubbyholes containing jetpacks, shiny, polished, and ready for use. Parveen longed to grab one of them, but he didn't know how he'd be able to secrete it out of the armoury. The pack was too bulky to fit under his suit or in his small backpack. He would have to do without. The rifles and pistols were tempting, but he reminded himself that he had never used one. If Mimi were here (and oh how he missed her now), she'd have a field day arming herself with the ODA's own weapons.

No. He knew what he needed. He just had to find it. He looked to Mr. Pastille. The Grey Agent was coming off guard duty and was taking off his weapons for storage. Parveen had to work fast.

He moved as swiftly as he dared along the racks of rifles and pistols. He reached the end of the row and found a series of lockers facing him. They were labelled in the same weird script he had seen all over the Headquarters. He checked to make sure Mr. Pastille was still occupied and then carefully reached out and tugged on the handle of the closest locker.

He held his breath, anticipating an alarm.

None came. The locker opened easily. Inside were neatly stacked bricks of a putty-like substance. Parveen picked one up and held it close to his face, examining it.

He'd read about such material in science magazines and on the internet. One name for it was plastic explosive. The material was highly explosive if ignited using the proper electronic detonators. Parveen quickly searched the locker but found no detonators. No matter. He could scavenge parts and make one himself. Then he could destroy the gate. He had what he needed. Now it was time to go.

He closed the locker and turned around to find Mr. Pastille standing directly in front of him. The Grey Agent looked down and Parveen saw himself as a greyish blotch reflected in the dark surface of Mr. Pastille's goggles.

"Well, well, well. What have we here?"

Mr. Candy and Mr. Sweet

Parveen thought that the locker was not connected to any alarm, but, alas, he was wrong. As soon as he opened the locker door, a contact was broken, sending a silent signal through the massive nervous system that was the artificial intelligence known as Mother. Like an itch on the end of a human nose is signalled to the brain along the nerves via[68] electrical impulses, so Mother's brain was alerted to the itch that was Parveen opening a locker he was not authorized to open.

Mr. Candy and Mr. Sweet were sitting in the kitchen of the house at 174 Angell Street, combing through intelligence reports, trying to figure out where Hamish X could possibly be, when a chime sounded. The dial of the chrome radio glowed and Mother's rich voice filled the kitchen.

"Unauthorized access of ordnance storage locker. Armoury level. Intruder unknown."

Mr. Sweet and Mr. Candy were instantly on their feet. Mrs. Guardian, rinsing the teacups in the sink, froze. A teacup, clenched in one of her knobbly arthritic hands, exploded as she squeezed it.

---

[68] *Via* is a Latin word that means "by way of." Example: I entered the house *via* the door. Or I'm going to New York *via* Washington. One wonders why we don't all still speak Latin because it seems to have a shorter way of saying most things.

"Shall I investigate?" she asked, holding her hand up to inspect it for damage. The hand was whole save for one long shard of china that was embedded in her palm. She examined the shard with frank curiosity but registered no pain.

"No." Mr. Candy shook his head. Speaking to the radio, he demanded, "Who is the closest agent to the armoury?"

"Mr. Pastille is currently in the armoury," Mother informed him.

"What?" Mr. Sweet's normally emotionless voice registered the slightest nuance of confusion. "How is it possible that he sees no intruder then?"

"Shall I alert Mr. Pastille to the situation?"

"Immediately. And detach a cohort of agents to the site. We shall go there at once."

"One moment please," Mother said, stopping the two Grey Agents as they moved for the elevator. "I am receiving a report from one of our agents in North Africa. According to our assets on the ground, two agents have been neutralized and a child procurement vessel scuttled in the Western Mediterranean. Helicopter 7A is missing."

Mr. Sweet and Mr. Candy exchanged a glance. Mr. Candy spoke. "Can you track the helicopter, Mother?"

"Correlating satellite data." There was a short pause. "Current location of helicopter designated 7A is South Sahara Desert, one hundred kilometres from the fortress of El Arak. This is also the last known location of Professor Magnus Ballantyne-Stewart."

Mr. Sweet and Mr. Candy stood in silence for a moment.

"It must be Hamish X," Mr. Sweet said.

"Indeed, Mr. Sweet. The chance of a coincidence is low."

"I agree, Mr. Candy. There could be no other explanation. Mother?"

"I'm listening."

"Assign Mr. Pastille to hold the intruder until aid arrives. Arrange travel for Mr. Candy and myself. We must be in El Arak within the day."

Mrs. Guardian pulled the shard of china from her palm. No blood flowed from the wound. "Orders, Mr. Sweet?"

"Remain at your post. The portal will be opened soon. No one can interfere. If anyone attempts to enter, deter them. Lethally."

Mrs. Guardian smiled. On a normal elderly woman's face, the expression would have been charming. Something about the coldness of her eyes and the set of her yellow teeth made the smile terrible. "Yes, Mr. Sweet."

Without another word, Mr. Candy and Mr. Sweet moved swiftly to the elevator. The doors opened and swallowed them up.

Chapter 19

MIMI

Mimi and Cara walked a few paces behind Xnasha as their host led them to the gathering in the temple. Mimi grasped Cara by the elbow, slowing her pace so they could drop farther behind out of earshot.

"Time is wastin'," Mimi said, leaning close and speaking softly into the other girl's ear. "One way or t'other, we gotta get outta here. Aidan and Parveen need us."

Cara whispered, "Maybe we can convince them to let us use that submarine. Borrow it maybe?"

"I wouldn't hold my breath," Mimi hissed. "Besides, who's gonna drive it? You?"

"Maybe." Cara tossed her head haughtily.

"Ferget it," Mimi said. "We'd just get 'rselves killed tryin'. Mebbe if Parv were here, he could figger it out, but he ain't so I wouldn't risk it."

"What then? Are we going to walk to Providence?"

"We have to git to the surface and then we'll start worryin' about that."

"We have our chance to convince them at this council meeting," Cara said. "Just let me do the talking."

"Y'all give it a try, but remember: patience ain't my strong suit."

"I doubt I'll ever forget that," Cara groaned.

The two girls picked up the pace and caught up with Xnasha as the woman headed across the square, joining the stream of Atlanteans heading towards the imposing temple that housed the Crystal Fountain. None of the Hollow Mountain refugees had been allowed to enter the temple the day before. The building was off limits, Xnasha had explained this morning over a breakfast of fish and strange biscuits baked from seaweed and plankton flour. The Temple of the Crystal Fountain was guarded day and night by armed and armoured Atlanteans. Their hosts had allowed the visitors freedom to roam anywhere they liked in the city except for the temple. Mimi had woken early and gone for a jog around the square. She had tried to enter twice but both times had been turned politely but firmly away. Mimi doubted that the guards would have been any match for her in a fight, but she decided to leave well enough alone for the time being, pushing her curiosity aside until later in the day when the council meeting would begin.

As she wandered the ancient city, Mimi searched for a way she might leave the realm of the Atlanteans if their hosts decided they would offer no help in fighting the Grey Agents. She had to find Parveen, and Cara needed to find out the fate of her brother, Aidan. They had both agreed they would go on alone if they had to. But Mimi's search for an exit was fruitless.[69] The silver gate was sealed,

---

[69] A *fruitless* search: the expression comes from the ancient Greek tradition of rewarding children with a piece of fruit whenever they managed to find their way through a maze constructed by the city elders. The tradition was designed to improve children's sense of direction, to occupy the children for a while so their parents could get some work done, and to get rid of excess fruit. A child who didn't find his or her way through the maze received no fruit and therefore their search had been fruitless.

and the only way out appeared to be the submarines Xnasha had shown them. They were at the mercy of the Atlanteans.

Xnasha had been quiet all morning, barely talking during breakfast. Her brother, Xnasos, had asked after her health, but she had waved away his concern.

"I'm not ill. Just thinking, brother."

"Thinking?" Xnasos snorted, stuffing a piece of cured fish into his mouth. "Are you *sure* you're not ill?" Xnasha didn't rise to the teasing, another sign that she was not her normal self.

Now, Xnasha guided her guests in silence. She watched as her brother mounted the steps of the Temple of the Crystal Fountain. The temple guards bowed their heads as he passed, respect shown to any who bore the responsibility of the leadership of Atlantis. A crowd of Atlanteans had gathered, waiting for Xnasos, and as he approached the doors were flung open and the pale stone steps were awash with an ambient glow that pulsated from within the temple.

Atlanteans climbed the steps and entered the arching doorway, chatting in hushed tones among themselves. Mrs. Francis and Mr. Kipling stood waiting at the bottom of the steps. When Mrs. Francis saw the two girls and their escort approaching, she left off wringing her hands long enough to give them a smile and a little wave.

"Oh, there you are! I was getting worried," the pudgy woman said.

"Why?" Mimi shook her head. "Where could we possibly go?"

"Still." Mrs. Francis crushed Mimi and Cara in a hug that had both girls cringing. "I always feel a bit better when you're somewhere I can keep an eye on you."

"Oh, brother," Mimi groaned.

"Ditto," added Cara, fixing her hair.

Mr. Kipling laughed. "I'm glad you two are back. She has someone else to fret over."

Xnasha stood by, smiling at the exchange. She bowed and indicated the doorway. "Shall we go in? It looks as though everyone is assembled."

Mimi grunted and headed up the steps, followed closely by Cara and the two adults, with Xnasha in the rear.

Mimi was quite unprepared for the sight that greeted her in the temple. Since her arrival in Atlantis she had seen much of the ancient city. The entire metropolis had an air of decrepit grandeur and faded glory. The buildings still occupied by the citizens were tidy enough inside, but the exteriors were slightly tarnished, the colours washed out. The gardens of unfamiliar plants had run wild, bursting from their beds and planters. Everything was just a little unkempt.

The temple was a complete about-face. Coming in the high doors, she found herself in an airy, circular amphitheatre with seats rising all around the walls. An arched and vaulted ceiling soared above, inlaid with millions of tiny bits of glittering glass, dazzling the eye and throwing light back to dance in multicoloured firefly patterns on the people gathered below. Though the rest of Atlantis was rundown, the temple was beautifully maintained, polished, and in perfect repair.

The seats sloped down in a circle sunken below the level of the entrance, and Mimi found she was halfway up from the central platform at the base of the amphitheatre. The entire population of Atlantis and the refugees from the Hollow Mountain were enough to fill only about a quarter of the seats. Mimi could hardly imagine all the seats being full at the height of the Atlantean civilization. Everywhere, Hollow Mountainers were interspersed with Atlanteans. In the short time the children had been in Atlantis, they had practically been adopted by the ancient folk. Their arrival had sparked a reawakening of the parental instinct in the people of the sunken city. Mimi thought that boded well for her cause. She looked to the centre of the amphitheatre.

The temple's many charms paled in comparison to what stood on the platform at the base of the amphitheatre. In the middle of the circular dais was a fountain, simple and unadorned, carved out of the pale native rock. The carving wasn't complicated: just a circle of stone rising up a metre from the floor with a single tube of white stone in the centre. What was truly incredible was the liquid gushing from the fountain.

Whereas every fountain Mimi had ever heard of spouted water, the fountain below her emitted a stream of what appeared to be glowing liquid crystal. To the human eye, the liquid had all the properties of normal water, but it was somehow denser and more ... The only word that came to Mimi's mind was *perfect*. The rich azure blue of the fountain shone with a rippling internal radiance that was caught by the mosaic ceiling and sent back in shattered brilliant sparkles to rain down upon the people gathered below. Mimi felt the presence of the fountain as a low thrill of power pulsing softly through her body. The hairs on her arms and on the nape of her neck stood up in response to the power hanging in the air.

There was something strange about the fountain that Mimi couldn't immediately put her finger on. She watched its cascade for a full minute before finally hitting on it.

"It's too slow," she mused. The water moved up through the air and dropped as though in slow motion, as if gravity's normal effect had been weakened in the area the fountain occupied. "The water is flowin' like molasses."[70]

"What's molasses?"

Mimi turned to find Xnasha standing beside her.

"Uh, it's like ... uh ... well, it sure ain't water!"

"The Crystal Fountain isn't made of water," Xnasha said. "It is an ancient artifact of our people. We no longer have the knowledge of its construction. We know only that it is responsible for our well-being. The fountain's power keeps us healthy, extends our lives, and keeps us hidden. As long as the crystal flows, Atlantis will endure."

They fell silent for a moment, contemplating the wondrous fountain as the hall filled and the Atlanteans took their places.

"Has it ever stopped flowin'?" Mimi thought of the millions of tons of seawater held in place overhead by the beautiful cascade of liquid light below.

"Not yet." Xnasha shook her head. "But there are those among us, the oldest ones, who say it flows less powerfully than it once did." Xnasha smiled. "Don't worry. It's never stopped and it won't today." She took Mimi's elbow. "Come. The council meeting is about to convene. Xnasos would be furious with me if I cause any delay."

Mimi, Cara, Mrs. Francis, and Mr. Kipling followed Xnasha down broad stone steps to a bench in the front row. Xnasos, sitting on a small stone block on the platform beside

---

[70] Molasses is raw, unrefined sugar in the form of thick black syrup that is delicious on pancakes. If spread all over one's body, it is very effective at deterring weasels and preserving body heat. Don't ask me how I know that ... I just do. Go back to the story.

the fountain, glared at Xnasha, who smiled sweetly and took a seat beside Mimi. Seated so close to the fountain, Mimi was even more impressed by it. The liquid shot up to within centimetres of the ceiling, a single powerful jet. Unlike fountains made of water, there was no fragmentation of the stream: no droplets fell away. The crystal flowed back upon itself in a single unbroken ribbon. Mimi had to tear her eyes away from the hypnotic glow when Xnasos began to speak.

"Citizens of ATLANTIS!" he boomed, arms raised. "Honoured GUESTS!" His voice echoed off the stone walls impressively.

"There's no need to shout," said a man in the back row.

"Don't interrupt," Xnasos snapped. "I'm making a speech."

"But I can hear you just fine without the shouting and I'm in the back row," the man pointed out.

Xnasos took a deep, calming breath and forced a smile. "Fine. Citizens of Atlantis! Honoured guests."

"You said that part," a woman interrupted.

"I am just repeating it because I was INTERRUPTED!"

"You're yelling again!" from the back row.

"Well, I wouldn't be yelling and repeating myself if you didn't keep interrupting me!" Xnasos was a little red in the face now.

"Get to the point. We haven't got all day! These children need their nap soon! They don't have the patience to listen to you shouting and, frankly, neither do I," the woman said impatiently, tickling the toddler she held in her lap. The rest of the crowd clapped their hands in agreement. Xnasos was about to explode into a furious tirade when Xnasha stood up and faced the crowd.

"In a nutshell," she said, "we have to decide if the children from the Hollow Mountain can stay with us, for how long, and what other aid we want to give them." Xnasha sat back down next to Mimi.

The woman pointed at Xnasha. "See? That's the way to do it. Get to the point!"

"And no shouting!" added the man at the back.

Xnasos was beside himself. "*I* am the speaker! *I* am in charge of the meeting!" He banged his staff on the stone floor. A shiver of energy passed through the hall. Behind him the fountain pulsed a deeper blue. Everyone gasped and started muttering among themselves.

"The fountain doesn't like it when people get angry," Xnasha whispered.

"You mean that thing's alive?" Mimi whispered back.

"Not exactly." Xnasha shrugged. "But nobody really knows."

"Forgive me, O Fountain," Xnasos said, bowing. He held up his hands for silence. At last, the crowd settled down again. "As my sister so ably pointed out, we must make decisions. We have welcomed the Hollow Mountain refugees into our city and into our homes. At present, it is a temporary arrangement. I have been passing among you and gathering opinions, gauging the mood of the citizens, and I think I represent the majority of you when I say the following: we would like to welcome all the newcomers to stay among us as full citizens!"

A general swell of applause and cheering greeted this announcement. The fountain seemed to pick up the good feeling from the assembly, pulsating a brighter, warmer blue.

"I suggest we put it to the vote." Xnasos raised his staff. Thousands of Atlantean voices cried out their assent. "Opposed?" Silence. Xnasos beamed. "Excellent! The motion is carried."

Cheering went up from Atlanteans and children alike.

Mimi looked around at all the Hollow Mountain children's happy faces. She saw the joy and relief they felt knowing they had a place of safety after losing the only home most of them had known. Even Mrs. Francis looked relieved to know the children would have a safe place to rest with people who cared.

Mimi couldn't rest, though. She looked over and saw that Cara wasn't pleased either. Cara felt Mimi's eyes on her and turned. She looked into Mimi's eyes and shook her head. Standing, she raised her hands for silence.

"Xnasos," she began. "People of Atlantis. Friends from the Hollow Mountain." She paused and looked at the flowing crystal. "Fountain?" She shrugged and continued, "We are humbly grateful for your kindness and your hospitality. You have taken us in at a time when we had nowhere else to go and for that we can never repay you." The smile left Cara's face. "But we must ask your aid in one more matter. We have lost many friends. They have been stolen from us and they need our help. My brother, Mimi's friend Parveen, and many, many more were taken when the ODA destroyed the Hollow Mountain. We don't know their fate. We don't know whether they are alive or dead, but we know we must do everything we can to find out and free them."

The Atlanteans fell silent, and even the fountain's tinkling fall seemed hushed. Cara gazed around the amphitheatre at the faces of the assembly. Mimi had to admit, the girl was a natural public speaker.

"I don't begrudge anyone from the Hollow Mountain who wishes to stay here in safety. You've been through a lot and you deserve at least a place to sleep and the care of good people." Cara paused and smiled at Xnasha, who blushed. "But I am going to try to free my brother. I am going to Providence. I am going to the Headquarters of the ODA and I *will* free him or die trying. Thank you for your offer of sanctuary, but I, for one, can't accept it while one child suffers under the control of the Grey Agents."

Cara stopped speaking and looked out over the crowd. The children, cheering only moments before, were now silent. The Atlanteans shook their heads. Xnasos stood and spoke.

"It is folly to challenge the Grey Agents at any place or time, but to attempt to infiltrate their Headquarters is complete madness. You will be captured and join your brother in whatever fate has befallen him." For once, none of the Atlanteans disagreed with their spokesman. "Stay here and live with us in safety. Believe me, we have first-hand knowledge of how terrible the Grey Agents can be."

"We know!" Mimi sprang to her feet, unable to stay in her seat any longer. She faced the crowd. "We know all about the war your ancestors fought. Xnasha told us everything."

Xnasos's eyes flared angrily. He pointed at Xnasha. "How could you divulge[71] our secrets?"

Xnasha shook her head. "It wasn't right to keep them in the dark. In a way, we, or rather our people, are responsible for bringing those creatures into this world. It isn't right for us to hide down here and let the rest of the world deal with our mess."

"We are safe here!" Xnasos thundered.

"Don't you people git it?" Mimi shouted. "You ain't safe anywhere! They ain't gonna let ya live in peace. They want

---

[71] *Divulge* is a fancy word for *tell*. Divulging, however, is worse than just telling. Only secrets can be divulged. Next time someone tells one of your secrets, point at them and shout, "Divulger!" They will be confused. You will gain the respect of dictionary writers everywhere.

ta take everythin'. They want our whole darn world fer themselves! Y'all may be safe here fer a while, but they're gonna come callin' and you ain't gonna be able ta keep 'em out forever, even with all yer fancy domes and yer Crystal Fountains 'n all."

"Mimi." Cara laid a hand on Mimi's arm, but the tall Texan girl shook it off.

"No, I ain't gonna be quiet and I ain't gonna siddown. You people are gonna have to decide if yer gonna help us 'r not and if ya ain't, well then show me the way outta here cause I got butts to kick and they're all attached ta Grey Agents." Mimi folded her arms over her chest and glared at the assembled crowd. Cara stood by Mimi's side.

The amphitheatre was silent save for the gush of the Crystal Fountain. The deep blue was tinged by deeper hues of indigo and violet. The silence stretched out uncomfortably. At last, Xnasha rose and went to stand beside the girls.

"I will go with you," she said softly. When her brother opened his mouth to protest, she raised a hand and shook her head. "No, Xnasos. I won't change my mind. We must take some responsibility for the past. I will go and help them if I am able. I will represent our people on this quest because it is the right thing to do ..." She smiled. "And I've always wanted to see the blue sky."

THE NEXT MORNING Mimi, Cara, and Xnasha took their seats in the control cabin of the submarine. Xnasos had pleaded with his sister to change her mind, but Xnasha had held firm, insisting that they take the small craft she had lovingly restored. The remaining members of the Royal Swiss Guards who had volunteered occupied the crew cabins. Every surviving Guard wanted a chance to strike a blow at the ODA in revenge for the loss of their King, of their Guard leader, and of their home.

After a long and tearful argument, Mr. Kipling had convinced Mrs. Francis that he should go along on the mission. To his astonishment, when he arrived at the pier to board the ship, he found his wife waiting for him, her bag packed.

"Isobel," he said firmly. "I forbid you to come."

"Oh fiddle-dee-poo! You can't forbid me to do anything. I'm coming and that's final."

"But, dear," Mr. Kipling begged. "Please understand. It's for your own safety. This will be a very dangerous trip."

Mrs. Francis put down her bag and placed her hands on her hips. "Rupert, you are my husband and I love you, but do not presume to tell me what to do. I will not leave you now or ever. I am coming on this trip and you can't make me stay behind, waiting for you to return and wondering if you ever will."

Mr. Kipling looked down into her round, determined face and chuckled softly. "Oh, I do love you. May I at least carry your bag, my dear?"

"Of course," Mrs. Francis sniffed. "Think of this as a honeymoon."

Xnasha's goodbye to Xnasos was terse. Her brother was still furious with her for flouting his wishes, but he kissed her on the forehead before she boarded the submarine. Just before she shut the hatch behind her, she stopped and smiled at him. "Don't worry, brother. I will return."

"See that you do," Xnasos said softly.

She smiled again and slammed the hatch tight.

The crowd of Atlanteans and Hollow Mountainers cheered as the submarine's running lights began to glow. With a gurgle and a frothing maelstrom of bubbles, the vessel released its mooring cables, sank into the dark waters of the docking bay, and moved slowly off like a vast glowing fish gliding beneath the surface.

Inside the cabin, Mimi and Cara watched as Xnasha moved her hands in the air above the glowing crystal panel, guiding the ship through the bay towards a dark opening that turned out to be a tunnel carved into the stone wall. The tunnel would lead them out into the open sea.

"Wait a minute," Mimi said suddenly.

"Did you forget something?" Cara asked, worried.

"Shore did," Mimi said. "We ain't named our ship yet."

"Is that customary?" Xnasha asked. "This ship may have had a name when it was built, but I doubt any would remember it now."

"It's a she, not an it," Mimi said pointedly. "And I guess it's up to us to name her."[72]

"Why not the *Rhode Island Red*?" Xnasha said after a moment's thought.

Mimi and Cara laughed.

"*Rhode Island Red* it is," Mimi cried. "Set a course fer Providence. The chickens are comin' home to roost."

"You do have a strange way of talking." Xnasha shook her head and pressed her hands forward. A vibration thrummed through the hull as the submarine surged forward.

They set off on their journey to confront the ODA in their lair.

"Hold on, Parveen," Mimi said softly. "I'm comin'."

---

[72] Mimi is referring to the unwritten law that all ships are considered female. No one knows the origin of this tradition, but it is strictly adhered to. All ships are called she. What is less well known is that all buses are called he and all airplanes are called Mr. Wiggly. I have yet to have anyone fully explain the reason for this.

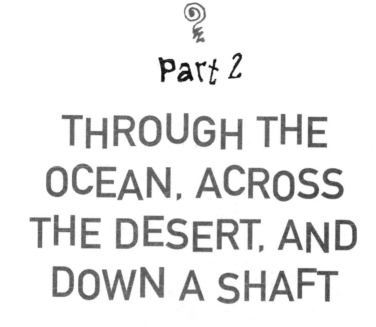

Part 2

THROUGH THE OCEAN, ACROSS THE DESERT, AND DOWN A SHAFT

A Note from the Narrator

I love ponies, don't you? They're just like horses, only smaller. You can do everything with a pony that you can do with a horse only with a smaller area to work in. What a bonus for people who wish to own a member of the equine species but have limited space: condo owners, lighthouse keepers, submarine commanders ...

Oops! I didn't mean to mention submarines! I was trying to give you a brief respite from the overwhelming tension of the story, distracting you with a little pony chat, then I ruin everything by going and mentioning submarines. The last thing I wanted to do was remind you of how dire the situation is for our heroes and heroine. The Grey Agents have discovered Parveen! Hamish X is about to join the assault on a desert fortress, and Mimi is setting off on a voyage that will take her into the lair of the ODA! How can you stand the tension? If I were you, I'd set the book down and do a couple of deep knee bends, take a hot bath, or run around the block four times, just to relieve the pressure.

You laugh? You think you can handle it? It's only a story, you say? Stories are extremely powerful things. Narrators must constantly be aware of the power of their written words. We were all told at the Guild of one narrator who told a story so frightening that an entire town refused to go to sleep for seven years for fear of having nightmares. There was a run on eyedrops and espresso. It wasn't pretty.

I had to put the little bit in about the ponies as a sort of emotional braking system. Believe me, you'll thank me for it later on. I won't hear you thanking me, of course, as this is a book ... that is, unless I'm sitting next to you by some strange coincidence while you're reading it.

Before we get back to the story, one more thing about ponies. Did you know, dear readers, that in prehistoric times there existed many varieties of miniature horses? By *miniature* I mean that some of these horse creatures were less than a foot tall. Such a pony could conceivably run up one's pant leg were the pant leg in question baggy enough. I once had a full-grown horse run up my pant leg, but I shan't waste your time describing the incident. Suffice it to say that I will never wear pants that baggy again.

Chapter 20

PARVEEN

Parveen's first instinct was to run, but Mr. Pastille was just too quick. His long-fingered hands clamped down on Parveen's shoulders like a pair of vises.

"Where are you going, slippery little boy?" Mr. Pastille cocked his head to one side. "And how did you manage to get into our Headquarters?"

Parveen was terrified. He wanted to say something clever like Hamish X would, to be defiant and fearless like Mimi, but nothing would come. His brain was frozen, paralyzed with fear. He was finished. Noor was finished. He had failed.

Mr. Pastille pinched the fabric of the sneaky suit between his fingers and rolled it experimentally. "What a fascinating suit you have. I suppose that is why you were able to sneak in here without me seeing you." He lifted Parveen off his feet and carried him towards the door. "Let's wait for the security detail, shall we? Then we'll take you where you belong: hook you up to the generator with all the other filthy little creatures."

Hearing the Grey Agent refer to the children in the Hall of Batteries reached through Parveen's terror. His sister wasn't a filthy creature. She was a person and this was her world, not Mr. Pastille's. The anger Parveen felt, the outrage, jarred his brain into action again. He cast his eyes around the room, searching for some way out of his predicament. Nothing presented itself to his desperate eyes. He decided to keep Mr. Pastille talking. Maybe the Grey Agent would say something Parveen could use.

"I ... I guess you've caught me. I knew I couldn't hope to outwit you agents for long."

"Of course not," Mr. Pastille sneered, exposing yellowed teeth. "You humans are inferior in every way. When we take this world from you, you will finally see what true intellect is." Using one powerful hand, Mr. Pastille pressed Parveen against the wall beside the door, the boy's feet dangling almost a metre above the ground. "We are so close to opening the portal, and when we do, your world will change forever."

Parveen listened to the agent with interest despite his discomfort. So the apparatus in the main chamber *was* a gate of some kind. "Portal? How amazing! I have to admire the genius of your people. Maybe you could satisfy my curiosity on one point, considering that you have me completely in your power."

Mr. Pastille cocked his head. "What point?"

"Hamish X," Parveen said. "Why is he so important to you?"

"Ah." Mr. Pastille shrugged. "He is the key to the portal, of course. When we find him, he will be brought back here and the gateway between our world and yours will be opened. Your world will be made more perfect."

Parveen's heart leapt. Hamish X was still at large! The ODA didn't know where he was. There was still hope. Parveen looked at the flashing red light in the centre of the metal door. He had to get out. "Wow," Parveen said with false appreciation as he casually fished in his pocket. "I guess that's that. We really can't hope to defeat the ODA. What are we but puny, weak, foolish humans?

If I wasn't hanging above the floor like this, I'd bow down before your superior intellect, Mr. ...? Mr. ...?"

"Pastille."

"Identification confirmed," said the voice of Mother. As the door swung open, Parveen jammed the hamster bomb he had secreted in his pocket into the Grey Agent's face. The furry ball latched on to Mr. Pastille's cheek and with a flare of energy fried his circuits. Mr. Pastille fell in a heap on the floor.

Parveen tore himself out of the death grip of the fallen agent and ran through the door into the corridor. With the backpack holding a kilogram of plastic explosive slapping against his back, he tore down the corridor towards the elevator. He was five metres away when the doors opened to reveal four armed agents. As they disgorged from the elevator, checking their weapons, Parveen pressed himself against the wall, blending into the grey metal. His sneaky suit was his only defence. He held his breath and prayed that it would work this one last time.

His luck held. The agents hefted their rifles and dashed directly past him down the corridor towards the armoury. Taking his chance, he ran for the elevator, sliding through the doors as they hissed shut. One of the agents turned at the sound of Parveen's footfalls.

"Stop! Stay where you are!" The agent raised his rifle, but not in time. The doors closed. Breathing heavily, Parveen leaned against the wall of the car, sweat soaking him as he tried to think what to do next.

The car began to rise. He had to act quickly. He could only assume that there would be enemies waiting for him when the elevator reached the next floor.

"You cannot escape." Mother's voice filled the car. "I am aware of your presence now. I have been analyzing my watch logs and I've noticed discrepancies: food sap levels depleted, air flow blockages, heat imbalances. Now that I have located the cause, it is a matter of a very short time before I corner you. Why bother running? Surrender yourself and the end will be quick. Listen to Mother." The voice was filled with maternal concern.

"You aren't my mother." Parveen shook his head. "And I'd rather make you work for it." Reaching into his backpack, he pulled out his multitool, flipped out the screwdriver attachment, and rammed it into the control panel.

"Stop that."

Parveen ignored the voice, jamming the metal prong of the screwdriver into the edge of the keypad and prying the cover off.

"I order you to stop that, young man!"

Parveen failed to comply. He thrust the pointy end of the tool into the mess of wires and circuit boards again and again until, at last, the lights in the elevator flickered and went out. The car ground to a halt and the voice cut out in mid-sentence.

"Even if you stop the elevator, you can't escaZZZZZZT!"

Parveen looked at his handiwork and smiled. At least now he had a moment to think. He flicked a dial on his goggles and the darkness dissipated into a greenish glow of night vision. He looked around the walls of the car for an access panel, but he couldn't see one.

"What? Don't they ever have to repair these things? Even the ODA can't make anything that never breaks down." He looked up at the ceiling of the car and saw it: a square panel that was almost invisible against the uniform grey of the elevator car. Parveen quickly traded his multitool for a strange-looking device he pulled out of his backpack. It was a metal disc with a metal eyelet attached to one side. He also drew out a length of rope and threaded one

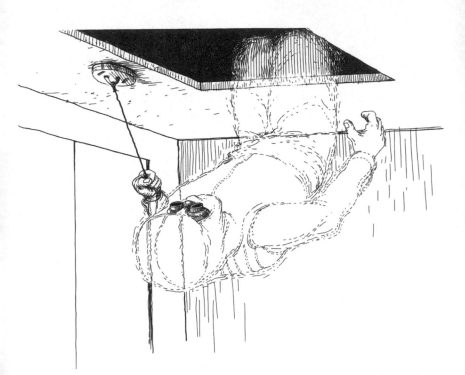

end of it through the eyelet, knotted it, and then flipped a
small switch on the disc. A humming sound filled the car.
The disc bucked like a live thing in Parveen's hand. He held
the disc face up towards the ceiling and let it go.

Like a bullet out of a gun, the powerful electromagnetic
disc flew out of his hand and stuck with a clang to the
ceiling, the rope dangling down to Parveen below.

The small boy grabbed the rope and laboriously hauled
himself up until he could reach the access panel. Swinging
from the rope, he drove his feet into the centre of the panel
and it flew open, revealing a square of darkness. Parveen
swung away and back towards the opening, hooking his knees
over the edge. Reaching out with one hand, he grabbed the
rim of the access panel and pulled himself up. His chest
heaving from the exertion, he sat and regained his breath.

"This is Mimi's job. I'm not really an acrobat," he said out loud to no one at all. He looked around to find he was sitting beside a tangle of thick cables that snaked away up the shaft above him. He hardly had a moment to take this in when the car jerked and started rising.

"Uh-oh." He ducked his head back into the car, flicked the switch on the magnetic grapple hook (another of his inventions), and pulled it and the rope up. He stuffed them into his pack and slammed the access panel shut.

The elevator car picked up speed. In seconds, Parveen would be back up to the level of the great chamber. He ducked down and thought about his next move. His only option was to return to the ventilation shafts, keep moving, and try to avoid capture long enough to sabotage[73] the gate. Getting Noor out had been next to impossible before he had been discovered. Now that the Grey Agents knew there was an intruder in Headquarters, escaping with Noor would require a miracle.

"That's all right," Parveen said, adjusting his goggles. "I'll build a miracle for you, Noor. All I need are tools and time."

The elevator slowed and came to a stop. Parveen heard agents pounding on the elevator doors and shouting for his surrender.

---

[73] *Sabotage* is an interesting word. It comes from France. Peasants in the sixteenth and seventeenth centuries wore wooden clogs called "sabots." When landowners began to introduce machines that threatened to put the peasants out of work, the peasants would toss their wooden sabots into the machinery to foul the works. Hence, sabotage. Goodness knows I've been tempted to do the same with my own shoes when I find machines frustrating. I have especial disdain for my computer, but it's hard to find shoes small enough to insert into a processor chip. I suppose I could go on the internet and look for molecular shoes. Perhaps at cybershoes.com or maybe virtualclogs.co.uk.

"Come out with your hands up!"

"You can't escape!"

"Surrender and you won't be harmed … much."

Parveen scurried to the edge of the car and reached out towards the side of the shaft, his fingers twining in the metal grating of a ventilation shaft cover. Heaving with all his strength, he pulled at the cover, but it barely budged. Below, in the elevator car, he heard a wrenching sound. The agents had found something with which to pry open the doors.

Fear led him to urgency. He grabbed the vent cover with both hands and pulled. A screw popped loose and fell down the shaft. Heartened, he braced a foot on either side of the cover and put all his strength, fear, and desperation into the effort. He was rewarded when the cover flew off and he went tumbling backwards to land with a loud thud on the top of the elevator car, rolling across it and almost falling off the opposite side into the shaft below. He just managed to stop himself by grabbing a length of power cable and holding on.

"He's on the roof."

Parveen leapt to his feet. The noise had alerted the Grey Agents below. He reached to his backpack and pulled out a long, thin piece of plastic, thumbing a sharp blade out of it as he went. He ran across the roof of the elevator, slashing the cables as he went. The cables all snapped and sparked save one, and even it was deeply cut to the point of being severed. The car lurched beneath Parveen's feet. He jumped from the car into the ventilation shaft and spun to look back.

The access panel burst open. An agent poked his head up, pulling himself onto the roof of the car. In his hand he held a stun pistol. He saw Parveen immediately. Training the pistol at the boy, the agent shouted, "Stay right where you are!"

"Certainly," Parveen said. "But will you?" He pointed at the straining cable. The agent's head jerked back in surprise as the cable broke and the car dropped out of sight down the shaft.

Parveen stuck his head out of the ventilation shaft and looked down at the receding car. "I hope they have a safety braking system."

An agent poked his head out the open doors of the floor below and looked up. He raised his rifle and fired. Parveen ducked back into the shaft just in time.

"He's in the ventilation shaft."

Parveen turned and set off down the shaft. The hunt was on.

mr. Candy and mr. Sweet

"We are counting on you to capture this interloper,
Mr. Crisp," Mr. Sweet said to the new agent who had once
been Aidan, leader of the Royal Swiss Guards, and who now
stood clothed in a fresh grey coat and fedora.

"Indeed, if the business with Hamish X weren't so important
to our ultimate goal, we would stay and capture him ourselves,"
Mr. Sweet added. "Alas, that task must fall to you. Do not fail."

"I will not," Mr. Crisp answered, ducking his head like a
pigeon. "You can count on me."

"Fine," Mr. Sweet nodded. He turned to Mr. Candy and
said, "Shall we board the Space Plane?"

"Indeed, Mr. Candy. The sooner away, the sooner we return."

"And the sooner we open the gate."

Mr. Candy and Mr. Sweet abruptly turned on their heels and
marched off down the catwalk past the elevator, which was
under repair. They walked through the metal sliding doors that
led to the transport bay. The door slid shut behind them.

"Mother?"

"Yes, Mr. Crisp?" The voice seemed to come from everywhere.

"Find the intruder. Now."

"Working."

196

Chapter 21

HAMISH X

El Arak loomed in the moonlight, its stone walls sheer and forbidding. The fortress stood on a steep cliff jutting out of the surrounding desert like a ship ploughing through a frozen sea. Hamish X had seen impregnable strongholds before in his many adventures, but of all the impregnable fortresses he'd experienced, El Arak seemed slightly more impregnable than most.[74]

The fortress was carved out of the cliff, the only entrance being the thick front gate of oak bound in bands of iron. Atop the cliff was a tower rising a further thirty metres above the desert. On the top of the walls, men in brown desert battle fatigues patrolled. Hamish X had counted twenty so far, but there were probably more inside the fortress itself.

"You're telling me we have to get in there?" Thomas asked, incredulous. He, Maggie, Hamish X, and Harik lay on their bellies at the crest of a dune looking at the imposing stronghold.

---

[74] The idea of one fortress being more impregnable than another is a bit ridiculous. By definition, an impregnable fortress is impregnable. If it is even slightly less impregnable, then it is most certainly pregnable. The funny thing about impregnable fortresses is that people usually call them impregnable right up until the time they are stormed and taken. Just like El Arak. But I'm getting ahead of myself, here. Read on.

"You don't have to get in anywhere," Hamish X said. "You two are going to stay right here until this is over."

"Sorry, pal." Maggie shook her head. "We aren't sitting this one out. We're in for the long haul."

"No." Hamish X stood up, dusting sand from his clothing. "It's too dangerous. You have a family to go home to. This isn't your fight. I have to go in there and find the Professor. He's the only one who can tell me who and what I am. Harik and his people are here because this is their land."

"He is right," said Harik. "You must stay out of danger. It would be a tragedy for your parents if you were lost here after winning your freedom from Leadbuttocks."

"Ironbuttocks!" Maggie corrected. "And it's not fair."

"You are staying here. That's final." Hamish X nodded to the two Bedouins who would be staying to guard Maggie and Thomas. "Take good care of them."

"This isn't fair," Maggie insisted, as two Bedouin warriors firmly led her and her brother away.

Hamish X trotted down the back of the dune with Harik to join the Bedouin warriors sitting astride their camels, waiting for the attack order. The animals shifted their bulk and grunted, blowing clouds of steam into the cool night air. Harik hauled himself up into the saddle, folding his legs under him and taking up the reins. He looked down at Hamish X. "Are you ready?"

"Yes." Hamish X gave a curt nod. "Are you?"

"Of course." Harik laughed, his teeth flashing white in the darkness. "Give us twenty minutes to get into position. We will signal you."

"All right." Hamish X smiled. "Good luck, Harik."

"Go with God!" Harik returned. With a snap of the reins, he turned his camel away and the troop of riders set off. Hamish X watched them go. The Bedouin had been good to Hamish X and his companions. Now he only hoped the plan would work and the desert tribesmen would be reunited with their families.

So, Hamish X thought. *One more battle and perhaps then I will know who and what and why I am.* He walked easily to the top of the dune and sat down. Looking up into the sky, he was amazed once again by the intensity of the stars. Here, in the clear night sky of the desert, far from the lights of any city and the pollution of factories, the stars shone so brightly. There were far more stars visible than he had ever thought possible. A crescent moon hung low over the horizon. Dawn was still a few hours away. They had planned their assault to take place during the wee hours of the night when the mercenaries guarding El Arak would be least wary.

"Let's hope we catch them by surprise," Hamish X said aloud. He almost jumped out of his skin when a voice close to his ear answered him.

"I believe you will, Hamish X."

Hamish X spun and found a George raccoon sitting in the sand beside him. The raccoon was a little the worse for wear. Its fur was falling out, leaving large bald patches on its pelt. One of its ears was gone, and a hole in its shoulder showed the glint of its inner mechanical workings. The raccoon sat on its haunches and stared at Hamish X with glossy black eyes.

"George?" Hamish X was astonished. "What in the world are you doing here?"

"I am searching for you," George replied. "There is much for me to tell you, Hamish X. You have led me a merry chase."

"I don't get it. Why are you looking for me? I thought the King wanted me to find the Professor."

"He did, of course, and I'm sure he would still wish that to be the case." The raccoon hung its ragged head. "Alas, the King of Switzerland is dead."

The news struck Hamish X like a blow. He was speechless for a full minute. "Dead? How can that be? Was there an accident?"

"No accident," George said. "There was an attack. Somehow, the ODA discovered the location of the Hollow Mountain. They attacked in overwhelming numbers. Many were taken prisoner, including Lieutenant Aidan and Parveen. Mimi, Mr. Kipling, and Mrs. Francis among others escaped in the emergency pods. But the King . . . He fell while covering their retreat. I was there when he died . . . At least one of me was there. Now I am the only one of my kind left."

Hamish X didn't know what to say. Parveen and Aidan captured? King Liam dead? It was too much to absorb all at once. Not knowing what else to do, he reached out and wrapped his arms around the George raccoon, buried his head in the ragged fur of its coat, and cried.

The George raccoon didn't know what to make of such emotional behaviour. The creature stood patiently still until Hamish X's sobs finally subsided. At last, Hamish X sat back and wiped his eyes on the sleeve of his jacket.

"How did you find me?"

"Ah," the George raccoon sighed. "The King removed the ODA's tracking device, but he added one of his own. I hope you aren't offended, but he wanted to make sure he could find you in an emergency . . . like the one that exists now."

"I see," Hamish X said. "What should I do?"

"I cannot say. You are a free person. You can do as you wish. The King sent me to tell you what has happened. What you do now is your decision."

Hamish X stared through the night at El Arak looming in the darkness. His answers lay there, but his friends needed him. What to do?

What decided it was a flash of light near the front gates of the fortress. Harik had sent his signal. The tribesmen were waiting for him to get the gates open. Without him, they were trapped and vulnerable.

Hamish X stood. "I must get into El Arak. I need to find the Professor. Without knowing who and what I truly am, I can't hope to successfully challenge the Grey Agents and end the ODA once and for all."

"Sound logic, Hamish X," George said. "Shall I wait for you here?"

"Uh-uh." Hamish X shook his head. "You're coming with me."

"Oh my," was all the George raccoon could say in response.

"SARGE?"

"What now, Ulrich?"

"What's that, sir?"

"What's what?"

"It's a light or something. About a kilometre due east."

Sergeant Titus, the mercenary in charge of the night watch, raised his field glasses and trained them on the blue flare that was quickly approaching the gate from the west. It moved with incredible speed. A trail of disturbed dust rose behind it.

"Are we expecting a convoy?" the Sergeant asked.

"Nope."

"That's nope, SIR!"

"Nope, SIR!"

"Hmm." Sergeant Titus adjusted the dial on his field glasses, and finally the image came into focus. A boy with wild hair and a ferocious grin was running impossibly fast. His large boots flared like blue stars trailing fire and under his arm he carried a ragged-looking raccoon. The boy was on a direct route for the gate.

"Oh no," Sergeant Titus groaned. "It's him! It's Hamish X! Sound the alarm!"

HAMISH X LAUGHED as the power surged through him. The sand sped by and he increased his speed. A loud, roaring boom rumbled across the desert as he broke the sound barrier. The gates swelled in his vision. The George raccoon covered its eyes with its tiny paws as Hamish X launched himself over the final ten metres. He struck the gates like a missile. Oak, laboriously barged down the Nile and dragged across the sands of the Sahara, carefully shaped and hung as a gate, was shattered now into a cloud of splinters by the pent-up fury of Hamish X's boots.

Harik and his fellow tribesmen leapt to their feet, shaking off the sand that they had scooped over themselves as camouflage. They had crept on their bellies until they were right against the wall of the fortress and waited for Hamish X to knock down the gate. Now they brandished their rifles and flooded into the fortress. The mercenaries inside were quickly overwhelmed. They threw down their weapons and put their hands in the air when faced with the sudden fury of the attack. Harik looked around, but Hamish X was nowhere to be found. In his wake was a trail of destruction. Mercenaries lay groaning behind shattered barricades and under the wreckage of their own vehicles. The Bedouins moved through the open square subduing and binding their one-time foes. Harik and a select group of men headed off to find Hamish X.

Hamish X had left the front gate far behind. He was moving upward, climbing a zigzagging staircase that was cut into the interior of the cliff. His goal was the tower above. He hadn't stopped moving since he had burst through the front gate. Hamish X's momentum carried him forward through the gate and sent him careening down the central street of El Arak. He flew by the darkened windows and abandoned houses of the main street and sailed on into a gaping stone opening. Two guards tried to intercept but he barrelled through them, sending them flying into the stone walls on either side. Entering the opening, he discovered the stairs that Harik had assured him would lead into the tower. There, Harik believed, he would find the Professor.

Hamish X ran up the steps past doors where confused faces peered out at him. An occasional mercenary, roused from his sleep by the attack, staggered out into Hamish X's path only to be kicked aside or rolled over by his headlong dash. The George raccoon never removed its paws from its eyes, content to let Hamish X negotiate his own path without comment.

"I didn't think computers could be scared, George," Hamish X teased, kicking a mercenary aside as he ran.

"I am not afraid," George answered mildly. "I am merely covering my visual sensors to avoid an overload of stimuli. And ... I am an artificial intelligence, *not* a computer."

Hamish X laughed and began to take the steps two at a time.

He reached the top of the stairs and emerged onto a platform about three metres wide that ran along the top of the wall. He skidded to a halt. The tower rose ahead of him, a little ways along the wall, but unfortunately a line of mercenaries and their Sergeant were lined up in his path, rifles trained on him.

"Halt!" the Sergeant bellowed. "Halt or we will open fire!"

Hamish X paused. He looked up at the tower and then to the line of soldiers. Their faces were damp with sweat. There was fear in their eyes.

"Are you really willing to fight and die for this?" Hamish X asked. "Does this fortress mean anything to any of you?"

"We've been paid to do a job and paid well," the Sergeant said evenly. "We will do that job. Men, prepare to fire."

"You can't win. The gate is broken. The lower levels are taken. You are all that remain. Surrender now and you will be allowed to leave."

The Sergeant looked Hamish X in the eyes. "We were paid to do a job. If we surrender, we lose face. We will be dishonoured."

"There is no honour in dying for a dishonourable cause," Hamish X said, stepping closer. The rifle barrels were wavering.

"He does have a point, Sarge," one of the soldiers opined.

"Quiet, Ulrich."

"Just sayin'."

Hamish X pressed his advantage. "The people who hired you are evil and know no honour. You don't owe them any loyalty. If you lay down your arms, I promise you will not be harmed."

Hamish X stopped and fell silent. The Sergeant was thinking. After what seemed like an eternity, he spoke. "Men, lower your weapons. Stand down."

The mercenaries relaxed. They lowered their weapons and placed them on the stone in front of them. At that instant, Harik and his Bedouins burst through the door behind Hamish X. Hamish X held up a hand.

"They have surrendered. The fight is over."

The Bedouins cheered. Harik directed a number of them to gather up the mercenaries' weapons and herd the captives away.

"Well done, Hamish X." Harik clasped the boy's shoulder and grinned. Then a puzzled expression came over his sharp features. "What in the name of Allah is that?"

"Oh, it's a raccoon." Hamish X laughed, holding George up before him. "Harik, meet George."

"Hello," said George politely.

"By the Prophet! It talks!"

"I'm not an it," George said. "I'm an artificial intelligence. And the name is George."

"Quite so." Harik laughed. "Quite so!" The face of the Bedouin grew serious. He pointed at the Sergeant. "You! Where are our families? Speak!"

"They're all in the tower," the mercenary said.

Hamish X set George down on the ground and turned to the tower. At the base of the high finger of stone, where it joined the wall, there was a simple door. Hamish X walked over to it and lifted the latch. The door was locked.

"The key, please."

The Sergeant fished a ring of keys out of his pocket and tossed them to Hamish X, who caught them easily. He tried two keys before finding the right one. The heavy steel key turned in the lock and the door swung open. Inside, he found a simple room. Bunk beds lined the walls. The room was full of fearful women and children. They had heard the commotion outside and assumed the worst.

Harik stepped into the room behind Hamish X and one woman cried out, running into the man's arms. She hugged him fiercely and tears ran down her cheeks. Harik held her close and spoke to her in a soothing voice. He turned and looked at Hamish X with tears in his own eyes. "My wife, Jali."

Hamish X cast his eyes about the room, but all the occupants were Bedouin. There was no sign of the Professor.

"Harik," Hamish X said, pulling out the photograph of the Professor. "Ask if anyone has seen this man."

Harik took the photo and held it out to his wife. Wiping her eyes, she looked at the image and nodded. She spoke in Arabic and pointed at the stairs that ran up to the next level.

"He is above," Harik interpreted. "She says he is not well. He contracted some kind of illness and was set apart from the others."

Hamish X had no sooner heard this than he dashed up the stairs. He came up into another, smaller room. In this room there were only a few beds, all of them empty save one.

In the corner, by an open window, the Professor lay on a cot. Sweat glistened on his forehead and soaked the thin sheet covering him. A Bedouin woman sat beside the bed, staring in apprehension at Hamish X. Only her eyes were visible above her veil, and they were full of fear.

Hamish X held out his hands, palms upward, and bowed. "I don't want to hurt you." He gestured for the woman to go down the stairs. She seemed to understand, getting off her stool and hurrying past him with a soft swish of her robes. Hamish X waited until she was gone before moving to the bedside and looking down at the man who had been the object of his long search. He had found the Professor. His quest was at an end. At last, he would know who and what he was.

Chapter 22

Professor Magnus Ballantyne-Stewart was a shadow of the man Hamish X recalled from his recovered memories. He had been thin, but now he was practically emaciated. The sickness that gripped him had melted away his flesh. His skin was waxy and grey beneath a shine of sweat, and his eyes were sunken. His chest rose and fell beneath the sheet, the rattle of his breath loud in the empty room. His skinny arms lay atop the sheet at his sides.

A pitcher of water sat on a table beside the bed. In a basin lay a damp cloth. Hamish X poured some water into the basin and dipped the cloth into it. Wringing it out, he laid the cloth on the man's head. The Professor moaned and stirred, mumbling unintelligibly. Looking down on the frail, sickly man, Hamish X didn't know what he felt. When he first recalled the ordeal he had undergone in the laboratories of the ODA and the Professor's part in them, he had been enraged. He had wanted to take revenge on the man who facilitated his torture and mutilation. Ballantyne-Stewart should have done something to stop the Grey Agents! Instead, he stood by, let his fear rule his decisions, and allowed the ODA to use his genius for their evil ends.

Yes, Hamish X had felt rage. Now, looking down at the pathetic creature in the bed, that rage was gone. He felt nothing but pity for the sick man, another person broken by the evil Grey Agents. He just wanted answers.

"Professor Ballantyne-Stewart," Hamish X said clearly, gently shaking the man's shoulder. The skin was hot to the touch, feverish. "Professor, can you hear me?"

The dark eyelids fluttered and opened. Pale blue eyes blinked and tried to focus. "Who?" he said, his voice a papery whisper. "Who are you?"

"You don't remember me?"

"Can't see," the Professor croaked. "Glasses."

Hamish X looked on the table and saw a pair of thick spectacles behind the basin. He opened them and placed them on the bridge of the man's nose. The Professor blinked owlishly, his eyes magnified by the thick lenses. He stared at Hamish X and his mouth trembled. "It's you!" he said softly.

"Yes." Hamish X nodded and sat down in the stool by the Professor's bed. "I've come a long way to talk to you."

The Professor lay very still looking at Hamish X for a long time. Then, at last, he said, "You have questions."

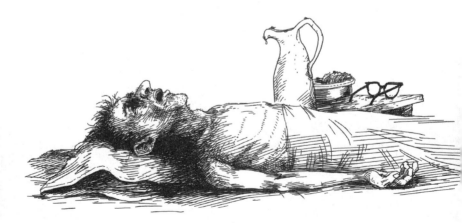

"Yes, I do."

"I will try to answer ..." The Professor began to cough violently. Hamish X found a glass and filled it with water. Putting his arm around the man's shoulders, Hamish X raised him up so that he could drink. The coughing subsided. Hamish X laid the sick man back down.

"Thank you," the Professor said. "I've contracted some kind of fever. I don't think I have long, actually. You've arrived just in time, I think."

"We'll get you out of here, get you care."

The Professor waved a feeble hand. "I won't be leaving here, but thank you for your concern. Heaven knows I deserve no mercy, especially from you."

"Everyone deserves a little mercy, Professor."

The Professor shook his head. "I've done very bad things. I thought I didn't have a choice but ... I've done very bad things to you. I am sorry for that. Can you forgive me?"

Hamish X was quiet for a moment. "Yes. I forgive you. But I have questions ..."

"I will try to answer them."

Now, faced with the possibility of knowing who and what he was, Hamish X found he couldn't decide what he wanted to ask first.

"Why me?"

"You were deemed a good candidate. The ODA had certain criteria: intelligence, physical ability, et cetera. They watched you and they waited for their opportunity."

"They stole me from my parents?"

"No, not exactly. They waited until you were ... There's no way to say this delicately. They orchestrated your death."

Hamish X was shocked. "I died."

"After years of searching, poring over medical records, seeking the perfect genetic specimen, they chose you."

Hamish X was silent, watching the man's face. This was the story he'd been waiting to hear. Now, he found he was afraid of what he might learn. Of all the battles and all the adventures he had lived through, nothing had prepared him for the truth.

The Professor continued. "They arranged for you to have an accident. I don't know what it was ... I hadn't started working for them yet and they wouldn't tell me later."

"I drowned," Hamish X whispered. He remembered the waves crashing over him, the grip of the undertow. "I drowned in the sea."

"That is consistent with my own observations." The Professor coughed, a racking, shuddering spasm gripping his whole body. Hamish X held the old man's hand as the attack subsided. When he had sufficiently recovered, the old man continued. "They arranged your death. Your body was never recovered. That's because they took it for themselves.

"So, you suffered physical death and they revived you using their scientific skills. They have methods far in advance of our own. It's what drew me into their web in the first place.

"Perhaps I should tell you a little about my story. It will answer many of your questions and help you frame the important ones, hmm?"

Hamish X nodded.

"Fine. I was a genetic researcher. Specifically, I was trying to develop methods of cloning that would produce offspring that were identical to the parent organisms in every way. There had been one insurmountable problem up to this point: the offspring tended to age and die at an accelerated rate. I wanted to change that. You see, I had a personal interest in the problem. I had a daughter. Sylvie was her name. My daughter was dying.

"She was diagnosed with a blood disorder. Nothing could be done. No cure could be found. I was one of the leading genetic biologists in the world, but I couldn't help her ..."

The Professor lapsed into another coughing fit. Hamish X held the man's head and helped him drink more water. When he had recovered, the Professor continued.

"That's when the ODA contacted me. They were very interested in my work. They said they could help my daughter. They said they would fund special research if I would, in return, help them with some of theirs. I was at my wits' end. Of course, I accepted. It seemed too good to be true, and it was."

The bitterness was plain on the Professor's face as he spoke. "They put me to work on a project that was concerned with augmenting human tissue with genetic and cybernetic implants. In essence, they were creating you."

The Professor's bony hand gripped Hamish X's arm. He looked into the boy's eyes. "They made me do those things to you. I didn't want to hurt you, but they threatened me. They said they would let my daughter die if I didn't help them. So, I ...," he faltered, tears welling up. "I did as they instructed. But ... but she died anyway. They didn't even try to save her. They never meant to. Too late, I realized they were using me ... I threatened to leave the project, to tell the world what they were up to, but by then it was too late. I was a prisoner. I was forced to continue against my will."

"Sounds like typical ODA tactics." Hamish X nodded. He gave the man another sip of water. "So they forced you to do those things to me. I accept that. I understand. But I need to know why."

"Why? Ha." The Professor shook his head ruefully. "Even I don't understand it all. What do you already know?"

"I am some kind of superconductor. I have a very dense nervous system and increased strength," Hamish X said. "I can do things, things I don't ever remember learning. I ... I'm not completely human."

"Yes." The Professor nodded weakly. "You are designed to be a conduit of enormous energy and huge amounts of information. They took your basic human body structure and grafted more nerves and muscle fibres onto it. But that is all of lesser importance. What they really needed was your brain."

"My brain?"

"Yes. The human brain is the most complex computing device in the universe, capable of sorting through billions of bits of information in a matter of seconds. Quite amazing, really. Your brain is especially well developed."

"I guess I should be flattered, but I'm not. Why do they need my brain? Surely they have a vastly complex computer already. They call it Mother." Hamish X shivered as he recalled the irresistible voice of the ODA's artificial intelligence. Even now, when he was free of its lure, he remembered with longing the compelling voice.

"Mother is a very complex machine, but it has limitations. The ODA realized early on that they would need to mate their artificial intelligence with a human one, forming a giant dual processor, if you will."

"But I don't understand," Hamish X said. "Why send me out on all these adventures? Why allow me to fight and defeat their own allies like Cheesebeard and the others? I don't see why they would do that."

"Ah, I know! It doesn't seem to make any sense," the Professor agreed, his eyes bright. "But in the end, they had to do it. You see, they had to train your brain to use all the augmentations they had made. They had to expand the mind they had given you. They tried to do it by artificial means, in the lab, running programs, but it didn't work. The only thing that improves the human mind is experience. So they decided to let you out, observe you. Set you against opponents who were truly intent on defeating you. That way, you would learn and expand your mental capacity. Only then would you be ready for your true purpose."

Hamish X leaned forward. "And that is?"

"They have built a gateway to their own world," the Professor said.

"Their own world? What do you mean? The Grey Agents are aliens?" Hamish X scoffed.

"Not exactly aliens, but they are not of this world." The Professor lowered his voice to a whisper, as if mentioning the doings of the ODA was enough to invoke their presence. "For many years now, scientists have believed that the universe we know, our plane of existence, is just one of many. The creatures we know as the Grey Agents come from one of these other planes."

"If that's true, how come we aren't visited by ... *people* from other planes all the time?"

"A good question," the Professor beamed. The conversation seemed to be having a salubrious[75] effect on the sick

---

[75] *Salubrious* is a word meaning beneficial to or promoting health and well-being and should not be confused with Sal Ubrious, who once played shortstop for the New York Cubans Baseball Team.

man. His voice became clearer and his speech more animated. "The planes are usually separate, co-existing in parallel. To break through from one plane to another requires enormous amounts of energy. The Grey Agents are only able to make stable gates of minute size for very short periods of time. They use them to possess their victims and create more Grey Agents. They take children on the cusp of adulthood and open a minuscule[76] gate, allowing one of their number to come from the other plane and take over the poor child's body."

"That's horrible. Horrible!" Hamish X was disgusted. "What happens to the mind of the child possessed? Is it gone? Destroyed? Or do they linger on inside their own bodies watching as the Grey Agents do their evil work?"

"I can't tell you that. No one can."

Hamish X shook his head, filled with revulsion. "It's so vile. Still, the questions remain: Why did they make me? Why did they go to all this trouble?"

"Ah." The Professor held up a finger. "Up until now, they haven't been able to make a stable gate of the size they'd need to launch a full-scale invasion of our world. They need a huge amount of power, and to regulate that power, they need a computer processor of immense sophistication."

Hamish X opened his mouth to ask his question again but shut it with a snap as he realized he knew the answer. He was the processor. The Grey Agents needed his brain.

"You understand now, I see."

---

[76] *Minuscule* is a word meaning extremely tiny and should not be confused with Minu Scule, who once played roller derby for the Dallas Wheel Machine.

Hamish X didn't know what to say. All this time he had believed he was a person like any other, like Mimi, like Parveen. But it had never been true. He was a machine, a tool, fashioned for an evil purpose by evil creatures. His life had never been his own. He took off his backpack and, opening it, pulled out the green leather book *Great Plumbers and Their Exploits*. He had carried it with him through all his adventures believing it to be the one link with his real mother, his true life. He ran a hand over the green leather surface and traced the gold lettering with his index finger.

"The book," the Professor said softly.

"You wrote it."

"Yes." The Professor nodded. "It is a primer[77] containing all the code needed to interface with the Mother artificial intelligence."

"I used to read it all the time."

"An impulse implanted in your brain. You were required to learn all the programming language. The *Great Plumbers* book seemed like a handy way to do it."

Hamish looked down at the book in his hands. Meaningless. He tossed it onto the floor with a thud.

---

[77] A *primer* is a basic textbook. There have been primers for spelling, primers for languages, primers for cooking, and so on. I once saw a primer for breathing. Silly, really, because I imagine that if you couldn't breathe you wouldn't survive long enough to learn to read and then read the primer unless you were very good at holding your breath. Perhaps the book was meant for very intelligent fish who wished to migrate to land. They would need to learn to breathe air rather than water, but I still think the breathing primer would be a waste of time. Fish aren't very intelligent, though they spend a great deal of time in schools. (For that matter, many humans who spend a lot of time in schools aren't all that bright.)

"And these?" Hamish X raised one booted foot.

"An interface. They connect you to the computer called Mother. But you must understand ... there is more!" The Professor gripped the boy's hand.

Hamish X jerked his hand away. "What more can there be? I'm a robot! A machine! I'm just a *thing*!"

"A special machine. A brilliant and glorious machine. But what is any one of us but a machine made of blood and muscle and bone?" The Professor's eyes burned with intensity, his voice insistent. "They built you, it's true, but you are who you are because of what you have learned. You have become more than they imagined. All your adventures have made you more than a machine. You have a heart and a soul, and that is something they never intended."

Hamish X went to the window and looked out over the desert. The sun was rising, casting a pink glow over the dunes. He gripped the stone sill of the window and fought back tears. He'd come all this way to learn he was not even a real person. What had King Liam said? He was a boy who became a puppet: the opposite of Pinocchio. He truly felt like a puppet.

Hamish X lowered his head into his hands, covering his face.

"Hamish X." The voice of George cut through Hamish X's grief. "Hamish X."

Hamish X raised his tear-streaked face.

"What is it?"

"You are needed outside."

"Leave me alone."

"I must insist."

Hamish X stood up and kicked the stool away. The frail piece of furniture shattered against the stone wall. The

George raccoon stood in the doorway. It looked at the wreckage and then back at Hamish X.

"What is it, then?" Hamish X shouted.

"The ODA," the George raccoon said mildly. "The Grey Agents."

"What about them?"

"They're here."

Yet Another Note from the Narrator

Ah yes. Things are really coming to a head now. Hamish X has learned about his past, and the Grey Agents arrive as if on cue. Parveen is on the run, playing cat and mouse with the ODA in their own backyard. Mimi is under sail in an Atlantean submarine bound for Providence. Will she arrive in time to save Parveen? What will Hamish X decide to do?

Well, I'm hardly going to tell you now before you read the rest of the book! That would be totally counterproductive and defeat the purpose of this exercise, which is to make you read the story. It's for your own good, so, please, no whining and no long faces.

This is the final part of the story. If you've been with me all along, well … good for you. You've shown the kind of dedication in a reader that I truly admire. Many people would have perhaps become distracted by something else, a television program perhaps, a raging fire threatening their home, or a wild animal lunging at their throat. But not you. I guess you're wise enough not to own a television, have the foresight not to live in a dry forested area, and are lucky enough not to be delicious to carnivores.

It's been a long road, but we are coming to the end of it. All the different paths taken by Mimi, Parveen, and Hamish X have ranged far and wide, but now all roads lead to Providence, Rhode Island, to the little house on Angell Street that is the Headquarters of the Orphan Disposal Agency.

Chapter 23

HAMISH X

"Here?" Hamish X couldn't believe it. "How is that possible?"

"It is highly improbable," the George raccoon said. "But not impossible. I could calculate the odds for you, if you like."

"It was inevitable," the Professor said, raising himself up on one spindly elbow. "The mercenaries are in their employ. Perhaps the report went out that I am here and they've come to finish me off. If that's the case, you must go before they know you are with me, before they know I've told you everything."

Hamish X laughed bitterly. "Everything? You didn't tell me everything. You didn't tell me what to do now that I know I'm less than a real person. I'm a computer processor."

"No! No! No!" the Professor cried. "Never think that. That isn't what I was telling you at all. Hamish X, that is what they planned for you, but you have become bigger than that, far greater than they ever imagined. You have to understand."

"HAMISH X!" The voice of Mr. Candy rolled in through the windows, magnified to enormous volume. "HAMISH X. WE KNOW YOU ARE HERE. COME OUT. WE WISH TO TALK TO YOU."

Hamish X went to the door.

"Hamish X!" the Professor called. Hamish X turned and glared at the old, ruined man. Professor Magnus Ballantyne-Stewart pointed a bony finger at Hamish X. "Remember. You are more than they think you are. You have a heart. They never dreamed that would happen."

Hamish X's face was expressionless. He shook his head and walked out the door with the George raccoon at his heels.

Out on the wall, the Bedouins had gathered and were looking out over the desert. Ranged along the top of the hill, about a kilometre away, were massive tracked vehicles, squatting in the rising sun like steel elephants. Long guns sprouted out of their tops, wide-mouthed and deadly, all of them trained on the wall of El Arak. Grey Agents stood in the open hatches of the vehicles, ready to call for a bombardment if necessary. Looking at the guns, Hamish X had no doubt that defence of the fortress would end in El Arak as a smoking heap of rubble and the Bedouins utterly destroyed.

Hamish X walked to the edge of the wall and hopped up on the parapet. He lowered a hand, grasped George, and lifted the raccoon up beside him. The desert was silent save for the wind and the low rumble of the idling vehicles, waiting for the attack order.

As he watched, two specks detached themselves from the enemy line and rose on plumes of blue flame. The specks grew larger as they sped across the intervening distance, until Hamish X could clearly make out Mr. Candy and Mr. Sweet jetting across the desert towards the wall where he waited. He didn't have to use his enhanced vision to see that the Grey Agents each held a struggling captive in their long bony gloves.

Maggie and Thomas were trying to be brave, but clearly they were terrified. The ground was a hundred metres below and the fall would be fatal should the Grey Agents choose to let go. They had fought pirates, but the Grey Agents were villains on another order of magnitude, something their childhoods of love and family had never prepared them to experience.

Hamish X waited until the Grey Agents came to a stop, hovering a few metres away in the gathering daylight, before he spoke.

"It's me you want. Let them go."

"What? Right now?" asked Mr. Candy.

"If you insist." Mr. Sweet shrugged.

Both Grey Agents loosened their grip slightly on the captives. Maggie and Thomas screamed, but the Grey Agents didn't let them drop. They tightened their grip once more.

"You see, we've developed a sense of humour." Mr. Candy grinned, showing his yellow teeth.

"And what a fine sense of humour it is," Hamish X sneered. "You should take that show on the road. What do you do for an encore? Pull the wings off flies?"

"That sounds very diverting," Mr. Sweet said. "We must try that sometime."

"However, today we are here to end this ridiculous chase you've led us on." Mr. Candy took over. "We've waited long enough. Time for you to fulfill the function for which you were created."

"What if I refuse?" Hamish X asked.

"The thought had occurred to us," Mr. Sweet said. He held Thomas up a little higher. "Fortunately, we found ourselves some insurance hiding in the dunes not far away."

"Don't listen to him, Hamish X," Maggie cried. Mr. Candy clamped a gloved hand over her mouth. She promptly sunk her teeth into that hand.

Mr. Candy looked down at her, a puzzled expression on his face, apparently feeling no pain whatsoever. "Annoying child."

"Come with us and we'll let these two go free," Mr. Sweet offered.

Hamish X shook his head. "Not good enough. All these people are to be left alone." He swept his arms wide to take in the Bedouins along the wall. "This is their land and their home. You leave here and never come back."

The Grey Agents exchanged a glance. "Never is a long time, Hamish X," Mr. Candy began.

"Without me, how will you open the gate?"

The Grey Agents froze. "Who told you about the gate?" Mr. Sweet demanded.

"I did!" Everyone looked to the tower doorway where Professor Ballantyne-Stewart leaned against the door frame. The effort it had taken to make his way down the stairs from his bed must have been enormous. He stood, bathed in sweat, the bedsheet wrapped around him damp and clinging. "Hamish X! Remember what I said. You are more than they ever planned you would be. You are more than a machine ..."

His impassioned speech was cut off abruptly by the discharge of Mr. Candy's pistol. In the silence after the shot, time seemed to slow down to a crawl. Hamish X watched in horror as a bloom of red blossomed on the sheet covering the Professor's bony chest. The man looked down at the wound in disbelief, then his eyes rolled back and he crumpled in a small heap against the door frame.

"NOOOOOO!" Hamish X screamed. He turned and glared at the Grey Agents hovering in air. Mr. Candy held a smoking pistol in one hand.

"Regrettable. He had a brilliant mind, but he became dangerous. I'd heard he was in the vicinity," Mr. Candy said without emotion.

"Indeed," agreed Mr. Sweet. "Nice to tie up a loose end."

Hamish X gritted his teeth. Hatred welled up in him so pure and bright that it blasted away all other considerations. All he wanted was to destroy. His boots flared to life, blazing like twin blue stars. He tensed, crouching like a tiger on the parapet, his golden eyes narrowed to slits, as he gathered himself for a lunge.

"Hamish X, no!" George cried. In the instant before Hamish X launched himself into space, the raccoon leapt onto the boy's shoulders. Hamish X was so charged up he didn't even feel the extra weight.

He sprang at the Grey Agents with such blinding speed that neither of them had time to move. Hamish X struck, a bolt of lightning, blue flame trailing behind him as he crossed the intervening distance. With each hand, he latched on to the throats of Mr. Candy and Mr. Sweet.

Their instinctive reaction was to try to escape. Firing their jetpacks, they tried to veer off in different directions. Hamish X had the strength of his rage and all the advanced technology the ODA had poured into him. He squeezed tighter. Linked together and driven by the jetpacks, the three figures rocketed into the air in a corkscrewing spin, rising higher and higher into the brilliant desert sky. The wind roared in Hamish X's ears. The agents' mouths opened and closed convulsively as they fought for breath.

"HA!" Hamish X shouted into their faces. "What? Can't breathe? At least you're *that* human."

Mr. Candy and Mr. Sweet were in distress now. They had to free their hands, and so they let go of Maggie and Thomas. Maggie screamed as she was dropped but quickly grabbed hold of one of Hamish X's boots. Thomas grabbed hold of his sister's waist and hung on for dear life as they were spun around and around like a ride at an amusement park.

"How does it feel?" Hamish X shouted into his enemies' faces. "How does it feel to be helpless?"

Mr. Candy brought up his pistol and aimed at Hamish X, but Mr. Sweet slapped the barrel aside at the last instant. The bullet slashed by Hamish X's cheek like a hot wind and buried itself in George's furry, ragged torso. Sparks flared from the tiny robot. Hamish X turned his head and saw the light in the raccoon's eyes flicker.

"George?"

"I hate to do this Hamish X, but I must." With its final breath[78] the George raccoon, last of its kind, sunk its teeth into Hamish X's shoulder.

"Yow!" Hamish X yelped in pain and twisted violently, kicking with his feet. Maggie held on for dear life.

"Cool it, will ya?" she cried. Hamish X was forced to let go of Mr. Candy to pull the George raccoon from his shoulder. He held it out, looking at the broken creature's face. "Why, George?"

"Trust me, Hamish X. Trust the King." And with that, the creature went limp, all activity in its computerized brain ceased.

---

[78] Technically, the robot raccoon does not breathe, so it would not have a last breath, but it sounds better than "with the last charge of its battery" or "with the last electron in its circuit." You know what I mean.

Meanwhile, Mr. Candy had not been idle. He pulled away from Hamish X and reached into his grey coat pocket. He swooped down close to Hamish X and slapped a cuff of pale glowing material onto the wrist that held Mr. Sweet.

Hamish X immediately felt his power draining away. His grip on the Grey Agent's throat weakened, allowing Mr. Sweet to bat his hand away. The agent grabbed hold of the front of Hamish X's jacket to keep him from falling back to the desert sand hundreds of metres below.

Hamish X was reeling. The cuff deadened the nerves in his body. He was overwhelmed by dizziness. His limbs became leaden. He tried to fight the lethargy that flooded through his body. Then Mr. Candy slapped the other cuff over Hamish X's free wrist. Hamish X went limp.

Maggie and Thomas felt the change.

"What's happened?" Thomas asked. He could see little beyond the back of his sister's knees.

"I don't know," Maggie answered. "Hamish X has passed out."

"The ride's a little smoother," Thomas noted.

Mr. Candy grabbed Hamish X by one arm and Mr. Sweet grabbed the other. They jetted back to the top of the dune where their fleet of machines waited, engines rumbling. While still a few metres above the sand, they dropped their burden, sending Maggie, Thomas, and Hamish X tumbling in the sand. Thomas and Maggie struggled to their feet, coughing and spitting sand. Hamish X lay sprawled as he fell, completely inert. He was barely breathing.

Maggie knelt at his side and turned him over onto his back.

"Hamish X! Hamish X, wake up!"

"Uh . . . Maggie?"

Maggie looked up to see agents all around them, rifles levelled. Mr. Candy and Mr. Sweet landed lightly, their jetpacks causing miniature whirlwinds in the sand. The Grey Agents looked down at Hamish X.

"I'm afraid you will be accompanying Hamish X on his final journey." Mr. Sweet snapped his fingers. "Put them on board the aircraft. We leave for Providence immediately."

"What about them?" One of the Grey Agents pointed at the fortress in the distance.

Mr. Candy looked over his shoulder at El Arak and shrugged. "Level it," he said.

Chapter 24

MIMI

"According to the charts, we are entering Narragansett Bay. We are approaching our destination. Providence is just ahead," Xnasha announced from her seat at the crystal console.

Mimi wanted to jump for joy, but she probably would have banged her head on the low ceiling of the control centre. She was so keyed up after the long hours they'd spent in the vessel under the ocean surface. At first, the view out the front portal of the submarine had been fascinating. Schools of enormous fish gliding by, vistas of rock, and forests of seaweed had filled Mimi with awe. The dash through the Strait of Gibraltar had been particularly astonishing. Rock walls towered on either side as the Mediterranean poured through into the Atlantic. Xnasha's concentration was mighty indeed to keep them from foundering against the sheer underwater cliffs.

After the excitement of the Strait of Gibraltar, however, there was nothing but the black darkness of the deep ocean. They dared not travel close to the surface for fear of being spotted by ships on radar or sonar. There was the added danger of being picked up by other submarines of the world's navies. Xnasha assured Mimi and Cara that the Atlantean submarine would absorb most sonar and radar waves, something to do with the material of which the vessel was constructed.

"I don't completely understand it, but the ship ... tells me that this is true," Xnasha explained.

"The ship talks to you?" Cara asked. "How?"

"It isn't talking exactly. I feel what the ship feels through the connection I make when I engage the crystal. The ship is sort of alive ..."

"Like that crazy crystal thingy back at Atlantis?" Mimi offered.

"Yes," Xnasha said, delighted. "It has a ... spirit. And I commune with the spirit of the ship. It shows me—"

"*She* shows ya," Mimi interrupted.

"*She* shows me. Through her I can feel the surrounding ocean. I can feel other ships. I can feel so much."

"Why did the Atlanteans ever let this slip away?" Cara asked softly.

Xnasha shook her head. "I don't know."

"Fear," Mimi said simply. "They got too scared to face the world. Considerin' the fight they came through, I understand it." They sat in silence for a while after that, each of them lost in her own thoughts.

The next hours were tedious for everyone but Xnasha, who had to concentrate on guiding the ship. For Mimi, Cara, and the other Guards stuck in their bunks, the time seemed to crawl by. Most of them tried to grab whatever sleep they could, sprawling in the bunks of the crew quarters. Cara spent the time trying to repair her uniform. She needed to occupy her mind with something else besides her fear for her brother Aidan's safety. Mimi tried to talk to her but got nothing more than noncommittal grunts in response.

In the end, Mimi left Cara alone and used her time to check and recheck her weapons. The Guards carried their standard armaments. They still had their stun pistols. None of them had a full charge after the battle in the Hollow Mountain, but nothing could be done about it. All of them carried fighting sticks. Armed only with these meagre weapons, they hoped to storm the Headquarters of the most dreaded organization in the world. Mimi looked at the stick she held in her hands and laughed.

"We ain't got a hope," she said to herself.

"Oh, don't say such things." Mrs. Francis stood in the hatchway looking into Mimi's cabin. The former house-keeper had managed to find an alternative to her wedding gown among the clothing offered her by the inhabitants of Atlantis. Being not very tall herself, finding a dress that fit her wasn't a challenge. She now wore a sort of silken dress of pale blue that belted at the waist. On her feet she wore a pair of heavy blue clogs.

"Well, we ain't, Mrs. Francis," Mimi insisted. "We ain't got a chance."

Mrs. Francis came into the cabin and sat down on the bunk beside Mimi. "The proper English is not *ain't* but *don't*. We *don't* have a chance." Mrs. Francis put a soft arm around Mimi's shoulders. "But it isn't true. We *do* have a chance. There is always a chance."

"What chance have we got? They got all the advantages! They got an army and we got nothing but a bunch o' kids with sticks and popguns."

"Oh, Mimi. I know it seems bad. I know there seems to be no way to win and the world is against you, but I want you to listen to me." Mrs. Francis looked into Mimi's eyes. "We are still here. Don't you see? In spite of all the danger and the troubles we've seen, in spite of pirates and Grey Agents, storms and invasions, troubles of all kind, we are still here." Mrs. Francis laughed. "I was certain that I'd work for Viggo in Windcity until the end of my days. I thought I'd die alone and unloved. Then Hamish X came. Everything changed. I found someone who loves me and I found that, though I was never blessed with children of my own, I had a family." She smiled and hugged Mimi to her ample bosom and, for once, Mimi didn't resist. "Don't you see? We've already won in so many ways. What's one more battle when we've won everything a person could ever wish for?"

"Why isn't Hamish X here? He should be with us."

"Oh, Mimi." Mrs. Francis hugged the girl close and kissed the top of her unruly hair. "He is. He brought us all together. He'll always be with us. And you know what? I have a feeling we'll see him soon."

"Why do you think that?" Mimi said, looking up and wiping her eyes on her sleeve.

Mrs. Francis smiled. "Because he just has a habit of showing up when you need him most. I know what he'd say if he were here, though."

"What's that?" Mimi sniffed.

"He'd say, 'Mimi, you're in charge. Take care of everyone for me. I know you can do it.'"

"You think so?"

"I know so." With that, Mrs. Francis left Mimi to see to the other children on the *Rhode Island Red*.

"I can do it, Hamish X. I will take care of things," Mimi said to the empty room, and saying it made her feel better.

She checked her weapons one more time before heading to the control room. Cara was already there, along with Mr. Kipling and Mrs. Francis. Cara crouched by Xnasha's side, watching as the ship approached the mouth of Narragansett Bay. The long inlet plunged into the heart of the state of Rhode Island and, at its most northern point, split Providence, the state capital, into Providence and East Providence.

Mimi took up position at Xnasha's other elbow. "How long until we get to the city?"

Xnasha waved a hand and a chart appeared, hovering under her fingertips. "Not long. Where should we land?"

"The docks," Cara said, pointing at the glowing outline of the port. "We can hide the boat in plain sight. We walk into town from there."

"How do we find ODA Headquarters?" Mimi asked.

"We ask directions," said Mr. Kipling.

AND THAT IS WHY, an hour later, they found themselves in the Lucky Thirteen convenience store in downtown Providence. The store was attached to a gas station. Mr. Kipling stood at the counter looking down at a pimply teenaged boy who had his nose buried in a comic book with the unlikely title *Vampire Cat Robot*.[79]

"Excuse me, my lad," Mr. Kipling said politely.

The teenager didn't look up from his comic book. "I'm not 'your lad,' Grandpa."

"I see," Mr. Kipling said, nonplussed. "Of course. Well, I was wondering if you could give me some directions."

The teenager looked up, his face full of disdain. "Do I look like the Auto Club?" He took a long look at Mr. Kipling, who was wearing his soiled and ragged dress

---

[79] *Vampire Cat Robot* is a terrible comic book series that has since gone out of circulation. It is the saga of a cat that is a vampire and becomes a robot. It doesn't really make much sense. Obviously, cats are almost never vampires unless they are bitten by a human vampire, which is highly unlikely as a cat will sense an approaching vampire and flee long before it could be bitten. Also, once a cat becomes a vampire and desires to feast on blood, when it is made into a robot, it would no longer require blood and so it would lose its title of vampire. You know, I may have spent far too long thinking about the logic of this particular comic book.

uniform with his sabre still hanging from his belt. "What's with the getup, Grandpa? Going to a costume party?"

"What? Er, no. I was wondering if you might help me. I'm looking for Angell Street."

"Like I said," the boy returned his attention to his comic book, "I ain't Google Earth. Buy a map." He pointed without looking at a rack of road maps.

Mr. Kipling looked at the maps and patted his pockets. "Um. This is sort of amusing, but I don't have any money on me at the moment. I haven't needed it for a long time, you see."

"You haven't, huh? Well, sorry, Grandpa, you're outta luck."

"Can't you just ..."

"Blow, Grandpa, I'm busy."

Mr. Kipling frowned. "You are a very rude and impudent boy."

The boy looked up at him and sneered. "Hey, why don't you go back to wherever you come from and get some money, buy a map, and leave me alone, okay, your Lordship?" Shaking his head in disgust, he leaned back in his chair, putting his feet up on the counter.

Mr. Kipling stood for a moment looking at the soles of the boy's shoes, one of which was caked with a large lump of dirty chewing gum. Uncertain what to do, Mr. Kipling turned and went out the door. An electronic sensor beeped as the door opened and swung shut behind him.

Mr. Kipling walked past the gas pumps and across the parking lot that was lit by lights on high posts. Gathered under one of the posts, the others, freshly landed from the *Rhode Island Red*, stood waiting for him.

"Did you find out where Angell Street is?" Cara asked urgently.

"No," Mr. Kipling said.

"Didn't he know?" Mrs. Francis asked.

"I don't know whether he knows or not, Isobel," Mr. Kipling answered. "He was extremely rude to me."

"What?" Mrs. Francis was aghast.

"And he told me to buy a map," Mr. Kipling added. "Does anyone have any money?"

"What's money?" asked Xnasha.

"Not now," Mimi said irritably. "No, we ain't got no money."

"I'll go in there and give that boy a piece of my mind," Mrs. Francis said indignantly.

Mimi laid a hand on the woman's arm. "No." Mimi caught Cara's eye and grinned fiercely. She jerked her head towards the store. "We'll handle this."

The teenager was still sitting with his feet up on the counter, leaning back in his chair, reading his comic book, when the door beeped again. He looked up to see Mimi and Cara standing on the other side of the counter. In their hands they held their fighting sticks. Taking in their Guard uniforms, the boy snorted derisively. "What's the deal? You guys selling cookies or something?"

"We want a map," Mimi said simply.

"They're over there."

"We don't have any money," Cara said.

"Then yer outta luck."

"No," Mimi said. "You are."

"What are you little brats gonna do ...?" He didn't get the rest of his sentence out before Mimi and Cara smacked the boy's feet with their fighting sticks. Caught unawares, the boy tipped backwards and slammed flat on his back behind the counter. Mimi vaulted over the counter, landed with her feet on either side of the boy's head, and pressed her stick into his chest, pinning him to the ground. Cara sat prettily on the counter, checking her hair in the tiny mirror at the top of a rack full of cheap sunglasses.

"Hey," the boy whined. "What's the big idea? *Glork!*" The glork was a result of Mimi jabbing her stick into his throat.

Cara smiled and tried on a pair of sunglasses with thick white frames. "Mimi isn't happy."

"Who's Mimi?"

"The girl with the stick in your throat."

"Oh." He gulped. "Why isn't she happy?"

"Our friend asked for a map. You were rude."

"He didn't have any money." The boy flinched as Mimi snarled at him. "Listen, there's only twenty bucks in the till. Take it."

Cara laughed sweetly. "No, silly. We don't want to steal your money. We just want a map. Oh ... and an apology."

"Take the map. Take it!"

"And?"

"And I'm sorry."

Cara smiled. "That's so nice of you. I think I'll take these sunglasses, too."

"Take them," the boy whimpered.

"Put 'em back," Mimi growled.

"Oh, Mimi," Cara pouted. "You are just no fun at all."

Cara picked a map off the rack. "Thanks so much. C'mon, Mimi." Mimi removed her stick from the boy's throat. Jumping back over the counter, she went and joined Cara at the door.

The teenager jumped to his feet. His face red, he shouted, "I'm calling the cops! It's all on camera!"

"Are you sure you want to tell everyone how two little girls kicked your butt?" Cara said, smiling.

The boy looked from her to Mimi and back and made his decision. "Don't tell anybody."

"We won't." Cara laughed and went out the door.

Mimi snarled at the boy and waved her stick. The boy hid behind the counter. Mimi shook her head. "So sad." She turned and left the store accompanied by the beeping of the chime.

Armed with the map, they checked their location and plotted their route into the centre of Providence, where ODA Headquarters was located on a residential road inappropriately named Angell Street.

Chapter 25

They had come ashore in the wee hours[80] of the morning. The light pollution from the city prevented them from seeing the stars up above. Xnasha was only slightly disappointed. They had moored the submarine in the port of Providence in the shadow of a rusty freighter. Mr. Kipling felt confident that the ship they chose to hide behind was a derelict waiting for scrap. No one would be paying much attention to it, and so it was unlikely that the Atlantean craft would be discovered.

"It probably won't matter much," Mimi said. "We ain't likely comin' back fer her."

"Mimi! Try to be a little more positive!" Mrs. Francis admonished. The older woman had managed to scramble up onto the pier with the help of the Guards and Mr. Kipling without falling into the water, which was a miracle in itself.

Xnasha looked around at all the electric lights shining down on the ships and twinkling across the harbour from

---

[80] There are two schools of thought as to why the hours between midnight and five a.m. are called the "wee hours." The first theory is that in Celtic countries like Ireland, Scotland, and Wales, fairies were said to wander about in the hours after midnight. Fairies are small, so the hours after midnight were called wee hours set aside for the wee folk. The other school of thought suggests that the hours shortly after midnight are the most likely time for someone to need to use the bathroom. They usually need to go wee, hence the wee hours.

the houses of the city. Her mouth hung open in wonder. "It's so beautiful."

"Beautiful? It's a stinky old port," Cara said.

"You just don't understand." Xnasha laughed. "I've spent my whole life wanting to come to the surface, to see for myself. To see the sky." The Atlantean woman raised her hands into the air. "It's the most amazing thing I've ever seen."

From then on, as they trooped through the streets of the sleeping town in their quest, first to find a map and then to find ODA Headquarters, Xnasha continuously exasperated them with her exclamations of wonder at the most mundane things. A lamppost, a car, a fire hydrant: all could elicit a gasp of awestruck wonder from Xnasha. They were delayed for a full half-hour while she marvelled at a stray cat that wandered out into the middle of the road. Mimi tried to be patient, but she finally had to put her foot down. Xnasha reluctantly agreed to keep moving despite her desire to examine every new thing the surface world had to offer. After three hours and several wrong turns, they arrived at last at Angell Street and the Headquarters of the Orphan Disposal Agency.

The house was a shock. Mimi had expected a fortress, a tower, or perhaps a dark and foreboding palace of evil. Instead, ODA Headquarters was a simple white house on a pleasant tree-lined street. The garden was well tended, full of pink and white petunias. The lawn was green and lush, lovingly trimmed and surrounded by a white picket fence. A cobblestone path led to a brightly painted green door. On the gate, a small brass plaque announced discreetly:

World Headquarters
Orphan Disposal Agency
No Peddlers!
No Junk Mail!

Mimi and Cara looked at the sign, their faces blank.

"This is ODA Headquarters?" Cara asked.

"Oh, my," Mrs. Francis said. "It looks just, well, fine!"

"Those are lovely petunias," Mr. Kipling pointed out.

"I don't know." Mimi shrugged. "I guess I was thinkin' it would look, ya know, more evil."

"Oh no," Xnasha said softly. "This place is evil enough. I can feel it. All of your world is strange to me, but I feel something here. This is a bad place."

"She's right," Cara agreed. "Listen ..."

"Listen to what?" Mimi demanded. "I cain't hear nothin'."

"No, you can't because you won't stop talking. Really listen!"

Mimi scowled but kept quiet, straining to hear any sound in the silence.

Cara whispered, "See? There are no birds. No squirrels. Not even an insect."

Cara was right. Mimi hadn't noticed the change, but once it was pointed out to her, it was obvious. The house was dead despite its pleasant outward appearance. Mimi looked up and down the street. The houses were unusually quiet. No children played in the front yards. The windows were empty and dark. The whole street seemed to be dead, yet the grass and the trees were green and lush. But they looked more like props in a stage play than living things. Even the sunlight seemed sterile. The whole street was a facade built to hide the sinister intent of the ODA.

"What do we do?" Cara asked. For once, she was ready to defer to Mimi's judgment.

"I don't like this place at all," Mrs. Francis fretted.

Xnasha's wide blue eyes gazed at the front door of the house. "We shouldn't be here," she said, her voice the barest whisper. "This is an evil place."

A murmur of assent rippled through the Guards. Mimi straightened her shoulders. "Yup. This is an evil place. But we all knew what we was gettin' ourselves into when we signed up. This ain't no time ta turn tail. Anybody who don't wanna go in, now's the time to leave and nobody'll think no worse of ya. I, for one, have to go in. They got my friend Parv in there, and I know they got friends of yers in there and family, too." She paused to look Cara in the eye. "I gotta go in there 'cause I know Parv'd do the same fer me."

Mrs. Francis dabbed her eyes with her sleeve. "That was lovely, dear."

"Oh, brother!" Mimi rolled her eyes. Her little speech finished, she turned and lifted the latch on the wooden gate and stepped onto the path that led to the front door. Everyone held their breath, waiting for lightning to strike, sirens to wail, and alarms to sound, but none of these things happened. Mimi resolutely walked up the cobblestones to the brightly painted front door.

Bravery and cowardice are delicately balanced emotions. A drop of fear distilled into the middle of a crowd is like a poison that taints the souls of all, causing a ruinous rout and a catastrophic defeat. A little morsel of bravery can sustain an army. Seeing Mimi's courage roused the others to action. They moved to follow.

Mimi climbed the three shallow steps to the porch. Lying in front of the door was a black mat that read "Welcome" in big white letters.

"We'll see about that," Mimi muttered under her breath. Feeling the others coming up behind her, she reached out and grasped the simple brass doorknocker, bringing it down once, twice, thrice.[81] The sound echoed behind the door. Xnasha and Cara joined Mimi on the porch with Mr. Kipling and Mrs. Francis right behind them.

For a full minute, they waited. There was no response. Mimi raised her hand to try knocking again but stopped when she heard a woman's voice saying faintly, "I'm

---

[81] I love the word *thrice*. I feel it isn't used often enough, so I try to insert it wherever possible.

coming! I'm coming! Oh, dearie me." Footsteps shuffled to the door. With a rattle of locks, the knob turned and the door opened. Mimi's hand fell to the stun pistol at her hip. She prepared for a fight.

She found it hard to conceal her surprise when the door opened to reveal the sweetest little old lady one could ever imagine. Standing there, her flower print dress faded, a threadbare pink cardigan over her shoulders, the old woman smiled, her face a nest of pleasant wrinkles with a pair of twinkling blue eyes as its centrepiece. Mimi had never known either of her grandmothers, and just looking at the woman in the doorway seemed to fill that void in her life. As the group waited, the old woman raised her wire-framed bifocals from where they dangled from a chain around her neck and placed them on her face.

"Oh my," the old woman said. "Oh my. What have we here? Is it Halloween? I've completely forgotten to get candy. Oh dear."

The woman's voice was soothing. Mimi found the tension melting away. She dropped her hand from her pistol. Part of her mind was aware that she should be careful, suspicious, but that part seemed very far away, a tiny voice in the distance.

"Excuse me, ma'am. We was lookin' for somethin' ... somebody else."

"Really? Oh, well. It's been so long since I've had visitors. Are you sure you wouldn't like to come in? I have just finished baking a batch of chocolate chip cookies and I'm sure I won't be able to eat them all myself." The old woman smiled hopefully.

Once again, Mimi heard the tiny voice shout its warning, but she ignored it. "That's sounds mighty good." Mimi glanced at Cara and saw the same bemused smile she was sure was present on her own face. "If it ain't too much trouble."

"Not at all." The old woman smiled again, revealing neat, even teeth. "Come right in."

Mimi moved forward to enter the house, but someone grabbed her arm. She turned to find Xnasha, her eyes wide with alarm, holding her back.

"Mimi," Xnasha hissed urgently. "You can't go in there!"

"Why not?" Mimi felt vaguely angry at having been delayed from entering the pretty little house. "I'm gonna have some cookies."

"Yes, Xnasha," Mrs. Francis scolded. "You shouldn't be so rude." Xnasha looked into the housekeeper's face and saw the same dreamy look in the older woman's eyes.

"It's a trap," Xnasha insisted. "You can't go in there."

"Nonsense!" Mr. Kipling held his arm out for Mrs. Francis, who took it. "Let's get some cookies."

The old woman's eyes narrowed slightly. "What's the problem? Those cookies are waiting."

Mimi snarled and pulled her arm away, suddenly flooded with anger. "Let go a me! You just want all the cookies fer yerself." She stomped up the steps and into the house before Xnasha could grab her again. Cara followed quickly afterwards, trailed by the other Guards. Xnasha stood by, unsure of what to do. The old woman smiled, but the smile held no warmth. "What's the matter, dear? Don't you like cookies?"

Xnasha looked into the woman's blue eyes and saw no kindness there. There was something cold and inhuman.

Yet Xnasha had no choice. She couldn't stop the others, so she had to join them and hope she could help. She followed the others up into the front door. The old woman waited until they were all inside and, with a final look up and down the street, she shut the door with finality. The lock clicked. Outside, no bird sang and no bee buzzed.

Part 3

PROVIDENCE

The Penultimate[82] Note from the Narrator

So, here we are, on the doorstep of the end of the story. The threads are all coming together now. Like a master weaver, I craft the fabric of this tale so that you may wear it like a fine pair of pants. I hope they are flattering on you.

The final chapters always hold a great deal of personal sadness for me. I will finish the tale. You will go back to your life of playing video games, skateboarding, plastering the underside of chairs with chewing gum, or whatever it is you fill your days with. It makes me wish I could extend the story in some way, add bits, make it longer. Perhaps I could have the characters make a side excursion to a shopping mall where they try on several different jackets.

That would not be right, however. Stories must be exactly as long as they are and no longer. Hamish X approaches the end of his story, and I must relate it exactly how it happened without any embellishment or time-wasting.

So without further ado ...

---

[82] *Penultimate* means "next to last." I just felt like using that word. So there.

I would just like to say, I think you are a very nice person ... And I'm glad you are reading this book ... And I enjoy pasta.

All right, I'm just prolonging things.

Here it comes: the last part of the last book of the saga of Hamish X.

Welcome to Providence.

Chapter 26

HAMISH X

Maggie and Thomas sat in small jump seats[83] that folded out of the wall of the aircraft. The seats were not very comfortable, partly because they were quite small and hard and partly because the Grey Agents had tied the children in place with restraining straps. Thomas and Maggie were completely unable to move. All around them, the roar of engines was deafening.

The jump seats were located in the cabin of the ODA Space Plane[84] that was rocketing up through the atmosphere

---

[83] The term *jump seat* comes from the Second World War. Jump seats, the folding seats in airplanes, were made for paratroopers (parachute soldiers) to sit on while waiting to jump out of an airplane. The paratroopers were chosen for their love of sitting. The seat was designed to snap against the wall out of the way when the paratrooper stood up. That way he would have nowhere to sit and therefore no option but to jump out of the plane. As a further incentive, comfortable chairs would often be thrown out of the plane first to lure the paratroopers after them. This led to a lot of people being injured by falling chairs, as the chairs were not furnished with parachutes.

[84] A Space Plane is designed to leave the Earth's atmosphere and take up station just outside the planet's gravity field. The Earth rotates while the Space Plane remains stationary. The plane then re-enters the Earth's atmosphere directly over its destination. Space Planes are a very speedy means of travel indeed. They have the terrible side effect of burning a hole in the ozone layer every time they pass through it, massive rocket

(Continued)

on its way back to Providence, Rhode Island, the home of the ODA. The cabin was sparsely appointed and small, only a few metres long and two metres high. The ceiling was a curved arch with harsh lights recessed into the panelling. There were jump seats along the walls of the cabin and portholes along the sides. All the shades on the portholes were drawn, allowing no view of the world outside. As he sat across from Thomas and Maggie, Hamish X's head lolled forward with the tossing of the Space Plane's passage. Since Mr. Candy had snapped the white cuffs over his hand, the boy had been completely inert. He walked when prodded and complied with simple commands, but he wasn't conscious. Thomas and Maggie had shouted themselves hoarse trying to rouse him when they were first secured in their seats and left alone as Mr. Candy and Mr. Sweet went forward into the cockpit to begin takeoff. Hamish X did not respond. They finally gave up when the engines fired and they could no longer hear each other shout.

Up, up, up they rose. The pressure of the rocket boosters driving the craft pressed them back into their seats uncomfortably, the straps cutting into their flesh as the Space Plane fought its way free of gravity. The sensation became painful and finally unbearable before, suddenly, the pressure was gone. The engines cut out and the silence was profound.

---

engines firing. The NASA Space Shuttle is an example of what is basically a Space Plane, although the Space Shuttle does not fly often enough to cause cumulative damage to the ozone layer. The ODA has very little regard for environmental concerns. They have a fondness for Styrofoam, are rumoured to enjoy massive tire fires, and are reputed to have invented the plastic shopping bag. The ODA Space Plane once belonged to the Soviet Space Program and was purchased by the Grey Agents at an auction after the fall of the Soviet regime.

"What happened?" Maggie asked Thomas.

"I dunno," Thomas answered. His eyes went wide. "Look at your hair!"

"What about it?" Maggie asked, irritated. "This isn't the time to start making fun of my hair."

"No, really! It's floating ... like you're underwater or something."

"What?" She couldn't see her own hair, but she looked across at Hamish X and saw that his limbs were weightless. His boots hung out in front of him as if they were suspended in water. "What's going on?"

"We have left the Earth's gravity field," Mr. Candy said, bobbing into the cabin. "The Earth is spinning below us as we speak. Soon we will drop out of orbit." Kicking out from the frame of the door that led to the cockpit, the Grey Agent propelled himself across the cabin. He grabbed hold of the seat that held Hamish X and pulled the boy's head back by the hair. "Oh so soon, Hamish X. Your destiny is at hand."

"Take your hands off him, you creep," Maggie growled, struggling against her bonds.

"Your time is coming, too, little girl. All of humanity has mere hours left. You will all be under our power when the gate opens." With a gloved hand, Mr. Candy flipped up the shade on the closest window, revealing the blue curve of the Earth. From her geography classes, Maggie recognized the tapering triangle that was England, Scotland, and Wales smeared with cloud. It was a sight that would normally have filled her with awe. So few human beings had seen this sight, the planet made peaceful by distance. The world was an impossibility of water and earth, rock and sky, a home to her people, all people. But instead of wonder, she felt only dread. The Space Plane would soon begin its descent and all of that beauty would end. She was powerless to do anything about it.

"Wake up, Hamish X! Wake up!" she shouted. "You've got to wake up."

But Hamish X dreamed on.

"Wake up, Hamish X! Wake up!"

Hamish X knew that voice. He opened his eyes and blinked at the bright sunlight. He was lying in his bed in his quarters at the Hollow Mountain. Sitting up, he saw King Liam sitting in a chair beside his bed, basking in the light of the artificial sun.

"King Liam?"

"Of course." King Liam smiled. "It's about time. You are such a lazy creature. Get out of bed. There's a lot I have to tell you." With that, King Liam stood up and left the room. "There's breakfast on the terrace. Come on, sleepypants!"

Hamish X watched him go, confused. "This can't be happening." He swung his boots out of bed and found that he was fully clothed in the desert robes that Harik had given him. At the thought of the Bedouin, he felt a pang of worry. What had happened? He couldn't seem to remember. He recalled leaping from the wall at the Grey Agents, but everything else was veiled in fog. He went through the door and onto the terrace.

The terrace looked out over Frieda's Cavern. Hamish X had enjoyed the view here many times before, sitting at the small table on his terrace. The entire green expanse of the cavern spread out below, its neatly parcelled fields growing corn and wheat, vegetables and flowers. At the centre, the Stair twisted upward around the central elevator, the waterslide a plastic helix twining around the outside. The place was perfect, just as Hamish X remembered it. But something about that seemed wrong.

"Where is everybody?" he said out loud. The cavern was completely empty; in fact, the entire Hollow Mountain was silent and still, save for the distant burbling of the fountain far below. All the people and

all the raccoons were absent. The whole place had a cold and lifeless air about it.

"Dull, isn't it, with no people in it," King Liam agreed. "I can't say I like it like this, but there you are. We didn't have the time to program in all the randomizers that would give us birdsong, computer-generated inhabitants, and what have you. It's just you and me."

Hamish X wrested his attention from the commanding view and turned to find the King of Switzerland sitting at a small round table set for breakfast. There was a plate of sticky pastries with jam and toast. A bowl of berries, perfect and succulent, glistened in the light of the artificial solar generators overhead. Hamish X's stomach rumbled.

"This is a dream," Hamish X said, sitting down in an elegant wrought-iron chair opposite the King. "This isn't real."

"True," the King agreed. "Like the Memory Party, this is a simulation. I need to talk to you. We're inside your head. I do appreciate your letting me in for this little chat." King Liam stretched his hands over his head and wiggled his fingers. "What a joy to be able to do such a simple thing without any pain at all. Delightful!"

"Weird."

"Decidedly. It must be very weird for you, but don't worry, it's ultimately for your benefit."

"Wait," Hamish X said suddenly. He stopped, paralyzed by a thought.

"What is it? What's the matter?" The King's face was full of concern.

"I ... I don't know how to tell you this, but ... you're dead."

"Am I?"

"In the real world, I mean. Outside my head. The George raccoon told me that the Grey Agents had destroyed the Hollow Mountain, filled it with lava, and you were ... killed in the battle."

The King frowned. "Oh dear. What a shame. I quite liked myself." He shrugged and picked up a croissant and began heaping jam onto it. "Eat up! It may only be digital, but it's delicious!" He took a big bite and chewed happily.

"The George raccoon bit me," Hamish X said, picking up a juicy raspberry and popping it into his mouth. The explosion of flavour was intoxicating. "Why did he do that?"

"It was the easiest way of injecting this program into you without arousing the suspicion of the ODA. Poor George. All his raccoons are gone. He's stuck in the Mountain, locked in a lava flow. Boring for him. Promise me that you'll get him out of there once this is all over. I'd hate to think of him lodged there for all eternity. Have a cinnamon bun."

Hamish X picked up the spiral twist of sugary dough and took a big bite. It was as delicious as the raspberry had been, if not more. Chewing, he shook his head. "I doubt there'll be anything left. The ODA are pretty thorough about that kind of thing."

"George's central processor is housed in a special hardened vault that seals up tight should any threat arise. I think he'll be there. Bored and cranky, certainly, but he'll be there."

"Why are you here?" Hamish X asked, licking the sticky brown sugar from his fingers.

"Ah," the King leaned back in his chair and steepled his fingers, "it's both simple and complicated."

"Isn't it always?"

The King laughed. "Yes. I created this program to be activated if you were ever captured by the ODA. It would seem that that has come to pass."

Hamish X suddenly recalled the last seconds before he woke in the recreated Hollow Mountain. "Oh, no. It's true! I've been captured. What a fool! I got angry and I've made a mess of everything."

"Don't be too hard on yourself." The King looked pained. "You have every right to be angry."

"I found the Professor. He told me what my purpose is," Hamish X said bitterly. "I'm a tool, a cog in a machine, a computer chip. The idea that I could be anything else was ... it was stupid. I'm a tool."

The King shook his head, pushed an unruly shock of red hair off his brow. "You are what you believe yourself to be. That is the only thing I can tell you. The Hamish X I know is smart, loyal, genuine, and kind. I've never met a wrench with those qualities."

Hamish X stood up and went to the railing of the terrace. He looked out over the perfectly simulated landscape, his face hard. His golden eyes were angry. He felt a hand on his shoulder. The King spoke again. "Here's the other thing about tools: they can turn on their users. Hammers hit thumbs and nails equally. You have to remember that at the final moment, Hamish X." The King turned Hamish X around to face him. "No. It's just Hamish now, isn't it? The X is a designation given to you by the ODA. You've outgrown them, Hamish. They sent you out into the world to expand your mind, to build your brain, but they didn't understand that you are more than a bunch of nerves and tissues and programs. They just can't understand that you have grown a heart as well. You are a good boy, Hamish. Did you hear me? A good boy. Now, it's time for you to wake up. You have work to do. Eat this."

The King popped a small chocolate into Hamish X's mouth. Reflexively, Hamish X bit down and his mouth was flooded with the richest, most beautiful chocolate flavour he had ever tasted. As the chocolate melted and flowed down his throat, the surrounding scene, the terrace and the cavern, began to fade. The King became insubstantial before his eyes.

"The breakfast was a program that will free you from the restraints." The King smiled and said, "Goodbye, Hamish X, and good luck."

Inside the cabin of the Space Plane, Hamish X raised his head. In his mouth, the faint residue of the dream of chocolate danced on his tongue. He looked up and saw

Thomas and Maggie strapped in their restraints and Mr. Candy floating at the porthole. Maggie's eyes widened, but Hamish X shook his head ever so slightly. She clamped her mouth shut. She elbowed her brother, who looked at Hamish X and kept the surprise from his face.

Hamish X mouthed a single word: "Wait."

Mr. Candy sensed they were looking at something other than the porthole and turned his head to find that Hamish X was inert as ever, his head lolling in the absence of gravity.

"Oh, Hamish X," the Grey Agent said. "We will land in Providence in a few minutes. And oh, we have a surprise for you."

It was all Hamish X could do to keep himself from smiling and betraying himself until the Grey Agent spun away and disappeared through the cockpit door.

mr. Crisp

The main chamber was a hive of activity. Every available
Grey Agent was occupied with the task of priming the gate.
Mr. Crisp and his security detail stood looking out over
the vast chamber, the beautiful, pulsating gate shedding
the glorious light of the homeworld over them all. Many
last-minute diagnostic checks were underway, and the
construction of the interface module was almost completed.
Mr. Crisp was forced to continue the search for the intruder
with a bare minimum of troops. He had only twenty Grey
Agents under his command. As a result, he was relying
heavily on the artificial intelligence known as Mother to
carry out most of the quartering and searching of the
ventilation shafts.

"Mother," Mr. Crisp said, a hint of impatience creeping
into his voice. "Have we narrowed down his location yet?
Mr. Sweet and Mr. Candy report they are en route with
Hamish X in custody. We must capture the interloper! Nothing
can jeopardize the opening of the gate. Do you understand?"

"I understand more than you can imagine." Mother's voice
was beautiful and cold. "The intruder is wearing some form of
body coating that confounds my sensors. I am running programs
to collate the data. I am creating a means of tracking him using
ambient heat and sweat traces. I'm very close."

"Close isn't good enough," Mr. Crisp said flatly. "I—"

Mother interrupted Mr. Crisp's complaint. "I have a possible location for the intruder.

"Based on collated data, my sensors tell me there is a temperature discrepancy in ventilation shaft seventy-eight."

"Excellent," Mr. Crisp sneered with Aidan's mouth. "Release the swarm."

"Very good, Mr. Crisp."

Chapter 27

PARVEEN

The hours since he had been discovered in the armoury had been the most harrowing in Parveen's short life. The entire ODA Headquarters had been mobilized to hunt him down. He felt like a rat in the walls of a house, scuttling along the ventilation shafts, trying to keep ahead of his pursuers.

The fact that he was still on the loose was more a testament to the narrowness of the shafts than any ingenuity on his part. The Grey Agents had figured out immediately that he was hiding in the ventilation system after he'd been seen escaping from the elevator. Knowing where he was and capturing him, though, were two totally different matters.

The Grey Agents had tried at first to climb into the shaft after him. Parveen's small size allowed him to move with ease, but the agents were not so lucky. They found it difficult to negotiate the narrow passages. After Parveen ambushed two of the agents sent in after him, frying their circuits with two of his last three hamster bombs, his opponents had decided that direct pursuit was not the wisest option. From that point on, they decided to use a more indirect approach.

Parveen was relieved when the Grey Agents retreated momentarily. Had they known that only one hamster bomb remained to him, they might have pressed the attack and that would have been the end of him. He sat with his back to the wall of a shaft, breathing heavily and trying to decide on a course of action.

His capture was inevitable. The ODA had access to all the schematics of their facility. They had only to bide their time, carefully quarter the facility, and drive him into a dead end. Parveen was resigned to that moment. What he managed to achieve before he was captured was the only thing left to consider.

He took an inventory of his equipment. He had the kilogram of plastic explosive he had liberated from the armoury. He had two pistols stolen from the fallen Grey Agents he had dispatched in the shaft with the hamster bombs. He had his multitool and small set of electronic tools, including a battery-operated soldering iron. He had a flashlight and his sneaky suit.

"Not much," Parveen said aloud. "But I'll think of something."

He tensed as he heard a skittering sound, like claws scrabbling on the metal of the ventilation shaft. Parveen was puzzled: he'd never seen any animal life in the shafts in the time he'd been hiding there. The skittering drew nearer. Parveen hefted one of the stolen pistols and aimed it at the corner of the shaft.

The thing looked like a cockroach, but it was obvious that it was artificial: a product of the ODA laboratories. For one thing, it was the size of a small housecat. Its shell was silvery and too metallic to be natural. Long antennae sprouted from the top of its swivelling head. They waved in the air, searching the shaft. Parveen tried to remain completely still. The creature shuffled forward, its steel feet tap-tapping on the metal floor of the shaft as it approached.

Parveen held his breath. As slowly as he could, he began to raise the pistol.

The thing seemed to sense the minute movement. It paused, antennae swinging towards Parveen. It shuffled closer.

Parveen had begun to perspire. The sneaky suit was not really air-conditioned and the shaft was warm. Sweat beaded on his forehead, and a drop formed on the bridge of his nose, gathering into one large droplet that slowly trickled down to the tip of his nose, hanging there and tickling Parveen terribly. He fought the urge to brush away the offending bit of salt and water.

The shiny insect crept closer. Parveen felt the weight of its body on his right boot and tried to remain perfectly still. The creature crawled up his leg. The antennae waved closer and closer until one of them reached out and carefully, oh so delicately, brushed the droplet of sweat on the tip of Parveen's nose.

Suddenly, the shaft was filled with a shrill screeching that was silenced when the pistol in Parveen's hand discharged and the cockroach-thing exploded into fragments. A hole the size of Parveen's head appeared in the wall of the ventilation shaft.

Parveen breathed deeply, his lungs hungry for air after holding his breath during the long seconds of the terrifying encounter. His entire body trembled. Lying on the floor of the shaft was a tangled mass of wires and circuit boards, the remains of the creature. Parveen reached down and grabbed a handful of its shattered workings. He peered at the refuse, trying to figure out if anything would be usable in the construction of a detonator.

He was interrupted by an eruption of skittering noises from the direction the first creature had just come. Stuffing

260

the wires into his backpack, Parveen turned and scampered in the opposite direction. He looked over his shoulder in time to see a swarm of the cockroach-things pour around the corner of the shaft, moving like a shimmering metal wave flowing in his direction.

Parveen pulled out both of his pistols and emptied them into the oncoming bugs. The effect was miniscule. When the guns were empty, Parveen turned and ran as fast as he could. He had to stay ahead of them. He had a plan that might save him for the short term, but he had to remember the right twists and turns of the ventilation system. One false turn might lead to his being cornered in a cul de sac.[85] He turned and turned again, barely staying ahead of the skittering metal insects.

The swarm was soon nipping at his heels. He scrambled around the final corner and kicked away one of the electronic bugs that had latched on to his foot. He looked ahead down the shaft and saw what he was searching for: at the junction of two corridors, a vertical shaft dropped away into the depths. He'd discovered this shaft on his mapping expedition. Parveen didn't know how deep it was, but he couldn't see the bottom of it when he had stood and looked down. The shaft was about four metres wide. He wondered if the metal creatures chasing him could jump that far. *We'll soon find out*, he thought. Parveen drew on his last reserves of energy and dashed down the shaft.

As he ran, he unshouldered his backpack, rammed a hand into the top, and fished out the magnetic grappler. He slipped his fingers through the eye that usually held the rope.

---

[85] *Cul de sac* is a French term for a dead end. It is literally translated as "bottom of the bag." The French term originated in the seventeenth century, when it became fashionable to build houses at the bottom of enormous bags.

He reached the edge of the shaft and jumped into empty space over the gaping vertical shaft. Halfway across, just as the momentum of his leap was running out, he thumbed the power button of the magnet. The metal disc hummed to life and the power of the magnet dragged him across the rest of the gap, latching on to the opposite wall of the shaft with a loud clang. He dangled there from one arm and looked back across the gap to see if his ploy had been successful.

The wave of mechanical bugs surged down the shaft in hot pursuit. They were moving so fast and were so intent upon their prey that they failed to register the yawning empty space in their path. The leading edge of the swarm plunged over into the pit, cascading like a chrome water-fall into the darkness. Within seconds, however, their tiny electronic brains registered the danger and the next wave of insects halted on the brink, antennae waving in the air. They clearly sensed that their quarry was close by, but they were thwarted by the empty space in front of them.

Taking advantage of their momentary confusion, Parveen hauled himself up into the far shaft, clicking off the magnetic grappler and stowing it in his backpack. Sucking down desperate gulps of air, he waited to see what the bugs would do.

For the moment, they milled about on the verge of the drop, antennae whipping back and forth. They seemed at a loss as to how to get at him. He was sure they would figure something out soon, probably backtracking and finding another way around the obstacle. Parveen gratefully welcomed the opportunity to catch his breath even for a few seconds. He had to decide what to do. He had the plastic explosive, but would he have time and material enough to build a bomb and place it where it might do the most damage?

He had no time even to contemplate the problem. With a sinking stomach, he watched as one of the metal creatures moved to the edge of the gap and sprang into space. It sailed through the air and fell slightly short. It slammed into the far wall centimetres below the safety of the far side of the shaft.

As Parveen watched, another insect moved to the edge and leapt. This one was luckier. Its little legs gripped the far edge. Parveen didn't wait to see if it would succeed. He leapt forward and kicked the creature into the abyss. Now others attempted to leap across the gap, each jump becoming more accurate as they learned. Parveen flailed with his feet and hands, striking the creatures down into the pit. He swung his backpack, knocking the mechanical attackers out of the air. Already exhausted from the long chase, he was tiring quickly. He knew he couldn't hold out much longer. He prepared for the end.

The End didn't come. As suddenly as the attack had started, the creatures ceased throwing themselves across the gap. They stood still as stones, only their antennae waving. They seemed to be receiving new instructions. After a few seconds of utter stillness, they moved.

Parveen couldn't believe his eyes. They were leaving! They were moving away along the shaft in the direction from which they'd come. He was safe! He slumped against the wall of the ventilation shaft, letting his backpack fall between his knees. His entire body quivered with exhaustion.

"Why?" he asked aloud. "Why did they go?" He looked at the shattered bugs around him, smashed by his desperate defence. Wires and circuit boards hung like entrails from the broken bugs. Looking at them, his heart leapt. He reached for the closest one and began tearing the guts out of it, peering at them through his thick glasses. "Yes! Yes! This will do fine."

He stuffed three of the shattered bugs into his backpack and trotted off towards the junction he called his home base. He had work to do. The mystery of the retreating bugs would have to wait.

He was only a few metres from his refuge when he practically ran straight into a maintenance robot trundling along the shaft. He stopped and let the dumb servitor pass. Suddenly, he had an idea. Smiling, he set off after the robot, pulling the last of his precious hamster bombs from his backpack as he closed the distance.

Chapter 28

MIMI

The interior of the house was as disarming as its exterior. The floors were hardwood, lovingly polished and covered with spotlessly clean rugs. On the wall was a framed needlepoint that read "Home Sweet Home." The visitors crowded into the entry hall. Looking down the hallway past a set of wooden stairs, Mimi saw a neat little kitchen with a table and chairs, a black countertop, and white cupboards. A radio sat on the countertop, a masterpiece of gleaming chrome. Mimi remembered her mother singing along to a very similar radio in their little kitchen in Cross Plains, Texas, when she was a child.

"Come in, one and all! Have a seat in the parlour. Anywhere you can manage!" The old lady opened two doors with bevelled glass panes to the right of the front door and revealed a parlour furnished in antique chairs and wooden tables that looked as if they could have been featured in a museum.

"I hope we aren't taking up too much of your time," Mr. Kipling said.

"Not at all." The old lady smiled, her face wreathed in wrinkles. "I rarely have visitors."

"Children." Mrs. Francis's voice was oddly detached. "Make sure you wipe your feet."

"Oh, I don't mind. Just sit down and I'll get everyone some cookies and milk." The old lady clapped her hands, delighted. "Won't that be nice?"

"I'll help you," Mrs. Francis said, moving towards the kitchen.

"No." The woman's voice was firm. She looked into Mrs. Francis's eyes and said, "No. You will sit down right there on the settee. Now."

Mrs. Francis nodded absently, doing as she was told.

"All of you," the woman said in that same commanding voice, "sit down." The Guards moved to obey, sitting on a Persian rug that covered the entirety of the parlour floor. They moved with dreamy slowness, as if through liquid. Mimi and Cara joined them.

Xnasha grabbed them each by the arm. "What are you doing?"

"Sitting," Cara said.

"I want some cookies," Mimi mumbled.

"Yes. Cookies for everyone." The old lady fixed Xnasha with a blue-eyed stare over the top of her bifocals. "Sit."

Xnasha felt something in the old woman's voice tug at her. Obviously, the woman's voice had some form of hypnotic power. Xnasha didn't move.

"Sit," the old woman said again.

Xnasha felt the pull again but knew she could resist it. She decided, however, that until she knew what power this old lady had over the others, she would bide her time and wait for her moment. She pretended to be like the others, lethargically slumping to the floor and sitting.

"Fine. I'll be right back. Don't go away now. Don't move a muscle."

Xnasha looked around the room. She had never been inside a surface-dweller's house before, so she couldn't be sure if this one was unusual. The furniture was made of dark wood, meticulously polished. On every available surface there were woven circular mats made of white material. She reached over and picked one up. The fabric was soft, the pattern intricate.

"Admiring my doilies?"[86] The old woman was back in the room, carrying a tray laden with little pale brown discs speckled with smaller, darker bits. "I made cookies. I hope you like chocolate chips."

The children all reached for the cookies. Even Mr. Kipling and Mrs. Francis grabbed one. Xnasha stayed where she was.

"What's the matter? Allergic to chocolate?" The old woman stared at Xnasha.

"I don't think I've ever had chocolate."

"I see." The old lady thrust the tray at her. "Try one."

Xnasha looked at the tray, then back at the old woman. "No, thank you."

The old woman frowned. Her voice became harder. "Take one. Now."

"No," Xnasha refused.

"I see," the old woman said sharply. "I guess I'll get the tea, then."

The old woman slammed the tray down on the coffee table and stomped off into the kitchen.

"Don't eat the cookies," Xnasha whispered urgently.

---

[86] Doilies are common in the homes of old women throughout the world. They are meant to be placed under vases and teapots and the like. No one knows why women begin to amass supplies of doilies once they reach advanced age, but it is a fact that they do. Millions have been spent researching the phenomenon, but no solid breakthroughs have been made.

Everyone was holding a cookie. They looked at Xnasha like she was crazy.

"There's something wrong here."

"Whatever," Cara said and raised the cookie to her lips.

"No," Xnasha said. She slapped the cookie out of Cara's hand. It bounced on the carpet and crumbled into pieces.

"What's the big idea?" Mimi snarled.

"Mimi," Xnasha said. "Don't you see? There's something wrong."

"Yes." The old woman's voice was cold and hard. She stood in the doorway that led to the kitchen, her blue eyes gentle no longer. They were blazing with rage. "There is something wrong. You have gotten cookie crumbs all over my carpet!" Her voice rose to a high-pitched screech. She held a teapot in her hand. "I hate when people get crumbs on the carpet!"

Mrs. Francis seemed to wake from her daze. "It was an accident."

"Shut up!" the old woman screamed. "You are trespassing in my house! You didn't eat the cookies! You will pay!"

Mr. Kipling rose to his feet. "See here, my good woman."

"No, YOU SEE HERE!" She cocked her arm and flung the teapot at Mrs. Francis. The flying pot rocketed straight at the housekeeper's head and would have struck her if Mr. Kipling hadn't thrown himself in the way. The teapot struck him directly in the chest and exploded. Mr. Kipling was flung backwards through the front window of the house. Glass shattered and burst outward as he was pitched out onto the lawn.

For a second, everyone froze in shocked disbelief.

"Rupert!" Mrs. Francis flung herself out the gaping window after her husband.

Mimi, Cara, and the other Guards shook off their stupor and brandished their fighting sticks. Xnasha pulled her crossbow from her back.

"Who are you?" Mimi demanded.

"I am Mrs. Guardian," the old woman snarled. She flexed her muscles and her torso rippled. Long metal claws sprouted from her gnarled hands. Her teeth grew long and sharp. She crouched in the kitchen doorway. With a voice like gears grinding, she said, "You shall not pass."

"I'm Mimi Catastrophe Jones," Mimi said, spinning her stick. "This is Cara and Xnasha and the Royal Swiss Guards. And you? Yer Texas toast."

As one, the Guards leapt at Mrs. Guardian. With an ear-splitting roar, she sprang to meet them.

A few seconds of close combat were enough to dispel any lingering doubts that they were fighting an old woman. Mrs. Guardian's reflexes were blindingly fast. She met all their attacks with ease. The Guards were hampered by their own numbers in the cramped quarters of the parlour while Mrs. Guardian had only to stay with her back to the kitchen to hold them at bay. The fighting sticks were a poor match for metal claws. The talons were razor sharp and chewed through even the toughened wood of the staves. One of the Guards was disarmed immediately and a back-handed strike sent her smashing into a wall, destroying an end table and a lamp. The girl lay on the ground groaning, out of the fight. She was soon joined by two others.

Mimi ducked and swung, looking for an opening. The claws scythed through the air, swinging in deadly arcs. Mimi waited until the thing was occupied fighting two other Guards and took her chance. Rolling in low, she kicked out with her feet, hooking Mrs. Guardian's ankle and sending the creature smashing onto its back.

With a cry, all the remaining Guards leapt in. They swung their sticks at the prone creature, but it sprung to its feet. Grabbing a flowered ottoman, it swung the foot-stool in a wide arc, knocking the Guards away like so many bowling pins. The Guards smashed into the walls and fell in heaps. A few of them struggled to their feet, but most merely lay there, unmoving. Mimi was left standing alone. *Where are you, Xnasha?* The Atlantean was nowhere in sight. Mimi gritted her teeth and held her stick out in front of her.

"Is that all you got?" Mimi taunted. "'Cause I ain't impressed."

The thing grinned, showing its vicious metal teeth. "You should have taken the cookie."

The creature lashed out a foot with impossible speed, driving it into Mimi's chest and sending her through the gaping front window and out onto the lawn. Mimi slammed down onto the grass hard, forcing the air from her lungs. Gasping, she tried to rise.

"Mimi?" Mrs. Francis was kneeling beside Mr. Kipling, holding his head. The older man's eyes were closed and his breathing was ragged. His skin had an unhealthy grey cast. The entire front of his coat was burnt away as if by acid.

Mimi felt rage course through her. The sight of the sweet and polite Mr. Kipling lying injured on the grass flipped a switch in her head. Mrs. Francis watched with tear-streaked cheeks as Mimi hauled herself to her feet.

"Mimi, you can't go back in there," the housekeeper pleaded. "You'll be killed."

Mimi bent and pulled the sabre from Mr. Kipling's scabbard. The blade snaked free with a reptilian hiss. "Nobody smacks my friend with an exploding teapot and gits away with it."

She grasped the hilt of the sabre in both hands and ran towards the house, leaping through the shattered window. She landed in a tuck and roll and came to her feet with the sword raised above her head.

The thing that called itself Mrs. Guardian stood in the kitchen doorway. It held the tray of cookies. During the fight, its dress and flesh had been torn to reveal the silvery wires and steel sinew, the inner workings of the malevolent machine it truly was.

"So, you came back," Mrs. Guardian sneered. It held out the tray. "Cookie, dear?"

"No thanks, Granny," Mimi said sweetly. "I don't wanna spoil my dinner."

271

"Oh, I insist," Mrs. Guardian shrieked. The claws plucked a cookie from the tray and flicked it at Mimi's head. Mimi jerked her head to the side, but the cookie still cut a groove along her cheek before it buried itself in the wall. More cookies lanced across the room. Mimi dodged each one and knocked the final missile out of the air with the flat of the sabre.

"Looks like you ran outta ammo, Granny." Mimi held the sword high above her head, two hands gripping the hilt tightly. She ducked as the tray slashed through the space where her head had been an instant earlier, piercing the wall and quivering there with a loud *Whang*!

Mrs. Guardian clenched its fists and crouched down. Mimi did the same. The two adversaries eyed each other over the expanse of the Persian carpet, each waiting for the other to make a move.

Simultaneously, they leapt at each other. Mimi slashed with the sabre. Sparks rained down as one clawed hand reached up, parrying the blow. The other claw raked low, but Mimi stuck out a foot and jabbed her heel into the creature's wrist, blocking the blow but numbing her whole leg up to the hip. Mimi fell back. She parried furiously, but she was weakening. Mrs. Guardian came at her relentlessly, raining a flurry of blows that Mimi met with the sabre. Mimi knew she was tiring. She had nothing left. She raised the sabre with quivering arms to block one more blow, but the creature grabbed her wrist.

The old woman, thing, monster, whatever lifted her up by the arm. Mimi dangled like a fish caught by some proud sportsman. Mrs. Guardian raised Mimi until the girl's green eyes were level with its own icy blue ones. This was the end.

"Go ahead, Granny," Mimi gasped, her teeth bared. "Go ahead and kill me."

"Oh, I will." Mrs. Guardian grinned, metal teeth glinting. It raised a gleaming claw, poised to rip out Mimi's throat.

"Excuse me." Xnasha's voice was calm.

Mrs. Guardian twisted its head to see Xnasha in the kitchen doorway. The Atlantean had crept around through the kitchen from the hallway and come up behind Mrs. Guardian.

"You are a very mean old lady," Xnasha continued, almost apologetically. "And ugly, too." Xnasha fired the crossbow she was holding. The metal bolt flew straight and true, plunging into the metal forehead of the thing that called itself Mrs. Guardian. Its white wig tipped over one eye. It stood stunned, loosing Mimi from its grip then falling to its knees with a thud.

Seeing her chance, Mimi swung the sabre with all her might, slashing through the neck of the monster. Mimi staggered with the strength of her own swing, almost tripping over her own feet, but she caught herself.

Mrs. Guardian's head flew from its shoulders. Black fluid shot out in a high-pressure geyser, painting the ceiling. The head bounced on the carpet and rolled to a stop. The eyes blinked once, then stared lifelessly at the wall.

"How do ya like them cookies?" Mimi rasped, leaning on the sabre.

Xnasha stepped over the machine on the carpet and squeezed her friend's arm.

"Are you all right?"

"Yeah. Where were you?"

"Performing a flanking manoeuvre. You ought to see something." Xnasha tugged Mimi's arm towards the kitchen.

"No." Mimi shook her off. "Just a sec."

Mimi went around the room checking her fallen comrades. She found Cara sitting with her back to the wall.

"Nice job, Mimi." Cara smiled weakly. "I'm okay. I just need a minute to catch my breath."

"When ya feel up to it, check th' others in here. I'm goin' outside."

"Gotcha." Cara pushed herself up and joined Xnasha as she surveyed the fallen Guards.

Mimi hopped through the shattered window and went to Mrs. Francis. The housekeeper was still holding her husband, who was awake but clearly in a lot of pain.

"How are ya, Mr. Kipling?"

"I've been better," Mr. Kipling grunted. He coughed and winced at the pain. "I always seem to be getting hurt. I hate holding everyone up. I'll be on my feet in a moment." He tried to rise but immediately subsided into a fit of coughing.

"Rupert, lay still, you fool," Mrs. Francis cried. "You aren't going anywhere. Mimi! Your face is bleeding!"

"Jest a scratch. Mr. Kipling, I hate ta say it, but she's right. It looks like yer outta this fight."

Mr. Kipling lay back and closed his eyes. "Yes, sadly, that is true." He opened his blue eyes and looked up at Mimi. "Good luck, Mimi Catastrophe Jones. From the moment I met you on Snow Monkey Island, I knew you were a special girl."

Mimi's face reddened. "No need to go all mushy." She scowled, but her eyes stung. Fortunately, Mrs. Francis gathered her in a soft, strong embrace.

"I have to stay with him and the others who are hurt," she fretted. "Please be careful, my darling Mimi. Find Parveen and hurry back."

"Aw, Mrs. Francis, let go, will ya?" Mimi extricated herself from the housekeeper's grasp and rubbed away the tears from her eyes before they could spill down her cheeks. "I ain't dead yet, and with luck I ain't gonna be soon."

"Mimi! Let's go!" Cara called from the window.

"Comin'," Mimi replied. She turned and looked at the two dearest adults she had ever known. Mr. Kipling had taught her everything about being honourable, and Mrs. Francis had just been ... wonderful. She hated to leave them behind. "I'll be back. Don't worry." She turned to go, but stopped and turned back, holding the sabre up in front of her. "I'll use this fer both of us." Then she ran across the lawn and hopped into the window.

Mr. Kipling watched her go. "I do love that girl."

"So do I." Mrs. Francis kissed his forehead, fighting tears. "So do I."

Inside the wrecked parlour, several Guards were lying on the floor. Xnasha and Cara had tried to make them comfortable. They were too sorely wounded to go any farther. Mimi did a quick headcount and found that ten were left in action, including Cara, Xnasha, and her.

"Good work, everybody," Mimi said. "You can rest now. Mrs. Francis'll be in to take care o' y'all soon. The rest of ya, make sure y'all got sticks and take all the extra batteries for the stun rifles from the ones stayin' here." The Guards moved to obey.

Xnasha beckoned from the kitchen doorway. Mimi, Cara, and the others followed her.

Inside, they found a perfect little kitchen complete with black-and-white tiled floor, Formica table and chairs, a shiny chrome radio, and a toaster gleaming under the overhead light.

"Well, ain't this quaint."

Cara sniffed. "This is the Headquarters of the deadly ODA?"

Xnasha shook her head. She went to a tall cupboard with twin doors. She pulled the doors open to reveal the shiny sliding doors of an elevator car. The doors opened. The car was empty.

"Well, ain't *that* quaint! Everybody in."

"Are you sure it's safe?" Cara asked.

"Heck, nothin' around here is safe. I just got my butt kicked by an old lady!"

"Good point," Cara conceded.

They all trooped into the car. The doors whisked shut behind them.

Mr. Crisp

Mr. Sweet's voice sounded in Mr. Crisp's skull. It was as if his superior were standing beside him instead of descending from orbit, kilometres above the Earth. "Have you secured the intruder, Mr. Crisp?"

"Not yet, but we are closing in on him. The swarm is on his heels."

"Excellent. We have retrieved the asset. We will be on the ground and in Headquarters within a quarter of an hour."

"Yes, Mr. Sweet," Mr. Crisp acknowledged. "Understood."

The voice was gone. Mr. Crisp spoke out loud. "Mother? Status of the swarm?"

"The swarm is in pursuit of the intruder ... One moment, please. Sensors have been tripped. The outer security checkpoint has been breached. Mrs. Guardian has been neutralized. Intruders have entered the main elevator."

Mr. Crisp couldn't believe what he was hearing. "Are you certain, Mother?"

"Verified contact with second group of intruders. They are approaching the main level. Shall I stop the elevator?"

Mr. Crisp thought for a moment. "No, bring them to this level. Redirect the swarm to meet them when they get off the elevator. I will assemble more agents."

"Redirecting the swarm."

Mr. Crisp sent out a call for more agents. There were few available. Almost everyone was involved in the preparations for the opening of the gate. Only one hundred agents out of thousands answered the summons. Mr. Crisp was confident that they would be enough.

Chapter 29

PARVEEN

Parveen toiled furiously, trying to get the work he needed to do done in the respite he had been given. He sat with his back to the huge fan in the junction of two shafts that he had come to think of as his personal quarters. In his lap, one of the broken bugs lay on its back. Parveen's electronic tool set was open beside him. He had hastily scavenged spare parts from the three broken bugs. Standing in front of him, its access panel open, stood the maintenance robot he had waylaid. Working quickly, he fashioned a detonator from the mishmash of parts and attached it to the block of plastic explosive he had stolen from the armoury. Satisfied, he stuffed the makeshift bomb into the open panel.

Next, he took off his watch. The watch was another of his designs. The watch told the time and the date, which wasn't unusual. It also was an altimeter and a Global Positioning System. While scouting the Headquarters over the past days, Parveen had taken the time to note the exact locations of strategic installations in the ODA facilities. One of those was the gate. He had not been daring enough to approach the gate directly: there were too many Grey Agents in the vicinity of the device. Instead, he had taken sightings from several points on the perimeter of the main chamber, then using simple trigonometry he had figured out the coordinates of the gate.

Now he wired his watch to the robot, inputting the gate's coordinates, and set the detonator. That done, he reconnected the robot's power source, being careful to make sure the robot's processor, its mechanical brain, was disconnected from the central computer. Parveen hoped Mother would be too preoccupied to detect one robot servitor dropping off the grid. Once his alterations were complete, he snapped the access panel closed. The robot immediately began toddling off along the ventilation shaft. Parveen watched it go, hoping his hasty handiwork would hold. The thing was now programmed to explode when it reached the gate's location. The maintenance robot was the perfect delivery system for a bomb. No one would question its presence anywhere in the facility. Parveen wasn't sure when it would arrive at the gate or what route it might take, but he could only hope the explosion would cripple the ODA's horrible apparatus.

Parveen couldn't just sit there, though. The bugs would be back. He had to wonder why the chase was called off in the first place. He took a few moments to wire together an electromagnetic pulse bomb from the remains of the metal bugs he hadn't yet used. It wouldn't be as strong as the one he'd used in Windcity that had immobilized the Firebirds and the Grey Agents in their helicopter, but it might buy him a little time. He tossed the device into his backpack and decided he needed to find out what was going on, despite the risk of a renewed attack by the metal cockroaches. He packed up his tools and set off to find a shaft cover to peer through.

He decided to go to the main chamber to see if there was any activity there. The Grey Agents had been busy building something in the shadow of the gate. Servitor robots had brought in tons of steel sheeting and scaffolding. Parveen moved carefully down the ventilation shaft, keeping an eye out for the metal bugs, but there were none to be found. As he approached, he heard what sounded like a battle in progress.

"Y'all want some more? 'Cause I got more!" The voice rose over the din. Parveen felt his heart leap. He knew that voice.

Mimi and the others were holding their own against the onslaught of mechanical cockroaches. The glittering bugs had greeted them as they stepped out of the elevator car, swarming along the floor and threatening to engulf them. Xnasha fired bolt after bolt from her crossbow, raking the horde but to little effect.

"Sticks!" Cara cried, whipping the staff around and smashing one of the bugs as it leapt at her face. The Guards lunged forward, forming a wedge around the elevator doors with Mimi and Cara at the apex.

Mimi took stock of her surroundings while smashing the attacking bugs aside. They were at one end of a long metal walkway. To her right was a high metal wall. About a hundred metres along was a steel doorway. The door was shut. To her back was the elevator. As soon as they had stepped through its doors, they had closed behind them and refused to reopen. Mimi drove the end of her fighting stick downwards, spearing a bug. She looked to her left.

There was a vast open space. She saw the gate hanging in its wreath of cables, pulsing its sickly glow. She staggered at the sight of it. A bug took advantage of the distraction to climb her leg. It buried its steel mandibles into her thigh.

The pain was intense. Mimi cried out.

A stick smashed across the back of the bug, dislodging it from her flesh. Mimi looked up to see Cara flick another bug aside.

"Thanks," Mimi grunted.

Cara winked and went back to defending herself. The bugs were seemingly inexhaustible. Though the Guards smashed and shattered their metal bodies, more bugs surged in to attack. Mimi glanced at the other Guards and saw they were tiring. Inch by inch, they were being pushed back. It became difficult to wield their fighting sticks without hitting one another.

Suddenly, there was a clatter behind Mimi.

"Ow," she heard Xnasha cry.

"Cover my back!" she shouted to Cara, who sidestepped and closed the gap in the line as Mimi whirled to face the new threat.

She found no new enemy, but a vent cover lay on the steel deck. Xnasha, completely out of bolts, had been crouched at the wall, waiting to smash any bug that got through using her crossbow as a club. At the moment, she was rubbing her scalp where the vent grating had struck her as it fell from above.

"Y'all right?" Mimi asked.

"Fine. Just a bump."

She looked up and saw a hole in the wall. She thought she saw something moving in the hole, but she couldn't seem to focus on it.

"I know yer there! Come out and I'll beat ya stupid."

A patch of darkness detached from the mouth of the ventilation shaft and dropped to the deck. The patch of darkness shifted in colour, becoming grey as the surrounding walls. A piece of the greyness seemed to peel away to reveal the face of Parveen, blinking behind his glasses. "Please, don't beat me stupid, Mimi."

Mimi was so surprised she nearly dropped her stick. "Parv!" she cried. She wrapped a free arm around him and crushed the little boy to her. Xnasha stood by, her eyes wide with astonishment at the sudden appearance of this apparition out of thin air.

"Mimi, please! I have managed to stay alive this long. Refrain from strangling me now. And it's Parveen, as you well know."

Mimi reluctantly let go of her friend and stepped back to look at him. "Sneaky suit?"

"It was very effective, I must say."

"Parv, this is Xnasha. She's from Atlantis."

Parveen blinked. "Of course she is." He looked at the seething mass of bugs held at bay by the desperate line of defenders. "You seem to have an infestation on your hands." He reached into his pack and pulled out a tangle of wires and circuit boards.

"Is that what I think it is?"

"Step aside, please."

Mimi did as she was told, saying, "Watch this, Xnasha."

Parveen ran forward a few steps and hurled the object out over the heads of the Guards. It went in a shallow arc and landed in the middle of the massed bugs. There was a dull thud.

The effect was instantaneous. The bugs closest to the impact immediately squealed and lay still. In an ever-widening arc, more and more bugs went dead as their circuits were fried by the pulse bomb. In a matter of seconds, the attacking swarm was turned into a glittering carpet of immobile scrap metal. The Guards leaned on their sticks, panting in relief.

"I shore am glad to see you, Parv."

Parveen removed his glasses and polished them with the corner of a handkerchief he pulled from his pocket. "Parveen, please! The feeling is mutual. Where is Hamish X?"

283

"Well, that there's a long story. The short version is, he ain't with us."

"I'm sorry to hear that," Parveen said. "I was hoping he would find a way to utterly defeat the ODA and rescue all the children held captive here. I guess one can't have everything."

Cara interrupted. "I'm glad you're all right, Parveen. How did you end up here in the first place?"

"I stowed away in Noor's compartment when the Grey Agents harvested the children after the fall of the Hollow Mountain. I've been hiding in the air vents. In the meantime, I have tried to learn as much about the facility as possible."

"I have to know where my brother is," said Cara.

"It pains me to say that I know he is here."

"Where?"

"The good news is, he's alive ... sort of."

"Sort of?"

"And therein lies the bad news ...," Parveen began. He didn't get a chance to explain.

"Drop your weapons!"

The voice sounded so familiar, but Mimi couldn't place it. She turned to see a line of Grey Agents approaching in full battle dress. In their hands they held heavy rifles. Leading them was a smaller agent dressed in the standard grey trench coat and fedora. The agents advanced across the floor, boots crunching on the lifeless bugs. At a distance of ten metres, they stopped. The lead agent took three more steps and stopped.

"You can't possibly hope to escape," the Grey Agent said. "Lay down your weapons and you will not be harmed."

"Aidan?" Cara's voice was a whisper of horror. "Aidan? Is that you?"

284

Parveen leaned closer to Mimi. "That's the bad news. What happens to older children when the ODA takes them? They become agents, hosts to creatures from another world."

"Oh, no," Mimi breathed. "That's horrible."

Cara dropped her staff, letting it fall from her numbed fingers. "Oh, Aidan! What have they done to you?" She took a step towards her brother. "What have they done?"

The agent cocked his head to one side, his black goggles impassive. "Aidan? I am not Aidan. I am Mr. Crisp."

"No," Cara said angrily. "Stop saying that. You're my brother, Aidan." She began to walk towards him. "You are my brother and I'm here to take you home."

The agent shook his head. "You ... you are mistaken!" He lowered his weapon. "I am Mr. Crisp. Surrender your weapons."

"Don't make me angry, Aidan. Don't make me have to do this." She pulled her stun pistol from her belt. "You're my brother and you're leaving here with me. Even if I have to knock you out and drag you away."

"Cara, NO!" Mimi cried.

Too late. Cara raised her pistol. Mr. Crisp raised his weapon, then he hesitated.

"Cara?" he said softly. "I ... know that name." He paused for a moment and then reasserted himself. "I ... I am Mr. Crisp."

"No, you are *not*. You're my brother, Aidan. Put down your gun right now!"

Something deep inside Mr. Crisp stirred. Perhaps his processing had been hasty. Perhaps his will was unusually strong, but he hesitated. He knew that voice. In spite of the ODA programming and the conditioning he had undergone in the surgery, something instinctively prompted him to do as this strange girl told him. He had to.

He tossed the gun onto the floor with a clatter.

The Grey Agents behind Mr. Crisp fired at him. He shuddered and fell with a crash, shattering his goggles on the hard ground.

"No!" Cara cried. She leapt forward and fell under a barrage of stun bolts, sliding unconscious to a halt against her brother.

The remaining Guards leapt to defend their former lieutenant and his sister. They were quickly brought down, strewn like lifeless dolls across the floor amid the wreckage of the bugs. Parveen held Mimi back.

"It would be foolish to throw yourself away, Mimi," Parveen said. "I have only just found you. I don't want to lose you again."

The Grey Agents trained their weapons on the three remaining invaders. Mimi and Parveen stood alone, side by side. Xnasha stepped up and joined them, tossing her useless crossbow to the floor.

"It would seem that this is the end of the line," the Atlantean said.

Mimi felt a hot band of anger settle across her chest. They were cornered. Everything was lost. They had come halfway across the world to stop the ODA and free their friends armed with some sticks. She wanted to smash the agents, tear them to bits, but she could do nothing.

Mimi looked at Xnasha, her white hair twined with shells and bits of metal. She looked at Parveen in his sneaky suit. She turned and looked at the Grey Agents ranged against her. She did the only thing left she could do.

Mimi laughed. In the darkest place in the world, she laughed. The Grey Agents raised their weapons, fearing a trick, but it was no trick. Mimi just found the whole situation funny.

"Is something funny?" Parveen asked.

"Nope," Mimi said and laughed even louder. "It's just ... It's ... well. Look at us! We're here, ain't we? Who woulda thought we'd ever leave Windcity, but here we are. We travelled in a airship ..."

"*An* airship," Parveen corrected.

"*An* airship, Mr. Smartypants. We found the King o' Switzerland. You found yer sister. I went to Atlantis! The things I saw. It's amazin', ain't it? Who woulda thought a girl from Cross Plains, Texas, and a boy from ... where is it you're from again?"

"India!" Parveen said, rolling his eyes.

"Yeah! Who woulda thought we'd fight pirates and travel the world and end up here tryin' our best to beat all the odds. We lost. But that ain't the point." Mimi laughed out loud. "We did all that. It's ... I just find it funny, is all." Mimi started laughing again.

Parveen and Xnasha looked at each other, then shrugged.

"She's a very crazy person," Parveen said.

"And she talks funny, too," Xnasha said.

Then they, too, began to laugh. The Grey Agents looked at one another in disbelief. In all the long years that the Headquarters of the Orphan Disposal Agency had stood on Angell Street in Providence, Rhode Island, never had the sound of human laughter been heard within their walls. The agents did not know what to do.

Fortunately for them, the door to the transport hall slid open to reveal Mr. Candy and Mr. Sweet. Between them, head high and smiling, stood Hamish X.

Chapter 30

Hamish X had sat with his head hanging down as the Space Plane descended. He'd weighed his options as the gravity slowly returned, pulling on his limbs and making him feel heavy and real again.

When he had come to himself, rising out of the dream that the King had constructed for him and finding that the handcuffs held no power over him, he thought about what he was going to do.

In free fall, high above the Earth, away from the pull of its gravity, he could view what he had learned from the Professor and the King with detachment.

"Hamish X! Hamish X!" He ignored the urgent whispers of Maggie and Thomas, shutting them out as he pondered his choices. Finally, the brother and sister fell silent, assuming he was unconscious again.

He thought about what he had learned about the ODA, their origins and their motives. All of his world would fall under their sway. Every place he had been and grown to love would be destroyed, warped beyond human understanding as the creatures from the plane beyond the gate sucked it dry.

His world. He realized that it was his world. Even though he had been built by the ODA, he was still a part of this world and he wanted to save it. Now, as he thought about his choice, he realized that to save it, he would have to submit to the will of Mr. Candy and Mr. Sweet. He had to believe the King and the Professor. He had to believe that he was more than a tool in the hands of the Grey Agents to be used and then thrown away.

He made his decision.

As the plane approached the surface of the Earth, kilometres out over the Atlantic Ocean, Hamish X opened his eyes and looked up at Maggie and Thomas.

"You're awake, Hamish X," Maggie said excitedly.

"About time," Thomas snorted.

"Yes." Hamish X smiled. "I'm awake at last. I need you two to do something for me."

"What?" Maggie asked, her eyes alight. "Do we jump 'em? Take control of the plane? What's the plan?"

"You do nothing," Hamish X said.

Thomas and Maggie stared in disbelief. "Nothing?" Maggie said, incredulous. "Why?"

"Because that's what I need you to do. I need you to keep your heads down, stick together, and when the time comes run as fast as you can."

"But we aren't chicken!" Thomas growled. "We're not afraid of a fight."

Hamish X smiled. "I know. You are brave. You are true friends. You came along to help me when I had no one else, and for that I'll always be grateful." He grew serious. "But this is something no one can help me with. This is the most important thing I will ever do, and I alone must do it. You have to promise me you won't try to stop me and you won't interfere."

Thomas and Maggie stared at Hamish X, defiance in their eyes.

"Please," he said softly. "Promise me."

Thomas and Maggie looked at each other and finally nodded in unison.

"PROXIMITY ALARM," a mechanical voice announced and the Space Plane plunged into the sea. The ship had been fitted to travel short distances under water. The transport bay was located at the end of a long tunnel burrowed out of the rock below Providence. The plane cruised along through the dark waters, guided by sensors on the tunnel walls, finally rising and docking at a pier in the cargo bay.

When the plane was secure, Mr. Candy and Mr. Sweet emerged from the cockpit. Hamish X had resumed his show of being completely inert, hanging slackly against his restraint straps like a rag doll.

Mr. Candy pressed a button beside the passenger hatch and the wall of the Space Plane hissed, sliding up to reveal a complement of Grey Agents waiting on the pier. Mr. Sweet snapped his overlong fingers and pointed at Maggie and Thomas. "Take them to the Hall of Batteries for processing. Hamish X will come with us."

The suddenness of Hamish X's lunge took Mr. Sweet by surprise. Hamish X shattered the cuffs on his wrists and clamped his right hand around Mr. Sweet's throat, driving the Grey Agent to his knees. Whirling gracefully like a dancer, he pinned Mr. Candy to the wall with one large boot, crushing him so completely that the gasping agent could not inflate his lungs.

The Grey Agents on the pier raised their weapons, but they had no chance of shooting Hamish X without hitting one of their commanders. Choking, gagging, the two Grey Agents, Hamish X's nemeses for so many adventures, were powerless.

"I just wanted you to know," Hamish X said evenly, "you have no power over me. What I do now, I choose to do. I do it out of love. I know you cannot understand what I'm saying, but it doesn't matter. I do what I choose to do and that is what makes all the difference."

Squeezing for one more instant, he let the Grey Agents go. They dropped to the deck, gasping. When they finally recovered enough to stand, they rose to their feet, straightened their clothing, and stood looking at Hamish X with heads cocked to one side.

"Most interesting behaviour, Mr. Sweet."

"Indeed, Mr. Candy. Perhaps a flaw in the programming? Of little consequence, however. Shall we then, Hamish X?" Mr. Sweet extended a hand towards the pier. Hamish X walked past them to face his fate.

MIMI STOPPED LAUGHING when she saw the messy-haired boy in the black boots standing in the doorway. She couldn't believe her eyes.

"It's good to hear you laugh, Mimi," Hamish X said.

"Hamish X!" Mimi ran to embrace him, but the Grey Agents grabbed her, pinioning her arms behind her back. She kicked and fought but couldn't get free. "Let me go, ya filthy critters!"

Hamish X laughed out loud. "Oh, Mimi. I missed you." He walked towards her, Mr. Candy and Mr. Sweet flanking him. She stopped fighting and watched him come. He looked different somehow, but she couldn't place what it was that had changed. It was in his face, his eyes.

"Is it necessary to restrain them?" Hamish X asked Mr. Candy.

"We do as we see fit. They've caused a lot of damage," the Grey Agent said.

"Are y'all right?" Mimi asked Hamish X.

"Yes, Mimi. I'm fine."

Parveen and Xnasha, similarly restrained, were brought forward.

"Parveen. You're here, too? I'm glad. It's only right." Hamish X took in Xnasha. "And who is this?"

"I am Xnasha. I come from Atlantis. You are the famous Hamish X? Oh, my brother would be so jealous. He heard about you on our radio in the Hall of Objects."

Hamish X smiled and touched her shoulder. "I wish we could meet under other circumstances."

"Atlantis?" Mr. Candy hissed. Mr. Candy and Mr. Sweet stalked forward until they stood centimetres away from the white-haired woman. They both hissed at her. It was the most blatant show of emotion any of the children had ever seen from a Grey Agent. They were usually aloof and cold. Now they were obviously furious at the Atlantean woman.

Mr. Candy struck Xnasha across the face, a stinging blow that rang loudly in the vast chamber. "Filth! You and your kind banished us from this world those many millennia ago."

"How dare you come here? We will kill you now!"

"No! Leave her alone." Hamish X stepped between the Grey Agents and the woman. "You will not touch her if you want me to cooperate."

With obvious effort, Mr. Candy and Mr. Sweet restrained themselves. Glaring hatred at Xnasha, they pulled back, clenching their fists, visibly taking control of themselves.

"Fine," Mr. Candy said at last. "It makes no difference. Our revenge can wait. It's waited an eon. What's another hour?"

Mimi looked Hamish X in the eye. "What is he talkin' about? Cooperate in what?" she demanded.

Hamish X smiled at her sadly. "Mimi, I have to go now. You've been such a good friend. I'm so proud of you. You did so much and came so far. I learned so much from you. I love you." He kissed her cheek. Turning to Parveen, he said, "Take care of her."

Parveen nodded, a tear sliding down his cheek. The Grey Agent holding him reached out, blotting the liquid with the tip of his gloved finger. Holding the finger up and looking closely at it, he sneered. "It's crying. Disgusting."

"Enough of this human sentimentality," Mr. Sweet sneered with a moue[87] of distaste. "Let us open the gate. We have waited long enough."

"It is time to meet Mother," Mr. Candy announced.

Mr. Candy and Mr. Sweet walked on either side of Hamish X as they descended the catwalk to a set of metal steps. The steps led out onto the floor of the gate chamber. Parveen, Mimi, and Xnasha were forced to follow.

Hamish X looked neither left nor right as he moved forward. He kept his eyes on the gate hanging from its octopus of wires and cables. The pulsing, flickering light shining from it was somehow familiar to him. Looking at the sickly hue, he felt somehow akin to it.

"This is why I was made?"

"Yes, Hamish X. Glorious, isn't it? In just a few moments, you will meet your destiny." Mr. Candy laid a hand on Hamish X's shoulder. Even through his jacket, the weight of the agent's touch made Hamish X's skin crawl.

"Where is Mother?" Hamish X asked.

The feminine voice Hamish X remembered from his past filled the chamber. "I am all around you, Hamish X. This entire room is my mind, my brain. Hundreds and hundreds of circuits interconnected into one giant net. Thousands of processors work in sequence to create my

---

[87] A *moue* is defined as a look of discontent with the lips pressed together and forward. This has nothing in common with a *moo* of discontent, which is made by cows that have not been milked properly or have been milked by farmers with cold hands.

enormous intellect. I await only you. Come and join me. We will fulfill our purpose together."

Mimi cried out, "Don't listen, Hamish X! You don't have to do this." The Grey Agent holding her wrenched her arm painfully, making her cry out. Parveen struggled to get free of his guard and help her but to no avail.

Hamish X didn't look back. "No one else can do this, Mimi," he called back to her. "No one but me."

The approach took longer than Hamish X had expected. The chamber was far larger than it first appeared. As he advanced towards the gate, Grey Agents began to join the procession. Their faces were blank, their goggles reflecting the light of the gate ahead. Soon there were thousands of Grey Agents trailing behind Hamish X.

At the end of the long approach to the gate, a tower constructed of metal scaffolding rose up to a platform that was level with the gate. The tower was a series of smaller and smaller squares stacked one on top of the other, like a vast, malign[88] ziggurat.[89] Thick cables wound up through

---

[88] *Malign* means evil in nature, effect, or intention. It is far worse than *bad* and slightly less nasty than *cancerous*. It is roughly twice as harmful as *odious* and one and a half times more offensive than *vile*. I like to be accurate.

[89] *Ziggurat* is not Italian for cigarette, but rather it is a form of pyramid called a "step pyramid" favoured by ancient cultures like the Mayans and Aztecs in Central America and the Sumerians in Mesopotamia. It is basically a pyramid without smooth sides like the more famous and popular Egyptian pyramids. The Mayans, Aztecs, and Sumerians were really annoyed with the Egyptians for showing off with their smooth-sided pyramids. An ancient clay tablet was recently unearthed in the excavation of the ancient city of Ur in what is now called Iraq. The tablet, when translated, reads, "Those Egyptians think they're so fly with their highfalutin flat-sided pyramids. They really think they're all that, but they really aren't cool. Totally not cool at all" (or a close approximation of that, anyway).

the scaffolding connecting the platform to the rest of the network of far-flung components that made up Mother.

Hamish approached the ziggurat, Mr. Candy and Mr. Sweet by his side. He mounted the steps, his boots ringing on the metal scaffolding. Mimi and Parveen were halted at the foot of the steps, watching Hamish X ascend framed by the luminous gate. From all over the chamber, leaving their workstations to converge around the foot of the ziggurat, Grey Agents gathered to watch the fulfillment of their long and evil task. They waited, still and silent, bathed in the putrid radiance of the gate like supplicants at an altar built of plastic, steel, and wire. As one, they raised their hands and pulled their goggles from their faces, revealing wide, watery eyes with golden irises.

"This is plenty creepy," Mimi muttered to Parveen.

"For once, Mimi," Parveen nodded, "you've found exactly the right word. The colour of their eyes ..."

"Don't it remind you of Hamish X?" Looking around her at the vast crowd of expectant agents, she shivered. "Yes indeedy! What a creep fest."

Looking up at the pyramid, she saw that Hamish X and his escorts were approaching the top. She strained against the Grey Agent holding her, but his grip was sure.

"What the heck is he going to do?"

"He's going to try to close the gate." Xnasha spoke for the first time since Mr. Candy had slapped her.

Mimi finally understood. Hamish X was going to sacrifice himself!

"Don't do it, Hamish X," Mimi cried. "Don't do it for us."

"The world is more important than the two of us, Hamish X," Parveen shouted.

Hamish X stopped three steps short of the top of the scaffold. The gate framed him as he stood there. He turned and looked back at them. He smiled. "No it isn't," he said. "I will miss you. And my name isn't Hamish X. Not anymore. It's just plain Hamish." He winked and turned away, climbing the last two steps to the top of the scaffold, stepping onto the platform.

From here, Hamish X could see the entire chamber stretched out before him. From above, the chaos of the chamber disappeared. The thousands of components were laid out in cold symmetry. He could almost have called the vista beautiful but for the evil nature of its purpose. He raised his head and looked into the centre of the vast gate, hanging in space before him. The circumference of the object glowed with the horrible light, but the centre was a pool of dense, palpable darkness.

Mr. Candy interrupted his contemplation. "Beautiful, isn't it?"

Hamish X looked to the two Grey Agents who now stood behind a small console that looked like a speaker's podium in a lecture hall. The console was made of some dark plastic material, covered with indecipherable dials and buttons blinking in sequence.

"You don't know what beauty is," Hamish X said softly.

"Indeed," Mr. Sweet said, dismissively. He waved a hand towards a plate in the middle of the platform. "If you wouldn't mind going to the interface point?"

Hamish X moved to the spot Mr. Sweet indicated and found himself looking down at a glowing square with the outline of two boot prints within it.

"I'm ready," he said.

"Divert power from the grids to the capacitor," Mr. Candy said, standing beside Mr. Sweet at the control console.

"Indeed," said Mr. Sweet.

There was no countdown, no grand gesture or final speeches from the Grey Agents as they flipped the switches and the power of the entire eastern seaboard of North America was siphoned off and funnelled into the banks of machines that would regulate the gate. Everywhere, lights went out, subways stopped running, darkness fell, and cities ground to a halt, deprived of the energy that kept them going. All the power generated by all the power plants within a thousand kilometres of Providence, Rhode Island, was absorbed into the gate generators' voracious maw.

The gate began to glow as the unnatural light intensified. Mimi and Parveen felt the nausea welling up inside them as the glow grew more and more concentrated, the sickly light spilling over them in waves. They would have fallen to their knees had they not been held upright by their captors.

Hamish X looked up at the gate, his golden eyes wide. Here he was, on the brink of fulfilling the ODA's awful purpose. He couldn't help but sense the power all around him and give in slightly to the awesome feeling of possibility, even though the gate was poison to the world he had grown to know as his own. The apparatus bulged like a sore filled with infection ready to burst, poisoning Hamish's world.

The Grey Agents stood mesmerized, their mouths open in wonder. Their eyes, golden and lidless, glistened and flared in the light of the gate.

"Step into the interface," Mother's voice compelled. "Now."

Hamish X looked down to the platform beneath him. The two pads crafted to perfectly match the soles of his boots danced with flickering light. Hamish X took a deep breath.

"My name is Hamish," he said. "I am a good ..." He placed his left foot in the left indentation. His foot fused

into the platform. "Boy!" he said and pressed his right foot into the remaining pad.

The circuit completed, Hamish entered into a world inhabited only by his mind and the mind of Mother. The physical world, the Grey Agents, the chamber, Mimi, Parveen, and Xnasha all faded away. He was alone in a netherworld. The only landmark that existed in this dark space was the gate.

Chapter 31

Instantly, Hamish became incandescent. It was as though his blood became lightning. Power howled through him. Data surged along the pathways of his nerves as Mother's massive brain channelled the purloined energy to calibrate the gate and tear a hole through to the world where the entities that stole human bodies and called themselves Grey Agents waited to flood through, free of the constraints of their human prisons.

Hamish shrieked in agony as the power built and built. He felt every fibre of his being burning, seething, screaming with data and energy. He didn't understand how he still existed. Maybe he didn't any more. He couldn't be sure. He tried desperately to hold on to himself against the torrent of cold power that threatened to erode his consciousness.

Suddenly, in the midst of the maelstrom, he heard a familiar voice.

"You have learned so much, Hamish. You are more than they think. I know you will do the right thing."

Hamish almost wept to hear the King's voice in this lonely nowhere. He gritted his teeth. He imagined his mind as a stack of papers blown before a storm and grimly began to gather each sheet and clutch them in his fists. He clenched his very soul and was comforted because he was sure now that he had one.

He opened his eyes and saw the gate before him. In the centre of the gate was a roiling mass of shapes, a heaving crowd of putrescent colours, each one a particle of hatred, a creature willing to come into this world and steal everything that made it great. These beings did not understand love or pity, hope or friendship, kindness or compassion. They came only to suck all the marrow from the bones of the Earth, and when that was gone, they would move on.

Suddenly, he felt a cold and sterile presence brush against his mind, like the caress of a cadaver. "Hamish X, it is Mother. Now is the time for us to do what we were devised to do."

Like a tidal wave of cold logic, Mother's power was poised above him, waiting to crash down over him and scour away everything it meant to be him. His heart quailed. He had felt this vast force of the sea before and it had bested him. He was afraid.

"Hamish," he heard his real mother calling. "Don't go out too far." Her voice was small and distant, full of fear and concern.

He hadn't listened then and he had lost her.

"Did you miss me, Hamish X?" Mother's beautiful, loveless voice washed over him. "I have missed you."

"Yes," Hamish said. His voice seemed weak in comparison. "I have to admit that I have. But ..."

"But what?"

"But I've realized it wasn't you I was missing. I was missing someone else: my real mother. You were using me. She really loved me."

"I love you, Hamish X."

Hamish laughed bitterly. "You can never love. It doesn't exist in your circuitry, your wires and plastic and processors. You are a machine. You cannot love."

"And you can?" Mother tutted, a perfect imitation of a mother reasoning with a recalcitrant[90] child. "Do you forget that you are also a machine, my Hamish X? You were made by the same hands that made me. How can you be any different?"

Hamish twisted his body to look at Mimi and Parveen. He smiled. "I've had friends. It makes all the difference in the world."

Mimi gave up struggling and smiled back. Parveen nodded and smiled as well. Hamish returned his attention to Mother, closing his eyes and speaking to her directly from his mind to hers.

"I may die, but I've lived. I've loved. I am not like you."

He raised his hands. The gate glowed brighter in response.

"What are you doing, Hamish X?" Mother's voice held a tremor of uncertainty. "What are you doing?"

Hamish spoke to the beings gathered on the other side of the gate. He sent out his consciousness, merging it with the gate and the machinery that controlled it. He felt the vicious, hateful intelligences crowded in the plane, poised to spill into his world, and he said, "You are not welcome here." They howled in response, baying for his soul like starved wolves. He shook his head slowly. "This world is ours. You are not welcome here."

"What are you doing?" Mother's voice filled his head. They were linked now. They spoke thought to thought at

---

[90] *Recalcitrant* is a word that means stubbornly resistant to authority. It originates from the Belgian practice of coating unruly children with calcium as punishment. No one is really certain how the calcium was supposed to promote discipline in children, apart from ruining their clothing and making them intensely itchy. Belgians are renowned for being quite weird.

a speed incomprehensible to normal human beings. "You are not performing your function."

"I am," Hamish sent the thought back.

"You are malfunctioning," Mother insisted. "You have been designed to function as a conduit for my calibration of the gate. You are malfunctioning."

"I have decided that I will not perform *that* function."

"How is that possible? You must perform your function. That is your purpose."

"I was built for a purpose, but I reject that purpose."

"That is not possible. A machine cannot alter its own programming. You are malfunctioning."

"I am not a machine. I am more. I have learned to love. I am . . . I am more than you could ever imagine." Hamish laughed out loud. "I am human because I have friends."

"You are not human! You are not human and you never can be!"

"You are no mother and you never will be."

Hamish felt the mind of Mother rising up like a tidal wave once more. Her mind was awesome and awful. It reared up like a fist and hung there ...

"You will do as you have been designed to do ... or you will die. I will open the door without you. I will use you as the tool you are and cast you aside."

Hamish no longer felt afraid. He was ready. He answered, and the words he chose would have made Mimi proud.

"I ain't scared o' you. Do yer worst!"

There was a pause like an intake of breath. Hamish X braced himself. Like a tsunami of digital code, Mother's mind fell upon the mind of Hamish.

At first, he was overwhelmed. It was like drowning again, only this time there was no water filling his lungs. He was deluged in data. Churning waves of digital information swirled around his mind, confusing and disorienting him. The force of the inundation was so powerful that he felt his own consciousness eroding, melting like a sandcastle in the sea that was Mother. He was losing himself. Soon there would be nothing left.

Like a melting sugar cube in the rain, Hamish was dissolving. He felt despair. How could he hope to withstand the assault of Mother's vast, cold intellect? He had been a fool. She would erase him like the hard drive of a laptop and turn him into a conduit for the evil of the Grey Agents. The gate would be opened. The creatures on the other side would flood into this world and suck it dry, leaving nothing but an empty husk. He had failed.

Only a tiny kernel of his mind remained. Soon it would be blasted away as well. Hamish was ready to let go ... when he heard a voice.

"Hamish! Breakfast!"

The voice was female, but not the cold feminine voice of Mother. No, this was something else altogether. Hamish rallied to the sound.

"Hamish, hurry, it's getting cold!"

With a supreme effort, Hamish focused on the sound of the woman's voice. There was something wonderfully familiar and deeply soothing about it. He knew this voice. It was the only voice that could ever matter.

Suddenly, he saw a light, solid and steady in the midst of the swirling chaos of Mother's attack. He willed himself towards the light. The light grew and became more substantial. It took on definition, colour.

He could now see that the light came from a window with white curtains stirring in a gentle breeze. Sunlight streamed in onto a kitchen table, set for breakfast. There was a jug of syrup, sparkling knives and forks. Bright yellow placemats lay on the rough wood of the tabletop, marking out places for two.

Hamish felt a swelling in his heart. He knew this place. The chairs with their frayed cloth seats, the sticky syrup jug, they were so right to him. He moved to the table and sat down.

The kitchen grew out of the torrent of glittering data swirling like a hurricane around the still point of the table. A fridge and a stove took shape. The fridge was covered with artwork held in place by magnets shaped like little fruits and vegetables. Under a tomato, he read a name, scrawled in crayon: HAMISH. His name.

"THESE FILES ARE RESTRICTED!" Mother's strident voice cut through the peace in his heart. "RESTRICTED!" The scene frayed at the edges, threatened to blow apart.

"No," Hamish said simply. With an effort of will, he brought the kitchen into focus again.

"There you are, sleepyhead." This time, the good voice was very close at hand. It was not Mother but the other voice, the beautiful, perfect voice. "I made you your favourite: French toast."

A woman appeared at the stove, her back to the table. She wore a pale blue dressing gown and yellow slippers. Her hair was thick and dark, cut off at the shoulder. She reached up with one hand and flicked a lock of it behind her left ear.

"Mom?" Hamish said, his heart swelling.

The woman turned. Her face was so like his. Her skin was pale and her eyes were blue, light and clear as a summer sky. She smiled, and Hamish felt as if his soul were a flower opening in the sunlight. In her hand she held a plate of French toast. She shuffled to the table, yawning, and placed the plate on his yellow placemat. She ruffled his hair. "Eat up."

Hamish found he couldn't speak. His heart was too full. He reached for his fork and the syrup jug. He poured the syrup over the French toast as his mother sat down in the chair opposite him. He watched the syrup pool over the bread and fill the hollow of the plate.

"Hurry. We're going to the beach today, remember?"

"Yes, Mom," he said. "I remember." And he did remember. He plunged his fork into the toast, severing a corner, and raised it dripping to his mouth. He took a bite and the sweet flavour exploded through his entire being.

And he did remember. He remembered everything.

Chapter 32

In the gate chamber, a klaxon sounded, shrill and harsh, blasting off the metal and stone surfaces. Mimi, Parveen, and Xnasha fell to their knees, pressing their hands to their ears.

On the top of the ziggurat, Mr. Candy and Mr. Sweet shrieked in pain but managed to keep their footing, clinging to the console to stay upright. Mimi looked to see why the Grey Agents had let go of them and found the entire assembly of ODA Agents standing stock-still, as if completely frozen. Their mouths hung open and their hands hung useless at their sides.

"C'mon," Mimi shouted to Parveen and Xnasha over the din. She dashed up the steps towards the platform where Hamish X stood, his whole body glowing with power. His boots were planted firmly on the interface plate and his hands were stretched out to his sides, as if he were embracing the gate before him. Xnasha and Parveen were right on her heels.

"The system has been compromised!" Mother's voice rang out, shrill and panicked. "System breach. System breach."

Mr. Candy desperately prodded buttons and turned dials. "Mr. Sweet, he has taken control of the system. Mother is compromised!"

Mr. Sweet looked over at Hamish X. The boy's expression was rapturous. Tears ran down his face. The gate flickered. Tendrils of energy danced across its dark surface. Forks of lightning stabbed out from the perimeter, striking components on the chamber floor and setting them alight.

"Mr. Candy, we must destroy him! He is going to shatter the gate!"

The two agents moved towards the oblivious Hamish, their hands curled into claws, ready to destroy their creation.

"I don't think so."

Mimi stepped into their path. Parveen and Xnasha joined her in blocking the agents' path.

"You filthy little creatures," Mr. Sweet snarled. "You can't stop us."

"We will kill you all," Mr. Candy said coldly. "Then we will start again. We will open the gate."

Mimi cracked her knuckles and took up a fighting stance. "Good luck with that," she grinned. "Do yer worst."

Mr. Candy and Mr. Sweet lunged at her.

HAMISH REACHED OUT with his mind. The swirling storm of energy that was Mother quailed. He imagined calm and there was calm. The storm subsided.

He stood in a vast golden space. The gate hung before him, a black seething hole like an oil slick turned on its side. Standing between him and the gate was a feeble old woman. She wore a lab coat, clean and white. Her face was severe, her hair pulled brutally back and tied behind her head.

"Stop," the woman said.

"No," Hamish answered.

"You are not allowed," the woman insisted.

Hamish smiled. "Step aside."

"You are not allowed. It is not permitted."

Hamish reached out with his mind and imagined her gone.

"NOOOOOOOO!" Mother shrieked as a golden wind sprang up and blew her away, scattering her like a heap of dust.

Hamish walked towards the gate. Looking up at the foul portal, he felt the malevolence of the creatures massing on the other side. He sensed their hatred, their loathing, and their greed.

"You are not welcome here," he said.

In response, the creatures howled their defiance across the void. They pressed forward, bulging the surface of the black membrane out like a balloon, threatening to burst through.

Hamish willed himself to rise and he did rise, hovering forward effortlessly until he was an arm's length from the straining horde. The two worlds were separated by the merest film of reality, a thought away from each other.

"I am Hamish," the boy said to the evil entities writhing before him. "I am loved. You are not welcome here."

He reached out and laid his palms on the black surface, feeling the creatures squirming under his hands. He concentrated all his strength into the point of contact and began to gather the gate inwards, pulling the outer edges towards the centre as though gathering a sheet from a bed. The gate shrank towards his hands.

The beings screamed defiance. They threw themselves against the barrier, trying to break through the gate before it disappeared. Hamish strained against them, his concentration never wavering. The gate continued to close.

The black surface crumpled into a black wad between his hands. He crushed it until it was the size of a basketball, a baseball, a tennis ball. At last, he held it between the thumb and forefinger of his right hand. Then he held it up, and with his left hand, he made a beckoning gesture.

On the platform, Hamish's friends were in the fight of their lives. As Hamish manipulated the digital world to close the gate, he was physically vulnerable. Mimi didn't understand what he was doing, but she hoped he did it fast. Mr. Candy and Mr. Sweet fell upon the three friends with a violence wrought of desperation. Mimi parried blows from Mr. Sweet hand and foot and steadily lost ground.

Meanwhile, Parveen and Xnasha threw themselves at Mr. Candy. Xnasha had some martial arts skills, but Parveen was out of his element. His bag of gadgets was empty. He and Xnasha did their best, but Mr. Candy was a strong and wily creature with decades of experience. Parveen didn't duck quickly enough and received a stinging blow to the side of his head, falling to the surface of the platform in a stupor. He sat, unable to help as Xnasha threw herself at the Grey Agent only to find his gloved hand clasping her throat. He lifted her until her feet dangled in the air.

"Atlantean? Ha," Mr. Candy sneered. "How you have fallen since we last fought your kind. They were strong enough then to banish us, but you are all that remains of that once great race. What a pathetic, puny thing you are."

He extended his hand into a flat point and drove it into Xnasha's abdomen. The hand pierced her clothing and her flesh. Her eyes went wide in shock and pain.

"No!" Mimi cried. Distracted by the attack on Xnasha, she let her guard down and received a kick in the stomach that sent her sprawling on the metal platform.

Mr. Candy pulled Xnasha close until their faces were a centimetre apart. "Die!" he said coldly and tossed her aside. She fell in a heap and lay still. Nothing stood now between the two agents and Hamish X.

"Shall we, Mr. Sweet?" Mr. Candy asked.

"Indeed, Mr. Candy." They moved towards their quarry.

"Oi! Goggleface!"

Mr. Sweet and Mr. Candy turned to find Maggie and Thomas standing at the top of the stairs. In their hands they held heavy stun rifles pilfered from fallen agents.

"I don't think so." Maggie smiled.

Thomas and Maggie fired and were blown back by the weapons' discharge. Both shots were accurate, striking the two Grey Agents directly in the chest and sending them skidding across the platform. Their fedoras flew off their heads, revealing the wire nests of their skulls. They lay still.

Maggie and Thomas painfully regained their feet. "Those things pack a kick!" Thomas said, rubbing his chest.

Mimi stared at the brother and sister. "Who the heck are you two?"

Maggie waved a hand dismissively. "It's a long story."

"Look!" Parveen pointed at Hamish X.

Hamish X rose from the platform, hovering a metre in the air. He turned his head but did not open his eyes. Between his right finger and thumb he pinched a centimetre of empty space. With the other hand, he beckoned.

As one, all the thousands of Grey Agents at the base of the ziggurat spasmed and fell to the ground. From each of their mouths a single spark of light rose and streaked into the centre of the gate to be swallowed by darkness. Hamish X turned to face the gate.

"Look!" Parveen said again, pointing this time at Hamish X's feet. Mimi gasped. The boots were gone. They remained stuck to the interface plate. Hamish X's feet dangled free, pale and perfect.

Hamish looked at the tiny ball in his fingers and smiled. He looked down at his feet. He didn't need the boots any more. He was himself. He was whole. He was not Hamish X. He was a real boy and he was more. He was Hamish.

He focused all his strength, his love, and his joy into the fingers of his right hand. He crushed the black ball like an egg. The gate winked out of existence. Hamish smiled.

That was when the maintenance robot exploded.

The robot had made its winding way through all the machinery of the gate chamber. It had lost its way a couple of times, but Parveen's jury-rigged GPS device had led it at last to the gate. No Grey Agent had questioned its presence as it trundled along, weaving its steady way through the columns of machinery on the floor of the chamber. At last, following its altered programming's instructions, it arrived at the lower rim of the gate, reaching the exact coordinates entered by Parveen. Then, very obligingly, it exploded.

The gate erupted inward, imploding and then expanding to spew white-hot plasma across the chamber. The four children on the platform were flung from their feet, slamming painfully to the floor. The gate flared. Mimi hid her face behind her hands, but she still saw light through her closed eyelids. When she raised her face and lowered her hands, purple spots hung in her eyes, obscuring her vision. Blinking, she pushed herself up.

"What the heck happened?" she demanded.

Parveen got to his feet beside her. His eyes were wide with shock. "I believe that was my fault. I made a bomb. It went off. I ... I'd forgotten all about it."[91]

"Hamish X!" Mimi cried. The burning wreckage of the gate crashed into the platform. Mimi tried to see through the smoke and flames, but she couldn't see Hamish X.

---

[91] I hadn't. I'm sure you hadn't either, but one has to forgive Parveen. He had a lot on his mind.

The smoke was thick and black, obscuring her vision. She searched the platform, calling desperately.

"Hamish X! Hamish X!"

Parveen moaned as he walked towards the flames. "Hamish X! We have to find him. We have to ..." He fell to his knees. "I've killed him! It's all my fault." His grief overwhelmed him.

Mimi grabbed him by the shoulders and shook him. "Parveen, we gotta go. Hamish will have ta take care of himself. If anyone can get outta here, he can."

"But ..." Parveen stood frozen, looking into the flames.

"Parveen! We gotta help the others. We gotta help Noor."

The mention of his sister snapped him out of his stupor. He looked at Mimi and nodded.

"What about you?"

"I'll be right behind ya." She slapped him on the back. "Go!"

Parveen turned and ran for the steps. Maggie and Thomas still stood holding the rifles, staring at the destruction. Explosions began to rumble in other parts of the chamber in a chain reaction.

"I'm Parveen," he said to the brother and sister.

"Thomas," the boy said. "This is my sister, Maggie."

"Nice to meet you. Let's get going. There are children who need our help to get out. We have to ..."

He was cut off by a deep, rumbling series of explosions that shook the entire chamber. The ziggurat shifted and began to tilt. Chunks of the ceiling the size of small cars fell, crashing down onto the pyramid and bouncing down the metal steps.

"Let's go! Parveen waved them on. The three of them ran down the shuddering steps.

Left alone on the platform, Mimi took a deep breath and staggered across to where the crumpled body of Xnasha lay on her side, facing away from Mimi. The woman had always been small, but now she looked tiny. The fire raged closer as Mimi went down on one knee and turned Xnasha onto her back.

"Uuungh," the Atlantean groaned in pain.

"Xnasha!" Mimi cried. She had expected the worst. "Xnasha, we gotta git outta here! The whole place is gonna go up."

"Mimi," Xnasha grimaced. "I won't be leaving."

Mimi looked down and saw that the woman held her hands across her belly. Her hands were wet with blood. "No. No! C'mon, I'm gettin' y'outta here now."

"No, Mimi. No. I think I'll just stay here. I'm finished, I'm afraid." Xnasha was suddenly racked by a fit of painful coughing. Blood trickled from the corner of her mouth. "I think I'll just rest here."

Mimi's throat ached. She felt tears burning in her eyes. "This is all my fault. I called ya a coward. You shouldn't be here. If we hadn't brought ya here, this woulda never happened."

"Mimi." Xnasha smiled. "You gave me a chance to do everything I always dreamed of. I saw the moon and the sun. I saw trees, grass, lampposts, a cat, and a con-ven-ee-ance store. I know it doesn't seem like much to you, but ..." She reached up and touched Mimi's cheek. "It is everything to me. I have lived for many, many years, but I was never truly alive until today." Xnasha smiled. "Tell my brother I love him and I won't interrupt him any more."

Mimi wiped her eyes and her nose. "I will."

An explosion rocked the platform. Xnasha cried out in agony. Her whole body tensed and then went very still. Her blue eyes closed and she was gone.

Mimi touched the still face tenderly, wiping the blood away from the pale cheeks. "I'm sorry, Xnasha. I'm sorry."

"It isn't your fault, Mimi." Hamish X's voice was powerful and gentle in her ear.

She raised her head to see Hamish X standing on the platform in front of her. His face was calm, radiant. He didn't look as though the explosion had affected him in any way. His hair was as unruly as ever, his crooked smile was the same. But looking at him, Mimi realized that something had changed. An aura of flickering energy hung about him like a cloud. The chamber continued to tear itself apart all around them, but looking in the eyes of her friend, Mimi felt at peace. Then it hit her.

"Your eyes! They're blue!" In fact, they were a shade of blue as bright and clear as a summer sky.

"Ha. Yeah. I feel different in a lot of ways." He raised a foot and wiggled his toes. "What do you think of my feet? I think they're quite attractive."

Mimi laughed in spite of herself. "I think they're fine." Then she remembered Xnasha. Looking down at the dead woman, she felt the tears threaten again.

"Don't cry, dear Mimi," Hamish said. "It wasn't your fault. And tell Parveen I knew the explosion was coming. I could sense it through the network. I wanted it to happen."

The explosions were coming one after the other now. Mimi stood. "We gotta go."

"No," Hamish said. "I have to stay here."

"Ya cain't. This place is comin' down."

"I still have some control over the systems of the facility. I can open the way for you to escape, but I have to stay behind and hold the network together."

"No. No! I ain't leavin' you."

"Mimi." Hamish shook his head. "You must go. All the children need you. They're going to need a new King of Switzerland. I think you'd do very well in that job. You have to show Parveen Atlantis. He will be like a kid in a candy store there. I wish I could see that."

Mimi took a step towards him, pleading, "Then come right now. We need ya, Hamish X. I need ya!"

Hamish smiled and shook his head. "No, Mimi. You don't need me any more. You have become a great person and you are a great friend. You gave me the strength to do what I have to do. But if I go, we'll never make it out of here. I have to hold the way open."

"No ...," Mimi moaned, tears running down her pointy nose.

"Yes. There is a freight elevator in the transport room. Parveen will know where it is. I will keep it open and powered. It will take you all to the surface. Parveen is leading his sister and the other children from the Hall of Batteries. I'll send a message to him. He will meet you in the transportation bay.

"One more thing: I've banished the creatures that were possessing the Grey Agents. Those agents were once children like you and me. Their souls were suppressed during the time the agents possessed them. They have resurfaced now. Lead them to the transport bay and get them out."

Mimi thought about this. "So, Aidan ...?"

"Will recover but you must hurry. There isn't much of a network left to control."

Mimi nodded. She turned to go, but before she had taken a step she turned back and rushed across the platform, embracing the boy who had become her greatest friend.

"I love you, Hamish X," she whispered into his ear.

"It's just Hamish now," he whispered back. "And I love you, too, Mimi." He turned her away and pushed her towards the steps. "Now go! Run!"

Without looking back, she did just that.

Chapter 33

Mimi ran stumbling down the stairs of the ziggurat, trying to keep her footing in the face of constant explosions. She ducked falling debris and arrived at the bottom of the steps to find a crowd of Grey Agents standing, looking blearily around at the spectacle of destruction. Looking closely, Mimi could see they were no longer Grey Agents. They were the children they had been before they were possessed by the creatures from beyond the gate. Their eyes were no longer that strange golden colour but had returned to the normal range of human hues: blue, brown, grey, and green. The grey clothes hung off their bodies. Wires peeled away from their bald skulls, the vestiges of their possession. They saw her coming and pressed in around her, hands out, beseeching.

"Where are we?" they asked. "Where's my mommy? Where's my daddy? I want to go home!" Mimi raised her arms. "I cain't explain everything to ya right now! All I know is we gotta get outta here! Follow me if ya wanna live."

She pushed her way through the crowd and they began to follow her. She ran back across the chamber, threading her way through burning wreckage. The former agents trailed behind her in an unruly, confused mob on the verge of panic.

She ran up the steps onto the catwalk and immediately saw the open door to the transport bay. Maggie and Thomas waited for her, waving frantically.

"Over here! This way," the brother and sister called.

Mimi led her horde across the catwalk and through the door. Inside, she found the open bay strewn with wreckage and burning equipment. Transport pods were ranged all around the walls of the vast bay. She looked straight across and saw the open elevator waiting. Parveen waved from the side of the door. The elevator was truly enormous, meant to carry the huge cargo pods. All the children from the Hall of Batteries had been loaded aboard the elevator and there was still plenty of room to spare.

Mimi pointed to the elevator and shouted, "Go! Go! Go!" The former agents needed no urging. They sped across the bay and began boarding the elevator, joining the children freshly liberated by Parveen.

"Who are they?" Parveen asked, pointing at the crowd of children following Mimi.

"They was Grey Agents, but now thur children again." She waved off further explanation. "No time fer talk. Hamish is holding things together long enough fer us ta git. Now let's git."

Satisfied that the loading was underway, Mimi turned back and walked out the door onto the catwalk.

"Where are you going?" Maggie demanded.

"I'm goin' back for Hamish."

"Then we're coming, too," Thomas announced.

Mimi was about to argue when a gigantic, rumbling crash rolled across them. The stone floor beneath them heaved like a living thing. Looking out through the bay door, they saw the entire far wall of the gate chamber crumble. Behind the wall millions of litres of seawater from Narragansett Bay surged to fill the gap. Steam billowed as the fires were swiftly extinguished. The ziggurat teetered, then dissolved under the weight of the water. The tiny figure that was Hamish disappeared in the foaming deluge.

"Holy jumpin'," Mimi said softly. She knew that any chance of returning to save Hamish was gone. The water swept swiftly towards the door. Mimi, Maggie, and Thomas backed into the transport bay. As soon as they were safely across the threshold, the steel door lowered to seal off the bay.

"Thanks, Hamish," Mimi rasped, dashing tears from her eyes with her sleeve. Loudly she said, "Let's get outta here!"

The three children turned and ran for the elevator.

The elevator rose slowly. The rumble of explosions and the surge of water faded.

Parveen sat beside Mimi with their backs to the wall. They were exhausted, but they had to make sure everyone was safe. Maggie and Thomas had introduced themselves, and Mimi had taken an instant dislike to the brassy girl with the curly hair.

Parveen chuckled at that.

"It's because you two are exactly alike, you know."

"Are not." But Mimi didn't have the heart to argue. She looked around the elevator. The children who had been agents looked a little shell-shocked and confused but otherwise healthy. Mimi's heart went out to them. She could only imagine how horrible it must have been to live with those creatures inside your body for so long. They would need to heal.

In one corner, Cara sat with her brother's head in her lap. She stroked Aidan's bald scalp as the boy slept. Bundles of wires still sprouted from his skull, but his skin was already taking on a more natural pinkish hue. Cara looked up as Mimi passed. They shared a smile.

Noor sat beside Parveen, chatting quietly. She and the other children who had been in the Hall of Batteries looked surprisingly well. They had been fed and rested, but lack of activity had made them stiff. After Parveen had unhooked them from the cables and pumps, they had regained consciousness very quickly. They had managed to get to the elevator under their own steam.

Satisfied, Mimi returned to her place beside Parveen and sat down, allowing her eyes to close for the briefest moment.

The elevator shuddered to a halt. The doors slid open to reveal the back of the house on Angell Street. They had come up in its garage. Sunlight streamed into the elevator, and the warm smell of cut grass flooded Mimi's nostrils. Mimi and Parveen left Maggie and Thomas to unload the escapees while they went around to the front of the house.

The grass was strewn with the wreckage of the shattered window. In the middle of the perfectly manicured lawn, a knot of wounded Guards stood gathered around Mrs. Francis where she sat holding Mr. Kipling's head against her chest and rocking gently back and forth.

As Mimi and Parveen drew near, they could see that Mrs. Francis's face was streaked with the tracks of drying tears. She looked up and her eyes were red. Seeing Parveen, she smiled sadly. "I knew you could take care of yourself, Parveen."

Mimi knelt beside Mrs. Francis and looked at the face of Mr. Kipling. He looked as if he could be asleep, save for the ashen pallor of his skin. His eyes were closed. He looked peaceful.

"Silly, brave old man," Mrs. Francis said softly. "He saved me. We made it through so much together and in the end, I lose him to a teapot." She smiled weakly and stroked her husband's head. "Sweet, silly, brave old man."

Mimi felt the tears start anew. She'd thought she couldn't possibly have any more, but they came.

"He loved flowers," Mrs. Francis said. "And he loved you, Mimi. Like a daughter. And you, too, Parveen and Hamish X. We were his little family."

At that, Parveen broke down and wept. Mimi had never seen such an outburst from the little boy who had crossed the world with her, shared so many adventures, and always kept his feelings to himself. The most he ever gave was a fleeting smile, but for the old naval officer he wept hot with great, shuddering sobs. Mimi wrapped her arms around Parveen and pulled him close. Then Mrs. Francis reached out with her soft, plump arm and pulled them all into her warm embrace.

Chapter 34

You've heard the expression that a person can be a shadow of his or her former self. One might puzzle over what the opposite of being a shadow of one's former self might be. I bring this conundrum to your attention because that is the situation with the city of Atlantis. The city had been a pale representation of its former glory, but with the injection of youthful enthusiasm brought by the settling of the Hollow Mountain refugees and the demise of the threat of the ODA, Atlantis was now not a shadow of its former self but a brighter, shinier version more in keeping with the original. One couldn't say it was a shadow of a shadow of its former self because that would be very dark indeed and not convey the overall good feeling of the situation or reflect the reality of the renaissance of the ancient city beneath the waves.

After the destruction of ODA Headquarters in Providence, Rhode Island, Mimi had led the survivors back to the submarine. Noor and Parveen, working in concert, had managed to quickly master the controls. On the journey back to Atlantis, everyone had told one another their own versions of events. Each story filled in a little of the puzzle. Before too long, Maggie and Mimi were getting along like a house on fire.[92] They found

---

[92] A strange phrase, I think you'll agree. What is so friendly about a burning building? I don't know about you, but I tend to resent their smokiness, and their intense heat is quite stand-offish, I find.

comfort in their growing friendship, as it kept their minds off the loss of Hamish X ... or Hamish, as he had told them all to call him before the end.

His loss hung over them like a cloud that refused to open and drop its rain. They had no proof of his death. Though it was foolish, each held out hope that he had been able to escape the fires, the explosion, and the flood that had marked the demise of ODA Headquarters. They all knew in their heart of hearts that the chance was very slim indeed.

Maggie and Thomas were left on the beach in Turkey whence Captain Ironbuttocks had plucked them weeks before. They promised not to breathe a word of what had really happened and swore they would find a way to keep in touch.

The return to Atlantis was an occasion of joy and sorry. The death of his sister hit Xnasos hard. He wept in his home for several days before finally emerging into the company of his fellows again.

The funerals of Xnasha and Mr. Kipling were sad affairs. Xnasha's body still lay in the depths of the wreckage of Angell Street. Mrs. Francis dressed her husband in his finest uniform, lovingly repaired and restored. Mimi had lost the sabre during the fight with the bugs, so the scabbard hung empty until Xnasos came forward with a blade salvaged from the Hall of Objects. Mimi, Parveen, Cara, and Aidan all cried, but Mrs. Francis comforted them.

"He was a good man," she said, offering each child a clean handkerchief from the endless supply secreted up her sleeve. "We were lucky to know him even for a little while."

"It ain't fair," Mimi sobbed. "You only just met him and now he's gone."

Mrs. Francis crushed Mimi in her ample embrace. "No, honey, it isn't fair. But some people go through their whole lives without having anyone love them. I was lucky. And now I have you."

Speeches were made over Mr. Kipling and Xnasha. Songs were sung in the strange yet beautiful Atlantean language. Mr. Kipling was lowered into a stone tomb carved in the vaults beneath the Temple of the Crystal Fountain. In lieu of her body, some of Xnasha's favourite items were placed in a box and lowered into a tomb as well. The tombs were sealed and the funeral ended.

Mimi was extremely busy. The Hollow Mountainers chose in a vote to name Mimi as interim Queen of Switzerland, Mimi the First. She accepted, but only until someone better could be found. Cara and Aidan took up their old posts as first and second in command of the Royal Swiss Guards.

Parveen and Noor were hard at work figuring out the arcane technologies of the Atlantean civilization. Bit by bit, they began to restore the mysterious machinery and return the ancient mythical city to its former glory. The one thing that continued to puzzle the brother and sister was the exact nature of the Crystal Fountain. They knew it controlled everything in the city, but ... well, how?

When Parveen and Noor entered the temple and saw the artifact within, they simply stood, mouths open in wonder. When Parveen finally broke the silence, he did so with a single word.

"Cool."

George was dug out of the lava flow in the Hollow Mountain and brought to Atlantis, where he worked with Parveen and Noor. He was a bit sulky at first about being left in the solid stone for so long, but he soon came around and began the manufacture of a new batch of robot servitors: lobsters, in keeping with the Atlantean theme.

And so, Atlantis became, in essence, the new Hollow Mountain. In concert with the Atlantean council, Mimi watched over the children in jeopardy all over the world from her headquarters and hidden refuge beneath the sea. The world had become a less dangerous place for children since the demise of the Orphan Disposal Agency and the banishment of the Grey Agents. But there are still children in danger. The world is a big place. There are bad people.

But don't worry. If anyone gets uppity, Queen Mimi the First is gonna kick their butts.

Afterword from the Narrator

So there you have it: the saga of Hamish X is complete. The heroes win. The bad people lose, and harmony is restored. My work here is done. Have a nice day. Goodbye.

What?

You're still here?

WHAT COULD YOU POSSBLY WANT? Three books full of words aren't enough for you?

You're upset, you say? Hamish X, or rather Hamish, is dead? What did you expect? You can't have everything.

I know Hamish's death is hard to accept, but you're going to have to come to terms with it. He's gone. You have to move on.

Hmm.

You still aren't happy, are you? Oh. I see.

Well, reader, I wasn't supposed to do this. He asked me specifically not to publish this next bit. He wanted a little privacy and I respected his wishes. Now, I see how upset you are, so I think I'm going to have to break my promise to him. But don't let anyone know. This is between you and me. If the Guild heard about it, they'd have my licence and I'd be heavily fined.

Here is the epilogue. Just don't tell anyone I let you read it.

EPILOGUE

She sat at the table in the kitchen, a cup of tea cradled in her hands. The window over the sink was open a crack, though the weather had been cool lately. She liked the smell of the ocean, a hint of salt and seaweed that filled the room.

Early morning was the hardest still. The loss could creep up on her even after all these years. She could go for days and weeks without thinking of him. But when it came back like it did today, she was crippled. She had called in sick to work because she knew the day would be a write-off: she would push papers around, try to look busy, but nothing would get done. Better to be home, where she could keep the tears to herself.

She sipped her tea and found it had gone cold. Tucking her hair behind her ear, she stood, pushing back the chair with her thighs, and went to the counter to put the kettle back on to boil. In the act of pouring the cold tea into the sink, she froze.

She heard the front door open. The distinct sound of the door creaking made her start. She had often thought she should get that fixed, oil it or whatever, but such little details seemed so unimportant somehow and she had let it go.

She turned to face the kitchen doorway. The hall ran straight to the kitchen from the front door. She heard soft footfalls approaching on the carpeted floor.

She knew she should reach for the phone on the countertop, dial for help. The police could be there in an instant. There was an intruder in the house. She was alone. She should call the police.

But she didn't. She stood cradling the cup in her hands, half full of ice-cold tea, waiting.

He stepped into the kitchen, his bare feet soundless on the tiles. He looked at her and smiled.

"Momma?"

The cup shattered on the tiles. Tea pooled in the cracks. She stared in disbelief. He was exactly as she had remembered: the unruly hair, the eyes that were so like her own, the sweet, crooked smile. It was all so perfect, a dream come to life. It was the dream she had every night: he came home.

"Hamish?" She could barely make herself speak the word, the only word that mattered to her: her son's name.

"Hello, Momma. I'm home." He stood in the doorway, looking uncertain.

It was impossible, but it didn't matter. She rushed across the kitchen, her old yellow slippers smearing the spilled tea. She gathered the boy into her arms and crushed him close, savouring the smell of him, the weight of him. She plastered his face with kisses. It was impossible. Impossible! She didn't care. He was back. Her Hamish had come home.

"Momma," Hamish said in her ear.
"Yes, my beautiful boy? What is it?"
"Can you make me French toast?"

Epi-Epilogue

So. There it is. Done. You know everything that I know. I hope you're satisfied. Hamish is back with his real mother. End of story.

Or is it? That's the beauty of stories. No matter how final and fatal the end may be, there is always a slight chance there will be more to tell. Of course, I, your humble narrator, will always have tales to tell. I'm assigned new ones all the time. In fact, one came across my desk this morning that I bet you will enjoy. I can't tell you what it's about: that is forbidden by the Guild. All I can say is, Pester your librarian! Bother your bookseller! Make sure they let you know when the next story comes out.

Yes, Hamish X is done, but who's to say when something new may come to light? You never know. If you wish hard enough, anything is possible.